"IMPRESSIVE. WILD. THE
PACE NEVER FLAGS."
—*CHICAGO TRIBUNE*

"GREAT ENTERTAINMENT."
—*DENVER POST*

"TOP-NOTCH. A TIGHTLY
CONSTRUCTED THRILLER."
—*LIBRARY JOURNAL*

REMOTE
CONTROL

"A DAZZLING TALENT."
—TONY HILLERMAN

REMOTE CONTROL

CONTROL

Stephen White

A SIGNET BOOK

SIGNET
Published by the Penguin Group
Penguin Putnam Inc., 375 Hudson Street,
New York, New York 10014, U.S.A.
Penguin Books Ltd, 27 Wrights Lane,
London W8 5TZ, England
Penguin Books Australia Ltd, Ringwood,
Victoria, Australia
Penguin Books Canada Ltd, 10 Alcorn Avenue,
Toronto, Ontario, Canada M4V 3B2
Penguin Books (N.Z.) Ltd, 182–190 Wairau Road,
Auckland 10, New Zealand

Penguin Books Ltd, Registered Offices:
Harmondsworth, Middlesex, England

Published by Signet, an imprint of Dutton Signet,
a member of Penguin Putnam Inc.
Previously appeared in a Dutton edition

First Signet Printing, March, 1998
10 9 8 7 6 5 4 3 2 1

REGISTERED TRADEMARK—MARCA REGISTRADA

Printed in the United States of America

PUBLISHER'S NOTE
This is a work of fiction. Names, characters, places, and incidents either are
the product of the author's imagination or are used fictitiously, and any
resemblance to actual persons, living or dead, events, or locales is entirely
coincidental.

to my mother, Sara White Kellas

A good deed never goes unpunished.

—*Gore Vidal*

PROLOGUE

Remember?

Staging shots come first.

A baggage carousel spins empty.

Monitor screens direct deplaning passengers to the destination of their luggage.

A page echoes overhead. "Mr. Singh, Mr. J. Singh" is wanted at the white courtesy telephone, please. The noise level in the room jumps suddenly as the escalators spill a couple of jets full of people into baggage claim. Individual voices are lost in the white noise of travel. Automatic doors open with a swoosh and the drone of a diesel momentarily drowns out all other sounds.

The woman's camera finds a man wearing khaki Dockers and a plaid wool sport coat. He is exactly where he told her he would be. The man is taller than everyone who passes by. His hair is blond and full; not long, barely reaching his collar. His right arm hangs straight down his side, pressed against his ribs. Although he knows she is there recording him, he does not look toward the lens.

The camera stays with him for a full minute. When Geraldo times it, he pegs it at 59.28 seconds.

Finally, in apparent recognition of *something*, the man's passive face brightens and his eyes widen. The woman follows his gaze across the big room, her lens freezing on the bottom steps of the escalator.

Unscuffed black flats. Faded blue jeans. Long slender legs.

One step up, one step down.

Now, brown oxfords, pressed corduroys, nice socks.

The camera glides upward and finds their faces. The woman is much younger than her companion, maybe twenty to his fifty. They seem happy, smiling. One of the disparate sounds on the tape seems to be her infectious laugh. Both the man and the woman have a carry-on bag slung over one shoulder.

She grabs his sleeve to slow him while she steals a glance at the monitor.

The man in the Dockers already knows where they are heading and he calmly strides over to wait for everyone's arrival in front of carousel number three.

The camera follows him there and pauses. The focus fades, then sharpens. His right arm continues to hang stiffly.

The baggage carousel groans and jerks to life. The travelers are momentarily distracted from their conversations. At first no luggage emerges from the black cave at the top of the stainless-steel slide.

The man stands immobile, calm. The lens shifts away from him and follows the bags as they spill from the mouth of the machine, scratching down stainless steel, stopped by rubber bumpers.

The older man in the corduroys and the young woman in the jeans step in front of the carousel, momentarily filling the camera's lens. Focus jumps back to the man in the Dockers as his left hand snakes inside the right lapel of his coat.

He steps toward the carousel. Two steps, not too close, not too far.

The crowd is three-deep in places. The passengers are jockeying for position, everyone's eyes peeled for suitcases and garment bags.

The man's left arm emerges from the wool jacket and briefly there's the glint of metal.

One more stride, another.

Suddenly a woman wearing a red coat fills the screen. For a few long seconds the camera records nothing but the color red.

Blam. Blam.

Two shots are unmistakable on the sound track.

The red coat drops off the bottom of the screen.

The camera jerks around—up, too high, down—trying to locate the gunman. People fall to the floor. An instant of silent shock creates a hollow of hope before a chorus of screams fills the air.

The woman wearing the red coat is at the gunman's feet, staring straight up at his left hand. In a sweet, plaintive gospel refrain, she calls out, "Oh Lord, he's got a gun. Oh Lord, Oh Lord. He's got a gun."

The man in the corduroys has collapsed onto the carousel, his head on a Samsonite duffel. He is on his side, facing the camera. His white polo shirt is marred by two dark circles, one on his abdomen, the other up toward his shoulder. The circles appear too small to be serious wounds. They are no bigger than dimes.

His expression is one of shock, not pain.

The young woman with him turns to face the shooter. Her amber hair is tied back on the side of her head. Her sunglasses are askew and she rips them off.

The camera zooms and captures the resolve in her blue eyes. She doesn't cower from the threat. Instead she moves in front of her bleeding companion and spreads her arms as though to shield him. She is facing the gunman—facing down the gunman—and she is willing to take the next bullet.

It's in her face. It's in her eyes.

She's willing to take the next bullet.

The shooter knows it. His finger squeezes but he can't quite complete the pressure on the trigger to release the next shot.

He can't shoot *her*. He's not here to shoot *her*.

The carousel continues its clockwise rotation as a young man wearing a University of Georgia Bulldogs sweatshirt flies into the frame from offscreen, delivering a devastating tackle that flattens the assassin, separating him from his weapon.

The carousel comes back around.

The young woman is holding the man's head in her lap, kissing his face, saying, "I love you, Daddy, I love you, Daddy."

ONE

A car crawled into Lauren Crowder's view.

Below her, the street descended steeply. At the bottom of the hill the car's headlights brightened the falling snow with blunt tunnels of light. When the vehicle stopped, she guessed that it was about halfway down the block on the far side of the road.

Originally her plan had been to go back up the driveway and wait in the shelter of Emma's front porch. Now she wasn't sure she would have time to make it that far. Instead she watched the street, readied herself, and waited.

The headlights snapped off in a blink, the extinguishing of two vanilla flames. The driver's door opened and the dimmer glow of the dome bulb flashed on, then off. The silhouettes vaporized and the car and driver disappeared in the mosaic of the storm.

Lauren held a gloved hand, the left one, out in front of her at arm's length, her fingers spread, and tried to count her digits. She couldn't. Her anxiety sharpened. She rationalized, trying to write off the visual difficulty to the effects of the storm. She forced her focus to drift above her fingertips, beyond her outstretched hand, back down the street in front of her, so she could have even a prayer of seeing the approaching shadow she was certain would soon appear out of this thick fog of snowflakes.

The shadow would be coming for Emma Spire. Lauren wasn't going to have time to get back up Emma's slick driveway.

She threaded the index finger of her right hand through the trigger guard of the handgun she held by her side. Her shoulder was beginning to sag from the drag of the weapon's weight.

Her anxiety was abating now, her pulse slowing. That surprised her. Until this moment she had been ambivalent about the wisdom of her decision to come here tonight to protect Emma, unsure of the true meaning of the voice-mail message she had heard earlier.

Reminding herself, again, to focus on the present danger, she narrowed her attention to the street in front of her and waited for a man to appear from the frozen mist or to make a telltale sound as he approached.

There.

A flutter of darkness in the sea of white. Like flotsam. There for only a second, then gone, as though it had settled behind an ocean swell.

That was him.

Was it?

How close? Fifty feet? Seventy-five?

Loud enough to be heard over the wind gusting with the storm, she yelled, "Go away. Leave her alone. I have a gun."

Over the thunder of the pounding of her heart, she thought she heard a grunt in response.

Oh God.

"I mean it. I'm serious. Go away, *now.* I have a gun. I'll shoot. I'll use it. Leave her alone."

Would she really use the gun? She wished, desperately, that she could see more clearly.

A dense squall line of snow floated past, and for a moment a narrow seam ripped open in the sheet of white. In that instant, she thought she saw a face framed in a tightly cinched dark blue hood that quickly dissolved into a mask that seemed painted with rage.

She thought the man's eyes looked like fire.

She was frightened now. The air that entered her nostrils was icy and bit at her membranes like frozen steel.

The terrible mask reappeared. She thought she saw the mouth opening and she waited for the spectral figure to speak. In the twisted features of the face she saw the devil's own brand of rage, but instead of words, she heard a scream, something primitive and guttural and unintelligible.

Oh God.

A fresh gust of wind-whipped snow blew shut the tiny window of clarity and she felt the space narrow.

In fear, she raised her hand, the right hand, the one with the gun. She waited a moment, then raised the weapon farther.

There, that's high enough.

She watched. She listened.

She blinked away the snow.

Unsure, she tilted the barrel higher. The slope of the terrain was invisible to her. A bright spot—a distant light?—filled her vision. She aimed there, toward that spot.

That has to be high enough.

She was terrified now. A knot of pressure filled her gut.

Suddenly, the clap of a gunshot exploded in her ears, the flash reflecting off the snow the way candlelight dances off the facets of cut crystal.

The blast startled her.

The gunshot, she could tell from the kick, must have come from the weapon she was holding.

Was that high enough?

Her ears were buzzing as though her muffs were filled with a swarm of bees. The snowflakes seemed to sizzle as they vaporized on the hot barrel of the pistol she held in her hand.

Except for the torrent of snow, everything around her had again grown quiet, the wind had stopped swirling, and the air had ceased its frantic howl.

She continued to hold the gun perpendicular to her body, her left hand raised now to support the right. She made one more examination of the road in front of her. She saw no one. She removed her finger from the trigger guard and, without bending her elbow, lowered her arm until the snout of the gun was again pointing lazily at Emma's driveway.

She scanned the direction where the gun had been aimed and searched for signs of danger. Nothing seemed to be moving except the tiny white pellets that were dropping from the sky by the millions.

Huddled in her heavy coat in the shadow of a brick pillar at the end of Emma's driveway, she imagined herself a gargoyle, offering her new friend protection from evil.

She wondered if the masked figure had, indeed, been Emma's adversary. Had he turned and run? God, she hoped so. But she knew that he hadn't left the neighborhood; the door of the car down the block hadn't opened again. The engine hadn't started.

Where was he?

She decided to return to her original plan, to take the high ground, and the advantage. With her weapon still at her side, she backed up the steep driveway. She progressed slowly, taking careful steps, her leather-soled boots having trouble finding purchase on the ice-slick slope.

Barely two minutes later the headlights of a vehicle lit the road down the hill. She paid scant attention to the new car until it stopped in what seemed to be the middle of the street.

She heard the sound of the car door opening and, seconds later, closing. The car pulled forward—*what?*—twenty feet, twenty-five, it was hard to tell from the erratic movement of the headlights—then reversed itself. Again the driver's door opened, this time remaining ajar enough to leave the interior lights glowing for a while. To Lauren, every image was refracted and distorted, either too bright or too dark.

Finally, the car backed the rest of the way down the block, turned around, and headed out of the neighborhood. Lauren figured the driver had been lost, looking for an address obscured by the storm.

No more than five minutes later, an emergency vehicle, blue and red lights flashing, fishtailed around the corner and edged up the hill. Through the blinding snow Lauren struggled to see what was happening.

A patrol car pulled to a stop in the middle of the block, its sidemounted searchlights compounding the reflected glow. The beacons on top of the car continued to rotate, bathing the stark scene in a lurid splash of primary colors.

Two car doors opened and Lauren heard voices, male voices, and the dull drone of police-radio chatter. Momentarily, she forgot about the man who might be sneaking up on Emma. She wanted to know why the cops were on the block. Why now?

Had someone reported the gunshot already?

From the opaque white field, rhythmically streaked with sharp flares of color, came an excited young voice. "They were right, Lane. Shit, there is a body down here. Get an ambulance, get an ambulance. Damn, I think it's bad. Get a blanket or something."

Lane replied, "Damn it to hell. I don't believe this."

Lauren had stopped being able to feel her toes. She shifted her weight back and forth from one foot to the other, trying to prod her blood to circulate. She wanted to know what, or more precisely, whom, the police had just found in the street. But she also recognized that she was standing in the shadows of the porch of a house that wasn't her own, and was loitering in a quiet residential neighborhood in possession of a gun that she had just fired.

That state of affairs, she correctly surmised, wouldn't look good to any cop confused about why he had a body in need of an ambulance lying in the middle of the street in a blizzard.

She shivered. She couldn't tell whether it was from the cold, or from fear. Though she really couldn't see it anymore, she tried to imagine the terrain in front of her, the slope of the hill, the curve of the street.

She told herself she had aimed high enough. She *had*.

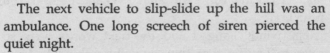

The next vehicle to slip-slide up the hill was an ambulance. One long screech of siren pierced the quiet night.

Two more patrol cars followed the ambulance to the scene. All over the block, residents turned on their outdoor lights and huddled in their front rooms, silhouetted in picture windows. A few brave folks ventured out onto the shelter of covered front porches to see what the hell was going on.

Part of what Lauren felt as she struggled to process the commotion unfolding on the street was relief. She couldn't imagine that the man who was threatening Emma would have hung around now that police were staked out all over the block. Lauren's duty as sentry could stop for the night. She could find Emma and help her rethink what to do next.

Through a fresh crease in the storm she thought she could make out a fat white swell in the landscape, like a big mogul, about where she thought Emma's predator's car had been parked.

If that's his car, he must still be around.

Where?

The paramedics hurried from the ambulance and hunched over the body in the street. Two patrol officers held umbrellas to try to shelter the EMTs. But the crazy winds picked up again, blowing snow in every direction but straight down, turning the umbrellas into affectations.

One of the paramedics said something that Lauren couldn't hear.

A deep baritone voice called back, *"What did you say?"* Then in a different pitch, "What'd he say? You hear him?"

The wind changed and the next words were so clear to Lauren that they actually seemed to blow right into her face. "I said I think this guy has been shot. He has what looks to me like a gunshot wound in his back, low, just to the right of the spine. We've got to evacuate him stat. His blood pressure is falling like a rock. I think he's going out."

The words registered slowly with Lauren.

This guy has been shot. . . .

She raised her right hand and stared with revulsion at the gun she gripped, as though she couldn't believe what it had done.

Aloud, she said, "Oh my God, I shot him."

*   *   *

A strong gust from the northeast returned the whiteout with a vengeance. Lauren used the shield of the thick snow as cover as she edged back down Emma's driveway to the sidewalk in front of the closest neighbor's house.

She knew she would have to turn herself in and tell the police she had fired the gun. The question was whether to do it here, or downtown at the station, or even at her office. If she turned herself in at work, at the Boulder County District Attorney's Office, she'd be sure to get some support from her colleagues. Whatever she did, though, she knew she couldn't afford to leave a trail to Emma's door. The stakes were too high.

The police could not know what she was doing up here tonight. If they discovered the reason behind her visit, Emma Spire would be as good as dead.

The wounded man was loaded onto a stretcher and then carried to the waiting ambulance. Seconds later it took off down the hill toward the hospital.

Lauren made her decision. She stepped off the sidewalk onto the street, walked up behind the closest police officer, and tapped him gently on the shoulder.

"Officer?"

He turned her way but didn't look at her. His dark hat was completely covered in snow. His mustache was caked with ice and his nose was running.

"What?" he barked.

"Officer," she said again.

He eyed her this time. She turned her head to the side and felt she recognized him, had seen him around, probably at the Justice Center or during one of her workday visits to the police department, but she couldn't pin a name on him.

"I'm Lauren Crowder, I'm a deputy DA here in Boulder County."

He was flustered. "Shit, that was quick. Who called you? We don't even have a detective here yet."

"I was in the neighborhood already, Officer, on personal business. I think that I may be able to be of some help. You know, with what's been going on."

"Well good, I could use some help. What a mess this is turning out to be. I woke up this morning already feeling like I'm getting the friggin' flu and standing out here like a polar bear is not going to help the situation any, if you know what I mean." His voice softened as he appraised her attractive face, and he took her by the elbow. "What do you say, let's get in the car. You can tell me all the ways you can help me."

"All right," Lauren said. She couldn't see his eyes, couldn't tell what part of her anatomy he was staring at. Still, she felt that this cop had started flirting with her and wondered if she could use it to her advantage. She was suddenly intensely aware of how cold she was, so cold that she had trouble forcing the muscles in her mouth to form the simple words of assent.

The cop yelled to his partner that he was going to do an interview and that the partner should get a perimeter up, and then he led Lauren over to the nearest patrol car, never removing his hand from her arm. He brushed as much snow off of himself as he could, slid into the driver's seat, and told her to get in on the passenger side.

She did, feeling her way cautiously around the car. The engine was running and the interior was warm. The patrol officer blew his nose loudly into a handkerchief that he pulled from inside his jacket and said, "So you know something about this?"

Lauren still had enough of her wits about her to ask, "What do you have so far, Officer . . . ?"

"Oh—Riske, Lane Riske. It's pronounced like it has a *y* but it doesn't. Boy, do I hate it when my mustache freezes. Hard to talk, feels like my face is going to crack. Anyway, here's what I got." He emphasized the personal pronoun. "I get a call not too long ago about a body in the middle of the road. Guy who called nine-one-one from a cell phone. Anyway, I get the call, I figure it's a crank. Maybe CU kids, maybe some imports from Denver, I don't know, I don't care, I mean, this isn't the type of neighborhood where we get too many unexplained bodies in the middle of the road, or anywhere else for that matter. Somebody just wants to fuck with us, you know, excuse my French, get some laughs, yuk it up making some cops climb up a mountain in a blizzard? You know how it is."

As his speech progressed he seemed to become more and more aware that he was sitting with a most attractive woman and he became more animated.

"So Loutis and I slalom up here and sure enough there's a big pile of snow in the middle of the road. Could be a body, I think, but most likely is just a drift. Maybe a dead deer. We get those sometimes up here. So I tell Loutis to get out and take a look and, yep, I'll be damned if it ain't a body, the guy looking like he's been run over. I mean, he has tire tracks still crusting in the snow on his legs. We cover the guy best we can and we call for an ambulance. Two minutes after the paramedics get here, they tell me the guy's been shot. Screws my night. So that's what I have. That's all I have. So what can you do for me that can help me feel better about my shift?"

Lauren briefly weighed whether Officer Riske's juvenile behavior provided her with any leverage. She decided it wasn't enough to make a difference in what she had to do.

She said, "I think, Officer, that you should reach into the pocket of my coat. Please reach in slowly. My hands will stay where you can see them. In my pocket, the one closest to you, you will find a handgun, a nine-millimeter Glock, with one round missing. The safety is on. I fired that gun tonight."

Riske looked down at her pocket, his eyes bulging. He didn't reach toward the gun. He didn't move a muscle. Finally, he said, "What did you say your name was? Do you have some ID with you?"

Her purse was in her car. Her car was in Emma's driveway. She wasn't about to tell him *that*.

"Not with me, no. My name is Lauren Crowder. I'm a deputy DA with Boulder County. I'm sure you've seen me around the Justice Center."

"You do look familiar. And you say you have a weapon in your pocket?"

"Yes, that's correct."

"Did you shoot this guy we found in the street?"

She wasn't sure how to answer that question. She said, "Not that I know of."

"But you fired your weapon?"

"Yes."

Riske stared at her for a moment before he said, "Please lean forward and place both your hands on the dashboard. I'm going to remove the weapon from your pocket now."

She did as she was instructed.

He tried to reach into her coat pocket but his thick gloves wouldn't fit into the narrow slit in the fabric. Using his teeth, he tugged the glove from his right hand and finally wrestled the gun from the pocket of Lauren's coat. When he removed his hand, he held the Glock G26 by the grip, using only his index finger and thumb.

"I am going to need to ask you to move to the backseat of the patrol car, ma'am. While we sort this out. I'm sure you understand."

"Yes," she said.

But she didn't want to move. In her mind, the backseat of a police car was just a waiting room for a jail cell. A one-way street she didn't want to be on.

Her loss of control would start the second she moved to the backseat.

"I am going to hook you up before I move you. Just a precaution. You understand why I need to do that?"

She wanted to argue that handcuffs weren't necessary. *I'm a deputy DA, you know you don't need to do that.* But she knew there was no point in protesting. She held out her hands. He cuffed her wrists loosely in front of her, then reached across her chest and opened the passenger door. In a moment he joined her outside the car and opened the back door on the passenger side. As she stooped to get in the car, she felt his hand guiding her head into the backseat.

She started to cry. That hand-on-the-head thing did it.

Now this mess was *real*.

She had an urgent need to call her husband, Alan, and tell him she would be late.

For five minutes or so she sat alone in the close, warm car, fighting the return of tears, saying quietly, "I'm not going to cry, I'm not going to cry." Snow wrapped the windows and collapsed the sense of space. The backseat was made of hard plastic and there were no handles for opening either the windows or doors. The blaring heater that had felt so good a few moments ago now felt oppressive. Awkwardly, she removed her gloves and laid them in her lap. She unbuttoned her heavy coat and pulled off her dripping earmuffs. She began to feel the ache of sensation creep into her toes.

Officer Riske returned and slid into the front seat. His voice had hardened and he didn't look her in the eyes. "I've been instructed to ask you for your gloves, ma'am. Were you wearing these gloves when you fired the gun?"

"Yes, I was." Immediately she doubted herself, wasn't sure she should have answered the question.

"May I have them, please?"

He reached his hand through a narrow opening in the metal mesh that separated the front and back seats of the car. Seeing the movement, she lifted the gloves from her lap, felt for the slit, and passed them through.

"Your earmuffs, too, please."

She had to scrunch them to fit them through the opening.

"Where were you standing when you fired your gun?"

She tried to look outside. All she saw was white. "I'm not sure. The storm, it's so confusing."

"You're not sure? Indoors or out?"

"Out."

"Around here, though? This neighborhood?"

"Yes."

"This block?"

"I think so, yes."

"On the street or in someone's yard?"

"I'm not sure."

"You don't recall where?"

"Not exactly, no. There was a light."

"A light? What about a light? You fired at a light?"

She didn't answer.

"How about approximately?"

"So much snow, it was so hard to see. You know, you've been out there."

"About what time was it when you fired your gun?"

"I'm not sure of that, either, exactly."

"Can you make a guess?"

"The last hour or so. But that's an estimate." She was sure one of Emma's neighbors would have heard the blast and would be able to time the shot. No point in trying to hide that fact.

No point in drawing them a map, either.

She caught herself.

God, I'm thinking like a felon.

"A guess then? Why did you fire your weapon, Ms. Crowder?"

"It's complicated."

"What does that mean?"

"Am I under arrest, Officer?"

"Should you be?"

"Am I?"

"At this time, my instructions are to hold you as a material witness in the investigation of a first-degree assault and, maybe—I don't know—an attempted murder. By now, who the hell knows, given the way that guy looked when we loaded him into the ambulance, a possible homicide."

The passenger side door opened. Detective Scott Malloy pulled himself onto the front seat. The act was not graceful. He was covered with snow and he moved his limbs as though they lacked the requisite number of joints.

"Hello, Lauren. Hello, Lane. May I have a minute or two here please, Officer Riske? See if we can clear this up." His demeanor was pleasant, his voice matter-of-fact.

Lauren managed to say, "Hello, Scott." She didn't add, "nice to see you."

Riske hesitated, pointed to the paper bags on the floor of the front seat, and said, "Her things, like you asked. The weapon, too." He opened the door and left the patrol car.

Lauren and Malloy had done a number of cases together over the last three years, since Scott Malloy made detective. They weren't buddies, weren't adversaries. She had always thought Malloy played fair, did his homework, and she couldn't recall his work ever being sloppy or backhanded enough to leave the DA's office looking like fools.

As for Malloy, he had always considered her to be a prosecutor with her toe slightly over the line onto the cops' side. She wasn't blatantly pro-cop like some DAs, but she was all right. He knew there were a few cops, even one or two detectives, who didn't trust her, considered her a Brownie.

Malloy wasn't dressed for the weather. His shoes were rubber-soled dress shoes, the ones he always wore on the job. And the unlined nylon shell he wore over his sport jacket was more appropriate for an Indian summer rain than for early winter snow.

"This cold, let me tell you. Stiffens me up. When you have kids, don't let them play football. I hate being stuffed in patrol cars."

Lauren didn't respond.

Scott Malloy, his voice different, all business, said, "So this is weird, isn't it, being here with you hooked up like that? What's going on? What's this about you firing a gun up here tonight? Is that true?"

She had already thought about what she was going to say. "I didn't fire *at* anybody, Scott."

He winced and a tiny moan escaped his lips. She wondered if it was an old football injury flaring up or indignation at what she had said.

He said, "A: Someone was shot in the middle of this street. B: Officer Riske says you admitted firing a handgun. Let's face it, it would be quite a coincidence if the two events are unrelated. This isn't D.C. or L.A. Maybe, you're saying, the shooting, it was like an accident?"

"Maybe. If, indeed, I shot anyone."

Scott Malloy was puzzled. He hadn't expected her to talk like a lawyer.

"What were you doing up here in a blizzard? You visiting someone? You don't live in this neighborhood, do you? I thought you and your husband lived on the east side."

No harm in confirming her place of residence. "That's right, we live in Spanish Hills."

"But you were up here with a weapon?"

She allowed the question to hang in the air.

"The Glock you gave to Riske, is it yours?"

"Yes."

"And I assume you have a carry permit for it?"

"Yes. Sheriff has the records."

"Has someone been threatening you?"

"Not recently, no. A while back, I received a threat from the family of a guy I was prosecuting. That's when I got the permit."

Malloy was perplexed at how the conversation was developing. Lauren was being cautious, holding back on him. As soon as he had heard the news that Deputy DA Lauren Crowder was involved in an apparent shooting, Malloy had expected that she would provide some acceptable explanation for the events of the evening. It might be something that would make her and the DA's office look foolish, but at least it would let him button this up and get home to his bed and his family before breakfast.

Instead, she was giving him *nada*. That worried him. Here he had a possible capital and a lady deputy DA was acting guilty. That, he hadn't expected.

"You going to tell me what happened? Why you fired your gun."

No response.

"You were in danger here, is that the way it came down? This guy attack you? Attempted rape? Carjacking? Robbery? What? Give me something here, Lauren, so I can unhook you and get you home to your husband."

Lauren recognized that Malloy was offering her a buffet of potential defenses from which to choose. The gesture felt generous, she would remember him for it. But he was also a cop who was trying to get her to talk. She reminded herself to remember that, too.

"Not exactly, no. I wasn't attacked. I was frightened, but—"

"Frightened? What does that mean? Did you feel, maybe, you were defending yourself?" Malloy couldn't believe his own words. He was handing her a ticket home.

She didn't bite. "I'm not sure, exactly. Things happened so fast. It was snowing terribly. And now I'm really very tired." She looked down at her lap and weighed her next words. "Can I go home, Scott?"

This was not a naive plea. She was asking him if he, as a peace officer, was restricting her freedom. If he was going to prohibit her from leaving the patrol car, then technically she was already in custody.

He cracked the knuckles on his left hand. Sequentially, starting with the pinkie. "Not with what you've told me so far. You know I can't do that. DA's office would kill me." The last sentence was a feeble attempt at levity.

She didn't appreciate the joke. "Then I take it that I'm under arrest?"

Scott Malloy thought carefully through the ramifications of what he was about to do. He said, "You're not helping me, Lauren. I'd love some assistance here."

She said, "I'm sorry."

He swallowed, fiddled with the volume on the squad radio, just to do something. "I'm in a hole right now. Can you give me a boost up, help me out at all? I don't like what I'm hearing so far."

"I'm really sorry, Scott."

He shifted his weight in the car, exhaled, and checked to see if he could see his breath turn into vapor.

"You're sure about all this? What you're doing? You've thought this through?"

"I think it's best, yes."

He stared at the crystal forms of the flakes caking on the windshield. "Okay, Lauren. If that's the way you want it, then I guess you're under arrest."

"If I'm under arrest, Scott," Lauren said, trying to keep her voice from cracking, "then I think I would like to talk with an attorney before I answer any more questions."

He'd been avoiding looking at her. Now he turned to face her, betrayal in his eyes. "What? An attorney? You're sure about that? Absolutely sure?"

She knew what he was saying.

He clarified, just in case she was missing his point. "That changes things, you know? Lawyers change things. Balls start rolling, they get hard to stop. You know what happens when the lawyers show up. I don't need to tell you, of all people, how this works.

Let's work this out—here, now—come on. You and me. We don't need lawyers."

"I know what I'm doing, Scott. I know that my request will change things."

"Then you'll reconsider? Talk to me." Scott wasn't bullying as much as he was pleading.

She could tell. She knew the difference. She also knew the rules.

"Scott," she said, exhaling, "I'm drawing my bright line now. This is my Edward's." The Edward's doctrine was the result of a U.S. Supreme Court decision that prohibited further questioning of a detainee after an unambiguous request for legal counsel.

Malloy couldn't believe what he was hearing. Only a damn lawyer could demand her rights *that* clearly.

He reached into his pocket for the card. He trusted his memory and didn't need to read the words. But he wanted to get it perfect this time.

"You have the right to remain silent, and anything you say can and will be used against you . . ."

✦

The police were cordial to her at first.

But everything changed when each cop in turn discovered that Lauren had asked to speak with a lawyer. Malloy had warned her it would. She knew it would.

Her friends in the department could no longer be overtly friendly.

Her enemies could now be openly gleeful.

You ask for a lawyer, you are guilty. Rule of thumb in the detective bureau. "There are exceptions," Sam Purdy had told her once. "They only prove the rule."

She hadn't bothered to disagree with him. She was a prosecutor back then, not an arrestee. Not an *offender*.

The blizzard outside felt warmer to her than the chill she experienced when they arrived at the police department.

After asking three different times, Lauren was finally given permission to phone her husband, Alan Gregory. She placed the call from a gray flannel cubicle in the detective bureau. She had already surrendered her watch and wondered what time it was.

Alan knew the time. When the phone rang, the clock on the microwave in their kitchen in Spanish Hills, east of Boulder, read 8:54.

He, too, had been late getting home. Expecting Lauren to follow him at any moment, he had showered, fed the dog, and started dinner. When Lauren didn't arrive, he grew more anxious. He stared down the lane searching for her car and tried, unsuccessfully, to raise her on her pager and her cell phone, dialing each number twice.

Out loud, he asked the dog if she knew why Lauren was so late. Emily, a big Bouvier des Flandres, looked at him curiously, wondering if he was offering a walk. He tried to lay the blame for his wife's tardiness on the blizzard. But given the events of the last couple of days, the storm was not a comforting culprit and he was worried.

A big pot of water for pasta had been simmering for thirty minutes already, and needed to be refreshed.

"Hello, it's me," she said breathlessly.

The somber tone of Lauren's greeting alerted Alan that something was wrong. "Hi," he replied, attempting to mask his nerves. "You're real late, what's up? You having some problems with the snow?"

"Alan—oh God—I'm in trouble. Maybe serious trouble. But it's not the snow. I need you to come to town, okay?"

He placed his wineglass too close to the edge of the kitchen counter, then reached back to move it farther away. "Are you all right? What happened?"

"No, no, I'm not . . . all right, that is. But I haven't been hurt. . . . You need to pay attention, okay? Stay with me here. They won't give me much time to talk with you."

"Of course. Who won't give you much time? What the hell's going—"

"Before you leave to come down here, you have to track down Casey Sparrow for me. I think you'll find her phone number in—"

Any remaining calm Alan possessed disappeared. "I know her phone number. Jesus, why do you need to talk with Casey?" Alan was a clinical psychologist and Casey Sparrow had served as guardian ad litem for one of his young patients.

"I may have some legal problems. It's real important that you find her and talk with her."

"What kind of legal problems? Is this about work? Why do you need Casey?"

But he was already thinking he knew what it was

about. *Why does anybody need a criminal defense attorney?*

"I'm at the police department, I'm being held for questioning . . . in a shooting. You're my first phone call since they took me into custody and it's beginning to look like I'm going to need some help getting out of this. I want Casey. The cops are being pretty hard-ass with me, playing it strictly by the book. The whole situation is a little complicated right now, to say the least."

A *shooting?* Struggling to stem a tornado of panic, Alan didn't know what to say. The chaotic events of the last few days spun in rewind and replayed in his mind. This whole mess had started with a shooting and now, it seemed, it was going to end with one.

The moment of silence lingered into seconds, the poignancy ripe, Alan's mind consumed by static.

"Have you been arrested?"

"Technically, yes."

It struck him that his usually precise wife was being vague.

He reminded himself to listen, to use his professional skills. Calm, Alan, calm. Hear her out. She'll tell you what you need to know.

"What happened, Lauren?"

"This isn't the best time for me to tell you that. Maybe we'll be able to talk later."

"You think someone is listening to you right now?"

"It's possible, yes."

"I can't believe this."

She said, "The police are saying that I shot a man. So things are an absolute disaster for me, legally."

Alan guessed the fact about the shooting was not in dispute with whomever she feared might be listening.

"They think you *shot* somebody?"

"Yes."

"Did you?"

Silence.

"You don't even have a *gun*, Lauren."

More silence.

"Do you?"

"Later, sweets."

He thought about lightning striking twice. "You can't tell me what's going on, can you?"

"No."

"Is the man dead?"

"Not yet. But apparently he's critical. They say it doesn't look good for him. I don't know whether or not to believe them."

Alan swallowed. This was his DA wife wondering if she could trust the police? *Jesus.*

"Did this guy attack you? What was he doing to you?"

What a night this was turning out to be. What the hell were you doing with a gun?

"No. It's not like that. He never got that close to me. It's not like that at all. He was almost half a block away from me when he fell."

To Alan, it sounded as though Lauren were admitting the basic facts. "Where did you get the gun? Why did you shoot it? What on earth is this all about?"

She exhaled audibly before she said, "You know," her voice barely a whisper.

Yes, he did.

"Your friend?"

"Yes."

Emma. *Damn.*

The level of complication jumped by the tenth power. He had been praying that this Emma mess might just go away.

"Jesus. Is she hurt?"

"I don't know. I don't think so. I haven't seen her since this morning. You know that she missed that motions hearing this afternoon? So I don't really know how she is. I was hoping you knew something. That would help me know what to do."

He did. But her caution was contagious and he didn't want to talk about Emma on the phone.

He asked, "Is Sam there? At the police department?"

"I haven't seen him. But they're mostly keeping me in an interview room by myself. Everybody's come down here to be part of this. To the police department, I mean. The chief is here, the commander, the legal counsel, half the detective bureau. I'm not sure they really know what to do with me, given that I'm a DA and everything. Most of these people like me, Alan. They seem truly upset that I've asked to speak to an attorney. They want me to tell them something to make this go away."

"But you can't?"

"You know better than anyone what's at stake. Her vulnerability right now . . ."

"Does Roy know that you've been arrested?" Royal Peterson was the elected DA, Lauren's boss.

"Maybe, probably. I haven't spoken with him yet,

but I'm sure someone has tried to find him and let him know what happened."

"If the case isn't Sam's, whose is it?"

"Scott Malloy picked it up. But I'm guessing that one of the detective sergeants will run the show on something like this. God, I hope I get lucky on that." Malloy was someone Alan had met but didn't know well. The detective who was not there, Sam Purdy, was a good friend.

Alan thought, *it's a little late for lucky.* "What do you mean, 'get lucky'?"

"It's a chain-of-command thing. There are two detective sergeants in the general investigation division. One of them is the man I had that trouble with on the ride-along, back when I was a baby DA. Remember? I'm just praying that he's not the sergeant who supervises this."

Alan did recall the story about the fateful ride-along. Lauren had caused the man a passel of trouble by supporting a brutality complaint a citizen had lodged against him.

"Is Malloy cutting you any slack?"

"None. He's been . . . businesslike. Respectful. Everyone's polite and apologetic but they seem to want to make sure that they're not doing anything that will let them be accused of giving me special treatment." Her voice softened, finally, reassuring Alan that she really understood the gravity of what she was facing.

"I'm so sorry, sweets. Who caught this in your office? Has anybody been by?"

"Elliot." Elliot Bellhaven was one of Lauren's favorite colleagues in the district attorney's office.

"That's good, right?" He tried to make his voice sound encouraging, but it felt trivial and silly.

"He stopped in and said hello. He was nice, but it won't make any difference. This will go upstairs immediately and then to a special prosecutor as soon as Roy can arrange to get one appointed. The commander of the detective bureau came by already, too, and he said he would permit me another call after this one. I'll use it to call Roy."

Alan exhaled through pursed lips. "You're sure this isn't just going to go away?" Alan wanted to hear that it was all a big mistake.

"No, not tonight it isn't."

"God."

"Honey?"

"Yes."

"I need my medicine. And my syringes, too. You know where everything is? Don't forget the alcohol wipes."

"Of course. I'll call Casey first and then I'll be right down. I love you, Lauren."

"Yes," she said. "Alan, there's something else—"

"What?"

"My eyes," she whispered.

"What?"

She stayed silent. This was a secret, too, from whomever might be listening.

Oh shit. She'd woken that morning with some intermittent pain when she moved her right eye. "More pain?"

"Worse than that."

Only one thing worse.

"You're losing your vision again?"

"Yes." Her voice was firm but he heard a crack in it.

"One eye or both?"

"Much worse in one than the other. But both now."

"Blurry?"

"In one. A big hole in the center of the other."

"You'll need steroids, honey. Right away. You know Arbuthnot is going to want to get started immediately, while the inflammation is fresh." Alan knew how aggressive her neurologist was about visual exacerbations. He also knew how much his wife despised IV steroids.

"Right now what I need is Casey Sparrow. The IV can wait. Please hurry. And bring the checkbook from my brokerage account. Casey may want a retainer for this."

"Casey will wait for her money."

"Bring it."

"Where is it?"

"Top right-hand drawer of my desk. It's the one with the gray cover."

The line went dead.

He said, "I love you."

✛

Casey Sparrow lived thirty minutes away in the mountains, near Rollinsville. When Alan phoned, she had been home from her treacherous commute for only a few minutes, and her shoulders were still tense from the drive. She was halfway through her first scotch of the evening and the stereo was blaring.

"Casey, hi, it's Alan Gregory."

"Hello, Alan." She was surprised to hear from him.

"I'm sorry to bother you on a Friday night but this is . . . an emergency. Lauren is apparently in some serious trouble and needs your help. Your legal help. Right away, tonight." As he was punching Casey's phone number, he had wondered how he would actually say it, how he would convey the fact that Lauren was in jail for shooting someone. The circumstances felt monumental, the words he had rehearsed ended up feeling pedestrian.

With her free hand, Casey flicked down the volume on the stereo. She was addicted to old Broadway show tunes and didn't like people to know it.

"You have got my attention, Alan. I'm waiting. Please go on."

She listened to his sketchy description of the situation. When Alan said, "Lauren's been arrested, or at least she's in custody. Somehow—I don't know what happened, I wish I could tell you more—somehow, she says the police think she shot somebody," Casey reacted by kicking off the sheepskin-lined clogs she wore around the house and hurried down the hall to her bedroom to change clothes. Her dog followed behind her, intrigued at the bustle of activity.

"Is she at the police department or the jail?"

"The police department, on Thirty-third."

"Okay, listen, I'm coming right down to Boulder. I don't know what it's like down there but it's snowing like crazy up here. The roads were awful on my way up here, and they'll be worse now. I'll be down as soon as I can, but you'll get there first. If they let you see her—which they won't—tell her not to say anything. I mean it, anything."

"Okay."

"Alan, I'm dead serious. She needs to wait for me. Your wife can be stubborn as hell and she may think she can turn this around without help. Are you listening to me? You must convince her to wait. She may want to think that because she's a deputy DA that the cops are her friends. The truth is that the cops stopped being her friends the moment that gun went off." Casey paused. "No, screw that, I'm going to type an order and fax it to them right now informing them I've been retained and instructing them to stay out of her face."

"You can do that?"

"I can do it. It's not binding but it's a reasonable shot across their bow."

"I'll do my best at this end . . . but, Casey, there's something else I think you should know before you actually see her."

Casey shed her jeans and sweatshirt and began to slide one leg, then the other into a pair of wool trousers. She squeezed the cordless phone between her cheek and her shoulder, hopped a little bit as she tugged the pants over her hips, and buttoned them closed. With her left hand she started to pull a brush through her long red hair.

"Yes, what's that?"

"Lauren is sick, Casey."

"What kind of sick?" Casey thought—*like, the flu, so what?*—that's the least of her problems, and tossed the hairbrush onto the counter, the whole time trying to figure out how she could pull a sweater over her head without interrupting the conversation.

"She needs medicine. If it's what I'm afraid it is, she may need to go to the hospital, tonight even, right away, to get the drugs she needs."

"Hold on a second, I'm sorry, but I'm freezing here." Casey exhaled, placed the phone on her dresser, and pulled a wine-colored turtleneck over her gooseflesh.

She grabbed the phone again. "What do you mean, she may have to go to the hospital tonight? What kind of sick are we talking about?"

Alan knew that Lauren may not have been planning to tell Casey about her illness. He also assumed that she might be angry at him for revealing it. He decided to deal with that later.

"You probably don't know this, Casey, but Lauren has multiple sclerosis. She just told me on the phone that she's losing her vision. If it's true, then it's serious, it indicates an exacerbation—a flare-up of her disease. She has some regular medicine she takes by injection—I'll be taking it with me when I go now— but she's probably going to need IV medicine right away, too, high-dose steroids. For the acute vision problem—it's called optic neuritis."

The details swelled and Casey was stunned.

"Lauren has MS?"

"Yes."

"And she's losing her vision? Are we talking 'losing-her-vision,' glasses—or 'losing-her-vision,' blind? How long has this been going on?"

"The vision problem is acute—today. The loss could be partial, or it could be complete. It could be one eye, it could be both. The pain started this morning. She just now told me about the vision loss. She was vague on the phone but I got the feeling that it's still progressing. I think she was afraid someone might be listening."

Good, thought Casey, *at least she's being cautious about something*. "But the MS, when did she—?"

"—A long time ago, Casey. She's had MS for a long, long time."

"Alan, while she's in custody they're not going to let her take any medicine without clearance from the doc who's on call to the police department or the jail. That takes time in the best of circumstances. This is a weekend, and a blizzard, not the best of circumstances. And she's going to have to tell the cops what it's for. That's true even for routine meds, let alone for something like you're describing."

"I'm not sure she's prepared to do that. To tell them she has MS."

"Revealing she has MS is the least of her problems right now, I'm afraid."

"She'll try to finesse this, Casey, you watch. It's a privacy thing for her. You said yourself that she's stubborn, and you're right."

Casey paused at the mirror and pondered what she had just learned. *Lauren looks as healthy as I do.* She'd known Lauren a long time. How could she not have known that Lauren suffered from a chronic illness? *Am I really that thick?*

She lost a moment trying to decide whether to apply some makeup and whether to brush her teeth.

No. *Maybe do makeup in the car. Chew some gum.*

"Alan?"

"Yes."

"If Lauren is going blind, how did she manage to shoot somebody?"

"I've been wondering the same thing. She's never told me she owns a gun, Casey. So I still don't even know how she got one, let alone why she fired it. The question of how she managed to actually hit her target is way down my list of concerns right now."

"I'll be out the door in two minutes. I'll see you at the police department. And Alan?"

"Yes."

"I need phone numbers, too, whatever you have. Beepers, cell phones, everything and anything I might need to reach anybody, whenever."

Alan dictated a long list of phone numbers, then said, "I'm on my way, be careful."

Casey Sparrow put her retriever, Toby, outside for a prowl, fearing a long night ahead. While the dog roamed, Casey sat at her laptop, typed a memo to the detectives at the Boulder Police Department, got the correct number from the police dispatcher, and faxed it to the detective division.

She pulled on a heavy coat, a hat, and gloves and went outside and called for Toby. The dog responded eagerly and pranced around the truck while Casey scraped snow off the windshield. Halfway through the task, she realized that she had already made her first serious mistake. When Alan arrived at the police department, he was not going to be allowed to see Lauren; instead, he would immediately be pulled inside a room and be interviewed as a possible witness.

After luring Toby back inside the house, Casey

jumped into the cab of the truck, started it to get the defroster working, grabbed her cell phone, and called Alan at home to warn him off.

No answer. *Damn.* She checked her list of phone numbers and realized the list didn't include one for his car. She found the number he had provided for his beeper and punched that in. At the voice prompt, she entered the number of her car phone.

"Shit," Casey said aloud, "that is going to be my last damn screwup on this case. The absolute last."

She double-checked her briefcase to be sure she had everything she needed with her and turned left out of her driveway onto the Peak to Peak Highway, choosing Boulder Canyon instead of Coal Creek Canyon to get to town. It was always a toss-up which one would have been better scraped by the snow plows. But she chose Boulder Canyon because it had much more consistent cell reception than Coal Creek.

Casey Sparrow had a few more calls to make.

✛

Driving toward town, Alan Gregory realized he didn't know what was in his wife's purse.

He'd never looked. He wondered if that was odd, if other husbands knew.

If pressed, he would have guessed lipstick, tissues, wallet, keys. Her pager. A small container to carry medication. Maybe her appointment calendar, some candy or gum—something to freshen her breath.

But he never would have guessed a gun.

Alan was stumped. He didn't know where she had gotten the gun. He felt chagrined admitting that to himself. But it was true.

For a couple of blocks, it left him wondering about other omissions.

But the gun was his focus. The gun was what got her arrested.

That, and the fact that the police thought she was somehow able to shoot a man with it from half a block away. In the dark.

Aloud, he said, "Lauren, what the hell were you doing at Emma's house with a gun?"

Alan had been to the police department many times to see Sam Purdy over the years. A few of those times had been after hours.

He knew the routine.

He parked his car on the street, avoiding the visitor's lot, and plodded through unplowed snow to the south side of the building, where the cops park their personal vehicles. He checked the rows for Sam's car, found it, then high-stepped back through the ankle-deep snow to the public entrance. The outer door of the vestibule was unlocked. Once inside, Alan lifted the telephone that was mounted on the wall. Someone answered after three rings.

"Yes, may I help you."

"Detective Purdy, please."

"And you are?"

"Dr. Alan Gregory."

"Is he expecting you?"

"Yes," Alan lied.

"You'll have to hold on a minute, it looks like he's on his line."

From his vantage in the glassed-in vestibule no activity was apparent in the adjacent lobby. The entrance to the detective bureau was in the far south corner of the waiting area. On the other side of that door, Alan guessed, things were hopping. Shootings were not routine in Boulder and the law enforcement authorities mobilized for them with zeal. Few major crimes went unsolved and clearance on murders was exceptional. It was a point of pride with the department.

Lauren had told Alan that the chief, at least one of the detective sergeants, the department legal counsel, and the DA on call had already arrived at the building. From prior experience observing a murder investigation up close as a psychological consultant to the department, Alan figured that an additional half-dozen detectives would have been called in from their homes, too. Throw in some crime scene investigators, some extra clerical support, and a weekend property person, and the detective bureau would be bustling like a retail business during an after-Christmas sale.

And all that would be for a routine attempted murder investigation. This one wasn't routine, though. This one involved a deputy DA, and . . . *who?*

Alan got lost, once again, wondering who the hell his wife was accused of shooting.

Behind him, the door that led outside from the vestibule opened. Before Alan had a chance to see who it was, he heard, "Hang up. Quick. Come *on.*" The voice was friendly and enthusiastic, as though the speaker were inviting Alan out for a beer with the boys.

When Alan turned, he found himself staring into the Adam's apple of Cozier Maitlin. Alan knew Maitlin socially, had met him while accompanying Lauren to lawyer parties. And he knew Cozier Maitlin by reputation. Maitlin was the only six-foot eight-inch criminal defense attorney in the Boulder bar.

"You're Alan Gregory, right?"

"Yes."

"Hang up the phone please, Dr. Gregory. Please accept my advice that it is absolutely not in your wife's interests for you to be paying voluntary visits to the detectives."

"But . . . I want to see her."

"Of course you do. The reality is that the police won't allow that to happen for a while. Trust me. Hang up, come with me, and we'll discuss what *will* be happening in the next few hours. Okay? Going in that door is a mistake. Allow me five minutes, please, to convince you. For her sake."

Alan followed Cozier Maitlin outside. A big BMW with the engine running was parked in the absolutely-don't-even-think-about-parking-here zone in front of the police department. Cozy slid awkwardly into the backseat. Alan followed.

"Let's boogie," Cozy said to the driver, a woman. The car glided off smoothly through the thick cushion of snow on Thirty-third Street, heading toward Arapahoe.

The music from the CD player was loud, the heat was on high, and the defroster was blaring away like a wind machine.

"Alan Gregory, that's Erin Rand up front. It's 'Doctor' Gregory, isn't it?"

"Yes."

"Dr. Alan Gregory, Erin Rand."

Erin waved a greeting from the front seat. Above the din, she said, "I'm real sorry about your wife." Then sardonically, almost under her breath, she admonished Maitlin, "Real good introduction, Cozy."

The CD that was blaring was reggae. Erin adjusted the volume down, clicked the fan blower to a lower setting, and cranked the car west at the light. Alan sensed a slight fishtail.

Cozy Maitlin held out his right hand and said, "I'm Cozier Maitlin, I think we've met before at some insipid legal affair or another. I do apologize for having to kidnap you back there, but Casey and I agreed that you shouldn't be talking with the authorities quite yet."

"You've spoken to Casey?"

"I'm sorry, we're both in the dark here, aren't we? Neither of us really knows what's going on." He raised his eyebrows. "For all I know, you're assuming that maybe Erin and I were out chasing ambulances and happened to stumble upon your wife's difficulties."

Alan didn't know how to respond.

"Well, what actually happened is that Casey called and thumb-nailed me about your call to her and asked me to assist with Lauren's defense. She's helped me out a couple of times when I've had cases in JeffCo. She knows the local jurisdiction there. I know it here. So I'm helping out. Anyway, I like your wife, I'm delighted to be of assistance. Lauren has a sense of fairness I've come to admire over the years. It never feels like it's just about winning and losing with her. And if Casey and I succeed in getting her out of this tussle without too much scar tissue—'' his voice rose ''—God, will she ever owe me big time.''

Erin spoke from the front seat. ''Since Cozy probably isn't planning to include me in this conversation any longer, for your information, I'm not his chauffeur. I'm a private investigator. And, Cozy, I would seriously like to get started doing my job. Do either of you know where the shooting was? I want to drive up there and check things out, see what's going on at the scene. Take some photos, talk to some strangers.''

Alan could guess that the shooting had taken place at, or near, Emma Spire's place. But it would only be a guess. And, given Lauren's discretion during their only phone call since her arrest, he wasn't sure how Lauren wanted to handle the whole Emma Spire situation.

Alan said, ''No, Erin, I'm sorry, I don't know where it happened. I know almost nothing.''

''Cozy, I know it's going to absolutely destroy your ability to concentrate, but I'm going to need to turn junior Marley off so I can hear the scanner.''

''If you must.'' Alan heard the Jamaican rhythms diminish, only to be replaced by the crackle of Erin's portable police scanner.

Cozy faced Alan as much as a person his size could in the backseat of a big German sedan. ''I think better with reggae on. Odd, isn't it? I think so, anyway. My, you're a shrink, aren't you, I'd better be careful about what I say. Oh well. Let's talk about Lauren, if you don't mind. She's in quite a jam.''

Alan's head was spinning. "Mr. Maitlin, Cozy—may I call you Cozy?"

"Sure. Unfortunately, virtually everyone but my mother does."

"Please don't be offended, but I don't really know you. And I don't want to screw anything up for my wife." Alan nodded at the car phone. "Do you mind calling Casey for me?"

"No, I don't mind. Quite prudent, actually. I pray the trait runs in your family."

Alan watched as Erin touched a speed dial button on the car phone. She passed the phone over the back of the seat, said, "Oh shit," and yanked the steering wheel so that the car glided back into the ruts that indicated where her lane was supposed to be.

"Have you ever considered buying snow tires for this boat, Cozy?"

"I have snow tires. But snow tires are for winter. This is still autumn."

"Snow tires aren't wardrobe, Cozy. They're for snow. Look outside, this is *snow*."

Maitlin ignored her.

Alan held the receiver to his ear. "Yeah," was how Casey Sparrow answered her car phone.

"Casey, it's Alan. I'm with Cozy Maitlin. Is that okay with you?"

"Good. Yes, absolutely. Do what he tells you. I'm parked behind a fishtailed cable TV truck just up the canyon from the Red Lion. Did Cozy catch up with you before the cops did? Please say yes."

"Barely, but yes."

"Thank God. I asked him to hurry, but with Cozy, you never can tell. I don't know what you know and

I don't want you to tell me over the air what you know, but I didn't want you inadvertently helping the detectives. Cozy will be assisting me on this. One pair of hands won't be enough, especially during these first few days. I'll be down to Boulder as soon as I can get past this stupid truck."

"So it's okay to talk with him?"

"Oh good. A tow truck has arrived, praise the Lord. Yes, absolutely, you can trust Maitlin. He may make you want to pull your hair out, he'll definitely make you want to pull *his* hair out, but, yes, you can trust him."

Alan, the psychologist, thought he detected an adrenaline surge in Casey's demeanor. He wondered if it was because of the case. Lauren had once told him that there was nothing as appetizing for a DA as prosecuting a high-profile capital crime. The same would probably be true for a defense lawyer.

"You want to talk to him, Casey?"

"No need, I've already yanked on my own hair plenty tonight. Hope to see you soon. Bye."

"Well?" asked Cozy.

"She said I could trust you."

"She implied I was difficult, too, didn't she?"

"Yes, she implied that."

"She's right. I am. I like to think it's one reason why I'm so successful at this." He paused. "That's how I rationalize my behavior, anyway."

From the front seat, Erin laughed loudly.

✛

Erin Rand removed her gloves and wrapped both her bare hands around the double latte she had ordered at an espresso bar on the Hill before she had driven the BMW up Baseline to the site of the shooting. She rotated her wrist to look at her watch. Ten-fifteen.

"Shooting was when, Cozy?"

Cozy answered her. "Casey thinks right around seven. Little before, a little after."

"This snow really screws up the scene. They're never going to find evidence till this shit melts, and even then half of it is going to get washed away." Erin had pulled Cozy's car right next to the crime scene tape at the end of the block. She and Cozy lowered the two driver's side windows so they could try to see what was going on. Snow as heavy as soggy cornflakes drifted inside the car and quickly melted on the warm leather.

Erin asked, "How long is this storm supposed to hang around?"

Alan said, "Not long, I heard that the upslope should break apart soon. Tonight, maybe tomorrow morning."

Cozy was gazing outside. He said, "The canopy is a nice touch, though, don't you think, Erin?"

A portable canopy had been erected on the side of the street in the middle of the block. It was about fifteen feet square and was centered over the spot where the victim had fallen.

Erin said, "Absolutely. I haven't seen one at a crime scene before and I admire their resourcefulness. But look how much snow is already under it. I bet they just got it up. If it keeps snowing this hard the damn thing will collapse from the weight, anyway."

Cozy said, "Still, you must admit, a nice touch. Someone up here is using his head. Perhaps a good sign for us, perhaps not. Time will tell."

Alan listened to the banter. Cozy was dipping a tea bag up and down, up and down into a cardboard container of hot water as though the act itself was an important part of whatever would lead to freeing Lauren from jail.

The trio had just slalomed to the crime scene above town, west of Chautauqua. The whole street was taped off and at least a half-dozen patrol cars remained. Everything and everyone was shrouded in snow. Occasionally, the wind stilled for a second or two and the storm blinked and for that brief moment everything was clearer.

Just as suddenly the whiteout would return.

Erin attached a telephoto lens to a Nikon camera body and took some shots with exposures that, to Alan, sounded way too long.

"How does this work? I've never been in a situation remotely like this before. When am I going to be able to see Lauren?"

Cozy responded without turning to face him. "Would you like me to be reassuring and say something that will help you feel hopeful? Or do you want me to tell you the truth?"

"How about the truth?"

He pointed at his car phone. "When Casey called again a few minutes ago, she was finally at the police department. Hopefully, she was on her way in to see Lauren. What the police have told Casey thus far is, that before she got smart, Lauren apparently admitted to firing her gun—"

"A gun. Lauren doesn't own a gun."

"Whatever. She fired a weapon. *Contemporaneously*, the authorities are alleging, a slug entered the victim. They will not be inclined to find this fact coincidental. The bullet entered the victim's back, I might add. He's unconscious now, in surgery. So—given Lauren's acknowledged discharge of a weapon and the subsequent injury by gunshot of a bystander close by, the authorities have plenty of reason to hold Lauren. Wait, she doesn't own any property up here, does she?"

"No, Cozy, she doesn't."

"Figures. Would have been too easy a defense. Bottom line: On a first-degree assault or an attempted murder, or even worse, if this goes capital, a homicide, they will definitely hold her over for two o'clocks unless we can prove unequivocally that she's not involved. Failing that she will get her first appearance . . . what's today, Friday? . . . She'll get her first appearance tomorrow. We can bitch and moan and threaten but there really is no way you will be permitted to see her until after the two o'clocks tomorrow. That's her first appearance. I'm very sorry, but that's just the way it is."

"So what are we talking, tomorrow at two?"

"No. Actually, on Saturdays the two o'clock hearings are at four o'clock. You might see her after that."

"What about bail?"

Cozy grew silent for a moment while he considered the question. "Assuming the case doesn't go capital, I think she'll bond out. If the man dies, the odds drop to fifty-fifty. There's going to be a special prosecutor appointed on this. To buy time, and to cover his or her ass, the special will probably ask for an investigation by the bond commissioner and for an independent psychiatric eval . . . mostly he'll just want to allow heads to cool and let the facts become clearer . . . so I'd say, barring complications—my best guess is that Lauren'll bond out by next Friday. Before that, not a prayer. Then again, given her reputation, maybe."

Lauren would spend a week in jail? "That's unacceptable. What are the chances of getting her out sooner?"

Cozy shrugged his shoulders. "I'm trying to be straight with you. Sooner, someone would have to go out on a limb. I don't see that happening. Maybe she'll draw a judge who's in a benevolent mood. I wouldn't count on it. If this guy goes out, a week is a reasonable guess."

Shit. "Do you know who the victim is, Cozy?"

"That's an excellent question. Casey says the cops won't identify him—it is a 'him,' by the way—and she suspects they are in the unenviable position of not knowing who the hell the guy is."

"Look," Erin said, pointing out the window, "they're checking cars."

A uniformed cop with a kitchen broom had begun cleaning the snow off a car parked against the curb thirty yards or so behind the canopy. Erin snapped long-exposure shots as fast as the long shutter speeds would allow.

"Can you get the license plate, Erin?"

"Wow, that's a good idea, Cozy. And here I was wasting my time trying to zero in on the registration in the glove compartment. Do your job, talk to your client. Leave me alone to do mine."

Cozy smiled in response. Alan's impression was that Cozy enjoyed her act.

The cop with the broom finished cleaning off the first car, a late-model Saab, and moved down the road, in the direction of Cozy's BMW. He started sweeping the snow off another car, a sport utility vehicle of some kind.

"Ah, intrigue, Cozy. Out-of-state tags on this next one," said Erin.

Cozy asked, "Is Lauren's car here, Alan? Do you see it anywhere?"

Cozy noted that Alan didn't even look around before he said, "I don't see it."

Alan was thinking, *but if you go up that driveway at the top of the hill and check the spot behind those three piñons, I think you may find it. That's Emma Spire's house.*

"Do you know anyone who lives around here? Know any reason why your wife would have been here?"

Alan recalled Lauren's caution about Emma Spire on the phone, considered the wild card of Emma's vulnerability, and decided he didn't want to answer Cozy's question. He was looking for a way to change the subject when it hit him that he still had drugs to take to the jail for Lauren.

"Cozy, I have some medicine with me that Lauren needs to take each night. I need to get it to Casey so she can give it to Lauren tonight, right away."

"What kind of medicine?"

"It's for a chronic thing she has. She's been taking it for a long time."

"I've heard rumors that she has something serious."

Jesus. "What have you heard?"

"It's not much of a secret in the Boulder bar that she has *something*. People respect her wishes not to talk about it. That's all."

As Alan digested the fact that Lauren's secret wasn't much of a secret, someone walked up from behind the car and blocked Maitlin's view of the crime scene. Alan recognized the person from his swagger and his overcoat.

"Hello, Mr. Maitlin."

Cozy shielded his eyes and lowered the window farther. He looked up. "Oh good evening, Detective Purdy. I see you pulled prime duty tonight. You must have infuriated someone downtown."

Purdy ignored the dig. "I take it that you're here on official business, Mr. Maitlin."

"It appears so, Detective, yes. I do hope that we're not in the way. You know I prefer to get started when things are fresh. Just like the police."

"You're not in the way yet, no."

"Hi Sam," Alan called.

Purdy leaned down and looked across the backseat, acting surprised to see his friend. "Hey, Alan, didn't expect to see you up here. I'm real sorry about the mess with Lauren. I'm still hoping we can straighten this out tonight and get her home safely tucked in bed. Do you know that people have been looking all over for you? I've heard we have some good video of you being kidnapped from the vestibule of the police department a little while ago."

"That would have been me offering him shelter from the storm, Detective."

"It is a little inclement out here. Mind if I come into the car, so we can talk a little more?"

Cozy thought about it, considered the pros and cons. They might learn something valuable. And then again, Alan was an unknown to Cozy, and might be a loose cannon. "Just a moment, Detective. Your window, Erin, if you don't mind."

The windows in the BMW powered up.

Alan said, "He's a good friend. He'll help us."

Cozy brushed hair off his brow. "Don't be naive. He's a good cop. He'll help them."

"He's sacrificed a lot to help Lauren out of trouble before. I think he'll do it again."

"You talking about the Utah thing?"

"Yeah."

"Nobody was watching him then. He got to be a cowboy. Cops like to be cowboys. So Utah doesn't count. All his colleagues are going to be watching him this time—closely. I promise. I think, though, that I'm going to invite him into the car anyway. This is what is about to happen: He wants information from you. I want information from him. This will be a dance of finesse. Be extremely careful what you say to him. Your wife's welfare depends on it."

Cozy lowered his window and invited Detective Purdy into the front seat. Sam brushed as much snow off himself as he could before he climbed into the car.

Cozy assumed the role of host. "I think you know everyone. In case you don't remember her, that's Erin Rand, one of my investigators. Sorry I can't offer you any refreshment."

"Just as well, I'm all coffee'd up, thanks."

"My mother taught me to be more gracious than this, Detective."

"Did Lauren call you for help, Mr. Maitlin? I'm surprised you're not down at the jail."

"No, I've not spoken with Lauren, exactly."

Sam looked at Alan who was looking at Cozy. "But you've been retained?"

"By the family, yes."

Sam knew that Cozy Maitlin had just told him that Alan had a lawyer. Sam looked back at his friend and wanted to know why the hell Alan needed one.

Alan, too, wanted to know why the hell Cozy thought Alan needed one.

"Is this your case, Detective?"

"No, I was on call and got pulled in to help work the scene. It's Scott Malloy's case. He's downtown, somebody else is at the hospital. You know how it goes when a big one breaks. Slow night till this happened. Accident alert is on. And your everyday creeps don't like to work in blizzards. So it's been slow. I didn't expect to spend my night out here, I can tell you that."

"Finding anything useful?"

"Lot of snow. A lot when it happened and more all the time. Hate these fall snowstorms. They're hell on the poor trees. Stand out there and you can hear the limbs crack."

"Neighbors see anything?"

"You know about witnesses, Mr. Maitlin. They hear things, they see things. Sometimes they think they hear things, sometimes they think they see things. A few folks heard a gunshot, nobody can agree on a time. Grain of salt, most of the time, especially in a whiteout like this."

"Who's the victim, Detective?"

Sam ignored the question; he figured he was just about done playing the part of the interviewee. He asked, "What was Lauren doing up here, anyway?"

Cozy said, "I can honestly say I don't know."

Sam watched Alan divert his eyes.

"Well, I can honestly say the same thing in regards to your question about the victim. I don't know who the hell he is. Alan, do you know?"

"Who the victim is? No. How would I know that?"

"Not who the victim is, what Lauren was doing up here?"

"No, Sam, I don't *know* that either."

"But, if pressed real hard, you might be able to make an educated guess?"

Cozy broke in. "I think that the product of all educated guesses will, for the moment, remain between my clients and me."

"I take it that someone, one of your associates, is down at the department with Lauren, Mr. Maitlin? You're not handling this by yourself, are you?"

"No. Actually, I'm the one who's assisting this time. I was brought on by Casey Sparrow. Do you know her? From JeffCo." From the lips of someone in the Boulder bar, it was like saying, "from the *suburbs*."

Sam Purdy smiled. "Yeah, I know her. I should've guessed. Casey's all right. She still have all that hair?"

"I certainly hope so. Wouldn't be the same Casey without it, would it? By the way, I want to commend you on the canopy over the crime scene. An inspired touch."

"Not my idea, but thanks. Those things are getting lighter and smaller all the time. I'll be sure to pass along your compliments."

"Erin would like to begin canvassing the neighborhood, interviewing witnesses. I assume that won't cause you any problems."

Sam looked hard at Alan, saw the pain and confusion in his face.

"Nah, it's fine by me, just stay outside the tape." Sam Purdy paused a moment, thought about what he would say next. He turned toward Erin. "If I were you, Ms. Rand, I would probably start my interviewing at that big house on the corner." Sam pointed in a vaguely southeastern direction. "Woman who lives there is quite a character. She's full of stories, loves to talk."

Erin Rand was flustered by the fact that she actually seemed to be getting a tip from a police detective. "Well, thank you very much for the advice."

"It's nothing. Well, although this has been pleasant, I do have to get back to work. Some vehicles to check. Most of them are easy, just residents' cars with Boulder County tags. Though nobody in the neighborhood seems to be able to identify that Nissan over there. Nobody has any unaccounted-for houseguests, no visitors' cars we haven't found. Curious." He was looking toward a big utility vehicle near the canopy. "Still need to find the damn slug that hit the guy, too. Wouldn't you know it, it went right through him. See you all later." He winked at Alan. "Hang in there, buddy. We'll make this come out all right."

Sam started to get out of the car.

Cozy stopped him. "Detective, some free advice. I'm not at all certain your officers have the right to sweep snow off private vehicles that aren't linked to a crime. The case law, I predict, won't support this as a plain view exception. You don't want to taint your evidence collection, do you?"

Purdy stared hard at Maitlin before asking, "Is this lawyer shit, counselor, or is this for real?"

"They're not mutually exclusive. It's probably both."

"I'll call the department lawyer then, and get myself some more free advice. A second opinion." He opened the door and eased himself out of the car.

Erin had started to pull on her gloves and hat. She stopped what she was doing and turned to Cozy and said, "I can't believe he told us all that. That's going to save me a ton of work."

"If he wasn't being intentionally misleading."

"Sam wouldn't do that to Lauren. He might not help us. He absolutely wouldn't set us up."

Cozy turned to Alan and said, "Well, if you're right about that, it seems you may have been correct about Sam Purdy's loyalties as well. Apparently, he's decided to provide us with some assistance. And now it's your turn to do the same."

"Of course, whatever I can do."

"I'm delighted to hear that. First what I'd like to know—what I *need* to know—is how does Lauren know Emma Spire? And, second, what might she have been doing up here with a gun?"

Erin Rand was about to venture out into the storm.

Now she decided she would rather stick around and hear Alan's answer to Cozy's question.

✛

The day had already been much too difficult for Alan. He doubted that he had sufficient energy remaining to do anything more than provide comfort for his wife. He was feeling imprisoned by this fancy lawyer's car, by this hellish snowstorm, and now by a question he didn't know how to answer.

The windshield was fogged and the interior of the car had chilled to the point that frost was building on the inside of the glass. He chanced a glance at his companions. Erin had turned to look at Alan. He could tell she wasn't going anywhere until he responded to Cozy.

Cozy's posture was erect, his face serious. Although his manner was formal and sufficiently respectful, the tone of his provocative question had carried the weight of authority, or at least, imperiousness. Alan recognized not only an ancient impulse to be accommodating to authority, but also a more recently cultivated desire to be obstinate.

He wasn't exactly certain whether answering Cozy's question about Emma Spire would fall into the category of being helpful to Lauren or not. He decided the only prudent course of action was to be intentionally oblique.

"Come on, Cozy, Emma Spire's life's an open book, we all know her the exact same way."

Cozy knew, of course, that Alan was referring to the very public events around Emma's father's death, specifically about the videotape of the assassination.

As a calling card, it was like asking how you knew about Rodney King or Reginald Denny or white Ford Broncos.

Two days after the assassination of Dr. Maxwell Spire a much more professional video than the one the assassin's wife had shot in the airport revealed new things about Emma.

A network-pool cameraman recorded her graceful movements as she mounted the three stone steps up the ornate altar of St. Matthew's Cathedral in Washington, D.C. Her eulogy of her father preceded one by the president of the United States.

The nation watched, live.

In the cathedral, at the pulpit, after thirty-five seconds spent composing herself, she said, "My name is Emma Spire."

Her voice cracked and tears filled her eyes. She gazed at her father's casket, beseeching him to rise from the box and assist her, rescue her.

"This morning I will bury a decent man, my father, in a grave beside a decent woman, my mother. And then, this afternoon, I will begin to resurrect my dreams. Because that is what they taught me to do. That is what they would have wanted me to do.

"But first, first, I . . . I want you to understand some things about my parents that might get lost if I don't tell you. My father was a wonderful physician and a dedicated public servant. Others, I'm sure, will tell you about that today. Believe them. Because those things are true. But

what is more important that you know about my parents is that their lives . . . blessed my life.

"They taught me about compassion, and they taught me about love. They taught me about values, and they taught me about dignity. That . . . man's . . . gun took my father's life. But his hatred cannot take what my daddy gave to me during every day of my life.

"I've already lived too long without my mother's touch or the wisdom she would whisper in my ear. And I will live, now, for too long without my father's embrace, his comfort, or his guidance. My life will be so much darker and colder without those things. I pray that I will rejoin my parents some day in heaven. Until that day, I hope and I pray with all my will, that I live a life that honors them and makes them proud."

Emma gazed down at the casket. Shutters clicked, catching the brittle light flickering in her eyes.

"I don't yet know how much I will miss you, Daddy. That . . . is a black territory in my heart. It's a place I'm still too terrified to explore."

The president, too, spoke that morning about Emma's father. He praised his surgeon general for his sense of duty to his country, for his ultimate sacrifice. He condemned those in the antiabortion movement who condoned the murder of Dr. Spire. The president spoke of the pornography of assassination, of the imperative that ours remain a nation of laws, not ideologues.

For America it was a CNN day. A video memory.

The president has many days.

But this day was Emma Spire's.

Live.

Later she went to Hollywood, ensuring she would not be forgotten.

Cozier Maitlin was exasperated. "That's not what I mean, Alan. I don't mean how does she know *of* Emma. What I want to know is how does Lauren *know* her? Here in Boulder. Are they friends? What? What was Lauren doing up here tonight?"

"You know that Emma came to Boulder to go to law school, right? After she decided not to marry that actor."

"Yes, of course. Apparently the poor man had done everything but straighten his cummerbund when she dumped him."

Alan ignored the invitation to gossip about Emma's aborted marriage. "Last spring some time, Emma applied to do an internship in the DA's office. Lauren got acquainted with her there. They've become friends."

The first part, the law school–in–Boulder part, was common knowledge. And the internship? *People* magazine had done a five-page piece about that. Maybe Cozy didn't read *People*.

"Was Lauren coming up here to see Emma tonight? Was this DA business or personal business?"

"I don't know how my wife spends her days, who she sees. She doesn't provide me with a copy of her calendar. I think Lauren should answer these questions, Cozy. I would be speculating, and that's not fair to either Lauren or Emma."

Cozy jerked his head quickly to face Alan. "Does the shooting have to do with Emma? Tell me that. What are we dealing with here?"

Alan was mildly appreciative of Cozy's interviewing technique. Alan could have taught him a few things about the use of non sequitur but a growl from his belly distracted him, reminding him that he hadn't eaten for a long time. Maybe that was the cause of the headache flaring in his brain stem.

"My wife shot somebody tonight. That thought is as baffling to me right now as if you told me aliens had landed in Boulder. I don't know what's what. Maybe my wife is sitting alone in jail because of Emma Spire. And then maybe not. I don't know. But I do know one thing, Cozy: If this does have to do with Emma, there are going to be more sleazy reporters camping out in Boulder tomorrow than have congregated anywhere since O.J."

Maitlin swallowed the last of his tea and reached forward to place the empty cup on the console between the front seats. "Although I am certain you have your reasons, I don't believe you. And I will admit to being wary and less than pleased that you are not being more forthcoming about this. Do you actually think the cops don't know that Emma Spire lives right up the street from here? I mean, really."

"From my brief conversation with Lauren tonight, Cozy, I'm working under the assumption that she feels she needs to hold that card close to her chest right now. I don't know the answers to your questions. Lauren does."

Erin interrupted. "I'm ready to start canvassing, Cozy. Alan, can you drive him back to town? The big boy's license is under suspension due to a proclivity toward trying to break the land speed record. And, Cozy, if you don't have somebody back up here in ninety minutes to give me a ride home, I'm going to tell the state bar about your account with Victoria's Secret. A cab is fine, I don't care. Pull some strings.

I promised the baby-sitter I'd be home by two-thirty. Nice meeting you, Alan." She paused and waited until he looked at her. "We'll do everything we can to make this come out okay."

Erin slid out of the car and walked around to the window next to Alan. She knocked on it. He searched around for the button and lowered the glass a few inches.

With one hand she held the hair back from her face. She whispered, "If I were in jail, he's who I would call. He's pompous, he's arrogant, and he's good. Keep reminding yourself to forget the first two traits."

In three determined strides Erin Rand disappeared into the storm.

Cozy was absolutely unconcerned about what Erin might have whispered to Alan. He suggested that Alan and he move up to the front seat.

"Erin's a good investigator, she'll come back with something," he said. "Especially with the wonderful treasure map that Detective Purdy left for her. People talk to Erin. I'm not sure I've ever understood precisely why, but they do. I found her inquisitive manner increasingly grating after we were married. Though I suppose it had its charms early. That, and the fact that the woman reached into my pants even before I'd ever dreamed of reaching into hers."

"You two are *married*?"

"*Were*, were. Ages ago, when we were young. And quite foolish. At least I was. She still is, I think."

"The kids with the baby-sitter, they're—"

"A different ex-husband altogether, thank you. Although I love them dearly. Twin girls, ten years old."

"And Erin works for you now?"

"Erin works for no one. She's independent, literally and figuratively. Has her own cute little business. My law firm employs her from time to time. Quite regularly, come to think of it."

"That's not difficult for you? Hiring your ex-wife, working with her?"

"The woman was dear enough to put me through law school without complaining too loudly. Helping her out with an occasional job seems the least I could do. And anyway, she's good, like I said, people open up to her, find her soothing. She always wanted to be a therapist, like you. That is what you do, isn't it?"

"Yes, it is. She has inviting eyes, Cozy. Compassionate. Maybe that's it."

"Maybe. It's something I'm told I lack—outward demonstrations of compassion. I've always thought that public empathy is thin ice for a criminal defense attorney. Society seems to feel that compassion should be bestowed most generously on the victim, don't you think, and not on the accused? Sometimes I'm not at all certain that I disagree. Other times things get turned around, though, and I'll admit to you that's not when I'm at my best."

Given the day's events, Alan was less inclined to concur than he might have been.

"But if that *is* your opinion—that Erin's manner is 'inviting'—a sweet word by the way, she would get a kick out of it, then perhaps I should assign her to interview you and allow her to ask you all the tough questions about your wife and Emma Spire that you're not inclined to answer."

Fighting hunger, fatigue, and shock, Alan paused

and thought before he spoke. "Don't misread me, Cozy. There are some complicated things going on. But this isn't about me. Lauren gets to make this call."

"Not Ms. Spire?"

"She's already made her calls."

"Ah."

"Hopefully, Lauren and Casey are sorting all this out right now, right?"

"Right, hopefully. Although this process, arrest and arraignment, is not as predictable as you might be inclined to believe."

"Assuming that they've talked, I would really like to head back to town and hear from Casey what's going on. I have to get Lauren her medicine before midnight. And I have the checkbook that Lauren needs if she's going to give Casey a retainer."

"Well, the retainer," said Cozy warmly. "Why didn't you say so?"

He placed his hands on the wheel and without facing Alan said, "Do you mind driving? Even if I still had my license, I admit that I have this neurotic thing about driving in arctic conditions."

TWO

**Tuesday, September 24. Late afternoon
66 Degrees, Sunny**

The sun was shining and the sky was clear, the air as sharp and fresh as the first sip of a cold beer.

Lauren played an adequate second base for Montezuma's Revenge, a softball team loosely managed by Alan's partner in clinical psychology practice, Diane Estevez. This game was against the Virga from nearby Broomfield.

Alan Gregory plopped down next to Raoul Estevez, Diane's husband, to watch the two teams warm up. Raoul said, "Great day for a game, huh? The opposition seems quite formidable, though, don't you think? All the parts of their uniforms match. I wonder if they have a shoe contract with Nike." Raoul was sitting with someone Alan didn't know.

"Alan Gregory," Raoul said, "this is Ethan Han."

Alan did know Han by reputation. Ethan Han was Boulder's entrepreneur du jour. The "Island Wunderkind," one of Denver's dailies had called him.

During a recent meal with Diane, Alan, and Lauren at the Zolo Grill, Raoul had described Ethan Han as "a special breed of entrepreneur. He has a unique vision of technology that extends far beyond commercial viability. With what he sees and what he wants to do with what he sees, he will either shake this world to its toes or he will die frustrated while trying. That is, if he manages to avoid the pressures of his creativity."

Alan asked, "What does that mean?"

Raoul thought about what he wanted to say. "His mind works much faster than his laboratory. He wants to explore the next idea, and the next, before he completes the necessary pieces of the first."

"He's impetuous?"

"No. He is like American food. He is unseasoned."

Looking for subtext in Raoul's crafty use of language, Alan said, "So I take it that you are going to work with him?"

"Absolutely. Who better? This man can change the human condition. Ten years, fifty years from now, his work will be remembered."

With Raoul Estevez and his conveniently awkward English, it was impossible to tell whether "who better" meant "who better could I find to work with" or "who better could Han find to help him achieve his vision than me." Alan assumed both possibilities might be true. No one had nannied more of Boulder's storied entrepreneurial successes than had Raoul Estevez. His résumé read Storage Technology, NBI, Minibyte, McData, Exabyte, and TelSat. Raoul's wet-nursing of these high-tech start-ups had earned him great wealth from stock options over the years, and apparently he was now involved with Ethan Han's medical engineering firm, BiModal.

"What's so visionary? What did I read, Han's company does electronic prosthetics, biological monitoring, and medical telemetry, right? How large a market can there be for that? Doctors and hospitals, who else needs that kind of equipment?"

Raoul dismissed Alan's limited perspective with a wave of his long fingers. "Saying that Han does 'prosthetics' is like saying that *Jurassic Park* was about lizards. BiModal already does incredibly sophisticated sensory myoelectrics for amputees. They are close to completing a prototype artificial retina. Astonishing things. You do not have an entrepreneur's vision, Alain. Telemetry, yes, Ethan knows it better than anyone. Biological monitoring, yes, cutting edge. But Ethan Han is not in this world to build a wristwatch EKG receiver so that cardiologists can monitor their patients from the golf course. His brilliance, his gift, is in creating software that decodes neural signals. And he knows things about business that young men don't usually know. The right technology creates markets, it doesn't fulfill them. Ethan has visions for what can be done with his technology that the rest of us haven't thought of, and won't ever be creative enough to think of. Education, entertainment, new forms of medical diagnostics. Consider Bill Gates here, not Henry Ford."

Alan's experience of Raoul was that he was such a good salesman he often sold himself first, so he said, "May I ask who recruited whom?"

"I don't understand." When Raoul wasn't comfortable with the twists of a conversation, his communication skills suffered drastic impairment, and he transformed himself back into a vestigial immigrant from Barcelona. The truth was that he was trained at

Harvard and Cal Tech and spoke English with more authority than most members of the U.S. Senate.

"Did you seek out Han or did he hear about you? Who was courting whom prior to this nuptial?"

"Nuptial? That is like a—?"

Diane, his wife, interrupted her assault on a quesadilla to cut in. "He's afraid that *nuptial* might be yet another Anglo-Saxon idiom for fucking."

"It means 'marriage,' Raoul."

"He knows what it means, guys." Lauren smiled warmly at Raoul.

Raoul refilled everyone's glasses with Crazy Ed's Chili Beer before he answered. "Ethan called me, just to talk, when I got back from Huntsville last month. He's having some cost-containment problems, heard I had some experience with that."

Over the last six months Raoul had been spending much of his time in Tennessee wrapping up his involvement with another start-up, TelSat, which was in the process of selling out to TCI. Diane had told Alan that she and Raoul were going to make a shitload of money in the transaction, too.

"And for your deal with BiModal, are you taking salary or stock options, Raoul?"

"The company is not rich with cash. R&D for the artificial retina and a . . . new project is killing them. Ethan is not wealthy, either. He is . . . what do you say?"

"Broke?"

"Yes, that. But I was thinking more . . . his existence is austere, frugal. I'm accepting options only this time. I think it is prudent. BiModal needs its cash. You may have read that Ethan turned down an unsolicited offer from HP two, three months ago?"

Alan had read about the solicitation in the paper. "Was it a good offer?"

"Yes, based on current revenues and conservative projections. A pittance for what BiModal should be worth in five years. Or even two, if Ethan's plans work out."

"So I should buy twice as much stock as I otherwise might consider?"

"Sorry, but you cannot. BiModal is privately held. Ethan and his family. A partner. A couple of big investors. That's it." His dark eyes locked onto a waitress who was approaching with the table's entrées. "Part of my job will be to stretch his capital. He wants me to streamline his R&D and help reduce costs of moving into production."

Again, Alan heard subtext. "What's the rest of your job?"

"It is—what—unspoken? I am to be his mentor, I think. To guide his imagination. To break his wildness, like a young horse needs. You know?"

"You make him sound capricious."

"No, 'unfocused' is a better word, I think. He does one thing for a while, then he gets excited about the next. A bad habit. It eats capital."

Alan had read that Han was twenty-nine, but reclining on the grass at the softball game, he looked twenty-five. He was wearing a Daily Bread T-shirt from the bakery on Pearl Street, some long cotton print shorts, and pale orange flip-flops. His dark black hair was unruly in an adolescent way and his tropical skin was as smooth and rich as melted chocolate. His sunglasses looked expensive.

"Do you know some of the players, Ethan?" Alan couldn't help wondering why Ethan had come to the park on a weekday afternoon to watch a softball game. It was a nice day for hanging out in the sun, sure, but most spectators were friends or relatives of the players.

"No, no. I only know Diane. Maybe I'll meet someone though, right? That's always possible." He didn't look at Alan as he spoke.

Alan said, "Raoul may have already told you, but I met my wife here. That's her at second base. Lauren."

Han had been looking that way. "She's quite attractive." His comment seemed offhand, as though he were approving of Alan's selection of a tie. "As a courtesy to you, I'll cross her off my list."

Han's humor was either as dry as a good chablis or he wasn't kidding. Alan couldn't tell.

"What about the left fielder? Whose wife is she?" He pointed to the outfield.

"She's new. I don't know her," said Raoul. "Maybe Alan knows who she is."

He did. The left fielder was a substitute, not a regular. Her abundant brown hair was tied back in a ponytail that flowed halfway down her back through the opening in her cap. She wore sunglasses that obscured most of her face. At that moment she was shagging whatever fly balls Diane's bat could loft that far and demonstrating a pretty fair arm.

Alan hesitated before addressing himself to Raoul. "That's a friend of Lauren's from work."

"She's a prosecutor, too?" Raoul asked.

"No, an intern. Law school student. Some of them spend some time in the DA's office."

Ethan was piecing together the riddle. "What's her name?"

"Emma," Alan said. "Her name is Emma." He wondered which one of them would bite.

Ethan Han leaned forward deliberately, as though being twelve inches closer to left field would yield him considerably more data. "*The* 'Emma'? That's Emma Spire out there?"

"Yes, one and the same."

"I read that after she left that actor on the altar she had come to town to go to school. I would love to meet her. Can I meet her, do you think?"

Raoul—who had never himself been introduced to Emma Spire, but to whom all things were always possible—said, "Of course you can. Diane will introduce you. Maybe we will all go out for pizza and beer afterward. Alain, yes? Won't that be fun?"

Before he answered Alan watched Ethan Han shift the rest of his weight forward and rest his elbows on his knees, his chin cupped in his palms.

Lauren was beat. The Broomfield Virga had won 14–3. Because of the Virga's exemplary batting skills, Lauren had been left standing in the sun at second base for extended periods of time. Alan knew she was exhausted and assumed she would want to skip dinner with their friends and head home and rest. He had his heart set on a Nick-N-Willy's garlic and basil pizza, anyway. He'd stop and pick up a ready-to-bake and throw it into the oven at home whenever Lauren was ready for dinner.

She walked over to find him under the ash tree and her face lit with relief at finding the shade. She lowered herself to the ground and sat, leaning her back against his for support.

He offered her a cold drink from his daypack and said, "Good game. How about Nick-N-Willy's tonight? You get to pick what kind." He really, really wanted her to choose garlic and basil. Sometimes she liked the one with feta. He wasn't in a feta mood.

"What do you mean, 'good game'? We got killed out there. And I hope you don't mind, but I told Diane that we'd join her and Raoul for dinner. Raoul is meeting with some new business associate of his. Diane figures they'll chatter on about initial offerings and SEC regulations and she wants someone to talk to."

Alan looked at Raoul and Ethan Han, who had ventured over near the backstop. "Raoul's new associate is Ethan Han—you know, the guy he was telling us about at dinner last week?"

"Really, so they *did* hook up." She was running the cold can of iced tea back and forth across her brow. "Then the evening might actually be interesting. Raoul's quite taken with him."

"Yes, he is. You're sure you're not too tired for this?"

"I'm fried, but I'll make it. We won't be out that late, right?"

"What about your medicine?"

"I gave myself a shot before the game."

Alan pointed across the field. "That man with

Raoul and Diane, over there, that's Ethan Han." Ethan was helping stuff catcher's equipment into a canvas bat bag. "Keep a close eye on him. I think he's about to put a move on Emma."

"No way," Lauren said. But Alan could feel her interest piquing.

"I was in on the planning. Watch."

"Sorry, sweets, but this fish don't swim. I've watched half a dozen guys try to hit on her at the office. She'll brush him off like a fly. She's not interested. In a funny way, she's kind of shy."

Alan shrugged and said, "We'll see soon enough, won't we?"

Not two minutes later, Emma Spire had accepted Ethan Han's invitation to join Diane and Raoul for dinner.

It looked like they were a party of six.

Raoul had suggested pizza and beer. Alan guessed Abo's if Raoul got his way, which he usually did, or Old Chicago if Diane was being obstinate, which she often was. But instead, at Ethan's urging, the group ended up at a big round table at MijBani feasting on creamed lentils and curried chickpeas and cauliflower and potatoes and chapati and naan.

With less than half of a tall Kingfisher in him, Alan was forced to admit that he had lost his yearning for pizza. Lauren, too, seemed to be rallying, although Alan couldn't tell if it was the good food that was responsible, or whether it was her fascination with the overt flirtation that was taking place between Ethan Han and Emma Spire.

Emma Spire's internship in the DA's office had started only a month earlier. Lauren had commented to Alan after the first day she had worked with Emma that her intensity during a personal conversation was remarkable. When you had Emma's attention, she made you feel like the center of the universe.

Royal Peterson, the DA, assigned Emma to Lauren, who tried hard to make the experience as normal as possible for Emma, for whom nothing seemed normal anymore. Lauren refused to be interviewed for the *People* piece, and convinced Roy to decline to permit the magazine photographer to shoot in the office.

Emma apologized to Lauren about the *People* intrusion. "If I give them this, if I let them have this piece of me, maybe they'll leave me alone for a while. Otherwise, I'm afraid they'll camp outside the DA's office the whole time I'm here."

Emma Spire knew this from experience.

In the nearly two and a half years since her father's assassination, her name had become one of those words that stand for *something* in the way that Jackie Kennedy's did in the post-Camelot years.

Since that CNN day—the day her father died in her arms on the baggage carousel—Emma's grace, compassion, and beauty entranced the public. But what cemented Emma in the nation's consciousness after that first sunny May was that she managed to bring clarity to the confused events around her father's assassination.

After Nelson Newell, her father's unrepentant assassin, was convicted of the murder of a cabinet official in federal court, Emma requested permission to be a witness at his sentencing hearing. The question to be decided by the court was simply heads or tails, life sentence or execution. The federal prosecutor scheduled Emma's testimony with trepidation, because she wouldn't give him a hint of what she planned to say. If she hadn't been Emma Spire, he would never have permitted her to testify.

Emma was dressed in a simple navy shirtdress with a black leather belt. Her hair was longer by a few inches than it had been in the fabled videotape of the assassination. She was thinner, more mature. Older, her eyes wiser. Watching your father being assassinated, she once told a friend, is a great diet aid.

She was sworn in and she promised to tell the truth. She took a seat in the witness box.

The federal prosecutor asked her relationship to the victim in this case, Dr. Maxwell Spire.

"He is my father," Emma said.

"You understand the purpose of today's proceedings?"

"Yes, I do."

"And what the court is being asked to do?"

"Mr. Newell has been convicted of murdering my father because of his hatred of my father's belief in freedom of reproductive choice. The purpose of today's proceeding is to determine whether Mr. Newell's life is to be sacrificed at the altar of retribution."

The prosecutor opened his mouth to speak. But Emma wasn't done.

"I will be as clear today as I am able to be: My father would not have wanted this man executed. Neither do I. I *understand* Nelson Newell. He believes passionately that violence is a way to solve problems. That makes him a dangerous man." She gazed at Newell then, it seemed with pity, not hate, and directed her next words to him. "I understand what you did, Mr. Newell. That day in the airport. If I'd had a gun—I would have tried to kill you, too. That would have been *my* solution and *my* rage and it would have been as vile as yours."

The prosecutor said, "Ms. Spire, the question—"

Emma looked directly at the judge. "Vengeance is still wrong. This man needs to be incarcerated forever. Please, do that. Don't compound my grief, do not soil my father's work, by killing . . . in his stead."

While the prosecutor was finding his next words, Emma said, "I don't think I have anything more to add."

Over the course of the next year, as she began to journey beyond her grief, Emma never attempted to hide her face. She became the focus of stories in national magazines and on tabloid TV. She *allowed* the world to watch as she moved to L.A. and started dating a young actor, Pico Hackney, and became part of the Hollywood scene. But she never seemed to *desire* that the world watch. That reticence only added to her allure.

With much fanfare, she became engaged to Hackney. Then, with the world's attention glued to their wedding, she left him alone at the altar.

"I'd become lost," she explained to Jane Pauley when she resurfaced a few weeks later in Boulder to live in her grandparents' home. "Hollywood was a drug I took to help me cope. Although I thought I loved him, I'm afraid that Pico, too, became a drug to distract me. That was my fault. Now I want to get my law degree. I want to live the life I might have lived if my father hadn't been killed. I hope people will forgive me my mistakes. I hope Pico can forgive me. I would like to be left alone now. It's time to place that other life behind me."

"What do you think it is about her?" Lauren asked Alan as they were getting ready for bed after their dinner at MijBani.

Alan couldn't tell how serious the question was. He answered, "Magic. Mirrors."

"No, what's so special? How can she be so captivating? You saw everyone knew she was there, staring at her in the restaurant."

Since Emma and Lauren had begun their friendship Alan had given the question of Emma's status plenty of thought. "I don't think it's all that complicated. I think it's the John-John factor."

"What does that mean?"

"Emma's the closest thing we have to the Kennedys. She lost a father to assassination like John Jr. She has Jackie's elegance and style. She has youth, courage, beauty—and especially, I think she intuitively understands her role."

"Which is what?"

Alan finished brushing his teeth while he thought about an answer. "Look at her, Lauren. She's whatever you want her to be. Emma's the daughter every parent's proud of, the sister everyone wants to confide in. She's the wife every husband wants to show off to his friends, and she's the woman every man wants to screw with the lights on."

"*Every* man?"

He smiled. "I'm speaking generally here."

"America's sweetheart?"

"Sure, fairy-tale stuff, don't you think?"

Lauren seemed to be considering what Alan was saying. She pulled off her T-shirt, slid into bed, and turned on her side. She said, "What did you think of Ethan Han?"

Alan said, "Not much. His ego is the size of Ohio. But his focus tonight was Emma; we were just extras on the set. Why, what was your impression?"

She fluffed her pillow. "If he was a defense attorney, I wouldn't want to face him."

"Is that a compliment?"

She laughed. "I'm not sure."

✛

The next time Alan and Lauren saw Ethan and Emma together as a couple was less than two weeks after the softball game. The occasion was a Sunday-night dinner party at Han's flat in the Citizens National Bank Building on the fourteen hundred block of the Downtown Boulder Mall. The invitation for the impromptu gathering had come only the Friday before, accompanied by a big bouquet of flowers and a handwritten note from Emma addressed to Lauren that read simply, "Please come."

Diane and Raoul had been invited to the dinner, too. Alan and Lauren met their friends for a drink downtown before the party. Over cocktails, Raoul explained that the other guests would be some investors in BiModal, including Ethan's partner, Thomas Morgan, whom Raoul described as more concerned with money than with technology.

Leaves were fluttering to the ground, many of the trees were almost bare, and a deep chill in the evening air whispered solemn promises of autumn. On the walk down the Mall toward Han's building, Lauren described how incredulous she was about the changes she had seen in Emma since she had met Ethan.

"I swear she's been absolutely unswayed by guys much more attractive and much more charming than Ethan seems to be. You know Anthony Tipton in my office?"

Diane said, "He's gorgeous. The one with the ass?"

"Yes, Tony, the one with the ass. She blew him right off."

"*No*," Diane said. "The guy is like an advertisement for infidelity. But if Emma was able to leave a hunk like Pico Hackney standing at the altar, she's a stronger woman than me."

Raoul coughed.

Struggling for an explanation for Emma's choice of Ethan Han over Anthony Tipton and Pico Hackney, Diane continued, "Maybe it's Ethan's brains she's attracted to, or his personality?"

Alan couldn't tell if Diane was being sarcastic or not.

Lauren said, "Ethan's exotic. Maybe she goes in for exotics."

Alan smiled to himself. His wife, he knew, was attracted to exotics. Alan had an alternative theory about Emma and Ethan that was less well thought out than he would like but he suspected that the women hadn't hit on the real issue yet, either. He thought that Emma's choice of lovers had to do with power and influence, not asses and brains.

"He's one of the few people in town with a stature that approximates hers. I think we're watching a true power couple here. She's dating her own kind."

"Like me and Raoul," said Diane.

Alan said, "Not exactly, Diane."

"More like Ted Turner and Jane Fonda."

"Or Arnold Schwarzenegger and Maria Shriver."

Alan thought it was beginning to feel like a parlor game. "Yeah, more like that. That's what I think the attraction is. It makes sense that Emma would be most comfortable with someone who has endured at least a taste of the kind of public scrutiny she has."

Alan could see Diane making skeptical faces.

"You don't like my theory?"

"It sounds kind of complicated, Alan. I think there's probably an easier explanation."

"Such as?"

"I have a feeling that Ethan's skin is as smooth as it looks and that he's probably damn good in bed."

"Which building is it, Raoul?"

Raoul seemed not to hear. Diane said, "It's the

macho one—the big old bank with all the pillars down at the dead end of the Mall."

They walked mostly in silence the rest of the way, enjoying the late-summer flowers and coleus, and the unexpected peacefulness of the brick-lined paths on an autumn Sunday.

Raoul said, "This is it," leading them through some glass doors into the lobby of the prominent stone building.

A stately staircase led to the second floor and from there a fire door blocked their path. The fire door off the second-floor landing of the century-old bank building was controlled by a doorbell-buzzer system. Raoul punched the button and they waited to be buzzed in. When no one came, he took out his keys and let them all in the door. A long flight of dark stairs led to the third floor.

Diane said, "I always thought this whole place was nothing but retail and offices."

"Was, I think," Lauren said. "Ethan carved out a small apartment in back. Emma said he has the whole third floor; he uses most of it for his computers and research."

No one greeted the group when they arrived at the top of the stairs, which led down a short hall to a spacious room lined with huge double-hung windows facing north. A big Heriz covered almost all of the red oak floor. The furniture consisted solely of butterfly sling chairs, maybe a dozen of them, in assorted colors.

"Interesting," said Lauren.

"Nice rug," said Alan about the Heriz. He knew rugs because his ex-wife had been a rug nut.

"I wish I wasn't wearing a skirt," said Diane, who couldn't figure how the hell she was going to get back out of one of those chairs.

Suddenly music filled the room.

Raoul, whose taste in music spanned the globe, said, "Hootie and the Blowfish," with obvious distaste just as Ethan Han entered from a door on the long wall opposite the windows. Han didn't smile much and he didn't smile then. He raised his arms, palms up, as though he was a pastor urging a congregation to rise and join him in prayer.

"Please," he said.

They followed him down a short corridor into a room that looked like a garage sale at Hewlett Packard. A hundred years ago, the old bank building had been built to be grand, with ten-foot ceilings of ornate pressed tin. The carved crown moldings around the room were at least fifteen inches high. The walls had long ago been painted a rich ocher that was now dull and solemn.

The room was lined on two sides with long counter-height workbenches covered with electronics. The east side was the computer wall. Four twenty-inch monitors, each glowing with whimsical screen savers, were spaced at even increments. Processors, drives, memory devices, keyboards, mouses, scanners, printers—enough for any dozen technojunkies—dotted the long laminated counter.

The opposing wall was covered with tools and instruments and microscopes and oscilloscopes and hundreds of color-coded bins full of electronic parts.

In the center of the room, Han's caterers had

erected a large round table covered with a cloth the color of autumn aspen leaves.

A waitress in a white blouse and black vest took coats and drink orders from the newest arrivals.

Two couples stood close to the table in the center of the room, cradling wineglasses. They made a quick assessment of the new guests and returned to their conversations. One of the men wore a sport coat and a tie, the other a linen shirt with a band collar. One woman was in high-end denim, the other in a long rayon skirt.

Across the room, Han's partner, Thomas Morgan, had begun pecking something out on one of the many keyboards. He turned as the new group entered the room. Han saw him, motioned with his hand, and said, "J.P., over here. I want you to meet some people."

Thomas Morgan saved to disc whatever he had been working on and brought the screen saver back up before stuffing his hands in his pockets and strolling over with long strides. Morgan was tall and slender and he wore his tight curls piled high on his head like a cap, the sides cropped to a buzz to accentuate his build. The haircut made his head look too long and narrow, as though it were a section removed from a totem.

Morgan nodded a solemn greeting to Raoul. Ethan made introductions. "This is Raoul's wife, Diane. And this is Emma's friend Lauren, and her husband . . . it's Alan, isn't it? Everyone, this is Thomas Morgan. We call him J.P."

Alan waited until Morgan faced him before holding out his hand for a handshake. Morgan kept his hand in his pocket, gazing at Alan's outstretched hand as though it were an alien life-form, and finally said, "I don't believe in handshakes."

To himself, Alan grunted, *Ah, Boulder.* He said, "Why do they call you J.P.? Are you related to J. P. Morgan?"

Stonefaced, Ethan said, "Hardly. The only thing the two have in common is an affinity for money. Thomas's middle name is actually Avarice."

That's when Emma entered the room.

Her smile. That's it. Maybe it's her smile that gets us.

Alan felt as though he finally had the missing ingredient of Emma's allure figured out. She was merely pretty until she smiled. Then her beauty took on dimension. If it brightened this big cold room—and it did—it could lighten any mood, reassure any doubt, and charm grumps and grandmothers alike.

Her full amber hair was down and lush and she wore a slip dress that was almost demure. Her only jewelry was a glistening pair of earrings that she had previously shown to Lauren. Ethan Han had given them to Emma on their second date—his first gift to her—and called them "antique jewelry." They were made from 100MHz Pentium processors.

Emma stopped in the middle of the room and shook hands with the two couples before proceeding over and joining the group by the door. After greeting everyone, she melded herself into the crook of Ethan's outstretched arm as though it were a cradle she had been waiting for her entire life.

Ethan's stiff reticence softened in her presence. She had the right word to welcome each of the new guests. Everyone in the room soon realized that, even if they didn't want to be, they were watching her every move.

Alan recognized that he wasn't watching her because she was famous. He was watching her because of what made her famous.

The caterers knew what they were doing. Dinner was fine, the service unobtrusive. Hootie and the Blowfish gave way to local rock and roll, mostly the Subdudes and Big Head Todd. Raoul seemed relieved. No flesh was served. The grain was quinoa.

Over the course of the meal, the two couples who completed the guest list at the dinner party revealed themselves as BiModal's major investors. Kenneth's wife, Georgia, was the head of an investment capital consortium. The other couple, Pete and Pat, he of the band collar, she of the denim, was already into BiModal for three million but were seriously considering "coming on board in a big way."

J.P., the only person at the table not part of a couple, was quiet except when asked by Ethan to address some point or another. His posture remained painfully erect through the whole meal. At Ethan's urging, as the entrées were being cleared, he explained BiModal's current financial situation.

"We're burning about 225K a month right now. That's above revenues, which are exceeding projections, up sixty percent over last year. The dilemma is that our current products can't support the development and start-up costs for the products that will be coming on-line in the next eighteen to thirty-six months. But R&D costs for the new products, especially the artificial retina, have skyrocketed, killing our cash reserves. Raoul," he nodded piously at Raoul, who smiled back over the rim of a wineglass, "has agreed to come on board to try and bring some of our efforts into a sharper focus. His experience as a specialist in cutting the fat out of development costs and reducing lead times for production start-up is just what we need. You all know his track record." Morgan gazed quickly toward Ethan and Emma.

Lauren said, "What, may I ask, is an artificial retina?"

Ethan touched a napkin to his lips before he answered. "It's an application of basic myoelectric sensing technology to human optics. Soon . . . we'll be implanting a tiny electronic device behind the eye of individuals suffering from retinal blindness. The chip, in effect, takes the place of the defective retina—that is, it converts light signals into electrical impulses and sends them down the optic nerve. The brain will experience the signals as visual images."

"You can really do that?" asked Diane.

"We're close." Han smiled. "J.P., is that it?"

J.P. seemed to puff up before he continued. "Almost. We've decided to try to keep BiModal privately held. Ethan finally agreed—after some rather heated philosophical arguments with me—that it is in the company's best interests to try to avoid a public offering to finance the next stage of our growth. We're hoping to generate some new investment enthusiasm tonight. Enough to carry us through release of the artificial retina. Revenues should be sufficient at that point . . ." he smiled at Emma, "to finance the newer products."

Alan turned to Raoul and said, "Are you and Diane thinking of investing?"

"No, they're looking for big money, bigger than us."

Alan teased, "I thought you guys were rich."

"As my wife tells me many times, Alan, 'we may be rich, but we aren't *rich*.' "

Before dessert was served, Ethan explained that he had prepared a demonstration that might provide a vision of the potential of BiModal's "next stage of growth"—the one that would succeed the artificial retina to the market—and suggested that everyone move into the front room and have a seat.

Diane, remembering the sling chairs in that big room, responded immediately, interjecting that she was tired of sitting, and she thought she might just stand for a while.

The autumn light was soft, the sky lit by a three-quarter moon. Everyone but J.P., Diane, and Ethan sunk down into a butterfly chair. J.P. leaned on one of the large window ledges on the far side of the room. The evening's focus was moving from finance to technology and Alan thought that J.P. assumed his secondary role reluctantly. From his perch he could watch everyone's faces in profile, but the guests would need to turn to see him.

Ethan left the room for a moment. He returned down the hall pushing a tall industrial cart that was neatly organized with a minicomputer and a large color monitor. He spent a few moments checking power supplies and cables.

"Diane," he said, "since you're standing, how about you? Will you volunteer?"

"For what?"

Han held up a device that looked like a radio collar for a big dog. He said, "This is Natalie." From the collar, two narrow hoses snaked off into an adjacent equipment room.

"Is this some kind of bondage thing?" Her voice tried to convey the question as a joke.

"Hardly."

"Will it hurt?"

"No, not at all."

She looked at Raoul for guidance. He was smiling knowingly. "Why not? I think you will have fun."

Her eyes said, Then you do it. Her mouth said, "Oh sure, why not?"

Ethan carefully fit the collar high on Diane's neck and tightened it into place so that it pressed firmly into the hollow at the back of her skull.

"Why do you call it 'Natalie'?" Diane didn't care. She was distracting herself.

"In homage to Natalie Wood. Her last movie was a science fiction film that predicted this technology."

"If I'm remembering correctly, she died filming it, right?"

"Unrelated events, I assure you."

"I'm so relieved."

Ethan wasn't interested in bantering with Diane. He turned his attention to the investors. "Basically, with the exception of the application program—the neural-signal-isolating software—which I consider my finest work to date, and the collar, which takes advantage of some recent quantum leaps in sensory dynamics technology, the equipment you see is off the shelf. High-end, mind you, and not just any shelf, but the computer hardware necessary here is not particularly sophisticated. The grandest requirements are for memory and processing power. Currently, we're using in excess of fifty gigabytes of memory for ten minutes of signal and over three hundred megs of RAM to run the program. With code refinements, the RAM requirements should be cut significantly. We *hope*. Raoul, write that down, that's your first job."

Raoul laughed but didn't reach for his pen.

"Natalie—the collar Diane is wearing—has sensors that are capable of picking up virtually all the neural signals that exist at the level of her brain stem. For those of you who have forgotten basic neuroanatomy, and I'll assume that's all of you—a brief lesson. By recording the electrical impulses in some discrete structures above the brain stem, we can reliably record virtually all sensory activity that takes place in the body from the face down, and some of the cranial nerve activity from the face and head as well. Motor and sensory signals from the trunk and the extremities travel down local nerve tracks and then up the spinal column to these structures above the brain stem. The cranial nerves that control the musculature in the face follow similar pathways but avoid the spinal column. We're still having trouble debugging the code that deciphers some signals, especially the visual and auditory ones. But for the purpose of the demonstration you are about to witness, those channels are not operative.

"Natalie is possible today because of advances by others in superconducting materials and supermagnetic technology. She senses the neural information—

really just electrical impulses—at the brain-stem level and transmits the data, via telemetry, to the processor.

"The software we've developed has the capacity to identify and separate the signals from literally thousands of discrete pathways, digitize them, and store them."

Han sensed he was losing some of his audience to technobabble. He opened his arms to his guests. "Let me simplify. Imagine a trunk line for a large telecommunications network, all right? With thousands of optical fibers—nerve tracks—and millions of discrete signals—conversations." He paused and waited for head nods. "These sensors are capable of remotely separating out the signals from thousands of fibers and independently isolating out, monitoring, and recording the individual conversations or data transmissions, all from a position that is external to that trunk line. Okay?"

Diane made a face that made everyone but Ethan laugh.

"Ready?"

"Said the spider to the fly?" she replied, nodding.

He hit a key and a computer-animated figure of a woman appeared on the large monitor. Without moving, Diane whispered to Alan, "Is that Natalie or is that me? Ooooh, I think that I like the way my butt looks in cyberspace."

Ethan explained, "The animated figure you see has been preprogrammed into the software. She is obviously nowhere nearly as attractive as Diane but she will represent her for our purposes this evening. Eventually, soon actually, we expect the software to be capable of defining a reasonable facsimile of the individual who is wearing the collar."

Alan thought that Ethan had been hoping for a more serious subject than Diane was proving to be. He wondered why Ethan had chosen Diane, who was always quick with a joke, and usually made no attempt to hide her irreverent side. Was Ethan that poor a judge of people?

"Diane, please take two steps forward and stop."

Diane stepped, goose-stepped, actually. The animated figure immediately mimicked Diane's motion.

"Raise your right arm."

She did. Her graphic representation did, too.

"Open your hand and spread your fingers."

Her obstinate side continuing to dominate, she first made a fist before opening her hand and spreading her fingers. But Diane, too, was growing transfixed watching the figure on the monitor do the exact same things she did.

"Lift your right leg."

She did. "Raoul, are you paying attention to what's going on here? Does this break any of our marital vows?"

Everyone laughed.

"Walk backward, please."

"Is this really just some high-tech sobriety test, Ethan?"

"I think maybe that's enough for now, Diane. Have a seat, please."

"Sorry, Ethan, even in the interest of science, I am not going to let you record the act of my getting my butt back out of *that* chair in *this* skirt."

Georgia, the venture capital specialist, said, "I'm beyond being simply impressed by what you're showing us here, Ethan. The entire signal that is generating that image is coming from the collar she's wearing? None of this is choreographed in advance? There's no video feed or infrared or anything to supplement the data?"

"No, none. Our sensors are responsible for the entire data input. Give her an instruction, Georgia. Any motor movement at all."

"Put your hands on your hips, please, Diane."

Diane had stopped enjoying herself and was beginning to feel like a marionette. She cocked one hip and followed the woman's instruction in an intentionally provocative and sultry way. Her animated double did exactly the same.

From across the room the image looked like the beginning of the trailer for an X-rated comic.

"Amazing," agreed Pete, the one with the "serious money."

Alan had already come to the conclusion that the purpose of the entire evening had been to impress this man and his wife. Technology was the featured attraction. Raoul was the extra added bonus. Emma was the surprise diva.

"How about," Diane said, "we share the fun and let someone else have a try, Ethan. Raoul, *honey*, could you please help me get this thing off."

Ethan jumped forward and turned to the man with the band collar. "Pete, would you like to have a go?"

The dinner party broke up abruptly a few minutes before ten, moments after the venture capitalist's baby-sitter phoned Ethan's flat with breathless news of projectile vomiting and other grave toddler distresses. Within a few minutes all of the guests were gathering their belongings and heading out the door.

The two money couples had arrived together in one car and they departed together. As the waiters were retrieving coats for the rest of the guests, Emma asked Lauren if she would mind walking her to her car. Although Boulder's downtown was usually safe, Emma's reluctance to walk alone to her car didn't surprise Lauren. Even at work, Emma usually sought company for the brief stroll to the parking lot.

Lauren said, "Of course. I would have offered, but I assumed you'd be staying here tonight. I take it you're not planning on—"

"No." Emma smiled, shaking her head. "Ethan needs to meet with J.P. about something. My car's in the parking structure on Spruce. Are you certain you don't mind? I can ask Ethan to walk me but I know he won't leave his computers alone until the caterers are packed up and gone."

"No, I don't mind at all. After that dessert, I'd enjoy a walk."

Alan overheard the conversation. "Lauren, why don't I go get our car? I'll drive around and pick you up on the Eleventh Street side of the garage when you're done walking with Emma?"

Lauren said that sounded fine to her. Ethan helped Emma into her coat, a simple gabardine trench. He flipped her hair out from under the collar and fingered it in a manner Lauren found affecting. The couple then held hands, left to right, right to left. Emma leaned in and they brushed lips quite gingerly, as though they were frightened of bruising each other. Emma's lips parted slightly, Ethan's didn't. When the brief kiss ended, Emma smiled. Ethan didn't.

"Talk to you soon," he said.

"Yes," she said. "Thanks for dinner. Your friends are nice."

Boulder's outdoor mall was almost deserted. Diane and Raoul walked east to their car, which they had left on Fifteenth. Alan kissed Emma's cheek, said, "Good night," and proceeded down to Thirteenth Street to find his car.

Lauren and Emma had the Mall to themselves for the next two blocks. The raised flower beds were bright with coleus and a light breeze rustled through the trees. The drying leaves crackling in the wind reminded Lauren of falling rain.

Finally, Emma said, "I can't believe it but I think I'm smitten."

Lauren said, "You really look smitten. I have to admit to some surprise. I've wondered whether you were even interested in men these last few weeks."

"After the fiasco in Hollywood, with Pico, I told myself I wouldn't get involved for a year. Oh well. You know, tonight, earlier, your question? Ethan didn't invite me to stay over. It feels odd. I'm not sure I would have, yet, I mean sleep there. But it feels odd that he doesn't want me to. Or at least that he hasn't asked me to."

"Do you know that he doesn't want you to? Has he stayed at your place?"

They stopped at the light on Broadway. No cars were coming in either direction. They jaywalked.

"It hasn't come up. I haven't asked. So far, all we do is, well, we kiss—and that's it. Which is fine, I'm not complaining."

Lauren felt perplexed at the lack of joy in her friend's voice.

"It's only been a couple of weeks, Emma. Give him some time. It sounds kind of innocent, refreshing." What she was thinking, and didn't say, was that entering into a relationship with Emma Spire had to feel complicated to any man. A man eager to rush into romance with Emma would, in Lauren's mind, be immediately suspect. Ethan's reticence was at a much safer end of the spectrum.

"I know you're right; I keep telling myself the same thing. But I don't trust my own judgment, I'm so wary of people. Since my father died, it seems I'm constantly on the lookout for people who want a bite of me. I'm not prepared for Ethan's caution. It's like you and Alan. I'm not accustomed to people who treat me like I'm normal. Maybe Hollywood made me too paranoid."

"Let's be realistic, Emma, if anyone has reason to be cautious of people's motives, it's you." Lauren found herself wondering if maybe what Ethan Han wanted from Emma Spire wasn't the same thing she was expecting him to want from her. Lauren decided to try to feel her out about it.

"What did you think of the party?"

"It was fine. The people were nice. Weird food."

"Did it feel kind of like a sales meeting to you? I

didn't get the impression that Ethan really cared much for anyone there but you."

"It's possible; he always seems to be thinking about his business. Other than all of you, I didn't know anyone but J.P. and the tension between them is pretty apparent. But Ethan does like to show off his toys, so I'm not surprised at the demonstration." She reached out and touched Lauren on the shoulder. "I really appreciate you coming to the party on such short notice. I'm not comfortable being places where I don't know anyone anymore. I feel like such a spectacle. With you guys there, at least I could have a conversation with someone, pretend I'm normal."

"You are normal, Emma. You're—"

"No, I'm not normal, Lauren, not anymore. People examine me in ways they don't examine you. People take liberties with me they wouldn't consider taking with you. Lately, I feel like everyone is waiting for me to screw up. I don't think people really want me to succeed anymore. Now it feels like they're just waiting for me to fail." She remembered something.

"Do you know that I had exactly two sips of wine tonight? And do you know why? Not because that's all I wanted. I was nervous enough that I wanted half a bottle. But I had two sips because, the reality of my life is this: if you or your husband get caught driving drunk, maybe, just maybe, it's worth one paragraph in the *Daily Camera*. If I get caught driving drunk, it's the cover of every news magazine for a week, the tabloids for a month, Betty Ford for six weeks of drying out, and the cop who stops me gets five minutes on *Hard Copy* like he's as important as the guy who caught the Oklahoma City bomber."

Lauren considered what Emma was saying and knew that it was true. In a tabloid world, the Emma Spires on the planet didn't get to make little mistakes. Blemishes became front-page melanomas.

"I understand your need for privacy. I live with something I don't want people to know, a secret, I guess, and I'm afraid that if it gets out, my life will change in ways I don't want, and that I can't control. For me, protecting that vulnerability is a small, but constant, part of my life. But for you the protection involves every step you take. It must be very difficult. I really can't imagine."

Emma took Lauren's hand and pulled her around the corner onto Eleventh Street toward the garage.

"Even people I consider friends have tried to tell me that not having any privacy is simply the price I have to pay for celebrity. But by leaving Pico, I had hoped I rejected celebrity once and for all. I don't want to have to pay a price for it. I'm not Demi Moore. I'm not Sandra Bullock. I'm just a kid whose father was murdered by a nut. I'm not cut out for this.

"I don't even know where to look for a life right now. I know I need to find one someplace, though. Maybe I'll go into international law and move to Paris. People would leave me alone there. The French don't give a damn about Americans."

Alan was parked just south of the entrance to the four-story brick garage in a no-parking zone against the curb. He had spent the couple of minutes he had been waiting watching a pair of rather older adolescents zooming up and down the ramps on BMX-style bikes inside the almost-empty structure. The driver's window on his car was open and Alan was singing along, badly, to the Rolling Stones' "Under My Thumb" on the radio. He extended his arm and waved at Emma and Lauren as they started up the staircase to the second level of the garage, continuing to sing along, oblivious to how poorly he was doing it.

The parking garage had been built to address modern security concerns. The stairwells were open to the street and the whole facility was brightly lit. The exterior walls of the elevators were glass so the passengers could be viewed from the sidewalk.

Emma's car was parked against the north wall of the garage about halfway up the structure. Emma killed her alarm remotely from ten feet away.

She said, "Get in, I'll drive you back down to your car."

Lauren replied, "No thanks, I'll walk. See you tomorrow at the office? Listen, let's get together soon for dinner, just you and me, what do you say?"

"Great idea, I'd like that. Thanks, and thanks again for coming tonight." She started the car, fiddled with the radio for a moment, and shifted into reverse.

The kid on the bike didn't scream in fear at the car pulling in front of him. Emma never even saw him barreling down the steep ramp from the next level.

She had checked her rearview mirror, had seen nothing in her path, and had continued to back up. The bicycle came around the corner, braking only at the last second, before sliding sideways into the rear fender of Emma's car. The rider flew off, his momentum carrying him across the trunk of the car to the driver's side. Emma Spire didn't see the rider until he was airborne, flying past the back window of her car.

Lauren was halfway down the stairs when she heard the brief squeal of bicycle tires and the crash. She listened, but couldn't tell what the noises had been. She hesitated between stairs, then heard the door to a car open and Emma's call, "Oh my God, are you all right?"

An angry male voice yelled, "Shit, did you hit him, man? Oh shit, lady, look what you did."

"I'm sorry, I'm sorry. I didn't see him, I didn't see him. Don't move him, don't move him, he could be hurt. We need to get an ambulance. I'll call for an ambulance."

Lauren started back up the stairs, pulling a phone from her purse. She had barely opened her mouth to speak when she realized she was walking onto a very different scene than the one she was expecting to find.

Emma was leaning over into her car, probably trying to punch 911 into her car phone. One kid, in a big flannel shirt, was standing behind her, looking furtively around the garage. The other kid was raising himself nimbly from the concrete deck, a knife in his hand.

"Emma, he has a knife!"

Lauren immediately wanted to take back the words and sound the warning a second time, this time without including Emma's name.

Immediately, the kid with the knife turned and faced Lauren. Although his face was in the shadows of the bill of a baseball cap, she could tell he was white. Like his friend, he was wearing baggy jeans and an oversize flannel shirt. The police would love the description. A *couple of white adolescents in baggy jeans, flannel shirts, and baseball caps*. There were maybe sixteen males between fourteen and twenty in Boulder that didn't occasionally fit that description.

"Go bitch, beat it."

Lauren fought to instill some calm in her voice. "Let her go. Take her purse. Let her go."

"Sorry, but I think we've made other plans." He laughed, thought he was pretty funny. "We're all going for a ride. But I suppose we can change our plans. You want to join her?" He seemed to be waiting for an answer. "No, didn't think so. Go, get the fuck out of here, or I cut her."

Emma turned, her face solemn and frightened, but not panicked. Her eyes said, See, what did I tell you? Her lips mouthed the word, Go.

Lauren backed into the staircase. Everything she had ever heard or read about self-defense said that, whatever you do, whatever you are forced to risk, don't let them take you someplace else. If they take you someplace else, they can do whatever they want to you.

That means rape. That means murder.

Lauren tore down the steps to get Alan. He was still singing along to oldies, oblivious to what was unfolding above him in the garage.

Lauren burst out of the stairwell at street level and caught his attention. "*Alan!* Back up the car, block the exit to the garage. Somebody's kidnapping Emma."

"What?"

"Back up, now, you have to block the exit. Someone has Emma, they're in her car."

He started the Land Cruiser just as he heard the squeal of tires from Emma's car. To stop her car, it was apparent that he would have to block both the entrance and the exit to the garage simultaneously. His car was big, but it wasn't big enough to do that; he was going to have to choose one or the other. From his position in the street he would be able to see Emma's car approach the gates for a distance of about twenty yards. That was it. If the driver was going fast, and Alan assumed he would be, then Alan would have about as much time to react to his chosen direction as a power hitter has to adjust to a fastball.

Emma's car came around the corner and skidded to a stop about fifty feet from the exit.

One of the kids, the one who wasn't driving, leaned out the window and yelled at Alan, "Get out of our way, man. We'll cut her."

Lauren was standing on the sidewalk, out of sight of Emma's car. Alan could see her clearly. In a voice that said "I know what I'm doing," she said to him, "Don't let them go. Time is on our side. They need out of the garage. They need Emma's car. Cutting her isn't as bad as the alternative. You can't let them leave with her."

Alan edged forward three or four feet. He prayed these kids didn't have a gun. He flashed on his brights.

The driver of the car gunned the engine and backed up another fifteen feet. Alan was well aware that Emma's car could out-accelerate his Land Cruiser off the line. But, he reminded himself, all he had to do was get in its path. Her car could not move a heavy Land Cruiser out of its way.

He checked his seat belt, wished he had a later-model car equipped with an air bag.

Lauren remembered her phone. She pulled it out.

The engine of Emma's car roared. The tires squealed on the slick concrete, fighting to get traction. The kidnappers had made their choice. They were coming out the entrance of the garage.

Alan had guessed that they would. He punched the accelerator and instantly jerked the wheel to the right. He swerved once and the bulk of the Land Cruiser filled the entrance lane. Trying to change course, the kid driving Emma's car clipped the brick railing of the garage and spun. Both doors opened and the two kids jumped out of the car, fleeing back into the garage, around a corner.

In three seconds they were gone, the bikes left behind.

Emma had been crammed between the two criminals on the front seat, her legs straddling the gear shift. Her hands were shaking and her face was chalky.

Lauren got to her first.

"I'm all right. I'm all right. I'm all right." Emma's tone was one of surprise, not reassurance.

"You're not cut? You're okay?"

Lauren slid into the passenger seat of the car and slowly held out her arms to Emma, who hesitated before folding in to them, whimpering, and starting to cry.

Alan leaned in. "Are you all right, Emma? Is she hurt, Lauren?"

Lauren answered, "She's okay, I think. Here's my phone. Call the police, hon."

Emma pushed herself violently from Lauren's arms. "*No!* Please, please don't call the police. This will never be over for me if you call the police. Let's just get out of here. We'll say it's a little car accident. I'll pay for everything, any damage. Get me out of here, please, now. Don't call the police."

She was begging.

It was the first time that Lauren had ever heard Emma sound desperate. She also realized that she, an officer of the court, had just witnessed an attempted kidnapping, and that she had an obligation to report it to the police.

Alan said, "We have to report it, don't we?"

"Why, who will know?"

"They were going to kidnap you, Emma."

"We don't know that. Maybe . . . it was a carjacking, or, or, just a mugging, or—"

Lauren reached over and held her again, forcing Emma's face into the crook of her shoulder. "That was no mugging. Those kids weren't looking for a joyride, Emma. That was a kidnapping, or . . . worse."

"Maybe they didn't know who I was."

"Maybe. You want to assume that? If they were waiting for you, they could try again."

"I don't want the police to know. Please. I can get some protection. I'll find someone to watch over me."

✛

After the terror in the parking garage Emma agreed to go home with Alan and Lauren. Sitting in their living room, she cradled a glass of wine and tried to explain what her life had been like.

"After my father was killed, the president was worried about me. Looking back, it's not too surprising. I was a wreck. Because of the videotape at the airport and all the news that followed I began to get a lot of mail, most of it supportive—I mean, really nice, inspirational even—but some of it was vicious and . . . a few letters were threatening.

"I was a guest at the White House for almost a week after the funeral and when I finally left, the president ordered the Secret Service to keep an eye on me. He can do that. That's when I met Kevin. He was one of the first agents who was assigned to protect me."

Alan asked, "And Kevin, this Secret Service agent, will help you again? All you have to do is ask? I thought you didn't want law enforcement involved."

"I only had the Secret Service protection for about a year. When I moved to California, the death threats stopped and there wasn't really any more need for protection."

"Who had been threatening you?"

"The threats had come from a few people who were part of the radical right-to-life movement, supporters of Nelson Newell. But after Newell's trial, and after I testified at the sentencing hearing, the Secret Service did a security review, concluded I was out of danger, and the protection stopped. I was relieved that they were gone. I didn't miss it then and I haven't had much trouble since. Some phone calls

I would rather not get, mostly. The biggest problem is always the press. The agents always told me they could protect me from a bullet but not from a camera."

Lauren asked, "But you could call the Secret Service again? They would help you, and they would agree to keep this whole thing quiet?"

"Keeping quiet wouldn't be a concern if they felt there was a security reason for it. But, no, I'm not eligible for Secret Service protection anymore. It's a whole different world in Washington now, isn't it? Kevin left the Secret Service not too long after my protection stopped. I get cards and an occasional phone call from him. He's stayed in touch."

"And you trust him?"

"God, yes. Most of the agents who helped me were great. Kevin was always especially sweet."

"And he lives around here?"

"Close enough. Near Colorado Springs. He started a security business after he left the Secret Service. Mostly corporate things, high-tech stuff; I never paid that much attention to what he was doing."

"You think he'll help?"

"Not himself, no, I doubt that he does this sort of thing anymore. But I think he'll know people who can tell me what I need. Whether it's a bodyguard, or just a better alarm system, or what. He's always told me if I need anything, I should call him. He'll give me good advice."

Lauren found a fresh toothbrush and a T-shirt for Emma to wear to bed. Once she was settled into the downstairs guest room Lauren moved back across the hall and snuggled next to Alan.

He waited for her breathing to slow before he said what they were both thinking.

"We made the wrong decision tonight. About not notifying the police. Emma's needs aside, it means that those two assholes—whatever their motives were—are still out there. Assuming that they weren't targeting Emma, they're going to pick another victim soon, right? And if they were targeting Emma, she has to know why, doesn't she, in order to determine the amount of danger she's in?"

"I know," Lauren said, scrunching into the crook of his shoulder. "I've been thinking the same thing for the past hour. But I don't see a way out of it at this point."

"What if you ran it by Roy tomorrow at the office, see what he thinks?"

"Want to know what Roy would think? He would be thinking about giving me a pink slip and figuring out how to handle the PR fallout. And Emma's internship would be history."

"You're sure?"

"Yes, absolutely. I have more credibility with Roy than Emma does. But, I think we'd both be gone."

"Everything happened so fast out there. We weren't thinking clearly."

"So?" she said. "What kind of an excuse is that? We're still expected to obey the law, aren't we?"

Emma slept with the big dog, Emily, at her side.

In the morning, Alan was out of the house at dawn to see an early patient, and Lauren made breakfast for two before she drove Emma back to her own house. While Emma showered and dressed, Lauren read the morning paper, reflecting how different the front page would look had Emma Spire notified the police of the attempted abduction the night before.

Before they left for work at the Justice Center, after continued prodding by Lauren, Emma finally called Kevin Quirk in Colorado Springs.

The receptionist at Tech Secure said Mr. Quirk was in a meeting, could he return the call later? Emma identified herself and said to please tell Mr. Quirk it was important. The flustered receptionist said, "Of course, Ms. Spire, I'm sorry."

Fifteen seconds later, Emma heard Kevin's familiar voice. Like the man, it was anvil solid and plain. Pure Iowa. If a voice could have freckles, Kevin Quirk's would.

"Emma, it's great to hear from you. Kim said it was urgent. What's up?"

"Hello, Kevin, how are you?" She tried to sound normal. Thought she had succeeded.

"Fine. Good. What's going on?"

"Not too much. But, um, there was an incident. And I think I may need your help, Kevin. Security-type help. Someone may have tried to kidnap me last night."

Kevin's tone lowered an octave and his words became clipped and efficient. "First, are you injured?"

"No, I was with some friends. They managed to help me before—"

"In order. Tell me what happened. From the beginning, don't skip anything."

She did. Lauren listened to Emma, occasionally

prompting her with some salient detail she was forgetting.

"You didn't call the police?" Kevin Quirk knew Emma well enough to know what she was going to say in response to his question.

"No. What would they do? I can't stand the thought of being back in the public eye that way, Kevin. I moved here to get away from that. This will pass. You know what the press can be like with me. They wouldn't let go for weeks."

Kevin Quirk stayed silent for a moment.

"I think you may have made the wrong decision last night, Emma. You need to reconsider bringing the police in, and given that it looks like it may have been attempted kidnapping, which is a federal crime, maybe the FBI. Whoever did this to you needs to be found. We need to know what they were up to, what their motives were. Get them off the street."

"Couple of kids, Kevin. That's all. I think it was a carjacking."

"I'm sure you would like to assume that, Emma." He knew he wouldn't convince her of an alternative position over the phone. "Listen, I'll come up to Boulder, we'll talk about it. Where's your house?"

"I promised the friends who helped me last night that I would stay with them or with somebody else until this settles out."

"Good friends? Do I need to check them out?"

"Good friends, Kevin. They're fine."

"Why don't you give me their names, just to be sure."

Emma smiled self-consciously, fought an urge to

shoot a glance at Lauren. "No, not now, Kevin. It's not necessary or possible."

"Okay, I'm relieved to hear that you're with somebody, but I want to see your house, or wherever you're actually living. Can your friends stay with you until I get there?"

Emma covered the mouthpiece and turned to Lauren. "He wants to see my house. Can you come by after work and stay with me? He doesn't want me to be alone there until he assesses the situation."

"Of course," Lauren said.

Emma mouthed "Thank you" to Lauren and spoke back into the phone. "Yes, Kevin, my friend says it's fine. Let me give you directions."

It was nearly seven that evening when Kevin Quirk pressed Emma's doorbell.

Lauren answered. "Mr. Quirk?" She held out her hand.

"Yes, Kevin Quirk." He reached out and took her hand, squeezed it gently, trying to mask his surprise. He had been assuming that Emma's friend was a man. The woman at the door was about his age, with eggshell skin and silky black hair that fell in a straight line to her shoulders. Her eyes were the color of coal smoke.

"Hello, I'm Lauren Crowder, a friend of Emma's. Thanks for coming by. I've been worried about her."

Emma came running to the front of the house with her hair wet from the shower. "Kevin! Kevin!"

She leapt into his arms, her momentum carrying them both around in a complete arc. To Lauren, Kevin Quirk didn't seem to be at all surprised at the exuberance of Emma's greeting. He hugged her enthusiastically, managing to get his fingers entangled in her wet hair.

The man was *solid*. That's the word that came to Lauren's mind. This body had been designed by an engineer, not an artist. No wasted curves or bulges. Kevin Quirk had a big forehead and a prominent chin and small eyes. For these initial moments at least, those eyes were only for Emma. Lauren caught herself looking for a wedding band on his left hand, found one.

He was married. She thought that he looked married.

Considering the exuberance of the greeting she had just witnessed, she wondered whether he would act married.

"You look great," he said, to Emma. He was holding her at arm's length, shaking his head back and forth, just a little bit, like a proud uncle.

"You too, Kevin," Emma said. "Look at you, you're letting your hair grow out. I told you it would look much better. You look a lot less like a marine than you used to." She took his hand and pulled him toward the back of the house. "Come on in, please."

The house was barely furnished. Emma noticed Kevin looking around at the emptiness.

"I still don't have much furniture, do I, Kev? All of my parents' stuff is still in storage. I'm usually so busy I hardly notice. You must be starved. Let me get you something. Do you want a beer?"

"You haven't changed, have you, Emma?" As usual, she seemed oblivious to her surroundings. His tone was approving. "If it's no trouble, I'd love a beer. It's a long drive up from the Springs."

Emma grabbed a bottle of Fat Tire from the refrigerator and brought it over to the sofa with a bowl of tortilla chips and some salsa. She plopped sideways onto the couch, right next to him.

He smiled to her once, said, "Thanks," and turned to Lauren. "Are you and Emma friends from law school?"

Lauren smiled. "Not exactly. Emma's been doing an internship at the Boulder County District Attorney's Office. We met there. I'm a deputy DA. I've been her supervisor for the past couple of months. We've become friends."

"Were you the one who was with her last night? During the assault?"

"Yes, I was. My husband and I."

"What can you tell me about it?"

"It was terrifying. It all happened very quickly. I had walked to her car. I should have just waited one more minute while she got the car started and pulled out of the garage."

"She's lucky you were there at all. God knows what they had in mind."

"I'm glad I was there."

"What do you think their intent was?"

"Do you mean do I think they knew it was Emma they were kidnapping?"

"Yes, I guess that's what I mean."

"I don't know. Before they attacked her, they were acting like kids, just speeding around the garage on their bikes. Maybe they were just waiting for the right victim, any victim. If it had been someone else in that car, I would have said that the assault was half-impulsive, and that the victim was chosen purely at random, just the bad luck of being an unaccompanied female in that parking garage on that night. But it wasn't anyone else. It was Emma. And because it was her, you can't assume they didn't recognize her. That would be absurd. So, the fact that it was Emma, that complicates things."

"Did they ever say her name?"

"Not that I heard. I did, though, when I called out a warning to her when I saw one of them had a knife. Up until that moment they might have just been after her car."

"Emma, did they seem to know your name, to know who you were?"

"Not that I remember, no. They never called me by my name."

"And they were definitely threatening to take you someplace else?"

"Absolutely. The one kid said that at least a couple of times."

"Not just out of the garage?"

"No, I had the feeling that they meant someplace else, they had a destination in mind."

Kevin concluded, "So it appears that they were after either the car or the woman. Not after money."

Lauren said, "I would agree with that. Though it still begs the question of whether they knew the identity of the woman they were kidnapping."

"You were all at a dinner party before this happened?"

"Yes."

"Who knew? Emma, who did you tell? Who knew

where you parked your car, where you would be last night, what time you would leave?"

"I can't think of anyone other than the people who were there, except for Jennifer, you remember my friend Jennifer? I still talk to her almost every day on the phone. I probably told her about the party, but she's back east. And there's a . . . there's a guy I've been seeing. I've been parking in the same garage whenever I've been visiting him. The dinner party was at his house."

Lauren waited a moment to try to gauge Quirk's reaction to Emma's announcement that she was involved with someone. His face revealed nothing.

Lauren said, "The guy she's seeing is a prominent businessman here in Boulder. I don't know if that might be important."

"Emma?"

She wrinkled her nose. "He wouldn't like that, being called a businessman. His name is Ethan Han. He owns a company called BiModal."

"Han, really? You're dating Ethan Han? He's kind of a darling right now, isn't he? He's what, from the Philippines or Taiwan or something? I know people in the Springs who can't wait for him to take that company of his public. Is it serious?"

"His work? Very, he takes it very seriously. And he's Hawaiian, Kevin. As American as you or me."

"I meant the relationship, Emma. Is the relationship between the two of you serious?"

Emma wasn't sure how to answer. "I . . . I like him, Kevin. But we've only been going out a little while, a couple of weeks at the most."

"Do I need to check out his place, too? Are you spending nights there?"

Lauren felt uneasy at the progression of the conversation. She realized she couldn't tell whether the questions that Kevin was asking were personal or professional in nature. She wasn't even sure whether or not Kevin could have provided an honest answer to that question.

"No, I'm not."

Lauren thought she detected the tiniest of sighs before Kevin Quirk stood up, loosened his tie, and said, "All right, show me around the house. Walk me through this alarm system. I can already tell you that the perimeter security is inadequate—you have too many trees, there's not enough light, and there is unimpeded access from too many directions. We have some work to do."

The neighborhood was composed of upper-middle-class homes in a corner of town that was isolated against a huge expanse of greenbelt. Most of the neighborhood had been constructed ten to twenty years earlier, which had allowed plenty of time for shrubbery to mature, trees to grow, and fences to be built. Emma's house was at the end of the block, high on a hill that abutted some of Boulder's abundant open space. Her backyard was unfenced and seemed to flow right into the golden grasses of the steep meadow.

Emma walked Kevin through the house and yard, pointing out what she knew about the alarm system, which she admitted to using "less than half the time."

"This won't do, Emma."

"What do you mean?"

He waved his arms in an arc. "What I mean is that your house is equipped to satisfy the security concerns of a typical neurotic suburban homeowner— you know, some guy who's a little worried about burglary and anxious about some of the things he sees on the news. This level of security might be sufficient for him and might deter a few amateur burglars. But it isn't sufficient for a house you're living in. This alarm wouldn't trip up a pro for more than a few moments."

"What do I need, Kevin?"

"Bottom line is this: You need to move to someplace more easily protected."

"No."

"I figured you would say that. As an alternative, you need to move out while I get the security upgraded here."

"No."

"Then you need a bodyguard for a while."

"Damn. I knew you were going to say that."

THREE

Friday, October 11. 9:25 P.M.
Heavy Snow, 20 Degrees

Although the circumstances were unfamiliar to Lauren, the interview room where she was being held at the police department was not. It was an institutional space about the size of a generous walk-in closet, decorated in a fashion more academic than penal. The decor was plain to the point of sterility; the room eerily quiet and windowless. Furnishings consisted of five aluminum arm chairs and a heavy laminated table. A big commercial tape recorder sat conspicuously on a built-in ledge in one corner.

Shortly after Lauren's phone call to Alan a female officer marched into the interview room with evidence bags and a pile of jail sweats. Lauren tried in vain to read the small rectangular name badge on the cop's uniform. She tried looking left and then right, glancing back obliquely at the tag. But she couldn't make out the letters, could barely locate the badge.

"I need your clothes," the woman said. Lauren thought the woman's voice sounded youthful.

"Why do you want my clothes?" Lauren asked, knowing why.

"I've been instructed to retrieve your clothing as possible evidence." The cop's tone was devoid of sympathy, and her silhouette transformed into a hands-on-her-hips pose. She said, "Are you going to need some help complying with this?"

Lauren wondered how this cop could be so young, yet already so embittered. The job? No, it wasn't just that, couldn't be. She figured her for two years on the job, tops.

"Your clothes, ma'am. Now, please. I'm expecting some cooperation, here."

Although many details eluded her, Lauren could tell that the officer was tall and thin, the kind of thin that comes without effort. Her build and coloring reminded Lauren of her little sister Teresa. Like Teresa, this cop probably grabbed size fours off the rack without a moment's reflection.

Lauren couldn't quite accept the fact that she was actually going to have to undress in front of this strange woman. She disrobed a garment at a time, pausing between each one, as though expecting a reprieve.

There has to be a way to avoid this.

Before unbuttoning her blouse, she hesitated once again.

"Is this really necessary? I was wearing a coat. They already have that."

"I'm waiting for cooperation here, ma'am," the cop said. "This is the easy way, believe me."

Lauren focused on the sensation of the fine fabric against her skin and tried to seal it in her memory as she folded each piece neatly before placing it near the brown paper evidence bags on the laminated table-top. The cop patted down each garment as Lauren removed it and then slid each one into its own bag, keeping an inventory on a clipboard.

"Can I keep my underwear?"

The officer didn't look her in the eye when she said, "Everything, ma'am. My orders are to retrieve *all* your clothing. Sergeant didn't say anything about you keeping your underwear. We will supply whatever you need."

I need privacy. I need my husband. I need my lawyer. And I need the clock turned back twelve hours. Can you do that, Officer?

Lauren reminded herself not to forget that one of her advantages, perhaps her only advantage, was that she was a lawyer. Curtly, she said, "I think you need a warrant to get my underwear."

"What?"

"You don't have a compelling reason to seize my underwear without a search warrant, Officer. You'll taint this entire evidence collection if you insist on that."

The cop didn't look up from the clipboard. "That's interesting information, ma'am. I'll make note of it when I'm studying for my detective's exam."

Lauren turned her back to the woman and reached behind her back to unclasp her bra. She slid it down her arms and immediately reached for the jail sweats to cover herself, pulling the sweatshirt down as far as she could over her hips before hooking her thumbs into the narrow waistband of her panties and sliding them to the floor. She realized, too, that she had just exposed her needle-bruised buttocks to the harsh fluorescent glare and the inquiring eyes of this young cop.

The room was not warm but Lauren was sweating, and a bead of perspiration dripped from her armpit down her left side. It humiliated her further. She told herself to get angry, not embarrassed.

She almost succeeded.

An initial sign that maybe someone out there cared about her came when she pulled the sweatpants over her naked hips. The size was about right. The smell was fresh. The fabric was *new*. A small piece of paper fluttered to the floor. She and the officer reached for the paper at the same instant.

"I'll get that, ma'am. Stand back." An order, not an offer.

Lauren straightened up and adjusted the waistband of the sweatpants as the cop bent down to pick up the paper. Lauren realized she could make a fist with both hands and bring it down on the back of the cop's head. She could picture the act clearly in her mind.

The very thought of retaliating revived her. She reminded herself, *I need to be prepared to fight.*

"Inspected by four. Hope that's your lucky number, ma'am. For a second there, I thought some admirer out there might be slipping you a note or something."

Five minutes after the young woman left with the brown bags full of Lauren's clothing the door to the interview room opened again. Lauren spotted a big person with a small head and short hair enter the room but couldn't discern the facial features well enough to recognize identity or gender. She tried looking back sideways, bypassing the blind spot that seemed to be growing ever larger in the center of her visual field, and finally recognized that her new visitor was Sergeant Wendell Pons.

Pons was the sergeant in the investigations division who she absolutely did not want to be supervising this case.

Behind her back, she called him Windy. The man said nothing succinctly. He was a poster boy for redundancy. Here, she intended to call him "Sergeant."

"Hello, Ms. Crowder. Difficult circumstances, but good to see you, as always. Hello."

"Sergeant." She was looking at the wall now, away from him, afraid how her eyes might appear to him as they darted around trying to find focus. She feared that he might think she was being intentionally disdainful of him.

"I want to get your Miranda warning on tape again. You don't mind? Just want to do it one more time, to be sure. I understand that Detective Malloy and you—"

"That's right, it's been done. I understand my rights better than you do, and I'm sure you know that I've asked for an attorney."

"She's on her way, your attorney. As a matter of fact, she faxed us this already. Said she's coming down from Rollinsville. You don't know anybody in town you could have used? I'm surprised." He was holding a sheet of paper in her direction, shaking it so that it crackled like fire. "Hostile tone in this little note, don't you think, the one from your lawyer? I was hoping we could all be friendly. You know, you a DA, maybe with somebody local helping us sort all this out. Somebody we know, somebody we can work with. But this isn't too friendly. A *fax*. Hostile. I find them cold. Faxes. Don't you? What's wrong with a phone call? If you can fax, you can phone, right?"

Lauren could see the white paper, but couldn't read it, and couldn't even tell if the side facing her was the side with the printing on it. She assumed it was a caustic warning from Casey to the cops that Lauren had retained her services and that her client had chosen to remain silent. Period.

Given her clear embracing of her Fifth Amendment rights, and if the fax said what she thought it did, Lauren knew that Pons shouldn't even be in the room with her.

Well, if Pons wasn't smart enough to back off, Lauren was willing to do her best to take advantage of his indiscretion. There were some things she wanted to know.

"How is the man who was shot?"

"The man you shot, you mean? That man?"

"How is the injured man?"

"Gut shot. Right through the belly. Clipped organs all over the place. Bowel, liver. Where did you get that round anyway? Doc operating on him says it opened up like a rosebud in July." Wendell Pons pronounced the word "Jew-lye."

"How serious are his injuries?"

"Like I said, the guy's gut shot, how do you think he's doing? Right in the belly, my worst nightmare. Main reason I wear the damn vest. Shit. Gut shot. I'd rather be hit in the head. Be quicker."

Lauren heard what she was hoping to hear. The pending charge was still first-degree assault, or attempted murder, not homicide. Not yet.

"Who is he?"

Pons stared at the fax in his hands, said nothing.

"Is my attorney here? I want to see her right away."

"Snowing like a son of a bitch out there. Need snowshoes to get down here from the Peak to Peak. Traffic guys in the State Patrol say there're accidents up and down the canyon. Really snowing, should make the skiers happy." He provided the weather report with some glee in his voice.

Translation: Don't hold your breath, bitch.

She was beginning to grow uncomfortable that Pons was remaining in the interview room with her after she had given a clear indication of her desire for an attorney. The man was a jerk, but he wasn't stupid. She wondered what he was up to. "Either turn the recorder on or stop speaking with me, please, Sergeant. I prefer to wait for my attorney. I have nothing more to say to you until she gets here."

He walked over to the corner of the room and flicked the tape recorder on. Lauren couldn't see well enough to know if there was actually a tape in the damn thing.

He read the Miranda warning off a card, stumbling twice over the phrasing, obviously out of practice.

"I'm also going to give you a copy of this to sign. You know, so we have a record."

"Fine."

He slid another sheet of paper in front of her. She looked down but she couldn't read it no matter how obliquely she examined it. The lawyer in her told her not to sign something she hadn't read. Couldn't read.

"I've changed my mind. I'm not going to sign anything. I'll wait for my attorney."

He shook his head, rebuking her, with a wide smile plastered on his face. As he turned to leave, he remembered the tape recorder and walked back and switched the machine off. He paused, debating with himself about whether to take a final cheap shot. *Hell, why not, she's earned it.*

"You know, there's some people out there who think we should be extra-special considerate to somebody like yourself, seeing all the good things you've done for the city. They say remember this case you did, or that case you did. Maybe you fucked up this time, but who knows, there's probably an explanation for what happened, right? Got to be an explanation. So maybe we should show you some special consideration, is what some people are arguing. Though it's hard to explain you wanting a lawyer, that's been real hard for everybody to understand. The wanting-a-lawyer part.

"But me, I say no. I remember once, years ago, a pup DA told me that good deeds don't mean shit if you cross the line. The law's the law, she said. So no, no special consideration tonight. I'm sure you understand, Ms. Crowder. About pup DAs and good deeds not being worth shit. Specially when someone wants a lawyer. Wanting a lawyer, now that's real hard to explain."

"Is my husband here?"

If Lauren could have seen clearly, she would have seen Pons take a cautionary glance at the tape recorder, to reassure himself that it was off. But she couldn't, and she didn't.

"Oh yeah, yeah. A while now, I think. Detective Malloy is having a little chat with him. Yeah, that's right. I can tell you that he's one boy who's not exercising any rights to remain silent. Mmm mmm, yes, a while now, I think. Well, I'll be going now, given your desire to wait for your attorney. I'm sure glad you and I are on the same page about special treatment. What goes around comes around, I always say."

Lauren thought she heard him chuckle as he was leaving the room.

She moved to a chair in the corner and sat in the space behind the door. She pulled her knees to her chest. Pons had said that Alan was close by and she imagined his warmth. She imagined him bringing her a cup of tea and some jelly beans. Emily, the big dog, was curled up at her feet, sighing that one big sigh that meant she was in for some serious slumber. For a precious moment Lauren was opening a book and being distracted by Mozart.

No, girl, you're in jail.

Casey Sparrow walked into the interview room without pausing to knock. Lauren had retreated into the corner behind the open door, as private a nook as she could find, and was startled at the *whoosh* of the opening door. She immediately grew concerned that some new indignity she hadn't anticipated awaited her.

"Hey honey, how are you doing?" Casey said in the softest voice she could assemble. She held out her arms and tried to look Lauren in the eyes without appearing to be looking *at* her eyes.

Lauren stood slowly, unfolding herself from her cocoon on the awkward chair. "Casey? Is that you? I thought you'd never get here." To Lauren, the indistinct red halo of hair around Casey's head looked much brighter from one eye than it did from the other.

"Yeah, it's me. I bet you could use a hug."

The women embraced, not one of those butt-out, bent-at-the-waist affairs that precede cheek pecks, but a soulful, bosom-crushing hug that temporarily filled Lauren with some much needed solace. Casey held on until she was certain she felt Lauren begin to pull back.

"I take it you're not having a very good day?"

Lauren managed a half-smile. "As my sister used to say, so far it's 'not just fine.' Seeing you here, like this—this is humiliating."

Casey considered saying something about there being no need to be embarrassed but she realized how insincere it would sound. Were the roles reversed, she knew she would be mortified to be in

Lauren's position. Lawyers, especially prosecutors, aren't supposed to screw up this badly.

Instead, Casey said, "Sit."

Lauren backed up, retreating to her chair in the corner. She reached down with one hand to find the cushion. "You too," she said. "It's been a while, Casey, how have you been?"

Casey had already decided to let Lauren take control of the conversation, at least initially. She wasn't surprised that Lauren preferred to spend a few moments ignoring the present circumstances and getting reacquainted.

"I'm doing okay. Jenny moved out a few months ago. I'm still getting over that. Otherwise, everything's been all right with me."

"I don't think I ever knew Jenny, did I?"

"No, I don't think so. We met in Golden. She's a manager in quality control at Coors. For her sake, we kept a pretty low profile as a couple. Coors has come a long way, but Jenny was never convinced that they were really ready for prime-time lesbians. Against my better judgment, I went along."

"I'm sorry it didn't work out."

"Yeah, thanks, I appreciate it, but lately I've been thinking that maybe the whole thing was doomed from the start." Casey smiled a tiny smile that Lauren couldn't see. "You know about lesbians and their dogs?"

Lauren shrugged.

"Well, I'm a devout dog lesbian and Jenny is a converted cat lesbian and I'm not at all sure that the two groups are romantically compatible. For now, let's just give thanks that I'm better at law than I am at romance." Casey forced a bigger smile. "You and Alan doing all right? That man better be nice to you *forever* after the way I saved his ass." Casey and her dog had once rescued Alan from an avalanche.

Lauren smiled. "Better than I ever hoped, Casey. It's been a dream, the marriage," she said, her voice trailing off. "I only hope we can weather this."

"They treating you fair?"

As casually as she could, Casey shifted Lauren's attention back to the current reality. She reached into her briefcase and fumbled around for a felt-tip pen and a green legal pad. She also pulled out a portable tape recorder and placed it prominently on the floor between them. It took her fifteen seconds to find the right button. One of her first tasks was to make some quick assessment of Lauren's state of mind, and she wanted to preserve a record of what she heard in case it became tactically useful.

"Here? They don't know what the hell to do with me, Case. But mostly it's all just crazy. Some of the people are sweet, some are businesslike." She grabbed the material of her sweatshirt. "They took my clothes, even my underwear; they're going to have some warrantless search problems. The woman cop who's keeping an eye on me is a first-class bitch. The whole gamut, so far." Lauren was staring at the vague shape of Casey's tape recorder. "What's that?" she asked.

Casey saw her looking at the recorder. "In case you say anything I can use for mens rea. You been keeping your mouth shut?"

"I've been good."

"Good or great? I'm looking for great, Lauren."

"Just good. I wasn't thinking clearly. I said some things to the patrolman on the scene before I made a clear Edward's."

Casey was encouraged that Lauren's thinking had enough clarity to describe the events so well, and simultaneously disappointed that her state of mind, her mens rea, was so lucid. Lauren being clearheaded wasn't going to help Casey make many useful points. And she didn't like the fact that Lauren had spoken to the patrolman before asking for counsel.

"We'll have to do some work on your act, then. Anything I can do to help right away, tonight?"

"You mean other than getting me out?" Lauren looked away. "I can't believe what I'm about to say, but there is something you can help me with. I need to pee. And I don't want anyone to watch me do it."

"Right now?"

"No, but soon." She rolled her eyes.

"I understand. I'll see what I can do. Maybe they'll cut you some slack. You're catching some breaks already, you know that?"

Lauren nodded, fingered the collar of her jail sweats. "New togs. My size. No lice."

"That's not your color, though, baby."

Lauren chuckled, mostly to please Casey.

"I didn't figure I'd get to see you until they moved me over to the jail. That's a break, too. I never really understood how alone people feel these first few hours in custody."

"The truth is that I've already been here for a half an hour. Just hanging around with Detective Malloy. He was giving me the royal runaround before I threw a tantrum and they decided to let me in here to see you. I think—"

"Scott Malloy is okay, Casey. I've worked with him, he's a decent cop."

"Boulder cops *are* generally a cut above, I'll grant you that. But you're going to have to stop thinking about the police as friends. I was about to say that I think that the only reason I'm being allowed to see you so soon is that they're hoping I can get you to tell them something that will make this whole thing go away."

"That's a question, isn't it?"

"I guess."

"It's not going to happen. I'm a guest of the county for now unless they're inclined toward personal recognizance or dropping charges. I'm amenable to either of those, nothing else. They haven't decided on charges yet, have they?"

"That would be too easy. What's your guess as to what they'll come up with?"

"They won't charge. They'll want us to agree to file later. But what are they thinking? First-degree assault, I guess. Homicide if the guy dies." This made Lauren remember the ephemeral scene during the storm. She looked at the floor, back up toward Casey. "Is he dead, the man who was shot?"

Casey was pleased at the careful language, the passive voice. "No, Malloy says he's still in surgery. They've got a detective at the hospital, hovering, hoping for a statement or some word from the doctors that will help with forensics. I don't think they even know who he is."

Lauren thought about it. "Whatever; they don't

need to decide now. They'll ask us to waive immediate filing at the two o'clocks tomorrow." Lauren suddenly felt too much like a lawyer jawing with a colleague. It was a seductive role for someone wearing jail clothes and cloth booties, but it didn't feel right.

"What are the two o'clocks?"

"In Boulder, appearances at the jail court are every afternoon at two. Everybody calls them two o'clocks. How's Alan? Have they cornered him yet?"

The Alan question could wait. "So your first appearance is tomorrow at two?"

Lauren smiled. "Actually no, on Saturday the two o'clocks are at four o'clock. A weekend thing. But I think they'll have me appear early or late in order to avoid the press."

"Alan's holding up okay. He's real worried about you. But I think, okay. And, no, he hasn't talked with the cops yet. I got Cozier Maitlin down here just in time. Cozy waylaid him and took him somewhere."

"Shit," Lauren said, "that means that jerk lied to me already."

"What? Which jerk? Cozy?"

"No. The detective sergeant—he told me they'd already interviewed Alan."

"He just now told you this? Like *after* your Edward's?" Casey was scribbling like mad.

"Yes."

"That's one mistake that this Detective Pons will wish he didn't make. I promise. Anybody else been in here walking over your constitutional rights?"

"Scott came back in and blotted my hands and face for gunshot residue."

"Just GSR? No Trace Metal Detection Test?"

"Only GSR."

"But he didn't ask any more questions?"

"No. Everything by the rules with Scott. And I don't think they'll find anything on the GSR. I was wearing gloves when I fired the gun and the gloves got soaked out there. So did my face. The GSR will be negative."

"But Malloy didn't try to question you further?"

"No, strictly by the book. But I'd already talked to Scott, a little anyway, before I was taken into custody."

"Do you remember what you said? I'm going to need every detail."

Lauren ran her fingers through her black hair, scratching her scalp with her nails. "Let me think about it for a minute, try to replay it in my head. You chose Cozy to help? I'm surprised." Lauren assumed that Casey would bring another lawyer on board quickly, though maybe not this quickly.

Casey said, "You chose me. I'm surprised."

"You're good."

"Uh huh. So's Maitlin. That's too easy. Though I am good, I've done exactly zero major crimes in Boulder County. Zero. Cozier Maitlin has done at least three murder cases that I know about. I figure at least a couple I don't know about. In Boulder County, with private homicide defense, he's it and you know it. The question isn't why did I choose Cozy. The man is good and he knows the ropes with capital crimes. The question is why didn't you call Cozy yourself? You and Cozy have a history I should know about? Is this going to be a problem?"

"I wanted a woman."

"You didn't answer my question."

"No. No problem with Cozy. I beat him sometimes in court. He may have trouble with me."

"Doesn't seem to, in fact he seemed quite eager to help. So why do you want a woman? Moral support? Sisterhood?" Casey had crafted a careful edge to her voice. Sharp enough to irritate, but not quite sharp enough to cut.

"I like women."

"So do I. It's public record. Don't dance with me on this, Lauren. The stakes are too high."

"This is complicated, Casey."

"Don't let all this red hair fool you, I'm not ditzy, I do just fine with 'complicated.' And if I'm going to be your attorney, I need to know exactly what's going on. And the first thing I need to know is why you hired me. I'm an outsider, is that it? Somebody you don't work against every day."

"Partially."

Casey sighed, wished she hadn't offered Lauren the facile explanation. "They're not going to let me stay in here with you all night, Lauren."

"How long do we have?"

"Malloy said thirty minutes, max. They want to move you over to the jail. I won't see you again until tomorrow morning. We have a lot of ground to cover."

Lauren lolled her head back and stretched the muscles taut on the front of her neck, then did the same thing forward left, and forward right. When she was done, she rubbed her eyes with her fingers.

"Do you remember that you once told me . . . about the time . . . when you were raped."

Casey's heart bounced.

"You were raped? Oh God." But she was thinking, *If this is true, I'll have you out of here in an hour.*

"No, Casey, I wasn't raped. I was preventing a rape, or trying to. That's why I had the gun with me."

"And that's why you fired it?"

"Sort of."

Casey slumped in her chair and exhaled deeply. "You weren't raped, right? Please tell me you weren't raped."

"I wasn't raped, Casey. I promise."

"But you stopped a rape?"

"I hope so. I really don't know."

"What do you mean you hope so? Isn't the potential rapist in surgery right now?"

"I not only don't know who the rapist is, I also don't have any idea who the man was that they found in the road with the bullet in him. But I can tell you that I wasn't the intended victim of the rape."

"Then why did you shoot this guy?"

"I'm not at all sure I did."

To Casey, this was beginning to sound as convoluted as Lauren said it would sound. "Then who was this man going to rape?"

"You promise to believe me?"

"Hell yes. You're in the business, Lauren. You know if a criminal defense attorney can't trust a client that they've just driven through a blizzard to see on a weekend, then the pope can't trust his priests, right?"

Lauren's laugh was genuine this time. She tried to look at the spot where she thought Casey's eyes would be and said, "What I was doing tonight, I was doing for Emma Spire."

Casey smiled and said, "Yeah, right." Then immediately, keeping her eyes on Lauren's, she continued, "Holy shit. You're not kidding, are you?"

"No, I'm not."

"Is she still in danger?"

"She may be, Casey. I don't know what happened up there with this man who I thought I saw heading to her house. And I sure don't know what might have been happening there after I left."

"Do the police know any of this?"

"No, they can't. They absolutely can't know."

"Because it's so complicated?"

"That's right. It's not just her physical well-being, it's her privacy that's at stake. And I think her life is at risk, too."

"Emma Spire *has* no privacy. She's been probed more times than a medical school cadaver."

"The police can't know what I'm telling you, Casey. You'll have to agree to that. I'll tell you everything, but the police don't know until I say so. When you learn more you'll understand."

"This is bullshit, Lauren. Absolute bullshit. You're facing a possible murder charge and you're asking me to defend you with one hand tied behind my back because you want to protect someone's reputation?"

"It's not that simple."

"Then what's so damn complicated?"

"Let's just say that if the police find out, if anyone finds out what's going on, the consequences for Emma will be worse than being raped."

Casey's imagination exploded with a Technicolor,

wide-screen, Dolby THX–quality flashback of twenty minutes of hell spent trying to fight off a drunk cowboy inside a goddamn Winnebago in a campground outside West Yellowstone when she was twenty years old.

"Tell me something that's worse than being raped. Go ahead, try."

"Casey, the only thing I can think of that would be worse than being raped once is being raped over and over and over again."

Casey looked at her wristwatch and said, "Shit. I can't argue with that. We have five minutes left, maybe. In those five minutes, I want you to figure out a way to bring me up to speed on this little conspiracy and let me know what the hell is going on."

"With Emma?"

"With Emma. And with this multiple rape thing." Casey watched Lauren squint at something across the room. "And I also want to know what the hell is going on with your vision."

"What?"

"Alan told me, Lauren. About your illness. And about your problem with your vision. I don't know why you feel you need to keep this a secret, but that's another conversation. Are you okay? What on earth can I do to help?"

Casey expected her client to look angry. Instead, Lauren looked relieved and, momentarily, fragile. "I think that I'm going blind, Casey. It's happened before and . . . I'm so scared."

"Alan says you need medicine?"

Lauren nodded. She started crying. "Probably. If I

get an IV started I have a better chance of avoiding permanent damage to my optic nerves." She wiped at her eyes. "At least the part of my eyes that makes tears is still working."

Scott Malloy knocked solidly at the door. "Time's up for now, we need to transfer Ms. Crowder to the jail for booking. You can consult with her more when you get there, if you want. I'll try to expedite it. Be a couple of hours, probably. Depends on how busy they are."

Through the door, Casey said, "She needs to pee—" then louder, "she needs to use the ladies' room first, Detective."

"Okay. I'm coming in." Malloy was holding a heavy jacket with Boulder County Jail markings for Lauren to wear and some canvas shoes for her feet.

Lauren looked down to try to hide the fact that she was crying. "I need the bathroom, Scott."

"Oh. Before you get to the jail?"

She nodded.

"I'll get Officer Lander. She'll take you in."

Casey said, "I'm happy to take her, Detective. Just show me where the bathroom is."

"It's right down here. You stay with her the whole time? We'll just pretend it's another interview room."

As Malloy guided Lauren down the hall, she looked back over her shoulder at Casey and said, "Thanks."

Handcuffs awaited Lauren when she was done in the bathroom. She had taken an extra minute to throw some cool water on her face.

Casey asked Malloy if he had to handcuff Lauren.

Casey knew that procedure would dictate that he did. She also knew there was no harm in asking.

Scott Malloy responded with a curt "Yes."

Lauren held her wrists out obligingly.

Malloy said, "No. Behind your back for the trip over to the jail. Sorry, regulations. I don't have a choice about some of this." She turned around and felt the heavy metal couple her wrists together.

They stopped by the reception desk on the way out of the detective bureau. Malloy bent over to sign some logs and a transfer form.

Casey decided that the time was right. With the clerk right in front of them, she had a witness. Lauren needed medical help. And she, Casey, needed some time to figure out what was going on with Emma Spire.

"Is there a nurse at the jail full-time?"

"That's right."

"What about a doctor?"

"On call at night. Has some regular hours occasionally during the day, I think they can tell you all about it when you get over there." He glanced at her sideways. "If you're hoping for tranqs or sleepers, don't hold your breath. It's not going to happen tonight."

Lauren was staring down at her borrowed shoes, not seeing anything but some faint colors and some blurry outlines.

Casey pressed on. "Could you please call the doctor and arrange to have him meet my client at the jail tonight? Right away."

"*What?*" Malloy was beyond skeptical. He wasn't interested in calling a doctor, all he was interested in was some gratitude for all the slack he had been cutting Lauren already.

"I think we have a medical emergency in progress, Detective."

He looked at Lauren. She appeared forlorn and beaten, not ill. "And what the hell might that be?" God, how he hated defense attorney antics, especially when he was already doing back flips trying to be reasonable.

"Your prisoner appears to be going blind, Detective Malloy."

"Don't play with me, Ms. Sparrow."

"Check yourself, please."

Malloy stared first at Casey Sparrow to try to see evidence of the lie in her face. He couldn't. He shifted his gaze to Lauren, who raised her head and looked toward him. Her left cornea was red, her pupils were different sizes, and she appeared to be trying to look him right back in the eye.

But she was failing by about ten degrees.

Suspicious of everything where prisoners and lawyers were concerned, Scott Malloy immediately wondered if Casey Sparrow had put some drops in her client's eyes to obfuscate something. He looked again at Lauren's face. She seemed to be scared, sad, and incredibly tired.

But her eyes? Even to Malloy, whose training in examining vision functioning was limited to the curbside tests used in identifying drunks, it was clear that Lauren was failing to track.

"Let me find Sergeant Pons," he said.

FOUR

No, really, Lauren, Ethan's expecting me. I'll be fine. Kevin's arranged for me to meet somebody tomorrow morning about personal protection until this thing . . . settles." Emma widened her eyes and offered a reassuring smile.

Lauren had pulled her car to a stop in the RTD bus cutout on the east end of the Downtown Boulder Mall.

"You're sure?"

"See, it's right there, only half a block. Don't be so worried about me." The Citizens National Bank Building was easy to spot, the largest and most architecturally interesting structure on the fourteen hundred block of the Mall.

Lauren felt uneasy. "Maybe I'll just wait here until you get inside. Look what happened the last time I turned my back on you."

"I'm fine, Lauren."

"I'll wait, anyway. Call me crazy. I have little sisters and brothers, I'm used to worrying. Call me if you need anything. Anything at all."

Emma assured her she would and said, "Thanks for everything. You've been great." She tugged down her hat, returned her sunglasses to her face, and smiled once more at Lauren, before walking with assured strides up the brick paths of the Mall.

Lauren waited, watching for two minutes until she saw Emma raise the bottom half of one of the big double-hung windows in Ethan's front room. Emma leaned her upper body outside and waved toward Lauren, who thought for the tenth time, at least, that Emma looked like royalty.

Emma wandered toward the rear of the flat and found Ethan sitting at a high stool in front of a keyboard. His eyes were intent on a twenty-inch screen, his hands were dancing over the keys as though whatever he was typing was coming straight from memory or was on a direct line from God. He wore a wireless telephone headset. He swiveled on his stool and waved a distracted hello to Emma without interrupting his conversation.

She approached him warmly, appreciating his smooth skin and his smoother manner, loving his baggy cotton clothes and the intensity of the relationship he had with his machines. Ethan was as serious about his work as her father had been about his. She was wary of that dedication to work—her mother had taught her to be—but she respected it. She also knew it attracted and compelled her in ways that someday she needed to slow down and understand better.

Tomorrow, she thought. She would do that tomorrow.

She kissed him on the ear, sliding in her tongue and probing gently.

He pulled away, pointing at the headset, indicating he was on the phone. Ethan wasn't speaking; the other person had been doing all the talking.

"You on hold?" she asked in a half-whisper.

He shook his head.

Emma studied Ethan's face and decided that although he was currently distracted, he wasn't uninterested.

Her confidence building, she walked a few steps, and pulled a high stool up to another computer. She touched the mouse to dissolve the screen saver. A long pattern of meaningless numbers, letters, and symbols appeared instantly, stark white columns on a black background.

Ethan screamed, "No. Emma, no. Don't touch that." She flinched as she looked at him, startled by his rebuke. He seemed to recognize that his reflexive command had been jagged and he quickly added, "Please."

He began to speak into the tiny microphone that dangled in front of his lips, his words the exotic sing-songy dialect of his youth. Emma knew that the phone call she had interrupted was long distance to Hawaii.

The first time she had eavesdropped on a call he was making to a friend in Hawaii, she had asked him about the speech pattern. He'd labeled it "pidgin," explaining that the language had developed from native Hawaiian, English, and Asian roots and was cemented with colloquial island slang.

Emma could decipher an occasional English word

in the patois but the totality of the dialect was foreign enough to be unintelligible. She guessed he was talking to one of his siblings, given the frequent use of the word "bro."

Emma's experience was that Ethan talked comfortably about only two things: his work and his family. He had two brothers and two sisters, all of whom still lived in the islands. His mother ran a dress shop in an upscale mall in Honolulu. His father had died of an aneurysm when Ethan, the youngest of the kids, was charging through his high school curriculum in two and a half years. The death of his father was the beginning of a litany of family tragedy that Ethan felt had yet to play its final notes.

Before he arrived on the mainland for his first year of studies at UCLA, his oldest brother had lost a leg above the knee and an arm below the elbow in a freak accident involving heavy machinery in a sugar cane field, and one of his sisters had lost a baby to SIDS. Another had been sterilized by hemorrhage after an abortion.

His brother's plight struggling with dual prostheses sparked an interest in medicine that Ethan wasn't aware he possessed when he left Hawaii for UCLA to study computer science. Before long he was hanging around with the engineers in medical technology more than he was studying in his field. After two years at UCLA he moved across town to Cal Tech and began to imagine the hardware and software that would lead to the products that eventually launched BiModal.

Ethan Han didn't see any reason that prosthetic

devices could not be programmed to "feel" in much the same manner as human skin.

The "technology" of human sensation is not particularly complicated. Sensors in the skin detect heat, pressure, light—whatever—and translate these sensations to electrical signals that are in turn carried up neural pathways to the brain for processing and decoding. Why couldn't electronic components replace any of the natural components responsible for sensory data collection and transmission?

Ethan's goal became simple. He wanted to design a prosthetic hand and foot that would allow his older brother to feel hot and cold and to sense pressure and movement.

By the time he began to develop his systems, improved battery devices had permitted major advances in myoelectric prosthetics. All Ethan had to do to improve upon them, he figured, was refine and miniaturize the existing sensory electronics and develop the computer hardware and software necessary to interpret and relay the signals to the intact neural pathways on his brother's stumps. If he could combine this new technology with the advances that other scientists were making daily with myoelectrics, a whole new generation of "sensitive" prosthetics would be possible.

When he was twenty-four years old, Ethan Han attended the fitting of his brother's first temperature-sensing prosthetic arm and hand.

And BiModal was born.

Emma moved away from the keyboard she wasn't supposed to touch and walked farther down the row of benches, parking herself at a Macintosh that wasn't powered up. She booted it, clicked the mouse a few times to locate the word processor, and typed, "I think I'm going to take a bath." She spooled the cryptic message to the printer, which came to life halfway down the bench toward Ethan. By the time she walked down there the message had been printed.

She retrieved the note, placed it gingerly on the keyboard in front of Ethan, kissed him again on the ear, this time without her tongue, and walked toward the back of his flat. She hoped he was looking as she made her way out of the laboratory. Without turning to see if she had an audience, she crossed her arms and pulled her top over her head. She reached behind her back and released her bra with her right hand and let it fall down her arms. As she passed through the door the garment was dangling from her fingers.

Although it was a role she occasionally enjoyed, she hadn't played the temptress in a long time. Hadn't desired to. She had never understood how public adulation could serve as such an aphrodisiac for Pico, her fiancé. For her, the pervasive attention deadened her, dumping novocaine on every erotic impulse she had.

But tonight she felt alive. She wondered if her lust was stimulated by Ethan's reticence. She decided she didn't care.

Odd, she thought, as she turned off the blow-dryer she had found in Ethan's bathroom. The music that was filling the flat was classical, not something she remembered hearing before in Ethan's home. When he was alone, he'd confessed to her, he almost always played the blues.

Still naked from her bath, she brushed her teeth with a toothbrush she carried in her purse, then applied a thin ribbon of eyeliner and a little blush. She painted her lips with a great deal of care. The progression of the symphonic themes energized her. She had forgotten the horror of the garage incident for the first time all day.

She grabbed a plaid bathrobe from the back of the bathroom door and crushed it to her face. The smell was Ethan's. It was the smell of skin after a day in the sun. It was the smell of fresh sweet male sweat. She pulled it on and went to find him to see whether he wanted to go out for dinner.

Dancing screen savers lit up the east wall of the laboratory. But Ethan was no longer there. She backtracked and checked the tiny kitchen and solitary bedroom. He wasn't there, either. The music beckoned from the front room but from where she stood it appeared that end of the flat was dark.

She called, "Ethan?" Her voice cracked like a preadolescent boy's, and hearing it, she realized that she was becoming frightened. Silently, she cursed the legacy of fear that Nelson Newell had bestowed upon her with those two bullets in the airport. Before her father's murder, nothing ever really frightened her.

"Ethan? Are you here?" She returned to the bench, scanning the surface for a note. Nothing. Briskly, she jogged down the length of the long workbench and

slid every mouse from side to side, prodding the
screen savers to disappear, hoping that a screen
would pop up with a message from Ethan.

Nothing but indecipherable code.

"Ethan?"

She was growing more frightened and didn't like
the feeling at all. "Calm down, Emma, calm down,"
she admonished. She lifted the receiver of a telephone off the workbench. Listened. The drone of the
dial tone was as reassuring as a heartbeat.

*He's gone out for a minute. No big deal. Maybe he's
picking up some food for dinner.*

She returned to the phone, thought of calling
Kevin. No. *Lauren?* No.

"Ethan? Where are you?"

Beethoven, not Ethan, answered. Deep bass shook
the flat.

The room was lit almost entirely by task lights, the
screen savers constantly changing the ambient lighting in the lab. The windows on the west wall faced
the rooftops of the adjoining building; to the east,
Boulder's sprawl and the prairie. To see *people,* Emma
would have to move to the front room. The Mall
would be full of foot traffic this time of night. She
convinced herself that she would feel safer there, by
the windows, waiting for Ethan to get back from
his errand.

The hallway was a dark tunnel, the door closed.
Did I close that door earlier? She tried to remember,
but couldn't.

"Ethan?"

The brass knob yielded easily to the pressure of
her fingers. The long room in front of her ran the

width of the building and was awash in shadows, lit only by the lights of the Mall that filtered in through thin curtains that had been pulled across the big windows. She remembered leaning out the window to wave good-bye to Lauren. The curtains hadn't been pulled then. Emma walked quickly to the windows and lowered herself to the deep sill. She pulled her knees to her chest and gazed down at the crowd, soothed by the presence of dozens of pedestrians strolling below.

Behind her she heard a noise—an electronic "click"—and she yelped involuntarily. She jumped up and turned toward the sound, reflexively pulling Ethan's robe tight at her throat.

Across the room, in the corner, just off the edge of the big Heriz, Ethan Han reclined in one of the room's many sling chairs. This chair was covered with bright orange canvas. Ethan's eyes were half-closed, as though he were dozing. The big cart of electronics that Emma had last seen at the dinner party hovered behind him. He was wearing the collar and headset that Diane had modeled during the demonstration.

At first, the setting struck Emma as clinical, as though Ethan were a patient hooked up in a hospital suite twenty years in the future. In seconds, however, the scene began to feel quite different.

Besides the collar, Ethan wore little else. His thin, muscled chest was bare, as were his legs. At first she thought he was completely naked but he was actually wearing a pair of nylon shorts. They were the color of dirty copper and seemed almost to disappear against his skin.

She whispered, "Ethan, are you okay?"

When Ethan smiled, the corners of his mouth didn't actually turn up as much as they widened. That happened now. She took it that he was happy to see her.

He said, "Shhhh."

"You startled me, you should have said something. I've been looking all over for you. I couldn't find you." Despite the fact that her anxiety hadn't entirely dissipated, she felt the surge of different tensions.

"I was enjoying watching you against the windows." His smile deepened. "You look lovely."

"Thank you," she said. "What are doing with that equipment? Is someone coming over again?" God, she hoped not. Not tonight, she wasn't up for it.

The monitor on the cart caught her eye. She realized that the animated figure floating in a lazy S-shape in the middle of the screen was *Ethan*.

Both Ethan and his cartoonlike image were perfectly still.

"I'm working," he said. "Collecting some auditory data to check some code enhancements."

"The Beethoven?"

"Yes. The Beethoven."

"The machine records sound, too? I thought it just recorded movement."

"Not sound exactly. It records activity on neural pathways. What it's recording are my neural responses to sound."

"But it will record all your movements, too?"

"Yes, it's recording all my movements." He raised an arm and waved. In real time, the computer-generated figure did the same. Ethan was confident enough about his technology that he didn't even bother to turn his head and look at the monitor.

Emma did.

"*All* of your movements?"

Ethan wasn't quick enough to catch her meaning.

"There are some technical parameters—thresholds, really—that are limiting. But for all practical purposes, yes, it records all of them."

"If I got close to you—really close to you—would it record my movements as well?"

"Not unless you were wearing a collar, too." He looked closely at her. "I could arrange that."

"Oh, thanks for the offer, but I've just washed my hair," she teased, running the fingers of one hand across her head. "Without wearing your little torture devices, though, no matter what I do, I stay invisible to the machine?"

"You would like that, wouldn't you?"

Emma didn't notice that his answer was not responsive to her question. She swallowed involuntarily. "Yeah, I fantasize about being invisible, Ethan. Usually, I feel absolutely on display." She raised her eyebrows. "And sometimes I fantasize other things, too."

"You had a bath?" he said.

"Yes, it was nice. I used your blow-dryer and I borrowed your robe." She fingered the lapel.

"I can see that."

This has to be the slowest dance I've ever danced, Emma thought. The tension in the room was electric. For her, the mood was erotic and seductive in a way she couldn't remember feeling since her daddy died. Not even with Pico.

What about Ethan? What was this dance like for him?
She could only guess; reading his moods the past
couple of weeks seemed as impossible to her as
understanding the code on the monitors in his
laboratory.

She wondered if Ethan's machine would graphi-
cally represent his erection. If it did, she decided, she
wanted a copy of the CD to play at home on her
laptop. *That* would be technology she could understand. She smiled at the thought, felt an enticing chill
run down her spine to her buttocks and her groin.

"What?" he asked.

"Nothing," she replied, stepping forward. She was
moving as involuntarily, it seemed to her, as Ethan's
computer likeness.

The butterfly chair on which Ethan sat was nothing
but canvas on an iron frame. Simple in design. She
decided she could work with it.

A step away from him, she stopped. She knelt, her
knees on the soft edge of the rug.

The toes of his right foot loosely graced the crimson yarn of the carpet. With her fingertips, she lifted
his foot and it seemed to float up to her as though
it were levitating. She raised her eyes and saw every
movement of Ethan's mirrored on the monitor. The
S-shaped figure now had a bend at one knee.

But she was nowhere to be seen.

God. I am invisible. She felt a rush of power, a force
that felt primal.

Ethan's foot had a high arch. She kissed the top of
his foot, above that arch, holding her lips there until
his flesh and her mouth were the same temperature.
Then she moved and did it again, this time down

near his toes. She flicked her tongue into the slit between his second and third toes.

She held it there, waiting to be told to stop.

She thought she heard a sound, something in the no-man's-land between a whimper and a moan.

She took his large toe into her mouth and caressed its shape with her tongue. She bit lightly on the soft pad in front of the nail.

Minutes later she floated deftly from the right foot to the left. It seemed to rise to her lips itself, as though it couldn't stand to wait its turn.

She loved the soft noises he was making and hoped that the sounds wouldn't stop. She hoped that the machinery would record them, too.

His shorts came off before her robe opened.
Dusk became night before her robe opened.
Beethoven boomed before her robe opened.
She had never felt so ready.
She had never felt so good at *anything*.

Afterward they lay naked, intertwined against the orange canvas sling of the butterfly chair. Ethan's digitalized form hung pretzeled above their heads like an apparition, the high resolution of the monitor revealing even the small detail of his chest as it rose with the deep breaths of recovery.

His coloring was dark, hair black and fine, skin the hue of wet earth. Emma was fair, her complexion and her coloring all neutral, the product of six generations of Protestant blending.

Behind them, the computer continued to hum. Voices, mostly happy, intruded from the Mall below. Beethoven clicked off.

She smelled of bath soap, he of sweat.

"Hello," she said after a while, eager to renew some contact with him, her voice husky and low from sex.

"Yes," he replied, "hello to you, too."

"That was good."

"No. That was great." She felt him hesitate as though choosing his words with care. He ran his index finger down the valley between her breasts. The finger came back moist. He tasted it, licking the salt from her.

Minutes passed and the room, to Emma, seemed to grow larger and larger, the windows bigger, the light more intense, the curtains more transparent. These were not new feelings for her. Often she felt circumstances around her evolve in ways that increased her feelings of vulnerability. The phenomenon had started days after her father's murder and was yet to stop.

She nodded toward the cart behind them. "If you play that tape back, I can watch you move exactly as you did as I made love to you, right?"

He chuckled. She had never heard him chuckle before and it froze her attention.

"What? What's so funny, Ethan?"

"Just a minute, I need my hand."

She leaned forward and he pulled his right arm out from beneath her body. With both hands free he unstrapped the collar from his head and neck and placed them on the floor next to the chair.

Emma looked up at the monitor. The dull golden glow of the previous program dissolved into a scene of a wave crashing over and over. Ethan had disappeared.

She mimed a frown, running a hand over his abdomen, below his navel. "Oooh. I think that I'm going to miss that little guy. So tell me, what was so funny before?"

"The 'machine,' as you call it, has much more sophisticated capabilities than I've let on. To understand what it can do, you need to conceptualize it in a different way. It's designed to record many things, not merely movement." She felt his pulse quicken against her, and wondered if he were again becoming aroused.

"Yes?"

"I don't talk about this comfortably. Almost no one knows what this equipment can do. Sometimes I'm not even sure I know what it can do. It's a scientific frontier. Technologically, this is virgin territory."

"What do you mean you're not sure what it can do? You designed it, right?"

"This stays here? You and me, that's it? No one else hears this?"

"Trade secrets, huh? Great, of course. I won't tell anyone."

He caressed her cheek with his finger, high, near her temple. "If you could experience anything on the face of this earth, any experience that some other human being has experienced but that you haven't, what would it be? I'm talking about something you would love to do but because you don't have the prior experience, or the training, or the intelligence, or the opportunity, or the money—or maybe simply the courage—to do it on your own, you haven't ever done it, and probably never will."

"What? Is that thing like a time machine? It will take me someplace else if I want it to?" She wondered if he was playing with her.

"Literally, no. Figuratively, yes. You would actually never even have to leave this room or the present time to take advantage of this technology."

"You said this is secret, right?" She was tantalized, but felt wary, too. "That goes for you, too, then. If I start spewing out my dreams, you don't tell anyone? I don't hear about this in the tabloids next week?" He nodded. "Okay, then, here's my secret, an easy one. Since I was a little girl, I've wanted to be an astronaut, to feel what it's like to be weightless."

He smiled. "With that intro, I was expecting something a little more perverted. Your fantasy is great. It's a wonderful desire. And with this technology, I can fulfill it. I can *give* you that experience. Not today, not tomorrow. Maybe next year, maybe not. But soon. Soon, I can make you an astronaut."

"What do you mean? With *this* machine?" She looked at the innocuous-looking computer equipment on the cart.

"Yes, with this machine."

"Ethan, *tell* me. What on earth are you talking about? What does it do? I thought it just turned live action into computer animation." She raised herself up on her arm to look him in the eye.

"This technology—let me try to explain." He reached to the floor and picked up the collar and helmet. "In here, in the collar, there are exquisitely sensitive devices capable of recording neural transmissions. The signals are simply electrochemical charges that run along nerves—wires. At the brainstem level—at the top of the spinal column—all the neural signals carrying messages from the body to the brain come together."

He gave the collar a little shake. "After the sensors deliver the neural impulses, the computer," he reached back and tapped the processor on the cart, "separates the signals, digitizes them, isolates them into tracks, and decodes them for storage and, later, playback.

"The end result," he ran his teeth over his lower lip, "is that now I'm capable of recording the *actual* sensory experience of an individual human being in much the same way and with much the same clarity that a compact disc records sound, or a digital camera records a visual event."

Emma was stunned. "The demonstration you did the other night? That's just a small part of it, then?"

He closed his eyes briefly. She wondered if he was planning on answering her.

Finally, he said, "The visual representation software is really just a toy, something concrete I decided to use to impress the investors. It has some potential uses, but I doubt that they are either lucrative or earth-shattering in any humanitarian sense. Believe me, it's a tiny piece of all this. I don't want people to know the extent of what I've done until I'm ready to proceed."

"Who knows? Does Raoul?"

"I can tell from his questions that he suspects I'm

stretching something, but no, he doesn't know the parameters. So far, only J.P. and, now, you. My brother, my family, have a general sense of it."

Her mind was stuck on the examples he had given. "But what's the equipment actually designed for? Other than entertainment-type things—pretending to be an astronaut? What can it do?"

"A million practical uses. I'm guessing I've thought of maybe one percent. Think of paraplegics. Or amputees, like my brother. It will grant the disabled access to experiences that they otherwise could never dream of having again. Think of pediatrics. A doctor who can't get a young patient to describe symptoms will be able to actually record those very symptoms and play them back for himself or herself and then know exactly what it is their patient is feeling."

Emma struggled to understand what she was hearing. It felt as though she were trying to grasp the edge of a cloud. "I don't get it. How does this differ from virtual reality?"

"Because this experience is not 'virtual' reality; it *is* reality. It's not a 'created experience' meant to trick the senses; it's an *actual* experience. I'm not talking about simulating experience for you, I'm talking about playing back what has already actually been experienced by someone else. What is recorded by the equipment is an individual's actual sensory experience of an event. What they sensed, what they felt, how their body responded to everything. *Everything. Anything.*"

She could tell that Ethan knew she didn't understand.

"Do you want to try sushi without having to go out to a restaurant? Buy the cuisine software. I'll be able to do a complete repertoire of world cuisines on a single disc. Right now only the rich can afford to drink old Bordeaux or Burgundy. Soon, it will be at your library for you to taste at any time. It will all be available on tape from BiModal. Taste the old vintages through Robert Parker's lips. Hear opera through Pavarotti's ears. I will provide all that."

The reality of what he was saying hit Emma like a truck. She stared up at the equipment cart as though she had just discovered a video camera hidden in her bedroom.

"What about just now, what exactly did you just record?"

"I'm not sure. I've never done this . . . before while wearing the sensors. So I don't know what's on the disc. I thought I was recording my responses to a Beethoven symphony."

"But what do you think you actually recorded?"

He hesitated.

She pulled as far away from him as the chair would allow.

"Ethan, did you just record us *screwing*? If I'm hearing you right, you can *play back* what we just did for yourself and get off again and again and again anytime you want?"

He sighed. "I don't know what I have on that disc, Emma. But, yes, it's likely that I may have been able to record my experience of making love to you. The key words are 'my experience' and 'you.' This technology is personal. This technology is intimate. That's not just sex on that tape. That's *us* making love. If I succeeded in recording what just happened, what is on that disc is exactly what it's like for me to make love with you. I find that thought wonderful."

She felt a rising nausea and sense of vulnerability. She jumped up from the chair and grabbed the robe from the rug. "Erase it. Right now. This feels absolutely pornographic."

"What? What do you mean?"

"Erase the damn tape, Ethan. I don't want there to be a tape of someone having sex with me. Two years from now is someone going to be able to rent this at Blockbuster? Or maybe just download it over the Web?"

She threw his shorts at him.

"Erase it!"

She saw the reluctance in his eyes: He didn't want to erase the disc.

He said, "This wasn't just someone having sex with you, Emma. It was me, it was us."

"I don't care. You did not ask my permission to record this. I didn't volunteer to model for your camera. And I want it erased, right *now*."

"You don't have to raise your voice. I didn't trick you. Sex tonight was your idea, not mine."

"Ethan, please. I don't regret the sex. But you should have warned me about the equipment, right away. It wasn't fair."

"You're overreacting. I don't even have the capacity to play back most of the tracks I'm recording, yet. So far, motion-in-space is my cleanest track. The monitor image, you know?"

"But you will, won't you, someday soon? You'll figure out how to play it all back?" She felt defenseless and unnaturally cold, and hugged herself around the chest.

"Yes, I'm confident that I will."

"When?" Her voice was small.

"There are a few technical challenges remaining."

She snapped, "Don't patronize me, Ethan."

He exhaled and began speaking quickly. "Okay, some of the code isn't running right; it's terribly complex programming and we're constantly finding bugs. The more sensory tracks we try to record or to run, the more memory problems we develop. Sensory data like this eats memory in massive quantities. I've got people working on ways of trying to compress the signals to reduce the memory consumption.

"The sensors we're using in the collar and helmet are running too hot. Even with all the advances in superconducting metals I need to find a better way of supplying coolant to the collar. Because of that problem, currently, I'm much more efficient at recording the neural signals than the transmitters are at feeding them back into the brain stem for playback. Follow?"

"So far."

"None of those glitches worries me, technically speaking. Whatever problems I don't solve, the advance of technology will solve for me. Higher temperature superconducting metals are just around the corner. The biggest single problem I have and the one most likely to turn out to be intractable is that there are resident signals already in the system—"

"What system are you talking about? Your computers?"

"No, no, no. In the human body—that system.

Even when the test subject is at rest, these neural pathways we're monitoring are carrying torrents of data up from the spinal column and down the cranial nerves. I need to find a way to block the resident signals so they don't compete with the signals we're transmitting in from system memory. Until I do, quadraplegics and amputees will provide my best test subjects, for obvious reasons."

"Those problems don't sound minor, Ethan."

"They're not. But I'm confident."

"That's great," she muttered.

She pulled the robe tight and walked over to the windows. She felt like the whole world could see her every movement and that the paparazzi were having their way with her.

She daydreamed of France.

Behind her, she heard him stir, slide into his shorts, and click off the computers.

"I want it erased, Ethan."

"It's late. I'm tired. Sleep on it. If you want it erased, I'll do it tomorrow."

"I'm not going to change my mind."

"Fine."

✛

James Morelli was the bodyguard whom Kevin Quirk had arranged for Emma to interview. Morelli had suggested that he come by Ethan's apartment at eight-thirty the next morning so he and Emma could go somewhere for coffee and get acquainted.

Emma was out of bed before Ethan. She showered and made herself some tea.

The tape, or disc, she had decided overnight, would have to go. Although she couldn't understand why, she knew there were people in the world who would interrupt their daily lives to be in her presence. There were people who would pay good money to read what banal things she had done with her week, where she was shopping for groceries, what kind of car she drove, what movies she went to, and whether or not she wore a helmet when she Rollerbladed.

She didn't doubt for a moment that there would be people who would pay good money to be part of this latest technological marvel, to discover just what it had been like for Ethan Han to have sex with her.

Could this equipment really duplicate that?

The thought made her shiver and she pondered the true value of technology that had the capacity to intrude on her privacy to a degree that vastly eclipsed all the prior assaults that had been made on her. She wondered if Ethan really understood the raw thrust of the technology he was creating.

Someone could actually experience having sex with her *without her permission*.

It was as though technology had found a way to invite strangers into her bed whenever they chose to enter. And they could do this, they could feel her mouth and her tongue and her flesh and her fingers and her—they could be *inside* her—without her knowledge that they were doing it.

The concept paralyzed her. *Have they stolen my will? Can my soul be far behind?*

She tried to juggle the image enough to make it real.

The skeptic in her wondered if Ethan was lying. The lawyer in her began to wonder about the legal ramifications of Ethan's technology and its effect on privacy, when she noticed the clock on his microwave change to 8:15. She decided to wake Ethan.

She was determined to have the data destroyed before she left his house for the day.

Ethan seemed distant when he awoke. Emma did not feel as though she was a particularly welcome part of his morning and considered the possibility that he had been feigning sleep until she left for the day so that he wouldn't have to deal with her.

She initiated an embrace. He touched her lightly on the shoulders and mumbled that he had to use the bathroom. When he came back he was wearing the bathrobe she had worn the night before. She hoped she had succeeded in mingling her smells with his.

"Listen," she said softly, "I'm going to need to go soon. That bodyguard I'm supposed to interview will be here any minute. I've decided that I definitely want to erase the disc, or whatever you call it, from last night, before I meet with him."

He looked at the floor, his hands lost in the pockets of the robe.

"You're sure?"

"Absolutely."

"That's disappointing." His face was impish. "I was really looking forward to playing that back someday."

"That's exactly why it has to be erased. I don't want to be 'played back.' Last night wasn't a performance I gave. It was a gift. *Love*. I don't want *anyone*, you included, having control over that. It's mine to give, when *I* choose to give it. I have so little left that feels truly private . . . please, erase it now. Ethan, last night will never be replayed, and that's fine. We can have plenty of time to do new versions, right?"

He nodded, reluctantly she thought.

"Okay. It's easy enough. Let's go do it," he said.

She followed him through the center of the laboratory and down the hallway to the front room.

The big windows caught the morning light at an acute angle and the room was alive with a shadowed brilliance that reminded her of beach light at daybreak. Down below, an industrial machine scrubbing the bricks on the Mall compromised the mood, filling the space with an annoying buzz.

Ethan stopped about five feet from the equipment cart and turned back to face her. "Don't be funny, Emma. It's too early in the day."

She stared at him. A streak of light cut at a diagonal across his thighs. The bathrobe hung open to his navel, one nipple exposed, a dark dot on his copper flesh. She found her breath shortening. She didn't know what he was talking about.

"What?" she said.

"What did you do with it?"

"What do you mean what did I do with it? What did I do with what?" An electric jolt of alarm covered her like a shawl and made her skin feel raw.

He was pointing at the cart. "The optical drive? The Bernoulli? Where did you put it?" He patted an empty space on the second shelf of the cart. She remembered the space had held a vanilla-colored piece of equipment about the size of a small VCR. "Where is it?"

"Ethan, *no!* What the hell is a Bernoulli? Are you telling me the tape is gone?"

"It's not a tape, it's a disc. You didn't take it, did you?"

"Of course I didn't take it. This isn't funny to me. I'm not even sure that I know what on earth an optical drive is."

"It's the storage device for the system." He waved his hand at the empty spot on the cart. "It was here last night. And now it's gone."

She wanted to scream at him. She wanted to attack him. Instead, she turned away from him, hugged herself, and cried until finally her sobs stilled, and her anguish turned flat, lifeless. All she felt was a dull ache deep in her gut.

She didn't know what else to feel. Violated. Defiled.

But no, this is worse.

Rape. This felt like rape.

Ethan tried to console her.

She pushed him away and cried out, "What about the program, the software, don't they need that? Did they get that?"

"No. Well, not last night, anyway," he said.

"What do you mean, 'not last night'?"

"The application program, the code, isn't on the optical drive. But three copies have been made without permission over the past few months. I have a computer security specialist looking into it, how it was done."

"So whoever has the disc may have the software, too?"

"Yes, they might," he admitted. "But they don't have the collar." He had told her five times not to worry about the stolen drive, the data was useless without the collar. And even if they got one, the technical problems that still needed to be solved . . .

Ethan retreated to the shower.

She slunk off to her favorite place in his flat, on the wide windowsill of the front room overlooking the Mall. She was staring at the cart of computer equipment as though it were as vile as the gun used to kill her father. The sound of the doorbell intruded—someone ringing up to the flat from the second-floor landing. James Morelli, her prospective bodyguard, she guessed, right on time.

She hit the buzzer to unlock the lower door and waited for the knock. Two sharp, confident raps soon followed.

She swung the door open. The person at the door wasn't her new bodyguard. It was the mailman.

She was surprised to see him. He seemed surprised to see Emma, looking at her twice, knowing that he'd seen her before, not quite able to piece together how he knew that face. "I've got a package. Mr. Han doesn't like me to leave them downstairs."

"Do I need to sign?"

"No." He narrowed his eyes. "Do I know you from somewhere else on my route?" He handed her the large padded envelope and a three-inch stack of Ethan's daily mail.

"I don't think so," she said absently. She figured that her identity would dawn on him later in the morning. He'd probably tell his wife about it at dinner. They would both be pretty excited.

Emma was baffled by it all.

She carried the stack of mail into the laboratory and placed it on Ethan's desk. The top envelope in the pile caught her attention.

"Oh my God," she said, looking over her shoulder to see whether Ethan was done with his shower. She listened intently, and thought she heard the water continuing to run.

Her heart felt as though it would erupt.

She lifted the envelope, hefted it. Standard business size, not too heavy. Two sheets inside, maybe three. She noted that the postage was first-class, not bulk rate. The address had been individually typed; it wasn't a label.

She placed the envelope back down. Walked away. Closed her eyes. She tried to catch her breath. She told herself the letter didn't mean anything.

But she couldn't leave it alone. She returned to the desk and raised the letter again, holding it up to the dull light that was coming from the western windows. The bond was too heavy; she couldn't make out a thing that was written on the paper inside.

Why is Ethan receiving mail from Operation Rescue? What does the right-to-life movement want with this man?

Emma took a deep breath and checked her watch.

"Screw the bodyguard," she said aloud.

She stuffed the envelope into the middle of the stack, scribbled a brief, talk-to-you-later note to

Ethan, and headed out the door. The bus station was a block away. She could find a cab there.

As soon as she arrived at the bus station, she used her cell phone to connect to Ethan's answering machine.

"It's me," she said. "Please don't tell the police what happened. If you figure out how the guy got into your flat, I want to know. I may have a friend of mine, a private investigator, call you to look into all this. His name is Kevin Quirk. Bye."

FIVE

The instant Scott Malloy left the interview room
to consult with Sergeant Pons, Lauren pounced
on Casey.

"You had no right to tell him—"

Casey held up her hand, realized that there was a
reasonable chance Lauren couldn't even see the gesture, and lowered it, feeling silly.

"Save it, Lauren. You heard me, I didn't say a
word to Malloy about your illness. And for now, I
won't. Not that it makes a hell of a lot of difference;
the fact that you can't see worth shit isn't going to
stay secret for long, anyway. And, if I understand
this optic—whatever it is—correctly from Alan, you
need medicine that you can't get in the infirmary at
the jail. And I need some more time with you to try
and understand what the hell is going on with your
friend, and I think I need it tonight. If you go to the
jail right now, I'll lose you for as many hours as
they decide to waste booking you. For the moment,
making them deal with you as a medical crisis case
will serve both of our needs."

Lauren was unswayed by Casey's logic, adamantly guarding a need to maintain a sense of control over *something*. "I didn't give you permission to—"

The frustration that had been creeping into Casey's voice exploded out. "I don't *need* your bullshit permission to untie my own hands. I will do everything I can to accommodate your desire for privacy. I won't, however, permit you to interfere with my ability to defend you. If you insist on *that* freedom, I'm walking out of here right now, and you can find yourself a new lawyer. Given that we're approaching midnight, on a weekend, in a blizzard, good luck. You'll stew in the damn county jail with a public defender—someone you may well have antagonized in court last week—until you make your first appearance tomorrow afternoon. Maybe that's what you want—to be some kind of sacrificial lamb. I can no longer tell what your agenda is."

Casey recognized the impact of her intensity on Lauren and softened her tone. "I *can* tell you I don't like seeing you here in handcuffs. I am truly frightened by whatever is going on with your health. And I absolutely don't want to see you spend even a minute in the Boulder County Jail."

Lauren was suddenly terrified that her only true ally in this awful place was angry at her. A renewed sense of vulnerability blew over her. She recognized an impulse to apologize, but instead stood speechless, frozen by the sound of footsteps echoing down the hall in her direction.

Scott Malloy was back. He'd been gone less than five minutes.

His face was somber. He glanced once at Lauren's eyes before directing his words to Casey Sparrow. Casey detected the tautness in his jaw and guessed that Detective Malloy did not like whatever message he was being asked to relay.

"Sergeant Pons says there's a nurse at the jail. 'A good one, a fine one' is what he said to tell you. She'll examine Lauren and make the call as to whether or not the doctor gets paged tonight. Let's go, there's a car waiting outside."

"I'm not sure that delaying seeing a doctor is a prudent decision, Detective. There are liability questions to consider, don't you think?"

"Well, it's not my decision and liability right now is not my concern. And as far as I can tell, Ms. Sparrow, you're not a doctor. I sure as hell am not a doctor. The consensus seems to be that we have a good medical opinion waiting for us a few miles away. What do you say we get over there as quickly as we can and see what the nurse has to say?"

"I'd prefer that my client be taken directly to the hospital from here. For evaluation and treatment."

"I'm sure you would prefer that. It's just not going to happen." He turned to his prisoner. In a pleasant, cajoling voice, he said, "Come on, Lauren, let's go."

Casey wasn't done protesting. "Speak to me, Detective, not to my client. I—"

Malloy glared at the attorney. "You're not going to win this one, Counselor. I suggest you save your energy."

Scott helped Lauren pull the coat up high on her neck and led her down a long corridor to a heavy steel door with an EXIT sign above it. Without any further warning, he pushed open the door and led her into an enclosed dock. A patrol car, newly cleaned of snow, engine running, was waiting ten feet away. Malloy guided Lauren out to the car, helped her onto the cold backseat, and slammed the door. He realized he had been leading her as though he believed she were, indeed, half-blind.

The transfer happened so quickly that Casey Sparrow didn't get a last word with Lauren.

When Malloy came back inside, he was prepared to end his diplomacy.

Casey disarmed him. "Thanks for your help tonight, Detective. I know you gave her some consideration that you weren't required to give her. If I was abrasive with you, I'm sorry. I don't mean to be difficult. I'm just trying to do what's best for my client."

Malloy narrowed his eyes, wondered if the conciliatory tone indicated that the attorney was playing some new game. He said, "I hope that Lauren's vision problem isn't serious."

"She thinks it is. So I have to take it seriously. Detective, there's one more thing you can do for me, if you don't mind."

"Yeah? What's that?" His voice carried a tractor trailer full of skepticism.

"Can you give me directions to the jail? I don't have any idea where it is since they moved it away from the Justice Center."

He laughed, and said, "Come on, I'll draw you a map. You know where the Boulder Airport is?"

She took two more steps, and said, "Boulder *has* an airport?"

Cozier Maitlin directed Alan to beach the BMW in the no-parking zone in front of the main entrance of the police department.

He did. Immediately after shifting the transmission into park, Alan announced, "I'm going in to see her."

"No, you're not. Not if you care about her welfare."

"Why the hell can't I go in?"

"You can't go in, Alan, because the detectives are dying to interview you. And because Casey and I don't know whether you know something important or not, so at this time we don't want them talking to you. They will not let you see your wife, regardless. So your efforts would be futile."

"What about her medicine?"

"I'll take it to her."

"Will they let you see her?" Alan felt defeated. "If they do, will you tell her that I love her?"

Cozy smiled warmly, his face conveying a degree of compassion that surprised Alan. "I probably won't see her until after she's booked over at the jail, if at all. Casey will be the one to meet with her. If the cops decided to do Lauren a favor, then Casey may have already spoken to her. And . . . I think we may discover the answer to that mystery momentarily."

"How?"

Cozy pointed out the windshield of the car at a figure huddled in a heavy coat, jogging flatfooted out the front door of the police station. "If I'm not mistaken, I think that shimmering red hair belongs to Casey Sparrow."

Cozy waited until Casey was ten feet from the front of his BMW before he reached over in front of Alan and pressed on the horn button for about three seconds. Casey started at the sound and slipped onto her butt in the snow, her briefcase flying.

Alan jumped from the car and offered his hand to help her to her feet. He said, "Casey, you okay?" as she eased herself up and started to wipe snow off her clothing.

"Did you blast that horn at me? Jesus Christ, Alan, what the hell were you thinking? You almost gave me a heart attack. Where's my briefcase?"

"No, it was Cozy, he's in the car. He hit the horn. I don't think he meant to frighten you, I'm sure it was inadvertent."

"You don't know him, do you? Cozy doesn't have accidents. Cozy causes other people to have accidents."

"Casey, were you able to see Lauren? What's going to happen? How is she holding up?"

"Let's get out of the snow, and I'll tell you what's going on."

Alan Gregory returned to the driver's seat of Cozy's car. Casey Sparrow slid into the backseat.

Casey said, "Hey, Cozy, I owe you one. Thanks for helping Lauren out tonight."

Alan's ear told him that two messages were being communicated. Casey was not only warning Cozy about upcoming retribution for the horn thing, she was also thanking him for being so responsive to her urgent plea for help on a weekend night. Although his experience with Cozier Maitlin was extremely limited, Alan guessed that Cozy was disposed to hear only the latter of Casey's two messages.

"What do you know so far, Casey?"

"I know Lauren's on her way to the jail and that we need to get over there so I can talk with her some more. Because I still don't understand what happened tonight. So move. Alan, why are you driving Cozy's limo?"

Cozy answered for him. "There are actually two reasons that Alan is driving. First, I am temporarily without possession of my driver's license, and second, I don't believe in driving in blizzards."

Casey made a scolding face at him. "No license? A DUI, Cozy? Really?"

"Hardly. A speed trap thing."

"Speeding is only a few points. How many times? What are we talking, *ten?*"

"Four, thank you. On one occasion I apparently exceeded the speed limit by a factor of three."

Casey shook her head. "You're a slow learner, Cozy. Alan, you know where the jail is?"

"Yes."

"Then why don't we head out? I'll fill you in on what I know. And you can tell me if you discovered anything."

Alan said, "Let's take two cars. Yours and mine, leave Cozy's here. It's not made for snow, anyway."

"Good idea. I'll take Cozy in my truck. We'll meet you over there."

Cozy said, "Wait a second," and whispered something to Casey. She listened and nodded her head.

Cozy faced Alan. "Alan, there's no point in you

going to the jail. You're not going to see Lauren tonight. After hours, like this, they won't even let you
inside and you'll end up sitting in your car freezing
in the parking lot until we're done. Give Casey the
medicine you have with you. She'll take it in to
Lauren. Then, if you still want to be helpful, go back
up the hill and get Erin. She'll be done soon. Then
go home and try and get some sleep; you'll need
it. Lauren will have her first appearance tomorrow
afternoon. You can see her then."

"At the Justice Center?"

"No. At the jail. There's a courtroom there that
they use for pretrial appearances. But we'll be in
touch before then."

Alan began to protest, "Casey—"

"He's right. Do what he says. It's best." Her voice
was soft.

Alan turned his head away and got lost in the
static of the falling snow. Reluctantly he handed over
the medicine and opened the car door.

"My beeper is on now, okay? You'll call me with
any news, right? I mean anything."

"It's better this way, Casey. We don't need him
pacing around outside the jail."

"I know. But I want to take my truck."

"Fine. You talked with her?"

"Yes."

"And?"

"She's emotional, she's scared, she's humiliated,
and despite it all, she's managing to keep her dignity.
They haven't wrestled that from her yet. I don't
know if I could go through what she's going through

without some self-pity. I don't see any in her, at all. I truly admire that."

"That is all nice and humane and compassionate of you, Casey," he said with mild rebuke in his tone, "but at the moment I'm actually more interested in her view of the events of the evening that led to her arrest."

"Wheat from the chaff time, Cozy? Bottom line is that she's basically saying that she doesn't think she did it."

He smiled in the dark. "Gosh, now that's a novel defense. I've never used it before." Cozy was intent on getting a reading on his colleague as much as he was eager to get a feeling for his new client.

The windows of the BMW were plastered with a mix of ice and snow. The inside of the car seemed to Casey Sparrow like the igloo of a wealthy Eskimo.

Casey said, "You know Emma Spire, don't you? You know she lives in town?"

"Of course."

"Well, our client is maintaining that this all has something to do with Emma Spire and that Lauren was at her house protecting her against a rape of some kind. Lauren is insisting that we leave Emma out of it. I don't know the hows or the whys. We were interrupted before I got the details. You know about her illness?"

"Obliquely."

"Her vision is deteriorating badly."

"The illness is . . . ?"

"You don't know?"

"People say she has something bad. That's all I know."

"Apparently, it's multiple sclerosis. A big secret. I don't see how she could have shot a man from that far away."

MS? thought Cozy. "The cops won't care if it was a lucky shot. They care about pulling the trigger and hitting the target. They don't add or take away points for luck. But the Emma Spire angle? I knew she lived up there. I asked the husband about it. He, too, is being quite circumspect. I think he knows the details, at least some of them. I'm afraid we need to proceed tonight as though our client may be more culpable than either of us would like to believe. What did you mean, by the way, by 'a rape of some kind'?"

"I don't know what I meant. That's one of the reasons I want to talk to Lauren again tonight. Lauren seems to think Emma Spire is still in some danger."

✛

If there were a more forlorn circumstance on the face of the planet than a journey to jail in the backseat of a squad car at midnight in a blizzard, Lauren was having trouble imagining what it might be.

She was actually most frightened of the isolating quiet, of being ignored as though she had no physical presence at all. In the time it had taken her to squeeze a handgun trigger, her status had devolved from that of esteemed citizen to that of offender. As far as the justice system was concerned, it was as though she had checked her identity and her worth and her humanity into the evidence locker along with her clothing.

She wondered if she would ever get any of it back.

The pain behind her eyes hadn't diminished. That meant the episode with her vision wasn't over and that she might suffer even more vision deterioration before the night was over. The gray fuzz on the edges of her perception might soon grow as black as charcoal.

She felt the car slither into another slow turn. They were now on Valmont. One more turn to come at Airport Road. Then a minute later they would be at the *jail*.

God.

She slunk farther down onto the seat. Silently she mouthed, "Alan, where are you? Please help me. Please."

Lauren had never entered the jail through the garage before.

On the back side of the building, away from the public entrance, the black-and-white patrol car stopped at a speaker mounted on a pole. The officer opened his window and pressed a button. A voice responded. In the backseat, Lauren couldn't understand what was being said. An icy wind blew snow into the car. The officer who was driving identified himself and said he had a prisoner for booking. A security camera that was directed at his windshield monitored the whole interchange.

In front of them, a big industrial door opened slowly, revealing a starkly lit garage big enough to hold four vehicles in two lanes. The patrol car pulled in alongside a patrol car from the Longmont Police Department. The Boulder County Jail, staffed by the Boulder County Sheriff's Department, served the whole county, from the eleven-thousand-foot mountains to the wheat-carpeted plains.

The big door closed behind the Boulder patrol car as soon as it entered. Most nights, the deputies closed the door quickly as a security concern. This night they were more interested in keeping the ferocity of the storm outside.

A female sheriff's deputy waited on one side of the garage. Malloy had called the jail and warned the booking sergeant that a female prisoner was on the way. The sheriff's deputy waited until the driver of the patrol car had pulled himself out of the car, then she opened the backseat door and half-lifted Lauren out into the garage.

The Boulder cop came around the car. The deputy said, "Miserable out there, huh?"

"Awful. I hate these fall snowstorms. We almost got sideswiped by a pickup on Valmont. He barely missed us. I'm still shaking."

"People can't drive in the snow."

"Wish I owned a body shop tomorrow."

"Ain't that the truth."

The deputy finally turned her attention to Lauren and said, "This way," tugging Lauren to the north side of the garage where she stood her in front of a blue screen marked "Video Search." The deputy patted Lauren down much more thoroughly than she had been searched at the police department. Lauren felt the deputy's hands go places that she had never considered someone's hands would ever go without her permission. Still cuffed, Lauren was then led through a heavy steel jail door into a small window-lined anteroom that was all cinder block and metal.

The deputy said, "Take a seat," pointing her finger at a stainless-steel bench that folded down from the wall across the room.

Lauren couldn't see well enough to tell exactly where the little bench was and since her hands were still hooked she couldn't feel for it. Finally, she thought she had figured out where it was, stooped to sit, and tumbled off the edge to the floor.

The deputy asked the Boulder cop, "She drunk? High on something?" and began to help her prisoner to her feet.

The BPD officer said, "Didn't think so, nobody told me anything about that. Just told me to keep my damn mouth shut."

Lauren blinked hard and said, "I've been having some trouble with my vision."

The deputy looked at the patrol cop. Her expression said, *Yeah, right.*

"You have glasses, honey?" She had changed her tone; she was talking to Lauren as though she were a drunk. She asked the cop, "She have glasses with her?"

"Maybe Detective Malloy has them. I don't. He's on his way over in a while to do the arrest paperwork."

The deputy guided Lauren to the bench and pushed down on her shoulders until she was perched on it. "Lift your feet now, one at a time."

Lauren did. Wearing latex gloves, the deputy pulled Lauren's wet shoes off, then her socks, and carefully examined the insides of her shoes and the soles of her feet for contraband or weapons.

To the officer who brought Lauren over, the deputy said, "She's clean. You can unhook her now."

He pulled out a key and released the restraints. "The cuffs aren't mine. They belong to Detective Malloy. Just hold 'em for him, if you don't mind. Like I said, he'll be over here soon enough."

"We can't start booking her until he logs her in. You want to do that part before you go? It'd speed things up. I'll get you some coffee."

"No, just park her in a holding cell. She can wait to be booked. Anybody tell you that she's a deputy DA?"

"No. No shit." The deputy gazed down at Lauren, still seated on the stainless-steel bench, as though she had just realized her prisoner was still in the room. "Here? Boulder County? What'd she do?"

"Yeah, here. She shot somebody is all I know. Half the brass in town is at the department tonight frettin' about this and that. Cross your t's and dot your i's on this one, that'd be my advice."

"Huh, I appreciate you telling me. In that case, I think I will leave her out of the pit and stick her in a holding cell until the detective gets here to log her in. Maybe let my sergeant handle this." She fingered the sleeve of Lauren's police department sweats. "You want these clothes back? I can get her changed out before you go."

"Not my problem. Work that all out with the detective. I'm out of here. Night."

Lauren was terrified.

She knew the jail terrain and although it had never

frightened her before, it did now. The booking room lay on the other side of the far door. She knew the booking room well, knew most of the faces and some of the names of the sheriff's deputies who staffed it. She knew what the computers did and where the cameras pointed. She knew where each of the holding cells was located and she knew which door led to the courtroom.

She knew where the print roller was.

She knew that a handful of minor-league felons would be in the pit grumbling about being busted while they watched whatever drivel was on the color TV that was mounted high on the wall out of their reach.

She felt so alone at that moment that she feared she had to remember to breathe and that she would somehow forget and she would just die.

"Come on, ma'am, let's go. Get you some jail clothes. Hope you like blue."

Lauren dreaded the next few steps. She figured that everyone wearing a uniform in the booking room was waiting for her entrance. She hung her head as she was led through the booking room, then quickly out the other side, and down a hallway to a small dressing room with a shower. She imagined the glares of the deputies in the booking room, the odd mixture of disdain and pity on their faces. She wondered if the sergeant who ran the booking room was there. She was fond of him and didn't want to face him under these circumstances.

From previous visits to the jail, Lauren was familiar with the changing rooms. Once inside, she felt along the wall for a bench and sat. "You want underwear? We got bras and panties. I'm going to let you keep those shoes, though, they seem to fit you okay."

In response to the question about the underwear, Lauren, who was usually incredibly picky about her underwear, said, "Please." Her voice felt tiny, entirely too small for someone in need of grown-up undergarments.

Thirty seconds later the deputy threw the underwear and the navy blue jail issue into Lauren's lap. Other than the color and the big BCSD stenciled on the back, the outfit was reminiscent of surgeon's scrubs.

"Let me know if these don't fit. I'll try to get you some others, but mostly I'm pretty good with sizes. Used to work a little retail over the holidays and such. And—trust me, you don't want to ignore this— if you need to use the facilities, these commodes in here are a lot more private than what you're going to find out in the holding cells. I'd recommend these."

Lauren began to cry.

"Jeez, honey, don't go crying. We'll get you down to the infirmary and see if Demain's free. After that, we're going to isolate you as best we can. Can't really risk having you in the women's module or hanging out with the customers that are still in booking, you know what I mean. Those folks might recognize you. Can't have that given what you may have already done to them."

Lauren knew that all these things represented special treatment from the deputy. Her horror was in realizing how terrible this felt even with the additional favors.

How bad can it get?

She remembered what Emma was facing and shuddered. Right now, she thought, I'll take the assault on my freedom and privacy over the assault on hers.

✛

Despite the horrendous weather conditions she faced at the scene of the shooting, Erin Rand settled into her usual investigatory routine. For Erin, that meant doing the easy things first. She liked to feel oriented.

After yanking her hat down tight and tugging her collar up to her chin, she high-stepped through the snow, methodically covering the perimeter of the crime scene tape, stopping every so often to add a detail to a diagram she was trying to sketch.

As she strolled, her notepad became soaked and she gave up trying to add new details. She hiked the taped perimeter once more, this time letting her camera do the recording. The snow complicated everything.

She decided to move her action off the street and begin to try to goad some neighborhood residents into speaking with her. Maybe one of them would even invite her inside and let her warm her fingers and dry off.

Recalling Detective Purdy's advice, Erin aimed herself at the house on what she thought was the southeastern corner of the block. The porch light was still on, though, and she focused with total determination on the climb to the front door. A long staircase rose from the sidewalk to the house. The treads had disappeared under the snow and from Erin's vantage the path up appeared to be nothing more than a steep hill awaiting the first sled of winter. With the toe of one boot she felt for the first step, grabbed the wrought-iron railing, and began to pull her way up the slope.

Before she reached the top of the stairs the front door opened and a sweet, high-pitched voice said, "My goodness, you're a brave one, aren't you? Come on in, dear, you must be freezing your cheeks. We need to get you warmed right up."

Grateful for the enthusiastic greeting, Erin muttered, "Thank you, God. This almost makes up for having to spend another night schlepping Cozy." She forced a smile onto her frozen face and tried to form words with her icy lips while she brushed snow off her clothing.

Finally, with great effort, she managed to say, "Hello, I'm Erin Rand, I'm an investigator. I wonder if I might ask you a few questions about what happened here tonight."

"Not while you're still outside, you can't, dear. I simply won't hear of it. It's cold enough to freeze cats out there and I'll be darned if I'm going to stand in this doorway and chat with you. Come in, come in. And don't worry about the snow on your boots, all those others certainly didn't."

Erin's surprising hostess was a woman in her sixties. Erin pegged her as at least five-ten. She was elegant, with shoulder-length silver-blond hair, and wore a dressing gown that Erin suspected was made of cashmere. Her face was thin and pale and remarkably unwrinkled.

The floor onto which Erin dripped melted snow was tiled with beautiful green marble. The entryway table was a stunning restored antique fruitwood.

But at least two aberrations to this picture of wealth and sophistication were immediately apparent to Erin.

First, her hostess's deep blue irises were swimming in a sea of red, wormy lines.

And, second, her gorgeous house reeked of cannabis.

"Leave those boots right where they are and follow me, dear." Erin gladly shed her footwear and followed the woman, who still had not introduced herself, down a hallway toward the back of the house. On the way they passed a living room and a dining room furnished as tastefully as the foyer. When the woman reached a closed door toward the end of the hallway, she reached up and put an index finger in front of her mouth to shush Erin, who was already feeling as speechless as she ever got, anyway.

"Arnold is in there," she whispered. "He doesn't know about any of this." Erin found herself wondering what species Arnold might be. She guessed potbellied pig.

The room at the end of the hallway did not disappoint Erin, who quickly concluded that it wouldn't have disappointed Martha Stewart, either. The kitchen was spacious and charming, with big windows that would welcome the morning light. An octagonal sunroom adjoined the kitchen. "Sit, sit," said the woman, pointing Erin toward a big round table cluttered with a few days' worth of newspapers.

Erin said, "I'm so sorry, but I didn't catch your name."

"I'm Lois, dear. Always have been."

"Lois . . . ?" The investigator in Erin wanted a last name.

Lois smiled. Her teeth were in fine shape.

"Well, hello, Lois, I can't tell you how much I appreciate your hospitality, inviting me in, and—"

At the mention of hospitality, Lois squeaked, "Oh," and was off to the kitchen as though she had just remembered she had left something cooking on the stove. She reached for this and grabbed that, frantically trying to assemble some refreshments for her guest. She threw open cabinet doors and mounted a frontal assault on the refrigerator. Erin stared, her mouth as wide open as Lois's pantry, at the speed with which the woman was putting together a tray of food.

"I would have just left these things out earlier, but I really thought I was done entertaining for tonight. My, my, I apologize. Do you eat fish in the evening? Some people don't. Personally, I sleep alone these days so it doesn't make any difference if my breath smells like an old cat food can."

Lois stopped and performed a neat pirouette in order to face Erin, who had pulled her hat from her head and was shaking out her fine blond hair. Lois eyed her guest approvingly, placed her hands on her hips, and cocked her head just a little. "Now, you're a pretty one, aren't you? I would wager that—unlike this old woman—the right side of your bed is never cold for too long. I always like to sleep on the left, don't you? Women should, I think. Arnold always thought he should have the side closest to the window. That makes no sense, does it? Left side women, right side men, I say." She paused, pondering something. "Though I don't know what the lesbians do. Now, that's a problem. I'll have to think about it some more. On second thought, looking at you, although it really is *none* of my business, maybe you should forget the smoked trout and stick to the Gouda. That would do fine, don't you think? And the gherkins shouldn't offend anyone too much, I wouldn't think. Although they can be just a little aromatic. I still have a plentitude of coffee. But if you're the iced tea type I can manage that as well, thank you very, very much."

Erin couldn't fathom what a polite response to Lois's soliloquy might be. She said, "Coffee sounds wonderful. Who's Arnold?"

"Cream?"

"No, no cream, thank you."

Lois searched in the refrigerator and said, "Just as well, I'm out of cream. You'll have to have your coffee without milk." Immediately, she changed her voice to a whisper. "Everybody knows my Arnold, everybody." Her eyes shifted away from Erin for a split second, down the hall toward the closed door.

"I'm sort of new in town," Erin said. She wasn't. "How does everyone know him?"

"From the greenbelt, dear. My Arnold is known as the 'father of the greenbelt.' " She spoke with naked pride about this. "Look out that window behind you. That's Arnold's doing. He was the driving force behind preserving the mountain backdrop for Boulder."

Obligingly, Erin looked outside. She saw white. "Really? The green-belt was his idea?"

"His idea. His organizing. His politicking. His arm-twisting. His *vision*."

"I didn't know. It was before my time, obviously, but I'm terribly grateful to him."

"We all are, dear. We all are."

Lois placed a lacquered tray right in front of her guest. Erin flaked some trout and placed it on a cracker, took a bite.

Lois watched intently. "You do sleep alone, too, don't you? I'm so sorry. You'll find someone, dear, don't worry."

"No need to be sorry, it's by choice, currently. I get offers, Lois. Though most of them aren't worth giving up smoked fish over, if you know what I mean."

"Do I *ever*."

"Can we talk a little about what happened here tonight?" Erin tried to make a charming face to go along with the abrupt change in subject.

"Yes, of course," Lois said, opening her eyes wide. Erin thought they looked like dirty brake lights. "You're not with the police, are you?"

"No, I'm a private investigator."

"Do you work for Emma?"

"I'm sorry, but I can't say who my client is. Do you know Emma Spire?"

"Of course I do. She's my neighbor. That's her house right next door. I'm not the type who ignores my neighbors, famous or not."

Erin couldn't have picked her neighbors out of a police lineup. She envied Lois's view of the world.

"Were you home all evening?"

"I couldn't very well leave Arnold, could I?"

"Arnold is not well?"

Lois shook her head.

Oh God. Erin saw a digression looming and chose to press her agenda as forcefully as she could, hoping to keep her hostess on track. "So you were home all evening. What did you see?"

"Next door? Or out in the street?"

Thinking, *this is great,* Erin said, "Either, both."

Lois stood and took Erin's hand. "Come on, let me show you something. This will be fun."

Erin's optimism took a dive. *Maybe this will be fun, though it no longer looks like it is going to be particularly useful.* The alternative, however, was a return to the blizzard, and the likelihood that the frightened, grouchy neighbors who shared this block with Lois would soon be slamming their front doors in Erin's face.

The room where Lois led Erin had once been a tiny bedroom, the kind of ten-by-eleven-foot cell that architects sentenced bunk-bedded children to in the late fifties. Lois and Arnold's children were long gone, though, and Lois had reclaimed the intimate little space with a vengeance.

If the telltale odor of cannabis was apparent to Erin elsewhere in the house, she thought that this cubicle smelled like a marijuana humidor. Cozy's reggae guru, Bob Marley, could have been happily entombed in this room.

"This is my retreat—my personal retreat—and I like *fabric,*" Lois announced. "Yards and yards and yards of it. Arnold would absolutely hate this room."

The room was cloaked in cloth. Florals and pais-
leys, tapestries and plaids. Upholstery, draperies,
throws—fabric everywhere.

"He hasn't seen it?"

"Besides his kidney problem, Arnold has glau-
coma." She said this as though to remind Erin of
something she already knew and should not have
forgotten. "It's so sad. But if he saw this room once,
he would never come back in here. Too *floral* for
Arnold. He gravitates more toward leather and buffalo and antlers and things." She mused wistfully.
"Arnold actually doesn't gravitate much anymore at
all, if you know what I mean."

Erin didn't but smiled politely.

In weather other than a whiteout, the room was
blessed with a remarkable view of Arnold's and
Lois's prized greenbelt. In front of the window, Lois
had arranged an impressive assortment of binoculars,
telescopes, and cameras, both still and video. "My
hobby is monitoring the greenbelt for wildlife and
birds. Arnold and I believe that the next political attack on Boulder's open space is on the near horizon
and that we can't have too much information ready
to fight back. I keep detailed records of the wildlife.
Sit, sit."

Erin did, on a comfortable overstuffed chair covered with a floral chenille. She was captivated by the
relative calm that had come over her hostess as soon
as they had entered her sanctuary.

"I saw it."

"What?" asked Erin.

"Tonight. What happened. The man, the gunshot,
the truck. I try to keep an eye on my neighbors. Espe-

cially Emma. She's too young to be living alone in such a large house, don't you think? She's a sad one. She's someone who would *never* eat smoked fish at night. She could learn something from you. Maybe . . . maybe you two could be roommates."

Erin deflected Lois past another fork in her meandering road. "You saw the gunshot tonight? Do the police know about this?" Erin swept her eyes around Lois's room.

Thank you, Sam Purdy. Thank you.

"Of course not. I couldn't very well invite the police in here, now, could I? I smoke *dope* in this room, dear. Can't you smell it? I could hardly bring them in here with this aroma. For all intensive purposes, I'm a criminal, am I not?"

Erin tripped over Lois's idiom, quickly deciding that this sweet lady had already managed to come to terms with her life of crime.

"But then again, I didn't really want to leave the police totally in the dark about what happened. So I gave them some hints. They seem smart, especially the big one. They'll figure it out."

"You gave the police some *hints*?"

"That's right." Lois was lighting up a joint that was rolled as tightly as a crayon. "Would you like a hit, dear? We'll talk."

✦

The jail nurse was a thirty-five-year-old black woman who had cut her health care teeth starting impossible IVs on impossibly blown veins in impossibly small bodies in a pediatric oncology center. For most of a decade she had labored there handing out emesis basins, holding tiny hands, and wiping away tears, too often her own. Demain Jones knew exactly what suffering was and precisely what "unfair" meant in the human lexicon of tragedy, and she had absolutely no patience for inmates who whined.

She greeted Lauren with a half-smile. It was Demain Jones's standard skeptical greeting for inmates. She figured that *maybe* half of the patients who walked into her infirmary actually belonged there, so she figured it was only fair to smile halfway until she determined which camp the current con belonged in.

With the deputy parked on a chair along one wall the nurse proceeded to examine Lauren. After retiring from peds oncology, Demain Jones had gone back to school and earned a degree as a physician's assistant. She was accomplished at physical exams and performed one on Lauren while peppering her with questions about her health history. Lauren knew the routine as well as she knew how to file a motion to suppress and was impressed with the nurse's thoroughness.

At the end of the workup, Jones reexamined Lauren's eyes and rechecked her reflexes, especially on the bottoms of her feet.

Demain Jones took a quick glance over at the deputy who was accompanying Lauren, then leaned forward as though she were about to check Lauren's eyes again. Looking straight into them without her scope, Demain said, in a tame voice laced with concern, "Honey, you know you have a positive Babinski?"

Lauren blinked, said nothing.

Demain Jones intended the pronouncement as a test to see how this patient of hers would react. Demain still wasn't sure whether Lauren was being straight with her. "You know what that means, having a positive Babinski?"

Lauren shrugged.

"One of two things. Either means you are the world's largest new-born baby, or you have something seriously wrong with your central nervous system."

Lauren was unwilling to give herself away. She tried to appear appropriately perplexed.

Demain Jones took a step back. "I was about to authorize a transfer to Community Hospital so that an ophthalmologist could take a look at those smoky eyes of yours, but I'm beginning to think that wouldn't be the right thing to do."

Lauren wanted desperately to get out of the county jail. "My vision *is* awful."

The nurse sighed. "Oh, I believe *that*. Your pupils have about as much in common as me and my ex-husband. And you can't track your own finger well enough to pick a basketball off your nose."

Lauren nodded, relieved that they were finally on the same page.

Demain Jones lowered her voice. In Lauren's ears it seemed to rumble. "Sister, don't you *dare* try to hustle me. You don't have the skills to hustle me. I spend five dark nights a week smellin' lies. Only the very *best* liars have even a chance to scam me. Now, be straight, hon, exactly what kind of doc should I be sending you to? It's not an ophthalmologist you need, is it?"

Lauren swallowed. "I probably need to see a . . . neurologist." Lauren hesitated, recognizing an opportunity, and she made an impulsive decision to try to take advantage of it. "And a urologist, too."

"A *urologist?*" Jones said skeptically. She had already surmised the neurology part.

Lauren leaned toward the nurse and whispered, "I haven't been able to pee."

"You have a diagnosis?"

"No," Lauren lied. "I'm being followed. They're ruling things out. You know what that's like."

"Mmmm mmm. I bet they are. You have names?"

"Of what they're ruling out?"

"Doctors' names."

"The doctors? Yes."

"Let's have 'em, honey."

Lauren gave Nurse Jones the name of her neurologist, Dr. Larry Arbuthnot—"I'm sorry, you are going to have to spell that one for me"—and her neighbor Dr. Adrienne Arvin, a urologist.

As she walked away from Lauren to consult with the deputy, Jones turned back and said, "If it turns out you're scamming me, I'm going to come and get you and we are going to be cellmates for a week and you are going to regret the day you were born."

Lauren couldn't see Demain Jones's face. If she could, she would have seen a smile in the nurse's eyes.

The sergeant from the booking room had to settle the dispute that soon erupted between the nurse and the deputy.

Jones had called the jail physician, who was home in bed, and who didn't even bother to open his eyes before he authorized Lauren's transfer to Community Hospital. Jones wanted Lauren transported to the hospital immediately. But the deputy argued that since the prisoner hadn't yet been actually booked, she wasn't officially in the custody of the county. That being the case, the Sheriff's Department couldn't transport her. The Boulder Police Department, the agency with legal custody, would have to arrange to have Lauren picked up and transported, or she would have to be booked first. Once she was booked a sheriff's deputy could transport her. Since the paperwork of logging her in for booking hadn't even started, a delay of ninety minutes was likely, and two hours was more realistic.

Demain Jones said that simply wouldn't do. She didn't know what the hell was wrong with Lauren's central nervous system but she didn't want whatever it was that was currently simmering erupting to a full boil in *her* infirmary in the middle of the night during a blizzard.

To complicate what was really becoming a pain-in-the-ass night shift, the booking sergeant had to cope with Lauren's two defense attorneys, who were now pacing around the pit demanding access to their client.

Scott Malloy finally arrived at the jail to log in his prisoner. The booking sergeant explained the situation to Malloy, and five minutes later, Lauren was hooked up again, moved to the backseat of Malloy's car, and was on her way across town to Community Hospital's emergency room.

*   *   *

Alan Gregory had already called Larry Arbuthnot at home and apprised him of what was going on with Lauren, both legally and medically, so Dr. Arbuthnot was not surprised at the call from Demain Jones at the Boulder County Jail, informing him that one of his patients was in need of his attention in the ER at Community Hospital.

Jones had a lot more questions for him.

But he told her he had to run. Actually, what he had to do was to try to conclude making love to his wife before he lost any more of his erection.

The urologist that Demain Jones called next was much more suspicious than Dr. Arbuthnot had been. Adrienne Arvin was Lauren and Alan's friend and neighbor, but she had never been Lauren's personal physician, and she did not know Lauren had been arrested. When the jail nurse called identifying one of Adrienne's good friends as a jail resident with a bladder problem, Adrienne suspected immediately that a serious game was afoot. If Lauren did not possess the sociopathic skills necessary to befuddle Demain Jones, Adrienne was an entirely different breed of adversary. Although Demain had no way of knowing it, she was now hitting against a big-league pitcher with incredibly good breaking stuff.

Adrienne listened to the nurse's story and said thanks, she would take care of it. She adopted a tone that was a mix of boredom and irritation. *Yeah, yeah.* She deflected Demain's attempts to get more history, said she'd get back to her after she examined her patient.

After hanging up, Adrienne phoned Alan, didn't get him, cursed him, said "screw it," and began the tedious process of bundling up her sleeping toddler for a trip across town to the hospital.

SIX

**Thursday, October 10. Late afternoon.
61 Degrees, Sunny**

God," Emma Spire said as much to the sky as to her companions, "this is humiliating. I thought that when the *Star* printed pictures of my high school boyfriends that it was the most mortifying black eye I would ever suffer. I was wrong. I am so humiliated right now I can't even find words for it."

The afternoon was warm, the air as dry as smoke. The early end to the day was the only clue to the looming winter.

Emma had phoned and asked Alan and Lauren to come over and go for a hike with her, explaining to Lauren that she would find it easier to talk if she was walking, and that she desperately needed to talk. To Lauren's surprise, Emma had specifically included the request that Alan accompany them.

They started the hike from Emma's backyard, cutting across a honeyed meadow of drying grasses until they reached a dusty, well-worn trail that led south toward the base of the Flatirons. Lauren walked on Emma's left side, Alan a step behind her to the right. Their backs were toward the city.

Alan was curious why he had been invited along.

The friendship that had developed between Lauren and Emma had never seemed to include him in any role other than Lauren's spouse. Even from a distance, though, he had felt the artificial magnetism of her celebrity. Lauren occasionally asked his take on Emma. Once, he'd said, "She wastes a lot of energy running in place, sweets. I think she's terrified of slowing down enough to find out where she is."

"It's understandable, don't you think?"

He was surprised that she didn't disagree. "Of course it's understandable. And when the time comes that she's not able to run anymore, she's going to be glad there's someone like you close by."

But on the trail, Emma's smile was absent and her eyes lacked any luster at all. Alan feared that the day had come when Emma could no longer run faster than her demons.

Lauren asked, "Emma? What's so terrible that you don't want to talk about it? Did your friend learn something about what happened at the parking garage? Are you in more danger than we thought?" Lauren feared that Kevin Quirk had uncovered some plot to harm or kidnap Emma.

Emma took two steps before she spoke.

"You know, maybe this wasn't a good idea. Maybe I don't want to talk about this after all. Why don't we just walk?"

Alan recognized the informal choreography that indicated to the psychologist in him the initiation of the ritual dance of resistance, and he guessed why he had been asked along on this hike. Emma wanted to be with someone who knew the matching steps, who knew how to follow her lead. Or how to take the lead from her.

Confronting her reluctance directly, he said, "Talking won't hurt, Emma. Maybe we can be of some help. Give it a try."

She took five steps before she spoke. She said, "I wish my mom were alive."

With that as a preamble, Alan figured that whatever words came next were going to be as measured as the last beats of a dying heart.

Alan said, "If she were here, what would you say to her, Emma?"

"I don't think I'd say anything. I'd just let her hold me. I'd tell her not to die. Daddy always thought I was a rock. Mom knew I wasn't ever as strong as I looked."

They had slowed so much that Alan was shortening his strides to accommodate Emma's meager progress. At this pace the Boulder greenbelt would loom as large as Yellowstone. Lauren and Alan both sensed the need for patience and tried to provide it, matching Emma's tempo both on the hike and in the conversation.

Before long they crested a small ridgeline, and Emma finally spoke again.

"Can we sit?" she asked in a weary voice while settling back against a big sloping rock lined with inky veins of granite, her knees pulled close to her chest. The hiking boots on her feet were scuffed with wear. Above the left knee of her jeans was a hole the size of a quarter. Her index finger slid into the rip and picked at the margins like a ferret tearing at a meal.

Alan and Lauren found perches close to where Emma was sitting. Emma's back was to the west, and they saw her silhouetted in profile against the foothills, which were already bathed in evening shadow.

"Last Sunday, at Ethan's apartment? Do you remember the demonstration Ethan did with your friend, Diane? After dinner, with the computer and with that . . . ?"

Alan and Lauren said, "Yes," simultaneously, in similarly subdued tones.

"Ethan recorded Diane's movements through that collar he developed?"

Another stereo "Yes."

"Well, last night . . ." She pulled some chickweed and tossed it aside and scuffed the hard toe of one boot into the dust. "Last night, he recorded me . . . while we . . . while we made love. He recorded me with the same equipment."

Lauren was relieved; she had been steeling herself for worse tidings than *that.* She looked askance at Alan, then back at Emma and said, "I don't think I understand. You wore that collar while you had sex?"

Emma looked away, not wanting to meet Lauren's eyes. She wasn't prepared to discuss her sexual activities with these two people. And she was bone tired already and wasn't sure she had the reservoir of energy that was going to be necessary to explain what had actually happened.

"No, he wore it. I didn't."

Her voice laced with relief, Lauren said, "So it recorded his movements, not yours?" Even a computer-generated parody of Emma's motions while having sex would cause a stir that Lauren knew Emma didn't want, or need. But Lauren couldn't see what trouble Ethan's animated likeness would cause without Emma's corresponding image on the recording.

"I wish it were that simple. God, how I wish it were that simple. Ethan was vague the other night during the party—the equipment he demonstrated records much more than movement. That night, at the party, he was only demonstrating a small part of what it does. But yesterday, last evening, he had the entire apparatus running, the whole thing, and what it recorded was his experience of having sex with me. Everything he felt while we made love was recorded."

The breeze was as loud as Emma's voice, and Alan and Lauren were forced to struggle to find her words in the wind.

Her eyes were down when she continued. "When I kissed him, it was recorded. When I sucked on his toes, it was recorded. When I had him in my mouth, it was recorded. When he was inside me . . . it was recorded."

An abrupt gust of wind rustled through the tall weeds and whistled through the gnarled pines nearby. Lauren pulled the collar of her sweater tight around her throat. She didn't want to hear these details and was guessing that Emma didn't really want to reveal them.

Emma seemed oblivious to the chill breeze. To herself, infused from some fresh reservoir of horror, she asked, "Oh God, I wonder if it records *his* lips and tongue. Oh God." Her imagination carried her to new depths of shame.

Lauren checked Alan's face, his raised eyebrows evidence he was as confused as she was. Lauren said, "I'm sorry I'm so dense about this. He recorded you? He used a camera?"

"Worse. No, no. It's much worse than a video-tape." She sighed the way a big dog does as it settles in to sleep. "Let me try to explain what Ethan's technology does. What he actually recorded last night."

Darkness seemed to descend faster than Alan's and Lauren's eyes could adjust. Emma's features faded into the bronze shadows.

Emma could feel the dusk as it surrounded her. It felt protective, like a cocoon. *To disappear* . . .

The gravity of the situation finally registering in his technologically naive consciousness, Alan said, "I assume you asked him to erase the disc with the data on it."

Emma nodded. "Yes, I insisted. He was reluctant, but he agreed."

"Then what's the problem?" Lauren asked, already guessing what the problem was.

The hole on the thigh of Emma's jeans was approaching silver-dollar size. "Someone . . . somehow . . . broke into Ethan's flat in the middle of the night while we were sleeping and stole the whole damn disc drive."

Lauren scooted to a rock closer to Emma and reached over and touched her friend's fingertips. "I don't know what to say. This must be a total night-mare for you. It would be a nightmare for any woman, but it's a total nightmare for you. If this became public . . ."

Alan, too, was anticipating the consequences of the disc being copied and disseminated, his imagination covering territory littered with obscene new violations of Emma's privacy. Like most of the American public, he had spent more than two years, through the newspapers, magazines, and television, as an occasional voyeur on Emma's life, never until the last few months considering the consequences of that scrutiny on her. Access to data like Emma was describing would be devastating to her. He winced thinking of the repercussions.

Emma waited until both Alan and Lauren were looking at her before she continued. "I don't know what to do. If this disc gets out publicly—if even the fact that this damn disc exists gets out publicly—I'm going to kill myself. That's it."

Alan listened for the threat, for the manipulation, for the cry for help that almost always framed such statements when his patients mouthed them. Listening to Emma he heard nothing but bald intent. He pondered how to intervene.

Lauren heard the hopelessness and targeted it. "Don't talk like that, we'll figure something out."

Emma's voice was minuscule. "No. No. You don't get it, what it's like. You can't. I never used to understand what it was like. When I was little, my parents knew lots of politicians and they always seemed to enjoy it, the notoriety, the attention. When I was engaged to Pico, he always seemed to get pumped up by it.

"But the difference is that they all chose it, they

wanted it. I didn't. I never did. I don't. I feel like my . . . soul has been kidnapped. My relationship with Pico made everything worse. That was a huge mistake on my part—moving to California."

She kicked at the dust, tracing circles in the dirt with the toe of her boot. "I love the water. I grew up at the beach in Delaware. Now, I don't even *vacation* at the beach anymore because I can't stand seeing swimsuit photos of me at the supermarket checkout the next week. Since Pico, I've stayed away from men because I don't want to feed the romance rumors that get ignited every time I'm seen with someone. I don't back causes, even ones I care deeply about. I watch what lectures I attend, what controversies I discuss. My friends buy the books I want to read and the videos I want to watch so that my tastes can remain at least a little private. And each night I go to bed, wondering which friend who isn't really a friend after all is going to sell me out."

Emma's eyes were focused on the eastern horizon, where a black ribbon of night had descended to wrap the planet like a gift.

"When my mother died of breast cancer, when I was seventeen, I felt that my world began to shrink. I literally felt it get smaller. She had meant so much to me, there was such a hole in my heart when she was gone. She was my best friend. My dad did his best to help but he didn't really know how, and then . . . when he was killed, I felt totally lost, my life . . .

"That day—the day of the shooting—in the airport, what I did wasn't what it looked like on that tape. See, I wasn't only protecting him, I was saving me.

As I was holding him on the carousel, I really felt that I couldn't go on without him. And then—bang bang—I had to survive alone. I had to find a way.

"The obsession the public has with me has been as much of a surprise as the gunshots. Maybe more. I knew there were people who hated my father for what he believed. But I wasn't prepared for the public ever wanting a piece of *me*.

"A week ago I would have told you that I thought I knew everything there was to know about losing control. About fateful moments. For two years now, I've had nowhere left to hide, almost nothing left to call my own. No close family. No privacy. No secrets. And now—with this stupid disc missing—I've somehow managed to lose control over things I didn't even know a person could lose control over. In the space of one technological leap, I apparently no longer even have a body I can call my own."

She hadn't been looking at her companions but suddenly turned to them. First toward Lauren, then Alan. "Do you realize that I am about to become *shareware*. Sex with me, by remote control. You, too, can screw America's princess-of-the-month. I wonder what it will cost. What is my virtue worth, anyway? What do you think? Twenty-nine ninety-five? Or a little more, forty bucks, like a Mike Tyson fight on cable? How long do you think I'll stay on the charts?"

Lauren took Emma's hand.

"They've won. Everyone who ever decided that they had a right to any piece of me that they could reach out and grab, well, they've won. I've lost everything now. It's that simple."

REMOTE CONTROL   219

"We just have to get that disc back," Lauren said.

Emma said nothing. Her eyes communicated her hopelessness.

"You can't exactly go to the police for help with this, can you?" Alan asked.

She scoffed, "You think they would manage to keep this a secret?"

"What about reporting it as a technology theft? Ethan's prominent enough, he'll get some attention from the police even on something as mundane as a burglary."

"Ethan backs up everything he does from here to Honolulu. Everybody who knows him knows that about him. For him to maintain that he lost valuable data and that he has no backup? It's just not plausible."

"We could get a restraining order, keep anyone from publishing it."

"That would be like advertising for the creep who stole it. You think the cyber freaks on the Internet are going to be deterred by a restraining order? This disc doesn't need to be published. It can be copied and recopied digitally a hundred different ways. Disc to disc, modem to modem. A restraining order? There would be no stopping it."

"What about your friend, Kevin? Can he help?"

"I called him earlier today." Emma sounded beaten, weary. She was talking now only because she was polite, not because this avenue of inquiry held out any hope. "He's going to talk to Ethan, see if he can figure out what happened, who might have taken the disc. Kevin will try, he's sweet. It's too late."

"Maybe Ethan's wrong about the technology,

Emma. Maybe he'll never debug it; maybe it will never work. Maybe the data is useless."

Emma said, "If it were you, Alan, would you be willing to take that risk?" She waited, letting his silence speak. "Alan, look at my life. It's a nice fantasy—but that's not the way my luck's been running."

Lauren tried to deter Emma's hopelessness one more time. "There are always options. We'll figure something out."

For much of a minute, Emma was silent. Then she said, "Yes, maybe you're right. Let's go back to the house."

Alan's impression was that Emma was buying into Lauren's hopefulness mostly as a way to indicate she was done talking. It was possible that Lauren had hit on something that resonated for Emma. But he didn't feel encouraged.

When Emma had said she would kill herself, Alan felt she meant it.

Lauren answered Kevin's knock and let him in the door.

Alan had completed a reconnaissance of Emma's refrigerator and pantry, and having failed to find sufficient ingredients to combine into a dinner for four, had picked up the phone to order a pizza.

Emma kicked her hiking boots onto the floor and curled into a ball on the sofa, her knees tucked close to her chest. When she picked up the remote control for the TV and flicked it on, she found herself staring at *Hard Copy*. She shivered for a moment as the anchor promised an exclusive report on Princess Diana's Caribbean holiday.

Emma started to cry.

Kevin arrived at her side before Lauren did. His embrace was a two-armed affair that shut the two of them off from the room.

The pizza was delivered by a young woman who was already aware that she was at Emma Spire's house. Although Alan opened the door only eighteen inches or so while he fished out his wallet, the delivery girl was trying desperately to peer around him into the house in hopes of catching a glimpse of the celebrity who lived inside.

Alan lied, "She's not home."

The girl's shoulders sank at least two inches. "Drag. She's so great, isn't she? I mean, she has such style. And right here in Boulder, can you believe it? Our hair's the exact same color, don't you think? Emma's and mine, I mean." The lanky kid fingered her honey-colored hair, which was at least a couple of shades lighter than Emma's.

"Just like hers. Exactly," Alan replied, tipping her an extra two dollars, hoping she would go away.

"Are you her boyfriend?"

"No, I'm not. I'm just a friend." To Alan, the conversation they were having felt absurd. He was discussing his relationship to Emma Spire with a teenager who delivered pizza.

"But you, like, *know* her, right?"

"Yes."

"Wow." She glanced down at the bills in her hand,

suddenly realizing the bonus built into her tip, and said, "Cool. I can't wait to tell my friends."

Alan closed the door and walked back toward the kitchen with the pizza thinking, *right there, that's exactly the problem that Emma's facing.* If the fact that you delivered pizza to her house is worth telling your friends, what is this damn disc of having sex with her worth?

Kevin Quirk carried his food to the couch where he sat close enough to Emma that he would have been able to protect her even if the roof caved in unexpectedly.

Kevin continued detailing the outcome of his conversation with Ethan earlier that day. "Your boyfriend has an elaborate alarm in his place, which he swears he *always* turns on at bedtime, except when he has houseguests, which is rarely. Disabling the various infrared sensors and leaving the perimeter armed has apparently caused him some technological vexation in the past—isn't that ironic? Like an astronaut being afraid of heights is what I think—so when he has visitors, he says he just leaves the whole thing unarmed. Emma, did he say anything about arming or not arming the alarm last night?"

She shook her head.

"And you didn't see him arm it?"

She shook her head again.

Kevin's voice took on a stern shadow. "You never met with that bodyguard I sent, did you, Emma?"

"The disc was already gone. It seemed pointless."

"I can get him back over here tonight."

She said, "No."

Kevin continued, his voice level again. "Ethan Han

tells me that he's guessing that entry came from the adjacent roof. Big old double-hungs provide great access. I went out there; one of the latches is scratched and bent. I dusted, collected some latents. I'll try and get somebody I know to run them through AFIS for me. Also picked up prints from the cart that all the equipment is on. Long shots, I know—they're probably his or yours, Emma, or one of his employees'. He says a half-dozen people are in and out of the lab every day.

"By the way, here's the list of the guests Han says were at that party the other night, the night of the incident in the parking garage. One of you want to take a look, check it for me?"

With the hand that wasn't around Emma's shoulders, Quirk offered the list. Alan took the sheet and perused it. He then handed it to Lauren and said, "J.P.'s not on it."

Lauren looked over Alan's shoulder. "That's right, other than J.P., I think it covers everyone who was there."

"Who's. J.P.?"

"J. P. Morgan. Ethan's business partner. What's his real first name, Lauren? Thomas?"

"I think so."

"He was at the party, too? A tall, skinny guy with a bad haircut? Looks like he's wearing a coonskin cap without a tail?"

"Yes, that's J.P."

"He came by today while I was talking to Han. I was never formally introduced."

Emma spoke for the first time in quite a while.

"J.P.'s a full partner in BiModal. He comes and goes as he pleases."

"What about this Raoul Estevez and his wife? Anybody know them?"

Alan said, "Diane's my partner and they're both good friends of ours. Raoul just began working for BiModal. They're beyond reproach."

"Nobody's beyond reproach. Does he have access?"

Emma said, "All the technical staff has access to the lab. Ethan's apartment in back has a separate key."

"And you all agree that you met these other guests, the money people, for the first time at this dinner party?"

They all said they had.

"Let's go back to the beginning. What good is the disc? What's the motive in stealing it?"

Lauren said, "Blackmail. Leverage. Money."

"Blackmail of whom? Emma or Ethan?" Alan asked.

Kevin answered. "I've been assuming Emma. Is Ethan vulnerable? Anybody?"

Alan said, "Maybe. BiModal is privately held. If Ethan tried to take the company public, data like this could be quite compromising to him."

"Are they contemplating an IPO?" The urgency of the question left Alan wondering if Kevin's next call would be to his broker.

"Apparently Ethan would like to. A huge capital infusion would take the pressure off R&D budgets, allow Ethan to develop his projects faster. J.P. has convinced him not to."

"Why?"

"This is according to my friend Raóul. J.P. would prefer to postpone an IPO until after the company's promise is clearer to potential stockholders. His argument is that if everyone is patient, when the IPO takes place the company will not only get the capital it needs, but that all the principals will become instant billionaires à la Bill Gates with Microsoft or Marc Andreesen with Netscape."

"Raoul said 'billionaires'?" Lauren asked.

Kevin nodded "It's not out of the question. After Netscape's initial public offering, its value jumped six hundred percent in four months. It's really a question of what the high-tech community thinks of the company's potential."

"Wow."

Kevin Quirk was still looking for suspects. "Who had the opportunity to steal the disc? Ethan says eight or nine people have keys to the laboratory area and know the alarm codes. Techs, partners, janitorial. Does anyone else have access? Emma?"

She shrugged "A burglar?"

"It's a long shot. A burglar would have taken other things. Could someone have come in while you two were—"

She stopped him. "The music was loud. It's possible someone came in. Maybe someone watched us through the windows. I don't know. I don't want to think about it."

Lauren asked Alan to help her clean up.

Alone with her in the kitchen, Alan said, "It has to be an inside job, a computer person. Who else could make use of that data?"

"What about Ethan? He could be pretending it's stolen just so he doesn't have to erase it." Lauren lowered her voice. "How serious is Emma about this? Can you tell?"

"What? About suicide?"

"Yes."

"I need to talk with her some more. But given the right, or wrong, precipitants, I think the risk is quite high. Her level of intent certainly is, I need to know what her plans are. I'll try to sit down with her before we leave tonight."

"What kind of plans are you talking about?"

" 'Plan' as in method—how she's planning on killing herself. If I knew that, it would help me determine the potential lethality of an attempt. Even with lethal intent, someone will survive a suicide attempt if they believe that five Tylenol and a shot of tequila will kill them. Lethal intent, low-risk method."

Lauren slotted the dishes into the dishwasher rack and began to rinse the glassware.

"But what's your impression of her clinically? She looks terribly fragile to me. I'm scared for her."

Alan began to wipe the counter. "I agree. She's barely treading water."

"Is she safe enough to be by herself?"

"You mean does she need to be hospitalized? Maybe. But I can't hold her on what I've seen. She's saying she'll kill herself 'if' something happens. That's not imminent enough danger for the mental health laws. And she would never admit herself voluntarily, the notoriety and fallout of being hospitalized would be absolutely unacceptable to her. I'll try and get her hooked up to see somebody on an outpatient basis first thing tomorrow. You'll have to stay here or she'll have to come to our house in the meantime."

"What about Diane? She'd be good with Emma."

"Too much of a conflict there, with Raoul working with Ethan. It will have to be someone else."

Lauren asked, "Can you believe this? This is . . . this is a nightmare. I mean, can you imagine what the release of this thing . . . this disc, would mean to her? What it would do to her?"

"It's like a digital version of rape," Alan said.

"No, it *is* rape, Alan. Multiplied by thousands or millions or whatever. It's rape on demand."

Alan knew instinctively that his wife had covered some moral ground about the philosophy of rape that he still needed time to contemplate.

"What's your impression of Kevin Quirk?"

He had hit a nerve. She slammed the dishwasher shut.

"What do I think of Emma's friend Kevin?" She twisted her head around to make sure Quirk wasn't listening. "You know what? The truth is I don't trust his motives. If this recording ever became available, my fear is that he'd be the first man on his block to get his Discover card out of his wallet. That's what I think about Kevin Quirk. That is, if he didn't follow Emma over there yesterday and steal the damn thing himself."

✜

Before Kevin Quirk had a chance to make an alternative offer, Lauren announced that she was planning to spend the night with Emma.

Alan thought Kevin looked ambushed. After mumbling something about needing to stay in Boulder another day, anyway, to follow up on what he'd already learned about the missing disc, Kevin said that maybe he would just sleep on Emma's sofa.

Seeing the look of distaste *that* idea precipitated on his wife's face, Alan suggested that Quirk come home with him and sleep in the spare bedroom instead of camping out on an uncomfortable couch.

But sleeping in a stranger's guest room five miles from Emma apparently wasn't what Kevin Quirk had in mind. "On second thought," he said, "I think maybe I'll just get a motel room."

Kevin asked for directions to the Holiday Inn. When he embraced Emma and left her house around eleven, he did so, Lauren thought, reluctantly. She tried to convince herself that Quirk's reticence was engendered by sincere concern over Emma's welfare, but she couldn't quite manage to sway herself. She harbored a concern that Kevin's motives were more personal than that. She tried to remember all the political celebrities who had ended up married to their bodyguards. Patty Hearst? One of Gerald Ford's kids? One of Princess Grace's kids? She couldn't recall.

Before Alan said good-bye he sat next to Emma and waited until she looked at him. He said, "I think you need to see someone, Emma, a therapist, right away. Tomorrow."

"I know. I've thought about it, too. You're probably right. What about you? Can I see you?"

"That would be great, but because we're already friends, it's not possible. But I know some people who are very good. Let me contact them for you, see if they have time to see you tomorrow."

"I'm pretty busy tomorrow. With school and everything."

"Emma. It's important."

She looked at Lauren, who was nodding her encouragement.

"Okay."

"I have your word?"

"Yes."

Alan drove home feeling that the agreement was pure capitulation on Emma's part. But he'd already made a judgment about her honor and felt confident that if she gave her word, she would keep it. At this stage he didn't require enthusiasm; he would gladly settle for cooperation.

Clinical instinct told him that emotionally, Emma Spire had an aneurysm that was threatening to blow.

Lauren, literally, tucked Emma into bed.

The bedroom that Emma chose for her own was the one that had once been her grandparents'.

A double bed with a simple steel frame and an oatmeal comforter took up the spot where the marital bed had stood. A tall nightstand of weathered pine stood beside it like a sentry. A large rectangular discoloration on the wall behind the bed still showed precisely where, for many years, a piece of art had hung.

Emma had placed nothing over the stain. The walls in the bedroom were bare. The windows were shuttered with wide slats that had faded to a dull white.

Along one wall of the bedroom stood a metal and glass étagère covered from corner to corner, back to front, with framed photographs of Emma, Emma's mother, Emma's father, and Emma's grandparents.

Lauren decided that the room felt like a monastic retreat. Or a safe house. Not like a home. Emma had been forced to move into this big house long before she was prepared to make herself a home.

Emma, in panties and a T-shirt that trumpeted one of her ex-fiancé's hit movies, tugged the comforter to her armpits. She rolled onto her side, facing away from Lauren, who sat on the edge of the mattress.

"It's not as dark as it seems, Emma."

For a moment, Lauren suspected that exhaustion and hopelessness had trapped Emma in sudden sleep. But Emma cleared her throat, pulled some hair away from her face, and said, "In my life, Lauren, it's always as dark as it seems. There's more I haven't told you."

Lauren stroked Emma's hair and felt a stab of dread. She said, "More what?"

"More . . . that's awful."

Lauren couldn't imagine what that might be. She said, "I'd like to hear what it is." But she didn't want to hear it. She wanted to run from the room, jump into her car, say hello to her dog, and be home in her own bed with her husband.

"It's about Ethan."

"Yes," Lauren said. She figured that.

"I think Ethan . . . I think he belongs to . . . Operation Rescue."

Lauren's lips were about to say "So what?" when her tired brain permitted the insidious connection to be made to Nelson Newell, Emma's father's assassin, and the radical right-to-life movement.

"Oh, God," she murmured quietly.

"Yes, oh God."

"Are you thinking he did this on purpose? Meeting you, dating you? Recording you like he did?"

Lauren's hand had come to rest on Emma's shoulder. Emma's muscles tightened noticeably before she spoke again. "I don't want to think that way about somebody I . . . I just slept with, but I have to consider it. I have to. Ethan seemed so sincere to me. But . . . maybe I misjudged him. Those people . . . would love to hurt me, Lauren. Nothing would make some of them happier than to drag me through the mud on top of my father's grave."

Had this really been the point of Ethan's insistent seduction of Emma? Had Ethan been setting Emma up for some major scandal in order to undermine her credibility with the public? That scenario seemed way too complex and awkward to Lauren. She guessed that—if Emma's supposition about Ethan and Operation Rescue were true—the motive was probably simple vengeance. And the opportunity was pure serendipity.

"Do you know this for sure?" Lauren asked. "About him being part of the antiabortion movement?"

"No. I saw some mail at his house, that's all."

"Did you read it?"

"No, it was sealed; it had just been delivered. But it was from them."

"Maybe it was just a fund-raising letter. I'm sure they rent mailing lists and send out solicitations to a lot of people."

Emma raised her voice. "No. It wasn't." She rolled onto her abdomen, her face almost buried in the pillow. "I just have an awful feeling that he's a member. Trust me."

Yesterday, Lauren mused, *I would have trusted you. Today, I'm not so sure.*

Lauren woke Emma around seven-thirty. Lauren was due in court at nine and before she left Emma alone, she wanted to make an assessment of Emma's mood and be certain she had plans for the day.

Emma's demeanor was much brighter than it had been the night before, and Lauren thought she actually saw a hint of a smile when Emma came into the kitchen after her shower and smelled fresh coffee.

"Thanks for waking me, I have a nine-thirty contracts class I absolutely can't miss. The teacher is a tyrant." She shook her head. "Actually he's a bit of a fool." She poured herself a mug of coffee and added a healthy shot of milk.

Lauren was relieved that Emma had something other than camping under the covers planned for the morning.

"What about after class?"

Emma smiled again, wider this time. "You want to know if I'm going to blow my brains out before lunch, don't you?"

Lauren almost choked on her coffee. She finally

managed to say, "No, that's not what I was thinking—" before she made a valiant attempt to match Emma's glorious smile and said, "Not entirely, anyway."

"The contracts professor may be a jerk, but his class isn't that bad. I'll be okay. I have another class at eleven-thirty. Then I'll come by the office. I don't know if you remember, but I'm still planning to attend that three o'clock evidence hearing on the Ramirez case. The one I researched the motion for?"

Lauren's legal calendar was one of the farthest things from her mind. "Thanks for reminding me, I'd forgotten all about that hearing. I'll see you in the office by two, then? We'll go over to court together."

Emma sipped some coffee. "Sounds good."

"Oh, and don't forget, Alan's going to call with the name of a therapist. You promised you would do that today, too. Will you see if you can get an appointment?"

"Yes, *Mom*. If my schedule allows it." The smile that accompanied the statement was the warmest one so far. Not quite as electric as Emma was capable of, but sufficiently heartening to satisfy Lauren that she could pack up her things and head home to change for a day at the office.

When she got there, she left Alan a long voice-mail message, filling him in on the latest twists.

A few minutes after Lauren's departure, Kevin Quirk called Emma.

"You okay?" he asked, concern in his voice.

"Yes, Kevin, thanks. Thanks for everything." Then she said, "I was too upset to go into it last night, but

I'm afraid this guy I'm seeing might be involved in the right-to-life movement."

Kevin didn't doubt her for even a second. "Then it looks like you've been set up, Emma."

"I wondered if there was some way you could check out what his involvement with them is."

"There are some people I can call."

"Kevin, there are *always* people you can call."

"What can I say?"

"Discreetly?"

"Without a trace. Leave it to me."

"What about your family, Kevin? Don't you have to head home, like, ever?"

"They're used to my sudden road trips. Part of the territory, Emma. What's your schedule today?"

She told him.

"You have a beeper, or a cell phone?"

"I have a portable phone."

"Number?"

She told him.

"I'll be in touch. I'm planning on finding that damn box and destroying it. That's my job. Your job is to be much more careful about whom you sleep with."

I am careful, she thought, stung by his rebuke. She managed to say, "Thanks for your help, Kevin. Bye."

Alan called next.

"Lauren told me the latest, Emma. How are you?" he asked.

Slightly exasperated, she said, "I'm getting tired of telling people I'm okay."

"That's fair. But we're concerned about you. I have

phone numbers of a couple of therapists who told me they could see you later today."

He was listening for evidence that Emma's despair had deepened. Instead he heard an energetic, "Great, give me the numbers." He did. She said, "I have to run. I'm late for class. I'll give one of these people a call when I have a minute."

She hadn't asked for details about either of the referrals. What are they like? Which one did he recommend? She hadn't voiced any second thoughts about seeing someone.

"You promise you're okay?"

"Alan, don't be so worried, I'm not about to blow my brains out."

He grew concerned all over again. Now he knew one of her methods.

⬦

Emma Spire's contracts professor thought Judge Lance Ito's policy of confiscating beepers and cell phones that erupted during court sessions was an absolute hoot. The law professor loved the idea so much that he instituted the same policy during his lectures. So far this semester he had bagged six beepers and two cell phones for his collection of booty. During lectures, he displayed his catch in a big zippered plastic bag on his podium. At the end of the semester he was thinking of having an artist do something creative with them—maybe something resembling a gavel, he thought—and having the thing mounted on the wall of his office.

Like big game.

As a precaution against confiscation, as she always did, Emma Spire turned off the power to her cell phone before she went into class.

As she often did, Emma failed to turn the power back on after class ended.

She missed Kevin Quirk's first call.

Kevin Quirk tried her cell phone a second time with the same result before he left a message on her answering machine at home. For good measure, he also phoned the DA's office. She wasn't in and his call was forwarded to a voice mailbox. He left his message there, too.

He was discreet. "Hi, it's me. I think I may have a line on it. I'll be in touch."

When Emma walked out of her late-morning class, the air was warm and no breeze disturbed the few leaves that remained on the trees on campus. An arctic cold front was barreling down from Canada, but was still four or five hours away from its inevitable collision with a huge mass of heavy, moist air that was lazily migrating north from the Gulf of Mexico. Like a cunning co-conspirator, an area of extreme low pressure was inching into position over the Four Corners and generating a healthy counterclockwise spin that would soon twist the two approaching weather systems together in a powerful flow against the eastern face of the Continental Divide.

The weather people called this configuration a classic upslope. By evening, the locals would call it a damn blizzard.

Emma was oblivious to the approaching storm.

She was wearing black jeans over modest black leotards. A Colorado Avalanche cap shadowed her face and her rich auburn hair was tied back in a neat French braid. Sunglasses hid her eyes. Dressed like this on campus, she knew, she would not be casually recognized. Unless the paparazzi had received marching orders from the tabloids that it was time for another Emma sighting, she was unlikely to draw any attention.

During that morning contracts lecture, all of her concerns about the missing optical disc had crystallized into hopelessness. She had come to the conclusion that whoever had stolen the optical drive took it because they already knew what was on it. And, she had decided, they took it because they were smart enough to recognize the value of what was recorded on it, and smart enough to have the data copied. Maybe once, more likely a dozen or a thousand times.

Despite Lauren's plea that a solution was possible, Emma felt that she had little left to lose.

Alan Gregory's day began to deteriorate shortly after three o'clock. He was with a patient when Lauren called and left a message that Emma hadn't shown up for the evidence hearing she had been so eager to attend. She wasn't answering her phone at home. Had he heard from her?

No, he hadn't. He wondered if either of the therapists he had referred Emma to had received a call from her.

An hour of phone tag answered that question. She hadn't phoned either therapist for an appointment.

At four-fifteen, Alan stuffed his hands into his trouser pockets and strode out to the waiting room to greet his next patient, Kendal Green, a fragile woman who was not only battling self-doubt but also enduring a vicious custody fight for her two young children.

The waiting room was furnished with a sofa and six chairs. An old pine table in front of the couch was covered with magazines. Kendal usually chose a seat facing the doors, one that permitted her to sit with her back to the farthest corner of the room. Alan looked for her there. But it was Emma Spire, not Kendal Green, sitting in that chair. Emma was fingering the spine of an unopened magazine that rested on her lap. Her gaze was fixed on the room's sole window.

Kendal sat anxiously on the sofa, her back as straight as a marine's, her Gucci-emblazoned purse in her lap.

Alan didn't know what to do. This appointment time was Kendal's. But Emma's surprise appearance raised many red flags and he guessed that of the two women in his waiting room, she was in greater immediate jeopardy.

Alan walked over to Kendal, leaned over, and said, "I have an emergency I need to deal with, so you and I will be a few minutes late getting started. Is that okay? I need to see this young woman briefly."

Kendal looked at Emma as though she had just

noticed that there was someone else in the room. Awareness flickered in her eyes.

"We're . . . not going to meet?"

"No, no, no. We'll talk. It will start a little late, that's all. This happens occasionally, something unexpected."

"I have that meeting tomorrow, with the custody people. You know that." Her tone was a mixture of admonishment and panic.

"I know. I apologize for the delay in starting. I really do."

Kendal finally realized who the younger woman was. "Oh my God," she whispered. "But I'll see you for the regular amount of time?"

Alan felt the gravitational force of Kendal's insecurity. Was her therapist, like her husband, going to discard her for a younger, more attractive woman?

"I hope so, but honestly, I don't know. Let me explore this other situation a bit and then we will talk about our meeting, okay?"

Kendal looked crushed.

Alan crossed the room and said softly, "Emma, would you like to come back to my office?"

She rose slowly, her eyes never meeting his gaze. To him, her movements seemed to require inordinate effort.

Once inside his office, she settled into a chair far from Alan and folded her legs beneath her.

He waited.

She stared outside. A harsh wind had begun blowing in advance of the cold front and the wind was bending the trees and whistling debris past the windows. The temperature had dropped thirty degrees in an hour.

She finally said, "Hi." She didn't look at him.

He tried to decide what to do.

Despair *should* be dark and brooding, with heavy eyes and oily hair, ratty clothing and fetid breath. But occasionally, Alan knew, despair was a chameleon, looking fresh and merely forlorn, as Emma did that day, in her jeans and leotards. After following her gaze outside and witnessing the ferocity of the invading front, he hoped she had a jacket in her car. Just as quickly, he realized that heavy clothing was the least of the protection Emma needed that day.

Relieved that she had found a way to start this conversation, Alan responded to her opening. "Hello, Emma. I'm glad you came. How can I help?"

He knew that at some time during this impromptu visit he would have to remind Emma that he was not ethically in a position to provide her with psychotherapy. He also knew that particular news could wait a few minutes while he assessed her mental status. He didn't expect to like what he discovered during the assessment and was already anticipating the possibility that he would be asking her to consider allowing a colleague of his to hospitalize her.

"I doubt you can," Emma said in a scratchy voice. The only distinct sound in the room was the sound of a clock ticking. Outside, the wind whined and squealed, syncopated by the tinny sound of autumn debris impacting the glass windows. Both Alan and Emma were breathing silently.

"But you came to see me?" he said. *Water the hope. Weed the despair.* Whatever else they ended up talking about, Alan figured that this conversation was about suicide. That's what he was listening for.

Emma cleared her throat. The scratchiness didn't entirely disappear. "I didn't want to go home. Didn't want to go to work. Couldn't pick up the phone and call my mom or my dad. I came here."

The desperation of the choices she perceived saddened Alan. Emma was looking for sanctuary from the most severe of storms and had ended choosing to sit in the office of a man she barely knew.

Bad choices, likely misperceived as *no* choices, hovered on Emma's horizon.

Alan had long considered that most of the time, day in and day out, psychotherapy was much like flying an airplane. Serious work, requiring serious attention, but mostly routine. To the passengers, the pilot's skills seemed magical. To the patient, the therapist's skills otherwordly. But to the professional, the daily tasks were mundane. Occasionally, though, a crisis was so acute, a problem so severe, that it required all Alan's skills to begin to understand it and to muddle through it.

This day, he figured that the airplane that Emma Spire was on had lost a wing.

Midafternoon, after court, Lauren had walked briskly back to her office. The temperature had started to plummet and she was caught without her coat. She settled in at her desk, read a memo that the chief trial deputy had placed on her blotter, and punched buttons on her speakerphone to retrieve her voice-mail messages. Since, as an intern, Emma didn't have her own extension, her infrequent messages were routinely forwarded to her supervisor's mailbox—Lauren's.

The person who had left the message hadn't identified himself, but Lauren thought she recognized the flat, accentless voice of Kevin Quirk, who left word that he thought he had a lead on the missing disc.

"Great," Lauren thought, as she pressed a button to save that message for Emma.

The next message was much more disquieting. A soft voice Lauren couldn't identify at first said, "The guy who has it says he's been thinking of a deal. He says I can have it back if I'll trade it for the real thing. Can you believe it?"

Lauren's mind translated the offer: *If you sing me a personal song, I'll give you back the tape of your concert.*

She replayed the message, stunned. *Who was that? Was that Emma?* It was.

Lauren realized that the subtext of the message was that someone was offering to return the disc to Emma, if Emma would agree to have sex with him. *Once.* Lauren pondered the dilemma and wondered what she would do.

What was worse, being forced to have sex against one's will once?

Or having the rape occur a thousand times, or a million, and never even knowing?

Emma was trying to explain the same conundrum to Alan.

She had found the message in an envelope placed under her windshield wiper. The offer, at first, had stunned her. Then angered her. She found herself vacillating, actually considering that a quick fuck, a blackmailed rape, might be the best solution. A way to make this all go away.

"So I can go and screw this guy, whoever he is, and he'll give me back the disc. In effect, I can trade being raped once for a promise of freedom from being raped every day by strangers. Or I can tell him no and suffer the consequences of the existence of the disc becoming public."

Alan could tell that Emma wasn't asking for advice. They both knew that there was no safe passageway through this minefield. Alan couldn't show Emma where it might be safe to step.

"Let's say you give him what he wants. You go ahead and . . . have sex . . . with him." Alan hesitated, then completed his thought after failing to find language that conveyed the oxymoron "agree to be raped by him."

"Yes?"

"What would force him to actually turn over the disc, Emma? Assuming he even has it."

She half laughed. "I can't exactly count on his honor, can I?"

Alan responded seriously, to be certain she understood. "No, Emma, you can't."

In a voice so low he had to strain to hear, she said, "He's already probably made copies. It'd be easy, if you knew what you were doing."

"Yes. Probably."

A lazy flurry of big flakes began to float diagonally across the yard like advance scouts checking the terrain, in no hurry to reach the ground. The low ceiling above was a mosaic of airy grays, a palette almost sufficient to paint the scope of Emma's despair.

For a full minute she was silent, then in a voice that felt as intimate as a diary entry she said, "I've never understood being anointed the way I've been. Why my life has felt important enough to become part of other people's lives—I don't think I'll ever know that. I've felt at times as though my very being—my identity—has become some wonderful new spice, something that people can take off the shelf and sprinkle on their own lives to enhance them.

"I've become a flavor enhancer. That's it. That's all I am."

Alan considered responding, didn't.

"Those first few days after Daddy died were a blur. I didn't realize, at first, that I'd been embraced by the media as some new *thing*. I was just so scared of what would happen to me, and I was so lonely, and so determined to live in a way that would have made my parents proud. When I started to come out of it—out of the haze—after the funeral, the next week, I realized that I'd become this *thing*, this *media* thing. It felt as though this girl on the news was really someone else, someone smarter, prettier, more charming than me. The president's people encouraged me to be available. They said it would honor my father, allow people to know him, through me, you know.

"So I did. I talked to Barbara Walters. I talked to Larry King. I did it all. I got to meet movie stars. But that wasn't good enough for me, so I even got *engaged* to one. What a mistake. I should have just disappeared.

"Why? I keep wondering why? What did I do to

deserve this? I told a crazy man not to murder my father. That's *it*. Then I got engaged to an actor. I'm not a brave person. I'm a wimp. Every day there are heroes greater than me. Read the papers. Watch the news. And there are a million women prettier than me—it can't be that. It can't be.

"So why won't they let me go? Whatever it was about me that they liked, that I liked, is dying inside me. Can't they see that? They're killing me. With each bite they take, they kill me. With each flash of the camera, they devour a piece of me. Slowly, but surely, whatever it's been inside me that they thought was so special, it's dying. Why does someone want to have *my* body on disc? God, how naked can they have me?"

Alan recalled that he, too, had thought nothing of keeping track of Emma's life before he met her. He never wondered if he had the right to watch. He never wondered if Emma Spire wanted to be watched.

He examined Emma, spirit frayed, eyes dark, before him.

His job was clear. All he had to do was give her a reason not to die today.

He asked the obvious. "Are you thinking of hurting yourself, Emma?"

She didn't look at him. She said, "Thinking?" She paused. "Of course. That's nothing new."

"Have you made any plans?"

Emma didn't respond. She seemed mesmerized by the snow outside, now falling in earnest.

He pressed. "Do you have any methods in mind that you've considered using to kill yourself?"

She knew exactly what he was asking. "I have a gun. It was my grandfather's. I have some drugs. I don't know if they'll work. I've thought about carbon monoxide, you know, with my car in the garage, the motor running. That should do it, but I'm afraid it's too slow, that I'd chicken out."

"Could you use the gun?" Alan knew that, statistically, women were reluctant to use firearms for suicide. The statistics didn't predict anything about Emma, however.

"I'm not sure. I wonder."

"What drugs do you have?"

"Some codeine. Some Atenolol."

Alan knew the carbon monoxide could be fatal. The codeine was dangerous, potentially lethal, especially if Emma mixed it with alcohol. He didn't know anything about the lethality of Atenolol. He thought it was a beta-blocker and wondered what she was doing with it.

"Do you have the drugs with you?"

"No, they're at home."

"Do you have the gun with you?"

She exhaled. "No."

He realized that he didn't believe her. That she might have the gun in her little leather backpack right then, right there, worried him. That she seemed willing to lie to him about it terrified him

"I'm worried about you, Emma."

"Me, too," she said.

He knew he was going to have to cancel the appointment with Kendal Green to handle this situation with Emma. "If I leave you waiting for a few minutes, you won't hurt yourself, will you?"

"Here? No. God, no."

"I have your word?"

"Yes." She finally met his eyes.

"I need to meet briefly with the woman who was in the waiting room a little while ago, to reschedule an appointment. When she and I are done, you and I need to talk some more, okay? We need to come up with some plans on how to handle this situation you're in. Here, tonight."

"You want me to wait out there? In the waiting room?" She was reluctant to leave his office.

"Please. It won't be too long. I don't have any other patients tonight No one else will come in. You'll have it to yourself. Then, together, we'll work out what to do next."

Her words still scratchy, she said, "All right."

Alan walked Emma back to the waiting room and watched her pick a seat and choose a magazine. He twisted the wand to shut the blinds. He asked Kendal to come back to his office.

She started talking before he sat down.

He interrupted her and explained that their session would need to be rescheduled.

He thought she looked like someone had killed her cat.

Alan finished rescheduling his appointment with Kendal Green, let her out the back door, and returned to the waiting room to get Emma.

She wasn't there. Alan's immediate reaction was that he wasn't as surprised as he should have been.

The note sitting on the seat of her chair, scrawled on a subscription card that had fallen out of *Mirabella*, read, "Don't worry. I'll keep my promise."

Alan said, "Damn," closed his eyes, and tilted his head as far back as he could, trying to stretch the muscles in his neck before his headache became intolerable. When he opened his eyes, the waiting room in his office was still empty.

Emma's note was still on the chair.

Aloud, he said, "If wishes were horses."

Alan heard a rush of slushy footsteps approaching the front door. The blinds were tilted closed and he couldn't see who was coming up the walk but he hoped that Emma had changed her mind and that she was coming back.

The door opened and Kevin Quirk, his hair and clothing pocked with big flakes of wet snow, burst into the room and stomped his feet on the mat.

Kevin looked up and saw Alan. His voice steady, he said, "Oh good, I caught you. Can you believe this storm? I though the weather lady said an inch or two. We've had that already. Listen, I've been trying to find Emma. You seen her?"

Quirk didn't appear to be someone who had been ambushed by the weather. He was dressed for winter, not Indian summer.

Alan said, "Hello, Kevin. She was here a while ago, but she left. I don't know where she went, maybe home."

"How did she seem?"

Alan hadn't fully considered yet the question of

whether the time he had spent with Emma that afternoon had changed her status and made her a temporary patient of his, or whether he had been merely providing counsel to a friend. The answer to that question was an ethical dilemma that could be as twisted as a pretzel and, if he managed to untangle it, would determine how much he could tell Kevin Quirk in response to his question.

Alan preferred to err on the side of caution. As nonchalantly as possible, he walked across the waiting room and began to straighten the magazines, a chore he probably hadn't done in a year. His first task was to swipe up the loose magazine subscription card from the chair in the corner and stuff it into his pocket.

"Distraught," Alan said. "Emma's distraught."

"She was going to see somebody for that, right? A shrink? Is that where she is now?"

"I wish. That was my advice to her last night. That was my advice to her this morning. But, no, as I said, I don't think she has an appointment yet."

"Maybe I have some news that can cheer her up. I just got a lead on that disc that was stolen. Hope maybe to get it back in the next little while. Tonight, anyway."

Alan decided to voice Emma's concern for her, see what Kevin's perspective was. "What real difference does it make? How can you be certain it wasn't copied?"

Kevin thought for about two seconds, then said, "I can't. No way. It's a digital record. A copy is as good as the original."

"That's the problem as far as Emma's concerned,

though I'm sure she'll be grateful if you manage to get it back. But she'll still be devastated that the genie's out of the bottle, that she can't be certain that copies aren't floating around. She's even terrified that people will be aware that the disc is out there." Alan watched Quirk's face, still rosy from exposure to the storm. "You know, Kevin, if I had stolen that disc drive, and I learned that someone with your background and abilities was after me, I'd give it back, too. But I'd copy it first."

"I've thought of all that."

"I assumed that you had."

Quirk's shoulders sank perceptibly. "I really like Emma, Alan. I think I know her better than maybe almost anyone. She's not that strong a person. She's full of self-doubt, insecurity. She's not like the media makes her out to be." He shook his head. "I'm just trying to help her. She's all alone."

Alan was surprised at Kevin's insight into Emma. He also reminded himself about the message that Emma had received that afternoon. The offer had been frank and obscene: someone had the disc and would return it to her for real live sex.

The source of that note was either the person who was scheduled to meet Kevin Quirk that evening.

Or the source of that note was Kevin Quirk.

Was this really just an elaborate ploy by Kevin to finally get Emma Spire into bed?

Alan wished Lauren was with him. She was much more confident in her perceptions of sociopathy than he was. She'd have a firm opinion about Kevin Quirk's motives. All Alan had were doubts.

He looked closely at the other man. Impulsively,

he said, "Let me go with you, Kevin, you know, when you go wherever you're going to go to get the disc. Maybe I'll be able to help you decide whether this person is telling the truth about making copies. Knowing *that* would help Emma feel better."

Kevin considered the offer. Alan figured him to be one of those people who was comforted by the illusion that mental health professionals could accurately distinguish a liar from an honest man. Alan always found the fantasy amusing, except when one of his colleagues had it about themselves.

"Okay," Kevin said. "You can come along. You'll do what I say?"

"I'm an inveterate chicken, Kevin. And I take orders like a buck-private." The cowardly part of the disclaimer was close enough to the truth, but Alan didn't even know exactly what a buck-private was, and responsiveness to authority was certainly not one of his more reliable personal traits.

Kevin asked, "Do you know where Eben Fine Park is? On Arapahoe?"

"Sure. Six, seven blocks from here. In good weather, we could walk there in ten minutes."

"This isn't good weather."

"It's right on Boulder Creek, Kevin, just down from the mouth of the canyon. That's where they're meeting you?" Not a bad choice, Alan thought. In the late afternoon, during bad weather, the little park on the west edge of the city would be one of the most deserted places in town.

Quirk looked at his watch. "We have a few minutes. Can I use your facilities?"

* * *

Alan called Lauren at her office to let her know he wouldn't be home on time. She wasn't in; he was connected to her voice mail and he left her a message that he'd be late and that he hoped Emma had called her.

He was gathering some papers from his desk when Kevin came out of the bathroom.

Kevin looked at Alan quizzically. "You going like that? It's miserable out there." He pointed to Alan's cotton sweater.

"I always keep a parka and a pair of boots in the car. This *is* Boulder."

Kevin pulled at the fabric of his jacket. "Me, too," he said. "I'm an old Boy Scout."

Alan had no doubt that Kevin Quirk had been the first Webelo in his pack.

"Who has it? The disc?"

"Don't know, yet. I'm almost certain it's somebody who knows Han. I'm assuming that Han was either in on this from the start with someone else and warned this person that I was after the disc. Or Han mentioned to someone close to him that I was snooping around, and the guy panicked. Either way, I just now got a call on my cell phone telling me where to go."

Alan flipped off the lights to his office. The falling snow outside seemed to brighten considerably. He said, "We'll know soon enough, I guess."

"Maybe. Maybe not. I think we're dealing with cowards. I'm willing to bet we'll get the disc back, primarily because they don't want me looking for it anymore. But I don't actually expect to see a soul in the park."

"Why the cloak-and-dagger, then?"

"Either to buy time for some reason I don't understand. Or to set up an ambush. Truthfully? I think they plan to drop the disc someplace obvious and they wanted a deserted location so that someone else wouldn't walk off with it."

From a determined examination of Kevin's expression, Alan couldn't tell what part of the prognostication had been serious. Alan opened the back door of his office, allowing Kevin to precede him to the side yard, where Alan's car was parked.

Alan asked, "Would you like me to drive?"

"No, I'll follow you."

Alan opened the back of his Land Cruiser and unzipped an old rucksack. He shook out an old parka and pulled it on, then tugged on the boots. If Ethan Han was in on this, Alan was thinking, everything was going to be more complicated. It would raise serious doubts that Ethan's romantic interest in Emma Spire had ever been anything more than an elaborate plan to compromise her integrity in order to punish her for her role as an involuntary poster child for the reproductive choice movement.

Alan had no doubt—none—that if Han had stolen his own optical disc drive, then there were already copies of the data secreted away.

Starting the engine of his car, he wished he felt more confidence about the reliability of Kevin Quirk's loyalty to Emma.

SEVEN

**Friday, October 11. Near midnight.
Snow, 16 Degrees**

Having reluctantly chauffeured Lauren across town from the jail to the hospital, Detective Scott Malloy was now stuck again. Regulations said that he was required to have a female officer present to monitor Lauren while she was in the examining room at the hospital. And dispatch had already informed him that they were not currently able to free a female officer for that duty. Maybe in an hour, they said. Malloy knew damn well that these doctors weren't going to wait an hour to examine Lauren. He would be left outside the exam room, unable to observe, and more important, unable to *hear* whatever was going on.

Shit.

Right after he and Lauren had arrived at the hospital, Malloy received word that the shooting victim had survived surgery and was on his way to the recovery room. Malloy's instinct was to race upstairs and take the lead in what he assumed would be an arduous process of negotiating with the surgeons about exactly when the detectives were going to be permitted to question the man. Danny Tartabull, the detective who had been assigned to shadow the victim, was marginally competent but, in Scott Malloy's eyes, a little too conciliatory. If the surgeons said "you can talk to him in the morning," Danny Tartabull would nod and ask the docs, "Is ten too early?" At the very least, Malloy wanted to get upstairs to make sure Tartabull didn't give away the store. He also thought it would be a good idea to bring Danny up to speed, in case they got lucky and Danny had a shot at a few questions.

The emergency room was dead.

Most people stay home during blizzards. Primary-care visits to the ER are reduced to nothing. The morning after the storm, though, things change. Heart attack victims begin to arrive by ambulance as out-of-shape homeowners try to shovel a few tons of snow off their sidewalks. Then, by midday, after the Rocky Mountain sunshine has a chance to put a nice transparent glaze on the ice, the casting room would be booked nonstop with broken bones from pedestrians who had failed to navigate on the ice, and motorists who thought antilock brakes could stop on Teflon.

But during a furious blizzard like this, blissful quiet.

The ER docs used the time to catch up on their sleep or make a dent on their charts or their managed-care paperwork. The nurses checked supplies, chatted, and relished the quiet.

Lauren was the only patient in the department.

The ER doc examined her efficiently, leaving Malloy out in the hall behind a closed door.

The doc returned to the desk, walking right past Malloy, ignoring his questions about his prisoner's condition. The doctor went into a back office to make a couple of calls, confirmed that the specialists were on their way in to see their patient, and returned to his pile of dictation. Lauren was stable and, to him, her diagnosis was not in question.

Malloy paced, frustrated that the doctor wouldn't talk to him and that he wasn't free to leave his prisoner. Not that he didn't trust her to stick around. He would have anointed Lauren his all-time-felon-least-likely-to-flee. But the book said don't leave your prisoner. The book also said a female officer should stand by a female detainee during medical examinations.

But the damn book wasn't written for the middle-of-the-fucking-night during a blizzard.

After pacing the hallway outside the open door to the exam room and catching occasional glimpses of Lauren falling asleep, Malloy decided he would cuff her to the gurney for ten minutes while he went upstairs to talk with Danny Tartabull and maybe even the damn surgeon.

What's ten minutes?

Lauren looked haggard. Her hair was limp and her skin ghostly pale under the hospital lights. She didn't stir from her sleep as Scott hooked up her left wrist and snapped the other end around the side rail on the gurney.

Another man loitering near the emergency department was as eager as Scott Malloy to talk with the shooting victim in the recovery room. He'd been assembling a plan that would get him past the cops and gain him brief access when he saw Malloy escort Lauren into the ER.

The man couldn't believe his fortune. Lauren was being delivered to him.

The man quickly scavenged a stethoscope and a hospital name badge from a white lab coat in an unlocked office. He pulled the top piece of a scrub suit over his turtleneck. From a safe distance, he watched the cop speak briefly with a nurse before proceeding to the elevators. Was the cop actually going to leave his prisoner unattended?

The man had no time to consider any options; this was too good an opportunity. He saw only one problem: the door to the exam room where Lauren was dozing was clearly visible to the nurse at the long counter that served as the nerve center for the ER.

He returned down the hall and watched the cop enter the elevator before moving to the nearest phone and asking the hospital operator for the main desk in the ER. He manufactured a few questions for the nurse who answered, posing as a parent anxious about an infection on his daughter's hand. Sure enough, the nurse's head went down and she scribbled notes the whole time they were talking.

He thanked her for her advice, hung up, and waited.

Although it took almost five minutes, during which time he would have sworn his watch had stopped, the phone finally rang again, and the nurse bowed her head to her pen.

Like a runner off the blocks, he made his move to Lauren's door. In seconds, he was in.

He entered with his back turned, quickly pulled a surgical mask over his face and an elastic hair restraint over his head.

Lauren was asleep.

He looked around and smiled at the propitious design of the room. He offered another prayer of thanks. The room had *two* doors, not one, the second leading out the far side of the examination suite. He poked his head out that door and quickly modified his plan to buy himself some time. He and Lauren were going elsewhere.

Despite the fact that she didn't have a spouse to help her take care of kids in the middle of the night, Adrienne, the urologist, arrived at the hospital before Arbuthnot, the neurologist, did.

Dr. Arbuthnot wasn't tardy; he knew pretty much what was going on with his patient. And he knew that thirty minutes wasn't going to make any difference in the treatment he was likely to order after examining her. Adrienne, on the other hand, was hurrying because it was her nature to move fast and because she didn't know anything other than that her good friend was under arrest and was asking for a urological consult, neither of which made any sense to Adrienne whatsoever.

She trundled into the hospital with her son, Jonas, in her arms, took a deep breath as she always did upon entering the ER, and recalled another night when she had watched her husband die in this very place. She handed her sleeping progeny to the nurse at the desk, taking a second to scan her face. Adrienne wanted to reassure herself that this nurse wasn't one she'd insulted or infuriated in the recent past.

She didn't think so.

"Find him a bed and don't forget to put up the rails. He migrates. Don't worry, he won't wake up. I don't think I'll be too long. Where's my patient?" She stared up at the big board that listed the patients currently bedded down in the ER.

The nurse gazed at the youngster bundled in her arms as though she'd just been handed a baby by a stranger on a street corner, and nodded down the hall. "She's in treatment one, Doctor. Right there."

Adrienne yanked off her hat and began to tug on the fingers of her gloves. In a much softer voice, she said, "Don't put him down in cardiac three, okay? I have a thing about that room."

Cardiac three was where her husband, Peter, had died.

Although Adrienne was small, she covered the ground to Lauren's room in a few squishy steps, trailing snow off her boots the whole way.

Two seconds later Adrienne's head popped back out of treatment one. She was significantly more irritated than when she had gone in. The nurse was already down the corridor in search of a bed for Jonas.

"She in X-ray or something?" Adrienne called out. Her accent seemed to twang in the empty halls.

The nurse stopped in her tracks. "What?"

"Where is she? Where's my patient?"

"In there. Treatment one."

"No she's not. This room is empty."

"*What?*"

He needed only a couple of minutes with Lauren, but he needed her awake.

She awoke in confusion—was this a dream that her gurney was moving and that her arm was hooked to the bed?

"Where are you taking me?" she mumbled, jangling the heavy cuff on her wrist and feeling it pull against the rail.

She tried to look around. Everything was either dark or blurred. She remembered that she was losing her vision. It felt unreal.

The person pushing the gurney stopped walking and moved alongside Lauren. She was on her side; he was behind her. He leaned in close and she smelled his sour breath. He touched the barrel of a gun to the soft tissue below her ear. "Stay quiet. I'll hurt you if I need to. I would prefer not to need to."

In her postsleep fog, Lauren wondered why the police were treating her this way. She thought she recognized the voice, but wasn't sure which cop it belonged to.

The nurse handed Jonas back to his mother and sprinted down the hall to Lauren's room. The nurse ran in, looked around, and came back out. She stood in the doorway, baffled. Her patient was gone. The gurney was gone.

"Just a second, Doctor. Dr. Matthews must have ordered something I don't know about."

The nurse marched past Adrienne, whose arms

were wrapped around her son, checked the desk, and found nothing revelatory on Lauren's admission paperwork or order sheet. She picked up the phone and punched the number for the room where Dr. Matthews was dictating.

"Clark, did you order anything new for the patient in treatment one?"

"No. The consults are ordered. Privates are coming in from outside. She's stable. What's up?"

"I don't know. The urologist is here to see her and the gurney is gone from T-1."

"Gone?"

"Gone."

"Where's the cop?"

"He went upstairs to see the gunshot that came in earlier."

"He didn't move her?"

"No."

"I'll be there in a second. Call X-ray, somebody must have taken her somewhere by mistake. And call security, just in case." In a voice intended to be calming, he added, "I hate it when this happens."

"Where is she?"

"Who?"

"You know who."

Lauren was wondering how the police had found out about Emma. She said, "I don't know."

"Don't say anything to anyone about the disc. Not a word."

How could they know about the disc? She asked, "What disc?"

He pressed the gun hard enough against Lauren's

skin to cause her to whimper. "Tell her to stay quiet about the disc. Or I'll put the damn data out on the Web."

Her mind finally as keen as her terror, Lauren realized that this man wasn't a cop.

Scott Malloy was surprised to see Sam Purdy pacing the third-floor surgical waiting room, his hands stuffed in the pockets of his overcoat. Sam had been assigned to work the crime scene, not the hospital.

"Hey, Sam."

"Scott."

"You're still working? What brings you down here?"

Sam said, "I've been spinning my wheels trying to track down the victim's clothes. Paramedics say they don't have them, that they're here at the hospital somewhere. Surgical nurse says the guy came upstairs without his clothes. Said I should check downstairs in the ER. I asked her to bring me the trash from his operating room before I head back down. So I'm waiting, what else is new. Typical bullshit."

Both men looked exhausted, wishing all this could wait until morning. "You had any luck?"

Scott knew that Lauren was Sam's friend. He couldn't tell from Sam's question whether "luck" would include the discovery of incriminating evidence or just the discovery of exculpatory evidence.

"Lots of lawyers but Lauren's quiet as a church mouse. She's scared, Sam, and . . . I think she's hiding something."

Sam Purdy remembered how coy Alan Gregory had been at the crime scene, remembered thinking the same thing about him. That he was hiding something.

Scott asked, "What did you find at the scene? Anything?"

"Snow and blood. Like Dracula spilled a Slurpy. But so far, no shell casing, no slug. One of the CSIs swept the area around the body and photographed the tire tracks that had compressed in the snow. He thinks whoever drove over this guy backed up and did it again for good measure. Basically, though, the scene is shit. It's like trying to find a snowflake in a snow cone. Soon, everything will be heading down the sewer. After the sun comes out tomorrow, hell, I don't need to tell you, we're going to need to get real lucky with forensics."

"But the CSI thinks two passes with the car, huh? He get pictures?"

"Tried. We'll know in the morning what shows up on film. I'd say fifty-fifty, given the conditions."

Scott nodded at the big doors to the OR suite. "Tartabull inside?"

Purdy said, "Yeah," with a smile. He knew about Detective Tartabull, too.

"I'm going in to ask the doc when I can see the guy. Maybe he saw some evidence of more than one pass by a car." Scott hesitated, then decided he needed to apprise Sam of what was going on. "Lauren's downstairs in the emergency room, Sam. She has some eye trouble. A doc is coming in to see her."

Eye trouble? "Why not just have the nurse see her at the jail?"

"Demain took a look. Thought it was serious enough to send her here."

That perplexed Sam. Demain Jones didn't transport

prisoners on whims. "Do you mind if I say hello to her? I'm on my way down to try and find this guy's clothes."

"No, go ahead. Don't forget the Edward's. The line is glowing."

"Not to worry. Just going to say hi. Who's with her down there?"

"Damn storm, dispatcher hasn't been able to free a woman officer to guard her. Lauren's sleeping, I just hooked her to the bed. She's not much of an escape risk, I don't think. Which way's the recovery room?"

Sam raised his eyebrows a little at the breech in protocol from Scott Malloy, who was not known to bend the rulebook. "Once you're inside the door, follow that line on the floor. It'll take you right to the nursing station. See you tomorrow, Scott."

"Yeah, Sam, thanks."

Sam Purdy rode down in the elevator with a hospital security guard who wanted to be a homicide detective when he grew up. The man peppered Sam with questions about the police academy and whether they would really hold stuff against him from when he was a kid, barely a teenager, really, when he didn't know any better. Purdy didn't want to answer any of the man's questions. Especially the one he assumed was coming about putting in a good word for the ex-delinquent with the department.

To distract the guard, Sam said, "What about you, what do you have going on a night like this?"

"Usually, nothing Bupkiss. Walk some nervous nurses to their cars. Jump-start some dead batteries. Occasionally—heh, big time—we get to subdue a drunk. Right now, the folks in the ER seem to have misplaced a patient. It's my job to find out where they left her. Probably some old lady whose flower's missing a few petals, know what I mean?"

"*Her?* You have a name?"

"Nah. But if you're curious, you're not doing anything, come on. Spend five minutes on my shift and you'll find out the true meaning of the word 'dull.' "

Since Sam was going there anyway, he followed the annoying man to the ER nurses' station.

"Who'd ya lose, Marian?" the guard asked with a cocked-hip smirk and a wink to Sam.

The nurse looked up from a paper on which she'd been writing. She wasn't in any mood for the security guard's attitude. "We're looking for a patient named Lauren Crowder. Dark hair, thirty-something. She shouldn't be too hard to find since apparently she's handcuffed to a gurney."

When the guard turned around to commiserate with his new buddy about this amazingly stupid state of affairs, he discovered that Sam Purdy was already gone.

As Sam ran down the closest corridor, sticking his head into every room large enough to hold a gurney, he radioed upstairs to get Malloy and Tartabull in on the search. Then he radioed dispatch and requested squad cars to watch for vehicles leaving the hospital. Then he yelled for the damn security guard and told him to get his ass outside and get his friends' asses outside and begin to secure the perimeter of this place.

"Hey, Sam, how ya doin'?"

Purdy spun around and had to look down to see

who had spoken to him. It was Adrienne, who stood a good foot shorter than him.

They were acquainted. Sam had investigated her husband's homicide.

"Adrienne, hi. Listen, I'm kind of busy, I—"

"I know you are. Just tell me where to look. I'll try to help you find her."

The man had pushed Lauren's gurney into an ultrasound room. The room was dark, lit only by the screens of some computer equipment that had been left percolating overnight, and from the inch-wide slit at the doorjamb. Neither Lauren nor the man could see anything more than each other's outlines.

He reminded himself he had to hurry, told himself he would allow one minute to complete this warning.

Lauren was having a vision of tremendous clarity. *Unless that weapon that is pressed into my neck is silenced, he can't afford to shoot me in here. As quiet as this hospital is tonight, everyone will hear it. I have to buy time. They'll be looking for me soon.*

"One more time. Where is she?"

The man's voice was impatient, but it was also unnatural, Lauren thought, as though the man was trying to disguise it.

Both victim and captor were aware of the seconds ticking away. Lauren considered screaming but feared he was close enough to quickly muffle her plea for help.

There had to be a way to make some noise.

"Just keep checking rooms, Adrienne. Holler if you see her."

The nurse called out to Sam from the desk. "She's not in X-ray. She's not in the lab. And the OR hasn't seen her."

In the waiting room, Cozy Maitlin was fast asleep, once again, on a bench in the children's play area. Casey Sparrow was watching the production unfolding at the nurse's desk and was just beginning to figure out from all the yelling that something was up that shouldn't be.

She hustled down the hall and confronted Sam Purdy.

"What's all the shouting about? Something going on involving my client?"

He considered lying to her, decided not to. "Lauren's missing, Casey. We can't find her."

"Oh, Jesus. She ran? Why the hell did she do that? If anyone should know better—"

"I don't think it's too likely that she ran, Casey. She was cuffed to her bed when she disappeared."

Casey felt a stab of dread. "Cuffed to her bed? Oh boy, you'll have to explain that to me later. Sam, something's going on that I don't know anything about. Do you guys know what it is?"

He shook his head.

Lauren managed to reach the power cord of a computer monitor with her free hand and she yanked the monitor from the top of a portable ultrasound machine. A crash echoed as the tube imploded.

Adrienne was closest. She was the one who heard the equipment shatter.

Fifteen seconds later, she rushed into the ultra-sound room. She found Lauren alone in the dark.

Lauren felt as much as saw the bright light sweep the room as the door opened, and she tried to scream, but the sound caught in her throat. She pulled feebly at her cuffed wrist. The futility sapped her of all of her remaining strength.

Oh God, he's back.

"Honey. Baby, it's me—Adrienne. Are you okay? Don't worry. It's going to be fine. You'll be fine."

Adrienne hurried across the room, leaned over her friend, and held her tightly until she stopped shaking, asking only if she'd been hurt. Adrienne kissed Lauren's limp hair and stroked her back and wished she knew what the hell was going on.

✦

Erin Rand thanked Lois warmly for her hospitality, promised to call her tomorrow, and descended the front steps to the street. She was praying that she would see Cozy's car waiting to drive her home, but she was not really expecting him to be there. Instead, she was steeling herself for the disagreeable but possibly necessary task of engaging in some serious flirting with whatever cops were left up here guarding the crime scene.

She was thrilled to see Alan Gregory walking toward her through the snow. Although the storm was abating, having begun its slide down the foothills toward Denver, she thought the temperature had dropped another ten degrees. She glanced at her watch. Another twenty minutes and her baby-sitter would be spitting nails.

Alan said, "Hi. I came back up here to give you a ride home."

With an aromatic belch evocative of smoked trout, she said, "Excuse me, that's wonderful. I didn't expect Cozy to remember I needed a ride."

"I felt like I needed to do *something*. The police have already transferred Lauren to the jail and they won't let me see her. Cozy and Casey are with her." He kept walking. "My car's at the end of the block. Come on, I'll take you home."

"Don't you want to know what I found out?"

Alan was assuming that Erin, like he, had been on a fool's errand. He didn't expect that she had learned a thing. For a moment he wondered if Lauren would consider these assumptions sexist. Probably, he allowed. He would disagree. He'd love to have the opportunity to argue the point with her.

"Of course I do. What did you learn?"

"It's . . . provocative. A witness saw the gunshot. But it wasn't from where the police are thinking. Might be important. I'll fill you in on the way into town. But it could be good, I think. I wish we knew what the cops knew. Cozy tell you anything helpful?"

"No." Alan's voice was small. "Where am I taking you?"

"I live near Valmont and Folsom."

He unlocked his Land Cruiser and opened the passenger door for her. She got in and he walked around and climbed in the driver's side and started the car.

She started telling him about a videotape the witness had taken after the gunshot. Although he was intensely interested, he had driven less than a minute when his curiosity got the better of him.

"Erin, have you been smoking dope?"

She laughed and sniffed at her clothing. "Before this is over," she said, "you just have to meet Lois. The lady is a trip, an absolute trip."

Two blocks from Erin's house, Alan's pager went off. He looked at the message and said, "It's your ex-husband."

✛

Purdy and Malloy unhooked Lauren and stood by while she was transferred to a new gurney so they could secure the old one for the crime scene investigators. They taped off the initial examination room and the ultrasound room. The dispatcher told them things were hopping elsewhere in the city and that it might be a while before the CSIs could get to the hospital.

The detectives were left pacing outside while the physicians—Arbuthnot, Adrienne, and the ER doc—examined Lauren as though she were the president of the United States and Community Hospital were Walter Reed Army Medical Center.

Sam Purdy and Scott Malloy were arguing with each other and with any of their supervisors who would answer their phones in the middle of this snowy night about what to do next. No one could decide whether Lauren's decision to invoke the Edward's doctrine regarding the crime for which she was a suspect meant that they couldn't question her about the kidnapping that had just occurred.

Frustrated, Malloy placed yet another call to the police department legal counsel, Lewis Skiles, requesting his opinion.

Casey Sparrow and Cozy Maitlin had already informed the detectives that their client was not going to be interviewed until she was medically stable, and unless they could be present with her during the questioning. Casey Sparrow and Cozy Maitlin didn't much care what Lewis Skiles had to say about Lauren's Edward's situation; their instructions to Lauren were to stay mum.

Alan arrived at the hospital frantic with concern for his wife. He immediately ran into Casey, who said, "She's all right, Alan. She's okay," before Alan even opened his mouth to ask. Casey calmed him down and told him what had happened.

"She wasn't hurt? You're sure."

"Terrified, but not hurt."

"Someone's with her now?" He couldn't believe what Lauren was going through. Every bit of strain was going to aggravate her medical condition. This night was like an avalanche of stress.

"Three doctors and there're cops right outside the door," Casey said.

"I want to go see her. Right now."

'I'm sorry, I really am, but it's not possible, Alan. She may be in the hospital, but she's still in custody. I need your help. Can you focus for a second? Medically, what's about to happen to Lauren?"

Alan tried to collect himself enough to respond. "Assuming the problem with her eyes is what I think it is, Arbuthnot, her neurologist, is going to be aggressive. He doesn't mess around with visual symptoms. I think he'll start her on IV steroids as a way of minimizing permanent damage to her optic nerves. But she has a history of susceptibility to blood pressure jumps on Solu-Medrol—that's the steroid they use—so she'll have to be monitored for a while, couple of hours at least. She'll get a big infusion of steroids once a day for five days, then oral prednisone for a few weeks after that. You gave her the medicine I brought for her?"

"Yes, I gave the ER doctor everything you gave me."

Alan, mystified, uneasy, said, "But I don't know about any bladder problem. That's news to me."

With a slight elevation in her eyebrows Casey explained, "The bladder complaint was a ruse to get her urologist friend down here to be with her. Pretty resourceful, I think, shows us she's thinking. So—I want to make sure I understand you correctly—she'll be in the hospital for five days?"

"Actually no, the treatment is usually done on an outpatient basis. She goes in, gets the IV, is monitored for a while, and goes home."

Almost to herself, Casey murmured, "I think I'll ask her doctor friend to keep her here. I don't want her at the jail."

Cozy seemed to be coming out of the residual stupor that had been caused by being awakened from too short a nap in the middle of the night. His beard growth was especially heavy on his chin and left his face looking unwashed.

He asked, "Did my ex-wife discover anything while walking through that blizzard?"

"Yes, as a matter of fact, she did. The witness Sam pointed her to thinks she saw someone fire a gun, so we know approximately where Lauren was standing when whatever happened happened. It's a good fifty feet from where they found the guy in the street."

"How reliable is the witness?"

"The good news is that she's a pillar of the community. The bad news is she smokes enough dope to supply a reggae festival in Kingston."

"That is a mixed bag."

"Same witness also shot some videotape right after she heard the gunshot. The woman swears it shows a vehicle driving down the middle of the street, stopping, backing up, going forward, backing up, and driving away. Erin says that when she watched it she thought it looked like a videotape of a snowstorm—and maybe, just maybe, some headlights snaking around in the distance. She thinks a pro, a video wizard, might be able to make something of it."

"Do we have the tape?"

"No, the lady wouldn't part with it. Erin is going to go back in the morning with her own VCR and a fresh tape and make a copy."

"Knowing Erin, she probably wants another contact high, too," added Cozy, wistfully.

Scott Malloy hung up the phone in the corridor outside Lauren's room and turned to Purdy.

"Somebody's after Lauren, Scott."

"Obviously. But why didn't whoever it is kill her

when they had the chance? That's what I want to know."

"Too risky? Or she knows something and they need to know what it is."

"What? What does she know?"

"If someone is after her now, maybe they were after her before, too, when she fired the gun. Is she claiming self-defense?"

"She's not claiming shit, Sam. She told us earlier she was firing at some streetlight, like a damn delinquent. She's not telling us who might have been after her before. She's not telling us who it was who took her just now. She's not telling us what the guy wanted. Sam, we *have* to talk with her about what just happened. Where are her goddamn lawyers? This is nuts. I swear, between her lawyers and her doctors I could end up killing somebody myself tonight. Am I being punished for something or what?"

An ambulance attendant named Ted Hopper stomped snow off his boots and plodded into the ER carrying a filthy, water-soaked parka. He saw the detectives huddled in the otherwise deserted hallway. Hopper was a veteran of the streets and had been around enough accident scenes to know cops when he saw them.

"Either of you Purdy?"

"Yeah, what do you want?" Sam said, without bothering to turn his head.

"Sam, take a look," said Malloy. "He's bearing gifts."

Hopper said, "My boss says you were asking about clothing from the shooting victim we picked up earlier tonight. Turned out someone had thrown this jacket behind the seat in the cab of the ambulance. I don't know how or why it ended up there, but here it is if you still want it. It's a mess."

Purdy stared at the garment with great interest. The jacket was an expensive Gore-Tex model, but it had suffered a bad night. It was oily in places, wet in more places, and was coated with the telltale shimmer of blood.

"You're sure it's his?"

"Yeah, my partner says she cut it off the guy to get an IV started. His pressure was zilch when we got there; he needed fluids bad. I was driving the bus. Did the guy make it?"

"So far," said Malloy.

"Good," the man said, sounding as though he meant it.

"Hold on there one second," Purdy said, as he hopped across the corridor to a red crash cart. On top was a box of latex examination gloves. He pulled a pair of gloves onto his hands and took the coat from the attendant, hanging it from its collar on his right index finger.

"Scott, do you mind getting his particulars? I want to take a closer look at this." Malloy fished in his pocket for a pad and pen and started asking Hopper for details.

Two doors down from Lauren's room Purdy found an examination table with an attached roll of white paper. He stretched out a double layer and gingerly pulled the jacket into some semblance of shape. He played with the light switches in the room until the big examination light above the table clicked on.

Thirty seconds later, he called out, "Scott, come in here. Look at this."

"No, you come back here. I don't want to leave the door unprotected again." Malloy had developed an unshakable paranoia about leaving Lauren unguarded.

"I have to show you something."

"It can wait. Come here and tell me."

With his discovery, Purdy had enjoyed a brief adrenaline rush that subsided with the same speed with which it had arrived. He became aware of beads of sweat on his brow and realized he was cooking. As he walked back to join Malloy, he began to shed his coat.

"What? What's so important with the jacket?"

"Burn marks on the fabric. Muzzle flash burns around the entry hole in the nylon."

"Bullshit."

"You go look for yourself, I'll stay here. Second door."

Malloy took off with long strides.

"Scott," Purdy called. Malloy stopped and faced him. "Get some gloves on, okay? We're all tired here."

Malloy's pace was much more deliberate when he returned a minute later. "Doesn't make sense."

"Sure doesn't. But you agree?"

"Yes, I agree, they look like flash burns. I even think there's some burned gunpowder particles embedded in the nylon. It means she's been lying to us."

"Lying about what? She hasn't told you squat."

"Sam, she was no more than two feet from him when that gun went off."

"Closer, twelve inches."

"Whatever. We have a victim shot in the back from close range. Sounds like a goddamn execution to me. She's not helping us here."

"Then again, Scott, the woman can't see, can she? How reliable a witness is she?"

"Are you saying she shot somebody at point-blank range and doesn't even know it?"

"I don't know what happened. Maybe the doctor who operated on him knows something. Is Tartabull still upstairs?"

Before Malloy could answer, two female uniforms marched into the ER. Malloy briefed them and stationed one at each entrance to the exam room. He tried to place one inside the room but as soon as she knocked and entered Adrienne barked at her in no uncertain terms to get out. Malloy didn't want a fight with the doctors and told the officer to keep a post right outside the door.

While Malloy was getting the guards situated, Purdy retrieved evidence bags from his car. He secured the jacket in one, and the paper it was lying on in another and returned both bags to the trunk of his car.

Purdy and Malloy walked together upstairs to try to find the surgeon who had operated on the gunshot victim. They had a lot of questions for him.

Malloy and Purdy walked up behind Detective Danny Tartabull just in time to hear the doctor's frustrated pronouncement.

"I don't know what your brother-in-law's operation was. All I can tell you is that, unlike your brother-in-law, *this* patient is not one of *those* patients who wakes up chatting in the recovery room, Detective. How many different ways must I explain that to you?"

Scott Malloy held out his hand and said, "I'm Malloy, Detective Malloy, you're Doctor . . . ?"

"Hassan." He sighed.

"Detective Sam Purdy."

"Hello, Detective. For what it's worth, you can't see him, either. One of you can't see him. Three of you can't see him. If ten of you show up, *ten* of you can't see him. He's not awake. His condition is critical. When he's awake and lucid and stable, you may see him. My brother's a cop in San Francisco; I know how it works. I'm not going to make this difficult." The surgeon looked much fresher than the detectives. But everyone's nerves were frayed.

"Can I ask a few questions, Doctor?"

"Certainly. If I can ask you one first. Who is he? I need some medical history."

"We're working on it."

"You don't know?"

"We don't know. May I ask my questions now?"

"Yes."

"Entry wound?"

"One, in his back. Above the pelvic bone, lower left quadrant."

"Exit?"

"Yes. Two to three inches lower, two to three inches closer to mid-line than the entry."

"No doubt about exit?"

"None, the slug's not in him."

"Was he run over by a vehicle?"

"It appears possible. Broken femur, broken ankle, crushed bones in his hand, other contusions and abrasions consistent with compression. Some internal hemorrhage not associated with the gunshot. Yes, I'd say it's consistent with being run over by a car. Wouldn't testify to it right now, but it's consistent."

Purdy asked, "Notice any burn marks around the wound? Like from a close-in shot?"

"No. The skin around the entry was free of burns, but he was outside, I assume wearing heavy clothing. The edges of the wound were cauterized, of course, by the slug. That's to be expected."

"You know what to look for?"

"I was a volunteer in Sarajevo for nine months, Detective. I know more about what gunshots do to flesh than I ever wanted to know."

Malloy held out a business card. "Detective Tartabull will be here the rest of the night. Someone will take his place in the morning. If anything comes up about your patient's condition, day or night, give me a call, please."

"No problem." Dr. Hassan pocketed the card without glancing at it.

The two detectives walked away.

Purdy said, "You really don't know who the hell the victim is, yet?"

"No. No ID. Car at the scene that you guys found that we can't place is registered to a business in the Springs. We're trying to raise the owner of the business. No luck so far."

"We have a photograph yet? Something to distribute to the papers?"

"Yeah, but Tartabull had to take it himself in the ER. We couldn't get a police photographer over here before John Doe went into surgery. The film's being developed. I hope Tartabull handles a camera better than he handles an interview. This storm is screwing everything up for everybody."

"Not for the bad guys. We need some luck."

Malloy scoffed. "This could end up being my first homicide, Sam, and what the hell do I have so far?"

An empty elevator arrived, the doors opened, and the men stepped in.

"I have a victim I can't identify lying underneath a blanket of snow in the middle of a rich man's block. I have an anonymous 911 call. I have no witnesses. I have evidence that somebody might have driven over my victim in a vehicle and then did it over again for good measure. I have a victim with a bullet in the back that forensics is going to tell me was fired at close range. And my best suspect is a lady DA I really like who is losing her vision for unknown reasons. She insists she fired her weapon from half a block away. And she has two goddamn lawyers who are driving me crazy. All my goddamn evidence is going to melt and drain away when the sun comes out tomorrow. Somebody seems to want to kidnap my suspect, and I'm so tired I could piss zzzzz's if I could take the time to find a toilet."

Sam waited a beat. Nobody had told Malloy yet. He couldn't quite believe it.

"You're leaving something out, Scott. You have another complication, too. A doozy."

"What the hell's that supposed to mean?"

"Emma Spire."

"What the fuck are you talking about? What do you mean?"

"I think it means Court TV for you, big boy."

The elevator deposited them on the first floor. Malloy yanked Purdy by the arm into a waiting area full of empty chairs.

"Don't mess with me, Sam, what does Miss America have to do with this?"

"That house at the end of the block? On the rise? That's her house."

"So?" Malloy's question was much more nonchalant than his tone.

"She's a friend of Lauren's. Works with her in the DA's office."

"I thought she came to town to be a law student, leave the spotlight behind."

"She's doing an internship, an outplacement."

"How do you know she lives there, in that house?"

"When she started with the DA's office, she did a couple of ridealongs with me. I took her home once. Sweet kid."

"Did you talk to her tonight?"

"No. There was no answer. House was dark. No car in the garage. But I think the car in her driveway might belong to Lauren."

"Can we get a warrant?"

"On the house or the car?"

"What do you mean?"

"See, that's the problem. We don't have plain view. The car's parked at the top of the driveway in a little cutout behind some trees. It's buried in snow. Can't even be sure it's Lauren's until we clean it off. It's complicated, is what Skiles says. Even more complicated in that we'd be giving a skeptical judge skimpy grounds to grant a warrant to search a celebrity's property. Judge won't be happy with that."

"Don't tell me—Skiles is thinking about all this, right?"

"You got it. My guess is he'll be done thinking when the snow's done melting."

"What's Emma Spire doing living in a big house in a ritzy neighborhood like that?"

"It was her grandparents' house. After her parents died, she moved in. Lauren told me once that Emma felt she needed to feel the proximity to her family."

"But she lives by herself?"

"That's my understanding."

"You don't know what this shooting might have to do with her?"

"No. But I bet it has something to do with the reason Lauren's not talking."

"We need to find her, then. Emma Spire."

"Yep."

"Do we know where to look?"

"Nope." Sam smiled. "We know some of her friends though. Maybe we can get them to cooperate."

"Funny, Sam."

Purdy placed a hand on the shoulder of his younger colleague and said, "They're not all like this, Scott, trust me. Some of them aren't this annoying. Some of them just pull your guts out a couple of inches at a time and put them in a blender and grind them up. Some of them rip your heart out through your throat and tear it to pieces and feed it to wild animals."

"So you're saying I should be grateful?" Malloy almost smiled.

"I'm only offering a little perspective, here, that's all. If you don't really need me anymore, I'm going to go check this jacket in on Thirty-third and maybe get some sleep before tomorrow. I don't want to get Vannattered on this evidence."

Lauren begged to be allowed to take a shower before the nurse started her IV. Adrienne hovered the entire time, shadowing Lauren, leading her from place to place, handing her things she couldn't see, steadying her as she dried herself off and dressed in a clean gown.

Lauren's terror at being secreted away by a man she couldn't even see had disintegrated into a jittery fatigue that was taking her prisoner almost as effectively as had the Boulder Police Department. She barely managed to remain awake while the ER nurse inserted a thin catheter into a vein in her wrist.

"Nice shot," Lauren commented after the nurse began taping the tubing in place.

"Cake," the nurse said, "your veins are like garden hoses." Lauren barely heard the reply, and she was fast asleep before the plastic bag of medicine was hung above the infusion pump beside her bed.

The ER doc was the first physician to come back out of the examination room into the hallway.

"Well?" asked Malloy, who did his best to get in the man's face.

"No apparent trauma from whoever wheeled her away from here. Other than being scared half to death, she looks the same as when I checked her over when she first came in."

"What about her vision?"

"Not good, and not my department. I'll let her neurologist deal with that. He should be out soon." The ER doc turned and started back toward the central desk to check the board.

"Just a minute, Doctor, I'm—"

"The neurologist will fill you in. I have a possible broken hip and an acute abdomen to see. Things are starting to pick up. Duty calls."

Arbuthnot, the neurologist, came out next.

"Doctor? I'm waiting for a report from you." Malloy used his most intimidating voice. He had reached a point of exasperation with the picket line of doctors and attorneys he was being forced to shuffle through.

Arbuthnot stuffed his hands into the pockets of his blue jeans. He wasn't a tall man but he was solid, with wide shoulders and thick legs. He had been a three-time member of the Canadian Olympic luge team and was someone who had never shown a particular susceptibility to intimidation; fear held a whole different meaning to someone who considered it recreation to shoot down ice troughs at seventy miles an hour on a sled the size of a cookie sheet.

"I'm sorry I can't help you there," Dr. Arbuthnot said to Malloy. "Lauren asked that I not divulge her medical condition to you or anyone else, Detective. She did authorize me to inform you that she is currently suffering an acute condition called a bilateral optic neuritis, which I am treating with intravenous medication. She'll be staying here with us for a few days." He offered a small smile as consolation.

Malloy didn't think he had any adrenaline left, but he felt *something* start pumping through his veins right then. His voice rose. "You don't have a choice about divulging her medical condition to me, Doctor. She's my prisoner." Malloy was about to lose his legendary cool. He had not anticipated any resistance from Lauren about access to her medical information and for the tenth time that night he asked himself why the hell she was making this so difficult for him.

"Detective? It's 'Detective,' isn't it? Ms. Crowder's a *lawyer*, and if she tells me not to talk, I don't talk. I've learned over the years to be exceedingly respectful to lawyers. And Ms. Crowder is my patient, and I'm not about to go against her wishes. If you get me a court order that says we should chat, though, we'll chat."

"But we're paying for this, for you. The city is."

"That's funny. She predicted you would say that." He took one hand from the pocket of his jeans and scratched behind his ear. "She's already authorized the hospital and me to bill her insurance and she's signed for full financial responsibility if we fail to collect. Good night, Detective. As far as I'm concerned this case is private pay. If it turns out otherwise, rather than deal with the city or the county, I'll comp her. I'm afraid I don't owe you anything on that count. Sorry."

Malloy wished he was having this conversation some place less public. He was inclined to get mean. "She's a *prisoner*, Doctor. She can't stay in the hospital without my approval."

Arbuthnot looked down at the floor then hard into Malloy's bloodshot eyes. "No, Detective, please permit me to tell you how it works. I decide if she stays in the hospital. You get to decide whether she stays here at Community or whether she goes to DG. Do you really want this woman in the prison ward at Denver General? Do that and you could have a major PR problem on your hands, don't you think? She's not much of an escape risk, is she? She's almost blind. And she's got friends in high places who won't take kindly to imperiousness on your part."

Malloy hissed, "I can't get a court order about something like this on a night like tonight, Doctor. You know that damn well."

Arbuthnot shrugged. "You can bully me about this until we both fall asleep on our feet, Detective. But it's not what *I* know damn well that matters. What matters is what *she* knows damn well. And what she seems to know damn well is the law. Talk to her about it. It's not my call. The medical information is hers to protect and she's chosen to protect it. Sorry, I just can't help you."

Malloy raised his voice and moved his face to within two inches of the physician's. "I can't talk to her without her attorney present. And her attorneys won't allow her to talk to me. It's a catch-22, Doctor, and I'm trying to solve a serious crime."

Arbuthnot didn't budge. "She also told me—in the event you became belligerent—to remind you who it was who left her unguarded earlier." Arbuthnot turned away from Malloy before he allowed a smile to creep onto his face. Lauren Crowder was one patient-lawyer he was not about to piss off. He'd much rather have an irritated police detective on his hands.

* * *

Malloy knocked on the treatment room door, pushed it open a crack, and said, "I'm coming in. Get her decent."

Adrienne, all four feet ten of her, was ready for him. She was standing at the foot of the bed with a finger in front of her lips. She waited until she was sure Malloy had seen the signal and then motioned him to the far corner of the room.

She whispered, "She's asleep. She won't be for long and I don't want her disturbed. Got it?"

Malloy had to look way down to see Adrienne's face, and he felt like he was being ordered around by a twelve-year-old with an attitude. "I just wanted to see her, make sure she's all right."

Lauren was curled on her side, a hospital blanket pulled up to her shoulders, a pillow under her head. The infusion pump burped rhythmically. Malloy envied her sleep.

"How's she doing, Doctor?"

"We won't know for a while."

"Why won't she be asleep for long? I'd think she'd be exhausted. Put me in that bed, and I won't wake up till Tuesday."

"The medicine. It has a mess of side effects. One of them is that it's a stimulant. It'll jack her up in the next couple of hours, maybe sooner."

Malloy nodded as though he understood even a little why doctors would give stimulants to someone suffering from acute vision loss. He was going to ask but assumed he wouldn't get an answer.

"She's really blind?"

"Her vision is severely impaired, yes."

"What about her . . . you know . . . her—?"

"I have tests to run on her bladder. Nothing definitive. It's probably not serious. Her vision is our main concern."

"You're her friend, aren't you? I mean, you're not just her doctor?"

"That's correct, I'm her very good friend. You have a problem with that?"

"She told you not to talk to me, too, right?"

Adrienne nodded.

Malloy yawned. "You know, I don't know her that well, I've seen her around court and all, done a few minor felonies with her. I knew she was bright. But I'm truly impressed with her. The woman is smart as a whip, and *clever*—shit. She's under arrest for investigation of first-degree assault, maybe a capital murder by morning, she can't see, and, still, she's not missing a trick, is she? She has all these doctors and lawyers making all the right moves. She's playing this like a chess master."

"Lauren doesn't miss much that I can tell."

"I'm trying to solve a serious crime here, you know. Could be an attempted *murder*." Malloy was attempting to play on Adrienne's sympathies, knowing that her husband had been the victim of a recent homicide.

The shot missed its mark. "I wish you good luck with that, Detective. I really do. I also suggest you look elsewhere. My patient is innocent. My friend is innocent."

"Unless proven guilty."

"Won't happen. Come on, let her get some rest. The best thing you can do for yourself and for her is to go catch your bad guy. You know the man can't be too far away; he apparently has absolutely no respect for visiting hours." She placed a hand on Malloy's back and pushed him from the room.

Malloy was unwilling to back down. "She may be making a big mistake here. There's somebody after her. We need to know more about that in order to protect her."

Adrienne looked at the female officers on sentry in the hallway. One of them turned and stepped toward the open door.

"Stay out," Adrienne said.

Malloy rolled his eyes. Adrienne noticed, pointed at one of the police officers. "She has a big gun, Detective. She'll protect Lauren."

Adrienne left Malloy and continued down the hall toward the waiting area to find Alan. She had a message that Lauren had asked her to pass along.

Alan saw Adrienne coming and met her halfway. They embraced. Adrienne whispered reassurances and promised she would watch Lauren like a hawk the whole time she was in the hospital.

Cozy Maitlin was finally wide awake, a fresh styrofoam cup of tea in his hand. He had sweet-talked a nurse into a toothbrush, comb, and disposable razor and looked almost fresh. Adrienne had never met him before and found herself impressed by his middle-of-the-night panache. Adrienne required about as much rest at night as your average vampire and had little patience for people whose blossoms faded after dark.

The man with the tea and the fresh face was not

wearing a wedding ring. She reminded herself that she was a recent widow.

After making certain she had everyone's attention, and after double-checking that Detective Malloy hadn't followed her down the hall, Adrienne said, "Lauren told me to tell all of you she'll be more forthcoming—those are her words, 'more forthcoming'—when you find Emma. The guy who took her was grilling her, looking for Emma. He said if she told the police anything that the disc goes public. Alan, she said you would know what all that meant. She asked me to remind you to be discreet."

He nodded.

"How is she, Doctor?" Casey asked.

"Please call me Adrienne." She smiled at Cozy, then directed her answer at Alan. "She doesn't need this stress, I can tell you that. Her vision is for shit. She's had previous optic involvement, hasn't she?"

"Once seriously."

"It resolved?"

"Mostly."

"Listen, hopefully, this optic neuritis will resolve again, like it did last time. I would love to stay and bullshit with you folks," she chanced another grin at Cozy, "but I need to schlepp Jonas back home and be here again in . . ." she glanced at her watch, ". . . in three and a half hours for an operation. I'll check in on Lauren in the morning, before I go into the OR."

She started to walk away, turned back. "You going to get home tonight, Alan? Do you want me to take care of Emily in the morning, let her out?"

"Please, Ren, that would be great, I don't know if

I'll make it home. With this much snow her dog run is useless to her. Do you mind putting her in the studio for a while in the morning? She still likes to hang out there and she doesn't like being in the house all day. You know where her food is?"

Adrienne nodded. "Get some sleep, Alan. You really look like shit. Jonas can draw people who look better than you. And the kid doesn't even know which end of the crayon is up."

As Adrienne retreated down the hall to retrieve her sleeping son, Cozy nodded his head in her direction and, with a smile, asked Alan, "Who was that masked man?"

Casey said, "Later, Cozy," and asked Alan if he knew where to find Emma Spire.

"I know a guy she's been seeing. I can go check his place, see if she's with him. But even if she's there, that only solves one problem. Because Emma doesn't have the disc that Adrienne was talking about. That's a huge part of all this. And I really don't think she'll be at this guy's place. She's still angry at him that the disc is missing in the first place."

"What's on the disc?" Casey asked.

Alan hesitated, then said, "It's complicated."

Casey said the same words at the exact same moment before adding, "You and Lauren practice this 'It's complicated' routine?"

"Basically, the disc is a recording of Emma that she doesn't want to become public."

"Video?"

"Not exactly."

"Audio?"

"Not exactly."

"I'm too tired for twenty questions, Alan."

"It's a computer thing, a digital recording." He spent five minutes trying to explain the implications of Ethan Han's technology.

Cozy didn't get it.

But Casey grasped both concepts immediately, finally understanding what Lauren had meant about a thousand rapes. "He can really do that? What he says he can do?"

Alan shrugged. "Not yet, but maybe soon. The technology is close."

Casey sat quietly for most of a minute, pondering the implications for Lauren. "First, I think I'll settle for finding Emma Spire. Solving one problem out of two sounds like a winning ratio to me right now. But, Cozy, one of us needs to be here when Lauren wakes up."

Cozy said, "That should be you, she'll need to see a face she trusts. Personally, I think we need to know just a little bit more about this young lady no one can find and we certainly need to know more about this disc." He looked to Alan Gregory. "Doctor, you're on. Let's go find this man she's been dating and you can begin to try and explain to me one more time why what's on this disc is so damn important."

The storm had skidded east and the blanket of clouds above Boulder had started to shred into wispy rags, releasing any warmth left trapped near the ground.

On the way from the hospital to Ethan Han's Pearl Street flat, Cozier Maitlin seemed less interested in the details of the missing optical disc than he was in providing Alan Gregory his unique perspective on homicide defense.

"Although it may not seem like it, we actually don't have many homicides or attempted murders in Boulder, and lately, almost no one has been arrested on a capital offense who could afford a private attorney. During my most self-indulgent moments—and if Erin were here, she would be arguing that we're talking the potential of Olympic-quality self-indulgence—I think that's a crying shame. Because big cases get my criminal defense attorney blood rushing like whitewater. I wouldn't miss a case like this for anything—anything.

"When Casey called me tonight the last thing in the world I had planned to do with this weekend was to spend it slaloming through this damn blizzard chasing cops and prosecutors around town. But when she told me what was up I told her 'yes' before she'd finished posing the question.

"In the next few hours we'll really get cranked up. The phone calls will begin flying—almost like a tennis match—to the chief trial deputy, and to the special prosecutor once they find one. By the way, I have fifty dollars that says Weld County will provide the special, Casey says it's going to be Arapahoe. She doesn't know it, but that's money in the bank for me. Soon, negotiations will begin over access, charges, bond, you name it, nonstop, every hour until the two o'clocks tomorrow. This one is big, too, once they get wind of Emma Spire's involvement, the press will be everywhere. By dawn, probably. Boulder, Denver, the wire services, the tabloids, the networks. The frenzy will be something to watch. The DA, I think, is in the process of hanging Lauren out to spin in the wind by keeping his distance. He's—"

"Royal won't do that, Cozy," Alan interrupted. "He likes Lauren. He'll stand behind her; he always has."

"You're being naive again. Has Royal Peterson called her yet to offer his condolences or his assistance? Has he contacted Casey or me to offer help? I know the man. If Royal is busy right now, he's busy looking for cover, not compassion; Teflon, not tenderness."

Alan thought about Royal Peterson not calling, not offering to help. Cozy was right. Alan wondered what Roy's posture would mean for Lauren down the road.

"Lauren's enemies in the defense bar—and as sweet as she might be to you, she has enemies, I guarantee you—and her enemies in the police department—ditto—are going to start telling stories to reporters. That whole thing she was involved with in Utah with the Supreme Court justice and the Mormons will come back like an old case of the clap and all the old wire reports will be rewritten in ways that make her look evil. The press will be calling Casey and me every two minutes trying to stir up trouble. It's going to be a three-ring circus."

Alan Gregory listened to Cozy Maitlin as dispassionately as he could. He was having trouble sharing

Cozy's excited anticipation and apparent delight over Lauren's impending prosecution and public scrutiny. He felt like screaming a reminder to Cozy that his wife was seriously ill and in jail.

Maitlin was oblivious. "I already have motions to prepare. The evidence gathering we saw earlier tonight is questionable at best, given the weather conditions. I can tie the prosecutors in knots on crime scene contamination, and the plain view aspects of sweeping off those cars that are parked on the street—that's a constitutional beauty. The supremes are going to love it. And Lauren's medical history is something else. She wants us to file a motion on her medical records staying secret, and, wait a second, I just had another thought."

He reached into his coat pocket and retrieved a phone that was about the size of a deck of cards. He punched in a number.

"Casey, it's me. Yeah. It's stopped snowing and the moon is out and it is soooo lovely out here. . . . No, no, that's not the reason I called. I have an idea. Lauren has a little vision left, correct? . . . Thought so. What do you think of this, we offer a deal to the cops? They still don't know who the guy who was shot is, do they? . . . Well, tell them that Lauren will visit the shooting victim in the recovery room and see if she can identify anything about the guy at all. . . . *Exactly*, there you go. Then you two retreat right after she sees the guy . . . yes . . . and then decide what she says to the cops, if anything. I agree, I agree, I think they'll go for it, what choice do they have? They need to know who this guy is. . . . We're almost there I think. Slow going out here in this muck. No traffic, thank God. . . . You'll let me know what happens? Adios then."

Alan asked, "What was that all about?"

"We need to know who the victim is. The police need to know who the victim is. We're going to offer the cops some cooperation in return for a peek at him, see if Lauren can ID him for us. I think they'll go for it. It's certainly worth a try."

"What if it's someone who . . . I don't know—"

"Complicates things for us?"

"Yes."

"Then Lauren, poor dear, it turns out, couldn't see well enough to recognize him. This one is win-win for us. My favorite kind of odds."

Alan pulled to a stop at the corner of Fourteenth and Pearl, on the edge of the Downtown Mall. In the middle of a night like this, the area should have been deserted. But it wasn't.

In the eerie stillness of the snow-cushioned night three black and whites and a few unmarked cars were clustered on the usually vehicle-free Mall bricks. The focus of all their attention seemed to be the ornate facade of the Citizens National Bank Building.

Alan said, "This isn't good, Cozy. That's where we were going. That's where Emma's boyfriend lives. Oh God, I wonder if she's gone ahead and killed herself."

Cozy digested the news but didn't get infected by the speculation. "Why does this man get the promotion? Ten minutes ago he's a guy she's dating, now they're a couple."

"It's awkward, that's all. I bet something is going

on here that involves him. Or, God forbid, her. I don't like it."

Cozy surveyed the police response. "No, that's not it. The police could handle an interview with Ms. Spire with a couple of detectives. This isn't a typical police response. Look there, up on the roof."

Three uniformed officers with flashlights were on the roof of the building adjacent to the old bank.

"Where does he live? Emma's beau?"

"A small flat behind his research laboratory. Third floor of the old bank building."

"That could be directly across from the roof they're taping off. Is there access from his place to the roof?"

Alan tried to recall the layout of Ethan's research laboratory. "There might be some windows that face in that direction." He gazed up at the roofline. "Those that are next to the roof where the cops are? I think they would go into the lab. His flat is behind that, above the alley."

"We have a choice to make here, Alan. We could get out of the car and walk over there and start asking questions and stick our noses into whatever investigation is going on in that building. If we do, the police will immediately recognize our interest in— what's this man's name?"

"Ethan Han."

Cozy was silent for a moment. "Really? Ethan Han?"

"Yes, have you heard of him? He's a medical technology entrepreneur who—"

"I know who the hell he is. Is there anyone involved in this case who isn't on *People* magazine's A-list?"

"Just you and me and Lauren, Cozy. We're the only regular folks."

"Yes, and I'm Daffy Duck. Well, anyway, if we go out there, the cops are going to learn about our interest in Ethan Han and very soon somebody is going to mention to them that Ethan and Emma are an item and the cops are going to realize that *we* are also concerned about Emma.

"So our decision right now is this: Do we play the Emma card and mosey over and see what's going on? Or do we make a tactical retreat? The police aren't stupid. It may take them an interview or two to sort it out, but they are not going to misread our interest in this crime scene, whatever it is."

Before Alan could answer, he was distracted by a loud noise.

⬌✛⬌

This time the car was Alan's Land Cruiser and not a fancy lawyer's BMW so Sam Purdy didn't even ask before he yanked open the back door and let himself in.

Both Alan and Cozy were startled and turned around. Purdy was delighted at the surprise on their faces.

"Hello, again, you two. Alan, you have a new hobby? You started listening to scanners or something? You're showing up at way too many crime scenes for it to be a coincidence."

"Hey, Sam. Too many for my taste, too. But we

just stumbled on this one. It's been a long night, how are you holding up?"

"I'm beat. The way the world is supposed to work is that when the snow starts falling in buckets, the felons hibernate, and detectives usually get to sleep in, or catch up on old business. Not this shift, I'll tell you. First Lauren's troubles and now this."

"Good evening again, Detective."

"Hello, Mr. Maitlin."

"What is *this*, this new situation?"

Sam ignored the question. "What brings you to the Mall at this hour? Shortcut across town from the hospital I don't know about?"

Cozy spoke before Alan had a chance to say something Cozy didn't want said. "Actually, no, Detective. We were on our way to my office—which is there," he pointed south, "just across the Mall on Fourteenth—when we saw the hubbub."

Purdy figured that a defense attorney as good as Cozier Maitlin could manage to lie to him with seamless facility, so Sam stared at Alan's face for clues as to whether or not Cozy's story was anywhere near true. Alan turned away from Sam.

Purdy looked back at the lawyer. "Let's say that's true, Mr. Maitlin. Let's say that."

"But it is," Cozy assured him with a face as straight as the Republican National Committee. "So what is going on in my quiet neighborhood that requires such a large police response?"

"Discharge of a firearm."

Alan swallowed. "A shooting?"

Emma? Ethan?

Sam loosened the three top buttons on his overcoat. He relished his advantage. "Two in one night. There have been some years I can hardly remember two shootings in this burg. Go figure."

"Anyone injured?" Alan asked.

"Let me think, it's been a hell of a night. Is there anyone you're particularly concerned about?"

Cozy considered warning Alan not to respond, but decided to see if Alan could recognize the trap and handle the big cop on his own. He wasn't going to be able to baby-sit Alan forever.

"In particular? No, I don't like to see anyone get shot."

"I forget sometimes what a humanitarian you are. It's one of the things I guess I like about you. Hanging with you is like slumming around with Amnesty International." He cracked open the door next to him and prepared to get out of the car. "Gentlemen, it's been sweet. Alan, you might reconsider exactly who you should be trusting, who really cares about who in this situation. And you, Mr. Maitlin, you can continue on your way to your office, and I'll pretend that I believe that was ever your destination. Is that benevolent of me or what? People moan about police brutality, but they never write poems about sweethearts like me."

Beyond the overt warning and the obvious sarcasm, Alan heard an edge in Sam's voice, an I-helped-you-out-earlier-didn't-I-and-this-is-what-I-get? tone. Alan wondered if Cozy heard it. He was inclined to think not.

"I was at a party there once, Sam. At the old bank building."

Sam rubbed his forehead with one gloved hand and pulled the door closed against the frigid air with the other. "We talking recently, Alan, or we talking, like, during the storied days of The Good Earth?" During the seventies, the top floor of the Citizens Bank Building had been the home of one of Boulder's more notorious nightspots.

"The Good Earth? You're talking before my time. No, more recently. The party was at Ethan Han's flat or lab or whatever he calls it."

"Lauren on your arm that night?"

Cozy was beginning to worry about the direction of the conversation. Sam was sketching out lines that would eventually connect dots. Soon, he would find the short line that connected Emma and Lauren. Until he and Casey understood that relationship a lot better, Cozy didn't want Sam Purdy tracing it. Cozy decided to allow just a little more line to play out before he reeled his client back in.

"Actually, Sam, I was on *her* arm during this particular soiree."

Sam smiled at that thought. "Figures. Then you probably know Han is the only actual resident of the bank building. The rest of the space is commercial."

"That's the way it looked to me that night."

"Big party?"

"Big enough. Catered."

"Meet somebody there . . . tall guy, looks like he's got an armadillo on top of his head?"

J. P. Morgan, Alan thought. How does Sam know J. P.?

"Yes, I think I remember seeing someone like that. Was he involved in the shooting?"

Sam ignored Alan's question. "Maybe remember a name to go with it?"

"Can't be sure about that."

"Well, as luck would have it, it probably won't surprise either of you to learn that it is indeed Ethan Han's place that is our second crime scene tonight. Coincidences are piling up deeper than the drifts around here."

"Was Ethan hurt?" The concern was Alan's.

Sam stretched his big neck from side to side. "First name basis? Is Mr. Han a buddy of yours?"

"No, just an acquaintance. I met him at one of Lauren's softball games."

"And the next thing that happens is he invites you to a fancy dinner? You must have really charmed the guy."

"We have some mutual friends."

"Ah." Sam was trying to decide whether he could believe Alan, whom he had never considered to be an accomplished liar. He couldn't decide. "This shooting's not my case. Lauren's shooting's not my case. But what I'm hearing is that it doesn't look like Ethan was injured in this latest fracas."

Alan exhaled involuntarily. He desperately wanted to ask about Emma Spire's whereabouts and her well-being, but knew he shouldn't reveal the connection if Sam didn't already know about it.

Cozy ran interference. He said, "Has the ambulance already departed?"

Sam Purdy hesitated, then said, "Don't remember saying that we ever needed one."

Damn, thought Cozy, but this cop's coy. Cozy still didn't know whether the ambulance wasn't needed because the victim was dead or because there *wasn't* a victim.

"I don't see any vehicles from the coroner's office, either."

Sam tried to suck free a poppy seed that had been lodged in his teeth since he'd eaten a midnight bagel and cream cheese, his meager dinner. He turned his head to face the cars on the Mall and said, "Nope, me neither."

Cozy was thinking of ways to pry some more information free from Detective Purdy and was coming up blank. He thought that he would probably enjoy a game of chess with this man.

Sam interrupted the silence by saying, "My guess is that we could help each other here. That'd be my guess, if everyone were so inclined."

"What do you have in mind?" Cozy asked. He loved horse trading, always assumed he'd end up with the thoroughbred.

"You two seem curious about the events that have transpired here tonight. I could shed a little light on that. I remain a little curious about why Lauren was firing a weapon just a few feet away from Emma Spire's house a few hours ago. I still have a feeling that, Alan, you might be able to shed a little light on that. Personally," he emphasized the word for Alan's benefit, "I might consider that a fair exchange of information."

Alan looked at Cozy.

"Seems one-sided to the lawyer in me, Detective. We give you information in a shooting *with* a victim. You give us information in a shooting without one. Where's the balance?"

"Who said there's no victim here?"

"No ambulance, no coroner. Two minus one, minus one, makes zero."

Purdy said, "How about I start off with a little goodwill, maybe give you a freebie? Do you know where I was heading when I got the call to respond here, Alan? I was on my way to Thirty-third to drop off some evidence when I get an order from Sergeant Pons to pick up a warrant to go search your house. Which is where I'll be heading as soon as I'm done here. You didn't hear that from me—either of you says you did, I'll deny it. But if I were you, I might put a preemptive call into Lew Skiles or the DA and see if you can negotiate access so that some bored detective doesn't knock down your door and tear up your house looking for something that probably isn't even there."

"They're going to search my house?" Alan was incredulous at how fast things were moving. "To-night? What are they looking for?"

Cozy replied, "They're fishing. It'll be a vague warrant, probably get thrown out." Cozy didn't believe his own protestations; most Boulder judges were strict with warrant requirements. But when around the police Cozy loved to cast as wide a net of doubt about the propriety of collected evidence as he could.

"It was Sergeant Pons's idea, apparently, the search. Felt that it shouldn't wait, even though Wendell is usually a patient man. A little redundant, some say, but typically patient."

Cozy reached over the seat and put a hand on the cop's shoulder. Sam fought an urge to slap it off.

Cozy said, "I do appreciate the advice. I think I'll phone the chief trial deputy as soon as we get to my office. I'm sure we can arrange convenient access for you and your colleagues."

Sam ignored Cozy and faced his friend.

"We're still looking for Lauren's car, Alan. It's a bitch finding a vehicle during a blizzard. In this much snow, an eighty-six Cressida looks exactly like a ninety-four Lexus looks just like a ninety-two Hyundai. And all the plates are totally crusted with ice."

"Maybe I could go out and look for it, Sam, and give you a call if I find it."

"Maybe you could just tell me where you might *go* to look for it and I'll do it myself."

"The plain view issues that we discussed earlier remain problematic, Detective Purdy. I don't know what a trial judge or the supremes might say about sweeping snow off a car to look at it. Or *in* it."

Purdy said, "Your warning has already been heeded, Mr. Maitlin. As a matter of fact, the puzzle is more convoluted than you think. See, I think the plain view problems would be compounded if the car in question was parked on *private* property that has not yet been linked to any criminal activity, especially if it were in a location that afforded no plain view from the sidewalk or the street.

"If Lauren's car were someplace like *that*, it might really curtail my freedom to examine it. 'Course, by midmorning, after a little Colorado sunshine, plates will have all dripped clean. Be easy, then. Be able to get a warrant. Who could guess how something like this could unravel by morning. Can you imagine the press, for instance, if it turned out someone prominent was involved in this mystery?"

As he finished speaking, Sam looked at Alan. The

detective's eyes smiled. Without an additional word, he was telling Alan and Cozy not to play him for a fool. He knew where Lauren's car was. He was waiting for someone to tell him *why* her car was in Emma Spire's driveway. He was also telling Alan and Cozy that they weren't the only ones looking for Emma.

Cozy Maitlin's mind was racing off in a direction he hoped would be more substantive than a discussion about the search of Alan and Lauren's house or the discovery and search of her car, both events which he knew from experience were as inevitable as the Colorado sun beginning to melt away the snow in the morning.

Cozy said, "I've been thinking. This is a large police response for a noninjury shooting."

"Huh?" countered Purdy, who despite his exhaustion, guessed instantly where the attorney was heading with this diversion.

"I count three radio cars, couple of detective cars, maybe more vehicles down on Fifteenth that I can't see. Big response for a no-bodily-harm firearm discharge. Fascinating."

Sam tried to recover the initiative. "It looks like it may be a 'make-my-day' situation. As a rule, the department's uneasy about them, investigates them carefully."

"Burglary then, or was it trespassing?"

Colorado's "make-my-day" law permits a resident to protect his or her dwelling with the use of deadly force, even if the only risk is to property.

"Let's say an attempted burglary."

"Someone tried to break in from the roof." There was no question in Cozy's statement. "Lord knows there should be a good trail of footprints to follow in this snow."

Sam Purdy realized that so far Cozy Maitlin was winning this battle of wits to see who was able to squeeze more information from whom. It really pissed him off.

"Who knows, Mr. Maitlin, depending on how things evolve here tonight, by morning you could have yourself yet another new client."

"And who might that be, Detective?"

"There's discussion going on among my colleagues right now about whether to arrest this latest shooter."

"A make-my-day situation shouldn't result in an arrest."

"What I may have neglected to mention, given that for some reason I sometimes lean toward being retentive around attorneys—maybe I should give you a call at the office, Alan, and take a look at that mistrustful side of myself in therapy—was that the shooter was a guest of the resident of the dwelling and not the resident himself. I'm told that the make-my-day law is a little vague about the rights of visitors to use deadly force to protect property that doesn't happen to be their own."

A *visitor*? Alan's heart was doing flip-flops. Was Emma, too, about to be arrested for firing a gun at someone? Or had J.P. been the shooter? Is that how Sam had met him?

Cozy said, "I'm happy to check the case law on that, if you would like, Detective. What was the relationship of the alleged shooter to the resident of the dwelling? Family? Friend? Invited guest? Uninvited guest?"

"Those are questions we're working assiduously to answer, Mr. Maitlin."

"Mr. Han isn't around to answer that question?"

Sam smirked. "I think I'm needed elsewhere. Good night, gents. Alan, make sure the bulb's screwed in tight. Pull the switch. Maybe you'll see the light."

Alan said, "Sam knows a lot, Cozy. He's sly."

Cozy said, "He's guessed at some things, but he's fishing, mostly. I doubt that the police have been able to confirm very much. They're wondering about a connection between Han and Emma Spire. They'll have it soon, maybe by morning, then the press will get ravenous and the pressure on Lauren to talk will be even more intense than it has been."

Alan started the car. "Do you really want to go to your office?"

"God no, I hate being there by myself. Especially at night. I'm such a wimp at being alone. You would think I would learn to be more masterful at relationships. My selfishness is actually quite maladaptive." The sudden injection of insight surprised Alan, who was once again reconsidering his assessment of Cozier Maitlin.

Cozy pulled his portable phone from his coat pocket. To Alan, he said, "Why don't you start driving east, toward your house. I think we should try and impede this search any way we can. That is as-

suming there is a search, and Sam Purdy isn't sending us off after the proverbial wild goose."

Cozy's call went through.

"Erin, listen—oh, did I wake you? . . . No it's not
Trevor, who the hell is Trevor? This is Cozy. Remem-
ber me, I'm tall, we were married once? I need to
ask you something. Is there a chance that Emma
Spire was at home tonight hiding out in the dark?
What did your nosy witness have to say?"

Cozy listened patiently to Erin's response and finally said, "No. Nothing much new at our end, she's
going to spend the night in the hospital. . . . It's
complicated. Go back to sleep, I'll talk to you tomorrow and fill you in. Alan said you're going to get a
videotape. I want to see it as soon as you have it."
He flipped the phone shut.

Alan asked, "So was Emma home tonight?"

"Erin's witness says not. Says she saw her leave
about an hour before the shooting. Never saw Emma
come back home and the old lady says she only left
her post by the window to go to the bathroom and
to check on someone named Arnold."

Alan said, "Well, we know Emma's not at home,
and she doesn't appear to be at Ethan's flat. I'm not
sure I know where else to look. Lauren might have
an idea on who else to call."

"Lauren needs her sleep. One thing at a time."
Cozy tapped in another number. "Listen to this; this
should be good." He pointed at his phone, which
was ringing.

"Wake up, Mitchell, it's Cozier Maitlin. We should
talk about your colleague, don't you think? . . . Yes,
Lauren, who else? How many members of your staff

have you arrested tonight? Sure, I'll hold on." Turning to Alan, who was driving east on Arapahoe about a quarter of a mile behind a pair of snowplows operating in tandem, Cozy said, "You know Mitchell Crest, the chief trial deputy, don't you? He's moving to another phone so his wife doesn't get homicidal. I'm glad I woke him up; I don't know why the hell I should allow him to get any sleep tonight. I want this playing field to be somewhere close to level when the starting gun goes off tomorrow afternoon."

Alan wasn't fond of "the gun going off" metaphor. Mitchell resumed the conversation.

Cozy listened, then said, "Yes, you heard right, I'm co-counsel with a sharp lawyer from JeffCo, a friend of the accused. . . . What do you mean, Mitchell? 'Humble' is my middle name. . . . But once again, your information is accurate. She's a bulldog, Mitch, and she won't be cutting *you* any slack and she's not going to fall for any of your tricks. You're going to end up happy to have someone as even-tempered as me around. Listen, I assume you're going to be wanting to move on a warrant soon and we just wanted to offer some cooperation . . . yes, that's me, always accommodating to the authorities. . . . What makes you think I heard something? I didn't hear anything, I just know the way you think, Mitchell; you're the one who sounds suspicious. . . . What's the deal? Basically, we help you out. We disarm the burglar alarm for you and—"

Cozy covered the mouthpiece and said to Alan, "You have a dog?"

Alan nodded.

"And we'll get their vicious watchdog . . . what do you mean? . . . I don't know—a Doberman or a Rottweiler or something, attack-trained I think I heard Lauren say once. And we'll agree to secure the residence in its current state if—are you still with me here, Mitchell?—if you get the police to permit us to observe the search and if you get the local constables to agree not to rip the place apart. That's it, that's all we want. We have nothing to hide."

Cozy covered the mouthpiece again and faced Alan. "The warrant's been issued. He thinks the police may already be at your house executing the search. I don't think he knows about the second shooting or the delays it's causing. Well, since I want to keep him from sleeping anyway . . ."

He turned his attention back to the phone. "You haven't heard about the second shooting, then, have you, Mitchell, the one on Pearl Street, on the Mall?" Cozy listened for a moment and raised his eyebrows to Alan. He raised a gloved thumb to indicate victory. "No. I don't know the details. Ran into it by accident, it's right by my office, a big police response, I can tell you that. . . . Yes. . . . I assumed that might slow them down. . . . That would be great. If you would make those calls, Lauren's husband and I will go right back to their house and wait for the police to show up. . . . I'm sure I'll see you tomorrow, Mitchell. . . . Of course, of course, I assumed you would want to postpone filing charges . . . yes, yes, we know there'll be a special assigned. I'll miss seeing your pretty face every day. Remember, though, I'm co-counsel here, Mitchell, I can't make any commitments before I talk with my client and my colleague. . . . You know, I hadn't thought of that: It *is* kind of like being married. We'll talk tomorrow. Try and get some rest. Bye."

"We're still going to my house?"

"Yes," answered Cozy. "I think we should. I would really like to be certain there isn't a schematic of Emma's neighborhood tacked up on your living room wall. That would complicate Lauren's defense considerably."

Alan didn't respond.

"There isn't one, is there?" After half a heartbeat, Cozy continued, "Alan, the swagger is an act. I could use some reassurance here."

"No, Cozy. There's nothing I know of in the house to worry about." But then again, Alan mused, he hadn't known that his wife carried a gun in her purse.

Once he turned from the recently plowed surfaces of South Boulder Road onto the country lanes of Spanish Hills, Alan had to feel his way gingerly to his home. In places, the snow was so deep that it challenged the clearance of his big 4×4.

He half-expected to see a convention of police and sheriff vehicles already mustered along the gravel lane that separated his modest house from Adrienne's renovated farmhouse, which was just up the hill. But the wide lane was devoid of vehicles—unless you counted the John Deere mini tractor with the snowblower attachment that Adrienne was driving to and fro with fervent resolve.

She was dressed in an electric pink snowboarding

suit, and from a distance looked like a neon rabbit making a battery commercial.

Alan checked the clock on the dashboard of his car and shook his head. Cozy raised his voice and said, "What on earth *is* that?"

"That's Adrienne. The urologist from the ER? She's my neighbor. She loves driving that stupid tractor, will use almost any excuse to get on it. Although the hour is a little odd, even for her."

"She's plowing snow now? Couldn't this wait until morning?"

"By the time morning rolls around for most of the human race, Adrienne's already in the OR."

"She does this routinely . . . in the middle of the night? One of these houses is yours, I take it? And you put up with this—racket?"

Adrienne had already cleared a wide swath from her double garage all the way to the lane. She had also cleared space for Alan and Lauren's two cars near their front door. For some reason Alan couldn't determine, she was now completing a third diagonal by clearing a pedestrian-size path from Alan and Lauren's house to the distant doors of the old tack-house on the south side of the property, a building that had most recently been Adrienne's recently deceased husband's, Peter's, woodworking studio.

"Which house is yours?"

"The little one."

"Good view up here?"

"You can see heaven from up here, Cozy."

"I should hang around until morning, then. It will

probably be my only opportunity for that particular vista."

Alan pulled to a stop in the cleared space near his front door, once again feeling some gratitude for Adrienne's hypomania.

She had completed the path to the old tackhouse and was heading back toward Alan and Cozy, the little headlights of the tractor dead in their eyes. Her entire outfit was frosted in tiny ice crystals. Her eyebrows were as white as spring clouds.

No one bothered speaking until she turned off the roaring tractor engine.

"Thanks for clearing the snow, Ren. You remember Cozier Maitlin from the hospital? Are you planning to get any sleep tonight?"

Adrienne smiled at Cozy but her lips were so cold she wasn't sure she could manipulate them well enough to risk speaking without embarrassing herself. She indicated to Alan with a nod that she wanted to go inside.

Alan unlocked the door and silenced the warning on the alarm. He led Adrienne into the small kitchen.

Cozy had been following but stopped at the doorway, removed his snowy shoes, and said, "I'm going to take a quick look around before the authorities arrive. Make certain that there are no surprises."

Adrienne felt the muscles in her face begin to thaw and looked to Alan for an explanation. "What did he say he was going to do? Does he need to use the john?"

"The police are coming to do a search of the house."

"In the middle of the night? You're kidding? What the hell are they looking for, a bloody glove?"

"Cozy thinks the cops are on a fishing expedition."

Alan suddenly realized that he didn't know who was watching Jonas and that his dog hadn't greeted him when he came in. "Who's with Jonas and where's Emily?"

"I took her over to my place. I have some company who's keeping an ear out for Jonas for me, and Emily's doing her watchdog thing at my house."

"Why were you clearing a trail to the studio? Was that for Emily, for tomorrow?"

"No, I was obliterating footprints."

Alan thought she was joking, getting into the spirit of the felonious themes of the night.

"I'm serious. When I got home, I discovered that we who live here on the Ponderosa have a visitor who broke into the studio to get out of the storm."

"Emma?"

"Bingo."

"She's all right?"

"She's not hurt."

"Thank God, where is she now?"

"My place, asleep I hope, listening for Jonas."

"Does she know about Lauren, the shooting?"

"Yes, I told her. She's real sorry that Lauren was caught up in this."

"Does she have the disc back?"

"No."

"Did she tell you the whole story?"

Adrienne shrugged. "Bits and pieces. She's not terribly effusive and she doesn't look much like the celebrity right now."

"Things are a mess, huh?"

Adrienne nodded. "She convinced me that somebody might really be looking for her, so I moved her car into my garage, got out John Deere, and obliterated her trail.''

Despite the events of the last twenty-four hours, Alan was still having trouble believing that such precautions were necessary. He said, "Thanks, I guess," and wondered if Adrienne had broken any laws. Emma wasn't a suspect in anything, so her footprints and tire tracks couldn't be considered evidence.

Could they?

✛

Casey Sparrow made the offer sound as generous as possible.

Scott Malloy tried to judge the proposal objectively, but the sheer volume of Casey Sparrow's red hair was distracting him. He leaned back against a mobile x-ray machine and focused his attention on her eyes, trying to avoid the crimson halo.

He said, "Let me make sure we understand each other."

A window across the corridor reflected his image back at him. Scott's left eye was much more bloodshot than his right, his beard was growing in unevenly the way it did sometimes, and he was trying in vain to control a muscle twitch that had started erupting in the corner of his mouth. He thought the twitch was a sign that he might be getting a cold sore.

Figured.

"Fine, understanding each other sounds great," replied Casey Sparrow. She knew she looked a lot better than he did. Hell, she thought, most of the patients upstairs in the intensive care unit probably looked a lot better than he did. She had stolen a minute in front of the mirror in Lauren's treatment room to add some blush to her cheeks and to apply some fresh lipstick. She couldn't have cared less how attractive she looked but she recognized the strategic advantage of making sure Scott Malloy was negotiating with someone who appeared immune to the consequences of pulling an all-nighter.

Scott explained how he understood the arrangements Casey had proposed. "We wheel Lauren upstairs to recovery or ICU or wherever this John Doe is, she looks sideways or upside down or however she has to look at him and sees if she recognizes him. You and she go somewhere private and have a tête-à-tête about the reliability of her vision. Then maybe you tell me what she saw, and maybe you don't."

"Yes. That's my offer."

"I want your guarantee that I can talk with her afterward."

"Then we withdraw our offer."

He looked at his feet. "I don't have much choice, do I?"

"No."

"Assuming your good faith . . ." He paused. "I accept. Is your client awake yet?"

"For a few minutes now, yes."

"What about the IV?"

"The first course of medicine is complete. They've removed the tubing. She still has some ugly plug in her arm."

"Let's go see John Doe then. God am I tired. How come you don't look as tired as I feel?"

"Clean living and good genes, Detective."

Malloy was so exhausted he actually looked down to see what was so damn special about her jeans.

The smells of the hospital, the sterile antecedents of hope and despair, seemed stronger in the corridor outside the operating rooms than they had in the ER. The emergency room had begun to come alive with the stirrings of minor catastrophe but the operating rooms still husbanded their middle-of-the-night silence like a mausoleum.

At the nurses station outside the recovery room, a scrub-suited nurse wearing brand-new cross-trainers was finishing up a twelve-hour shift.

She raised her head at the procession of strangers entering the recovery suite and yawned, covering her mouth with her hand.

Malloy saw her sleepy eyes and told himself he wouldn't yawn in response. He could control that. He *could*. He failed. He yawned, too.

Detective Danny Tartabull's chin was on his chest when he heard the sounds of the approaching posse. Tartabull tried to look alert. Instead, he ended up acting like someone who had just been woken up by a phone call and was trying to pretend he'd been awake the whole time.

Trying to mask his disdain, Scott said, "Hey, Danny, morning. Why don't you take five? Go to the can and splash some water on your face or something. Get some coffee."

"Sure. Thanks, Scott. What's up?" He rubbed his

eyes with one hand, pushed his hair from his forehead with the other. His shirttail was puffing out of
his trousers. Casey didn't know Tartabull, and thought
he looked like a guy auditioning for a part as a
derelict.

"I'll fill you in later."

Malloy's badge was hung over his belt. He faced
the nursing station and pointed at it.

"We need to take a look at the shooting victim.
Our John Doe. Your John Doe."

The nurse was tall and thin and her sandy hair
was cut shorter than Scott Malloy's. She had four
earrings on her left ear, none on her right. She said,
"I thought this was all worked out with Dr. Hassan.
He told me you promised you wouldn't disturb his
patient. Please don't make me page him for this, not
at this hour."

"We're not here to talk with the guy. We're just
here to *look* at him. This lady in the wheelchair may
be able to ID him for us."

The nurse manufactured a smile for Lauren. She
hadn't read the chart of the man still in recovery, but
heard he had been run over in addition to being shot.
She wondered if he and Lauren had been in the same
traffic accident. Her instincts caused her to be skeptical of the request that was being made; she figured
this was some cop trick that was going to get her in
a peck of trouble with Dr. Hassan.

"You just want to *look*?" The nurse's tone conveyed the kind of overt skepticism that a sorority girl
might employ to question a fraternity boy who said
he only wanted a peek.

Casey Sparrow stepped forward and held out her

hand. "Hello, I'm Casey Sparrow. I'm an attorney. The police officer is telling the truth. My client," she touched Lauren on the shoulder, "may be able to recognize your patient. As I'm sure you are aware, we need to know his identity in order to notify his family of his injuries. And I'm sure Dr. Hassan would love to learn his patient's medical history."

"How many of you?" As she asked the question the nurse's eyes focused on the uniformed officer standing five feet behind the other three.

Before Malloy had a chance to invite himself along on the look-see, Casey replied, "Two. My client and myself. It should only take a moment."

"We're going to transfer him to the ICU after shift change. Can't it wait till then?"

Scott Malloy exhaled, decided to ignore the nurse's lame protest, pointed at the recovery room, and asked, "How many doors go in there?"

"Two. One here, one on the other side."

"Would you mind showing the officer here where the door is on the other side?"

"There's already a cop there."

Malloy wondered why everybody except for Danny Tartabull insisted on arguing with him. He said, "Then how about you humor me and show him anyway?"

The nurse made a clucking sound with her tongue and the roof of her mouth that really irritated Scott Malloy, before she marched off with a loud, "Are you coming with me?" directed to the officer in uniform.

Scott pinned Casey Sparrow with his glare. "Two minutes, Counselor. Two minutes. Clock's running."

Casey mimicked the nurse's disdainful tongue cluck. "Are you always this charming, Detective?"

Lauren had started to sense the rank infusion of energy she always felt along with an intravenous gram of Solu-Medrol. The first day the energy boost was invigorating. The house would get cleaned, spotlessly. Her bills would get paid; her checkbook balanced to the penny. The dog would get the longest walk of her life. On subsequent days, though, as gram was added to gram, the stimulant qualities would go into overdrive, and she would have the equivalent of a Pratt and Whitney engine powering her Cessna body. The drug would steal her sleep and sour her mood. By the end of the week, depression and anxiety would replace euphoria.

The night's traumas had rendered Lauren's sable hair limp and stringy, and it fell in inelegant strands to her shoulders. She wore a hospital-issue gown and had a hospital blanket spread over her knees. She smelled of hospital soap. The area around the buffalo cap on her left wrist was stained bronze with Betadine.

Casey pushed Lauren's wheelchair into the recovery room. Only one bed in the big room was occupied. Casey wheeled Lauren's chair toward it.

The skin of the man lying on the mattress was inhumanly gray, the color of wet cement. Casey thought it should be easy to identify the man—how many gray people could possibly have been reported missing out there?

The patient's right ear was red-orange like the glow of a burner on an electric range. His left arm was confined from the biceps down in a splint and soft cast. His wide forehead was scraped raw on one side. A sheet covered him to his chest, which was hairless and strong. Bands of gauze and tape wrapped the area between the top of the sheet and his nipples. Monitor wires snaked off the gurney and two infusion pumps dumped fluids into his veins, while a drain gurgled and sucked waste from a tube in his abdomen. His arms were thick and defined by long ridges of muscle, even in sleep.

Casey guessed that the man was either in his late thirties or his early forties.

"Ready?" Lauren asked.

"What's the best way to do this? Do you want to try to stand up?"

"Peripheral vision is all I have, and my left eye seems better than my right. That's how I want to look at him, sideways from my left. Help me up, Case. I feel shaky."

Casey stood next to Lauren as she raised herself from the wheelchair and supported her under one elbow and across her back.

Lauren was wearing foam-rubber hospital-issue slippers. She shuffled them on the floor as she rotated ninety degrees and tried to focus her gaze on the man on the gurney.

At first the details were too hazy. He was the outline of a man, not a man at all. Lauren was bombarded with the image of the ghost in the blue hood in the storm. The rage.

She couldn't rely on memory, she had to know. She blinked, trying to clear her vision. Tilted her head a few degrees more, steadying herself with a hand on Casey's arm.

"Oh my God," she said.

"Oh, boy, here we go, I was afraid of this," Casey said, guiding her client, who was quivering, back onto the seat of the wheelchair.

"Five minutes alone, that's it," said Malloy. "I don't have all night to wait for the two of you to decide whether you're going to tell me what you saw in there."

"What is it with you and time? You're worse than a lawyer with that watch of yours."

Casey pushed Lauren's wheelchair past Malloy into an empty nurses lounge and closed the door, leaving the detective in the hallway. She hunched down in front of her client and put one of her hands on top of each of Lauren's.

"My gosh, your hands are so warm, Lauren. I take it that you know who John Doe is?"

Lauren nodded. "Yes. His name is Kevin Quirk."

"How do you know him?"

Lauren shook her head, trying to find some way to make sense of what had happened. "I just met him a couple of days ago. He was a Secret Service agent who was assigned to protect Emma. She really likes him. God, I hope I didn't actually shoot him."

As a denial from a client charged with attempted murder, Casey had been hoping for something a little more definitive.

Scott Malloy paced nearby outside the closed door, glancing at his watch, not exactly eavesdropping, not averse to stray sounds floating his way, either.

Through the heavy door, he was pretty sure it was Casey Sparrow who he heard say, "Oh shit."

Casey said, incredulously, "You mean Emma is still being protected by the Secret Service?"

"No, she's not. Kevin's retired. He owns a security company in Colorado Springs. She had asked him for some help recently."

"The Springs? Not exactly my favorite town. What kind of help did she need?"

"Protection."

"From?"

Lauren exhaled slowly and said, "It's complicated." She forced a smile. "Emma was . . . the target of a carjacking or kidnapping attempt a few days ago."

"I don't remember reading anything about that."

"We didn't report it. Emma didn't want the press to know."

"You said 'we' didn't report it?"

"Alan and I were there, too. See, Casey, I keep telling you it's complicated."

Casey laughed affectionately.

"It *is*, Case. Really."

"You no longer have to convince me. Put your lawyer hat on for a minute. This will have to be your call because, quite simply, I don't have enough facts to make it. Do we help Malloy out, tell him who this guy is, or do you play dumb?"

Lauren considered the ramifications of helping the police with the identification. Once the authorities had Kevin Quirk's name, it would lead the police directly to Emma Spire's door.

What had Kevin been doing in the middle of the

road in front of Emma's house last night? Why was he so angry when I saw him? Why wouldn't he identify himself when I called out?

She had plenty of new questions and no real answers to any of the old ones. She said, "I think we're talking 'blind,' Case, not 'dumb.' And, no, I'm not playing."

Malloy was livid. "What do you mean, she doesn't know who it is? That's bullshit."

"Our agreement, Detective, was that it was our prerogative to decide if Lauren could determine the man's identity. She's not one hundred percent certain and we've chosen to exercise that prerogative."

"But, I heard you—" He caught himself before he revealed his eavesdropping.

"You heard me what, Detective?"

"I heard you say you and your client would like to be cooperative."

"Nice recovery, Scott. Fatigue's catching up with you, isn't it? Sometimes when you roll the dice, you crap out. This is one of those times."

"The man's health is in jeopardy. His family could provide important history. You saw him; he's in critical condition."

"Have the doctor call me. Where's Lauren's bodyguard? I'm taking her back downstairs to her room. Want to come?"

⟵⊹⟶

Cozier Maitlin's cellular phone was chirping in his pocket as he rejoined Alan and Adrienne in the kitchen. He smiled at Adrienne and said, "No smoking guns," while he flipped the phone open.

"Maitlin," he offered in greeting.

"Hi, it's Casey. I've got some news."

For a full minute, Cozy listened to Casey Sparrow's account of Lauren's identification of the wounded man. Then he spent an equal amount of time explaining to Casey about the shooting on the Downtown Mall and the imminent search of Lauren and Alan's residence. He ended the call without bothering to say good-bye.

Alan interjected, "How's Lauren?"

"About the same. Casey says they moved her to a private room and gave her something to help her go back to sleep. Casey's going to spend the night there, at the hospital, rather than trying to go home.

"Lauren ID's the guy. Said to tell you it was 'Q,' that you would fill me in on who he is."

Alan's stomach heaved. *Kevin Quirk? God, that complicates things.*

Maitlin continued, "Casey must think that somebody involved in this actually has the ability to listen in on my cell phone. Anyway, for reasons I hope you are about to make clear, Lauren elected not to share the identification of the shooting victim with Detective Malloy, who, according to Casey, 'wasn't pleasant' and who has now departed the hospital for other pastures. I imagine, this one.

"So Alan, enlighten me. Who's Q?"

Alan turned his back to his guests and put a kettle on the stove for tea. He didn't want them to see his face as he considered Lauren's revelation about the shooting victim.

"His name is Kevin Quirk. He was a Secret Service agent who protected Emma for a while."

Adrienne and Cozy settled side by side on stools that had been handmade by Adrienne's deceased husband, Peter. Alan was distracted for a moment considering what Peter would think about this middle-of-the-night state of affairs, but yanked himself back to reality after recognizing that he missed his dead friend at the oddest of times.

Cozy said, "Our shooting victim is a Secret Service agent? That should make things easy for your wife. Jesus."

"Past tense, Cozy. Quirk retired from the Secret Service, is in the computer security business. He was helping Emma now as a friend, trying to help her get the disc back."

"He didn't have this disc with him when he was shot, did he? Does anyone know that? You said he was looking for it, right?"

Adrienne was uncharacteristically quiet.

Alan chose his words carefully. He said, "Yes, Emma had told him about it being missing, and had asked for his help in getting it back. I saw him earlier today and he was going out looking for it."

"And we don't know if he was successful in that endeavor, do we? At this point we are left to assume that searching for the disc is what got him shot. God, I wonder if the police have it."

Alan felt sweat beading on his temples and thought for a moment about how he wanted to respond.

Adrienne rescued him. She turned to Cozy with a seductive smile that Alan didn't know she had in her, and said, "I suppose we could walk over to my place and ask Emma."

Cozy said, *"What?"*

"Emma's here, Cozy. She came by sometime earlier tonight. Adrienne's been providing her with shelter from the storm."

✛

Emily, the dog, greeted Adrienne and Alan at the door with a sleepy, bent-ear, butt-wagging hello. She growled deeply at Cozy.

Adrienne reprimanded her, "Shhh. You wake my baby and our love affair is over."

Emma had pulled one of Adrienne's bulky cotton sweaters over her leotard. She was curled up on a corner of the sofa in the family room flipping mindlessly between the Home Shopping Channel and an infomercial touting a new piece of home exercise equipment. When tugged out from beneath the bed by a buxom woman dressed in a thong, the thing seemed to unfold like a giant spider that was ready to pounce and devour her.

Emma gave the trio entering the room half a glance.

Emily growled at Cozy again before prancing over to Emma and laying her head on the young woman's lap. Emma touched her absently.

Alan joined Emma on the couch. Her eyes, usually

so lively, seemed to sag, not only from exhaustion, but also with the burden of something infinitely heavier. Her usually electric smile was unplugged. She had been alone in the room before Alan and Adrienne and Cozy arrived, and she was alone in the room now that there were four people and a dog in it.

Alan was startled by the regression in Emma's emotional state and by the deterioration in her appearance since he had last seen her late in the afternoon. An office word entered his head and stayed there like an unwelcome visitor from out of town. The word was "decompensation." Clinically, it described the mental state of someone whose ego had succumbed to pressures greater than it could bear.

Cozy settled into a ladderback chair at a game table far across the room and said nothing, having an instinctual awareness that a quick, polite introduction wasn't called for in this situation. Adrienne offered a sotto voce "Hi, dear" and excused herself to go upstairs and check on her toddler.

Alan waited to see if Emma was planning to speak. When it appeared she wasn't, he said, "Hello, Emma."

She didn't acknowledge that he had spoken to her. She didn't look at him.

"It's Alan, Emma. How are you?"

She thumbed the remote and found an evangelist who was encouraging her to repent her sins. The man's nose was pickled with red veins that made it easy to believe that he himself had committed enough sins to know his way around repentance.

"Tough night for you. We've been looking for you, wondering if you were okay."

She flicked channels again.

"Is there anything that I can do to help?" Although Alan's impulse was to reach over and attempt to soothe away her pain, he was keeping his physical distance. He made his voice as soft as infant's hair, inviting her to join him in *some* human interaction. Anything.

She began to move her fingers in her lap as though she were typing. Both hands danced, her fingertips pecking out imaginary keys in a pantomime of communication that Alan found affecting.

After half a minute, she stopped.

Alan said, "I wish I could read what you just wrote. But I'm not able to. Perhaps you could say some of it out loud so I could hear it."

Her long fingers straightened and again she gripped the remote control. Quickly, she found the infomercial.

Emma's shoulders sagged half an inch and she sighed.

Alan glanced back at Cozy, who, given his vocation—defending individuals whose impulses had temporarily overwhelmed their judgment—had spent more than his share of hours fencing in the excesses of people whose emotional health was about as stable as a trailer park in a tornado. Cozy raised his eyebrows and shrugged his big shoulders to indicate he didn't know how to help.

Alan's clinical acumen was screaming that he was sharing a sofa with someone who was impaired enough to be placed on a mental health hold-and-treat. Even against Emma's will, he could hospitalize her and then get a colleague to care for her for up to seventy-two hours if he judged her to be "severely impaired" or a danger to herself or others.

He confronted her more directly. "Emma, did you hear about Lauren tonight? What happened earlier?"

No response.

"She's been arrested. She was trying to help you get the disc back. It's something about a shooting."

Emma said nothing but blinked twice in rapid succession. She'd heard him. She knew.

"She's been asking about you. She's worried about you."

Another pair of fast blinks. Alan was trying to decide whether or not to inform Emma that Kevin Quirk was the victim of the shooting. He guessed that the knowledge might serve to startle her from her withdrawn state, but he also feared that the news that a friend of hers had been shot might cause old nightmares of gunfire and death to resurface, and might precipitate a further disintegration of Emma's fragile emotional condition.

Adrienne poked her head into the room and sensed the poignancy that hung like an aromatic fog. She took a step into the room and leaned her head close to Cozy when she whispered, "There are a bunch of lights coming down the lane, maybe half a dozen cars. I think it's the police. I saw them out Jonas's window."

Cozy stood up and walked over behind the couch, silently cursing police timing. He lowered himself to one knee to diminish some of his height. He knew how intimidating his size could be to someone sitting, and fearful. Usually, he tried to use his size to his advantage. Not now.

"Alan, the police are here. We have to go back to your house."

"Give me a minute, Cozy. You go. I need a little more time. Tell them I'm in the bathroom or something. I won't be long."

Cozy warned Alan. "Don't let them get suspicious of this house, Alan. We don't want them coming over here. They're looking for Emma, too, remember that. We don't know what her involvement is."

"I know."

Cozy backed out of the room to greet the police.

Alan turned back to Emma and slid forward to try and see more of her face than her profile offered, and said, bluntly, "I'm really concerned about you right now."

After what felt like an interminable, almost excruciating delay, she said, "I am, too. . . . I keep remembering what Lauren said to me, that I don't have to kill myself. . . . I'm trying to believe it." Her voice was tiny and halting, as though she hadn't spoken for a long time and was trying to remember how.

"Lauren was right, Emma. You don't have to kill yourself. We'll find another solution. There's always another way. That's not the answer."

She still hadn't looked at him.

"Maybe . . . I guess."

"I have to go back over to my house to keep the police from coming over here. If I leave you alone here for a little while, you're not going to hurt yourself, are you?"

"I don't think so. I'm too tired."

As reassurance from a suicidal person, that rationale for avoiding self-destruction was lame.

"That's not good enough, Emma. I need your assurance that you won't hurt yourself while I'm gone. I need to go to my house to meet with the police. I know you don't want them to find you, so don't go outside. I'll be back as soon as I can. Will you give me your word that you won't hurt yourself?"

"You're coming back here, though? To see me, when you're done?"

"Yes, you're safe here. No one knows that you're here. Stay put, I'll come back as soon as I can. The dog will keep you company." That, he was thinking, is partly because the dog would go absolutely batshit if she saw a platoon of people dressed like mailmen invading her house.

"Okay."

"Okay, what? You won't hurt yourself?"

"Not before you get back."

As a palliative for an anxious psychologist, it wasn't much, but it was a step or two better than "I'm too tired."

The lane was lined with vehicles. Patrol cars and unmarked detectives' cars filled the plowed area around Alan and Lauren's front door. Two Boulder County Sheriff's Jeep Cherokees had joined the parade. Alan and Lauren lived in the county, not the city, and the sheriff insisted on having a representative on the scene during the search.

Scott Malloy, stoked with a huge cup of 7-Eleven coffee, was on the small concrete stoop speaking with Cozier Maitlin. Frustrated at what he wasn't accomplishing at the ER, Malloy had decided to personally oversee the search of Lauren's home. Alan had been hoping that Sam Purdy would be one of the detectives on the scene, but he wasn't.

Alan was reluctant to go home to watch what the police were planning to do to his home. Some insults, he decided, shouldn't be observed. He joined Adrienne on her front porch. She was surveying the activity, trying to blow vapor rings in the frigid air.

"I'm going to have to get someone to hospitalize her."

Adrienne blew another ring. "I figured that. Tonight?"

Alan gestured at the circus across the lane. "I think so. As soon as they leave. I should go home first, check things out. Will you keep an eye on Emma?"

"Of course. You have fun. Go watch your privacy get trampled."

A detective Alan didn't recognize broke away from the group that was huddled outside his front door and started down the path that led to the tackhouse, Peter's old studio.

Alan called out for him to stop. The studio was on Adrienne's property, not Alan and Lauren's. There was no way the cop had any legal right to examine it or search it. Alan didn't want them discovering the window that Emma had broken.

But the detective either didn't hear Alan or didn't care about his warning.

Adrienne wasn't so timid. She jumped on her John

Deere, which was parked nearby, powered it up, and aimed it straight at the detective, whose hands were stuffed deep in his pockets. Three times she flashed the beady little headlights of the tractor, while she laid on the horn as though she was intent on warning the officer about the imminence of Armageddon.

The detective raised his head and stopped, startled at the artillery that was approaching him. Before she pulled the tractor to a halt a few feet from him, he had backed off into a drift that reached to his waist. He asked what the fuck she thought she was doing. Adrienne responded in kind, and they proceeded to have a loud and heated discussion about the limitations of search warrants and about whose property actually belonged to whom.

Adrienne eventually prevailed in the argument— she was louder, and she had the tractor—and the detective retreated back down the plowed trail to join his colleagues in the other search, the legal one.

Alan walked across the lane and reluctantly went inside his house. After first asking permission from Scott Malloy whether he was allowed to sit, he collapsed on his favorite green leather chair and stared at the lights in the city. He was still wearing his coat, and, despite his intention to stay observant, he found it incredibly hard to keep from dozing off.

For the next half hour Adrienne patrolled the courtyard with John Deere, daring any of the authorities to cross the line onto her property.

When he wasn't keeping an eye on the cops, Cozier Maitlin was keeping an eye on Adrienne. He was beginning to enjoy her mildly deviant approach to the world.

When Sam Purdy left Alan and Cozy in Alan's car on the Mall, he returned to his department Tempo to wait for orders. Sam didn't relish his current role, which basically involved sitting around trying to stay both awake and warm until the brass decided whether or not he should assist with the execution of the search at Alan and Lauren's house.

Sam had already concluded that something smelled about the shooting Lauren was involved in and that something smelled about this latest shooting at the Mall.

Radio traffic sucked his attention away from the fact that he was starving. A frantic adolescent was reporting a no-bodily-injury drive-by shooting up near Chautauqua.

Sam considered the location of the shooting and allowed himself to conjure up some possibilities. He picked up his radio transmitter and told dispatch he'd be happy to respond to the scene. He thought the dispatcher sounded inordinately grateful.

Sam took his time on the messy streets and by the time he arrived at the site of the latest incident, the kid was irate. He told Sam he was sure he was the innocent victim of a drive-by by some punks from Longmont with whom he'd had some trouble after a recent football game.

Sam figured that what was more likely was that

the kid's windshield had been pocked by a stone. The resulting little chip in the glass had proceeded to grow from tiny pimple to bullet-size star when the mercury dropped precipitously with this damn storm. Happened all the time during cold weather in Colorado.

The puky, pea-green crescent of paint exposed at the roofline of the car made Sam think he was looking at an old Mazda. No tire tracks scarred the flat sea of snow around it. But the snow *was* compacted in a long line that led from where the kid had shuffled up to the car from a nearby house and was flattened in an irregular pattern in the spot where the kid had stood while he scraped the windshield. Sam could see no sign that the car had been driven since shortly after the snow had started falling in torrents late the previous afternoon.

He asked the kid, anyway. "What time did you say you parked here?"

"Before dinner. It was just getting dark."

That was consistent, thought Sam. "Was it snowing?"

"Not heavy, maybe some flurries."

Sam didn't feel much like talking about the weather. Fatigue made him forgetful and it made him cranky. He reminded himself to be thorough. "You haven't moved the car since then?"

"No, I've been with my girlfriend all night. She lives there." He pointed at her house.

Sam couldn't tell whether the kid was trying to be helpful or whether he was bragging.

"Is this going to take long? If her parents come home and see me out here at this time of the morning, I swear, it's not going to be pretty for anybody."

He plastered a "you know what I mean" smirk on his face in a manner that Sam found irritating. He wasn't predisposed to feel much sympathy for the young man's postcoital problems.

"And this hole wasn't here before, when you drove up?" Sam had his long flashlight focused on a small round crater in the windshield.

"I told them that already. Don't you people talk to each other? Jesus. How long is this going to take? I think I'd notice a bullet hole in the middle of my damn windshield."

Sam Purdy's patience was exhausted. Gruffly, he said, "I don't know if you'd notice a bullet hole in the middle of anything but your dick, wiseass. When I ask you a question, I want an answer, not evidence of your ignorance."

The kid stomped his boots, rubbing his gloved hands over his arms. "Can I get in my car? It's freezing out here. I want to try to get warm."

"No, you can't get in your car. Your car's a goddamn crime scene. It's *mine,* until I decide to give it back. You understand?" Sam was using the piercing eyes he usually reserved for felons.

The kid said, "Jee-zus Christ."

"If you want to get warm, go sit in my car. Go ahead. Get in the back. Wait. Give me your keys and your license first."

The kid fumbled around in his jacket pocket before handing Purdy his driver's license and a ring of keys the size of a monkey's fist.

Purdy tossed the wad of metal back, "Find me the right key. If it doesn't open the trunk, get me that one, too."

While the kid wrestled with his car keys, Purdy was wishing that the Boulder Police Department owned a helicopter. He couldn't tell for sure, but he was almost certain that this crappy Mazda's windshield was pointing on a direct line toward Emma Spire's driveway. If he had a helicopter, he knew he could determine, in about two seconds, if a straight line passed between the two points.

He was guessing maybe a fifty-foot change in elevation. Adjust for trajectory and he was willing to bet that if he stretched a wire from Emma Spire's driveway over the guy who almost croaked in the middle of the road, it would end at this guy's Mazda. My shield for a helicopter, he thought.

He trudged back to the car and found his street map of Boulder on the passenger seat under a two-day-old Burger King bag. He squinted and extended his arms until he was able to bring the tiny line indicating the street he was on into focus. Next, he found Emma Spire's street and scratched a dot at the approximate location of Emma's house and another at the location of the spot in the middle of the street where the guy with the bullet hole was run over by the car.

With a pencil, he drew a line between those two points and continued the line straight to the next street. The penciled mark led him to the spot where he was sitting.

He decided that the theory he was entertaining was possible. He ferreted out the implications and didn't like them. Every damn scenario seemed to indicate that there was a second gun involved in whatever had happened up here with Lauren.

He got on his radio and rousted his partner, Lucy Tanner, out of bed and told her to find a metal detector and bring him some coffee.

Sleepily, she told him to fuck off.

He said, "Please," gave her Emma's address, and knew he would see her in twenty minutes.

"We're going for a ride," Purdy announced to the kid in the Tempo as he pulled himself into the driver's seat.

"Where are you taking me? What the hell did I do?" The young man had completed a quick journey from feeling victimized by punks from Longmont to feeling victimized by the police.

Purdy didn't know what the hell to do with the kid. He couldn't leave him with his damn car. The kid might do something stupid, like move it.

"You didn't do anything. You want to get to the bottom of this, don't you? You and me are going to do some investigating. You can be like my sidekick. It wouldn't be fair of me to leave you there with your dick hanging out for your young lover's parents to find, would it?"

Sam expected that the kid had all his adolescent antennae tuned to recognize when he was being patronized. He was right.

"This is bull*shit*. Let me out of here. I'm the one whose car was trashed. You're treating me like I'm the goddamn criminal. I'm a *victim* here." He said the word as though the cop should consider it some kind of badge of honor.

Purdy pressured his brakes until the ABS took over and eased the car to a stop. He rotated slowly in his seat until he was staring the smartass kid right in the face. "How old is the girl you been screwing? Maybe I should investigate that, see if maybe we have another crime worth considering?"

Sam Purdy turned back to the business of navigating through the thick, heavy snow. He knew the twerp was done whining.

Eighteen minutes after Sam's call, Lucy drove up with the metal detector. She didn't have the coffee he'd requested, she wasn't wearing any makeup, and she wasn't in a good mood.

Sam walked over to the car.

"Don't say a fucking word, Sam. I was up late last night. Real late."

Sam said, "Luce, I'm way too tired to criticize. I'm *still* up late last night. Thanks for coming."

"You kidding me? You been up all night? You do look like shit. What's going on?"

He filled her in on the events of the evening, a concise version that would fit in *USA Today*.

"So what's this for?" She pointed at the metal detector on her passenger seat.

"Need to find a cartridge casing under the snow. I know where to look." He pointed at the adjacent driveway. "We start at the sidewalk and work our way up. That's Emma Spire's house, by the way."

"No shit? Is that important? Is she part of this?"

Sam shrugged and pointed to his gut.

Lucy nodded and got out of the car. She was wearing jeans that fit her like cellophane. They were tucked into the top of tan Sorels. Five minutes to get ready, or five hours, Lucy Tanner knew how to dress.

*   *   *

Within minutes they had located the cartridge casing on the sidewalk. Sam instructed the officers who had been guarding the earlier scene to extend the boundary to include the sidewalk in front of Emma Spire's house. He also called for CSIs to come back.

Sam and Lucy and the adolescent headed back to the Mazda on the next block. This time it took Sam and Lucy ten minutes to find the bullet, which was embedded in the backseat cushion of the kid's filthy car. Lucy taped off the area around the vehicle while Sam got patched through to the CSIs on the next block. He told them he had discovered a slug that he wanted recovered immediately.

A crime scene investigator arrived and efficiently recovered the bullet from the Mazda and turned it over to Lucy. She lofted the evidence bag and said to Sam, "You think this is the bullet from Lauren's gun?"

"Yeah. Fits the facts. She shoots a warning shot up in the air. The trajectory carries it here. I want to go back and get some quick ballistics on the casing and the slug. See if they're from Lauren's gun. I think they will be. If they are, then we have to start looking for a second shooter."

"Lauren fired only one round? That's certain?"

"That's the way it looks. Her weapon's a little Glock. One round missing from the magazine."

"Do you know why she fired?"

He shrugged his shoulders. "Like I said, I'd guess warning shot. Maybe accidental discharge. She has a lawyer. She's not saying. There's a reason though."

"And you and Scott are both convinced the victim was shot at close range?"

"Burn marks on the victim's coat are real tight. Forensics will bear it out. And that shell casing we found is—what would you say—maybe fifty feet from where the victim fell?"

"At least, maybe more. So what are you saying? Was the guy hit here? Or someplace else?"

"Good question, Luce."

She kicked some snow off her Sorels. "So if Lauren didn't do it, who did?"

He pointed at his belly again.

She scoffed, "*Emma Spire?* I don't want to hear it, Sammy. As a matter of fact, if your gut is right this time I'm going to tell everybody I never got out of bed this morning."

✛

When her automatic garage door began to creak and clang as it slid up on its tracks, and when the overhead light flashed on, Adrienne grew concerned. When the sound of an engine cranking to life roared above the drone of her tractor motor, and the headlights of Emma's car began to glow, Adrienne grew alarmed.

The little John Deere tractor was built for stamina, not for speed, and Adrienne didn't have enough time to get across the lane to intercept Emma before she pulled her car out of the garage and pointed it down the lane.

Adrienne knew that she certainly couldn't scream, "Emma, stop, don't go," in front of a dozen cops who were searching the county for her.

The uniformed officer who had been assigned to monitor the maniacal woman who was driving the tractor saw the car coming out of the garage, and the bundled silhouette of someone behind the wheel, and yelled to Adrienne, "Who is that?"

Adrienne answered, "That's my baby-sitter," before recovering her wits and saying, "What's it to you? That's *my* house. My garage. You have a warrant for that, too? If not . . ." She didn't finish.

Helplessly, she watched the taillights of Emma's car disappearing down the road.

Adrienne parked her tractor as close to Alan's front door as she could, killed the engine, and stomped past two cops. She was looking for Alan or the tall lawyer to give them the news about Emma's departure.

They would not be pleased. She felt like a sentry who had failed her platoon.

She found Cozy first. She whispered, "Our friend's gone. Drove away. Where's Alan?"

Alan couldn't figure any of it out.

Adrienne was dressed head to toe in pink nylon and was shaking his shoulders telling him to wake up. A man who looked nine feet tall towered above her saying, "Come on now, wake up."

Alan's dendrites were frayed. Whatever replenishment sleep was supposed to provide to the brain, he had enjoyed an insufficient amount. For a moment he wondered if he had suffered a concussion that he couldn't recall.

"What, what?"

Adrienne leaned over and whispered. "She's gone. I blew it. I'm sorry."

"Who's gone?" Alan's mind hadn't even decided which volume of current reality Adrienne was discussing. He was still trying to remember who the tall guy was.

Adrienne jerked her head in the direction of her own house. "You know."

"Emily ran away?" Alan's heart sank. God, he couldn't stand to lose another dog. Adrenaline jump-started his central nervous system.

Adrienne said, "No, the other 'she.' Remember— at my house—lying on the couch? The one with the problem."

Emma.

Oh God. The pieces came back, like successive images at a slide show. Lauren is in the hospital, under arrest. The tall guy is her lawyer. The cops are here— *in my house*—searching for God knows what. The optical disc is still missing.

And now Emma is gone.

"What? How?"

"She took her car, just drove away. I was on John Deere keeping the cops from my place. I didn't think she'd run. I blew it. I'm sorry."

He sighed. "You didn't blow it, Ren. I did. How many times can I misjudge somebody in one day?"

Adrienne apologized twice more before going back home to be with her son. Cozy stayed to see the last of the cops out the door.

Alan wanted to be alone. He also had a comforting urge to pick up the phone and page Sam Purdy and offer to meet him at the Village Coffee Shop for an early breakfast. He wanted to share a pot of bitter coffee or two and have a number five over easy with double hash browns and watch Sam eat a number three with sausage *and* a full stack of buttermilk pancakes. He wanted to tell Sam everything and get some advice about what to do. He wanted a friend.

Instead he had Cozy Maitlin.

Cozy said a final good-bye to Scott Malloy and suggested that the cop go home and get some sleep as he watched the parade of police vehicles slide back down the lane.

Cozy said, "No bloody socks in the bedroom. That's a relief."

Alan said, "I have to find Emma, Cozy. I think she's in serious jeopardy."

"Are you speaking as a psychologist—or as an amateur lawyer?"

"Both, I'm afraid."

"We're running out of places to look for Emma."

"We need to think of new ones, then. We need to anticipate what she'll do."

"She can't hide, Alan. By morning the press is going to be on this like white on rice. They'll find Emma for us in the next few hours. They or the cops."

"I'm afraid they'll find her dead, Cozy."

"I hope you're wrong. But right now, I think our attention, yours and mine, needs to be on getting your wife out of custody. Emma's welfare is secondary."

Alan was thinking about his wife's welfare. "Lauren's getting what she needs in the hospital. She's exactly where she'd be even if she wasn't under arrest. She didn't shoot anybody. Her legal mess will turn out all right as soon as we find Emma and the damn disc. I feel . . . totally confident about that. Right now our focus has to be on finding Emma."

Cozy's reply was suspicious. "Has Lauren told you something you haven't told me? How can you be so cavalier about her situation? Lauren doesn't even seem sure she didn't do it. The police love smoking guns. Your wife handed them one."

Alan rubbed sleep from his eyes. "Are you my lawyer?"

"Yes."

Alan slid his hands down his scruffy face and decided he was nearly twenty-four hours into a new beard. "Have we paid you anything yet?"

"No. We'll take care of that during business hours."

Alan removed his wallet and handed Cozy all the bills in it. Cozy counted eighty-six dollars.

"Is this a down payment, or do you really want to hire me for only twenty-three minutes?"

Alan allowed a smile before turning his back on Cozy and looking outside at the sky. He wished Emily was home. He liked the dog's company when he was anxious.

He said, "I know Lauren didn't shoot that man, Cozy, because . . . now that I know it was Kevin Quirk who was shot, there's a good chance that I did it."

Cozy swallowed hard and fell back on the sofa as

though he'd been pushed. In front of him, the western sky was black. His face could not have conveyed more skepticism than it did at that moment. "Yes, go on," he said.

Alan unzipped an inner pocket of his heavy coat and, with two fingers on the wooden stock, pulled a handgun from his pocket.

He said, "I think this may be the gun that shot Kevin Quirk."

Cozy eyed the weapon, which he pegged as a .38. His voice crisper than it had been, he said, "I'm assuming you're too tired to bullshit me."

"That's true. I am." With a loud *clunk*, Alan placed the weapon on the big coffee table.

"Is it yours? The revolver?"

"No. I don't own a gun. I don't even know how to fire one."

"But you somehow managed?" Cozy tried to say this without sarcasm, but he didn't quite succeed.

"I guess."

Cozy fought an urge to move into a rapid-fire interrogation while he pondered the ground they were on. He knew he had to tread carefully. "Do you have a tape recorder we might use? I'd like to record this conversation."

"Why?"

"To quote your lovely wife, 'I'm afraid this is going to be complicated.' It is, isn't it?"

"Yes."

"Do you have any coffee, Alan? Maybe something to eat?"

"I thought you were a tea man?"

"Some things require coffee. This is one."

EIGHT

Friday, October 11. 6:30 P.M.
26 Degrees, Heavy Snow

As Alan led the way down Arapahoe through the blizzard to Eben Fine Park, the first conclusion he reached was that Kevin Quirk was an arrogant man.

The only cogent explanation Alan could muster for someone to have arranged this rendezvous at Eben Fine Park during a snowstorm was to set up an ambush. The only explanation for Kevin Quirk agreeing to meet there was that he felt superior to his adversaries. Alan thought that Quirk's testosterone level probably needed adjusting.

The second conclusion Alan reached during the short drive was that inviting himself along for the ride was rank stupidity. If he survived this, Lauren was going to kill him.

Alan led Quirk west down Arapahoe, then across the narrow drive to the small parking area on the south side of the park. Theirs were the only two vehicles in the lot.

Quirk pulled up on the driver's side of the Land Cruiser and opened his passenger window.

Alan lowered his window. He asked, "Are we early?"

"No. You stay here. I'm going to go look around."

"You sure that's a wise idea?"

Quirk grinned. "What? Me looking around? Or you staying here?"

"At least tell me where you're going."

"I'm going to walk around the perimeter and approach from the other side. I think the optical drive will be stashed someplace obvious, maybe on a picnic table or something. I'll get it and come back here."

Alan looked beyond Kevin at the fury of the storm. "It's snowing so hard that I don't think you'll find anything out there, even if there's a bouquet of helium balloons tied to it."

"Just wait here."

Alan closed his window and killed his engine. He turned the key so that he could use his windshield wipers occasionally. Quirk disappeared from Alan's view five steps away from the car.

Having nothing better to do to manage his anxiety, Alan noted the time. He was in the midst of a silent argument with himself about how long he would wait before either going for some help or doing something inane like wandering into the park and looking for Quirk when a third car pulled into the lot. The driver chose to park as far as possible from the two vehicles already there.

Alan listened, heard a door thud shut. Just one. For a moment he thought he saw a flash of yellow and then the outline of a solitary person heading toward the park, but he couldn't be sure. He checked the clock on the dashboard. Kevin Quirk had been gone four minutes.

Alan got out of his car, told himself he would be careful. He followed a pair of fresh footprints and guessed he was about halfway across the grass center of the park when he heard someone bark a crisp order, *"Don't go down there. It's a trap!"*

Alan froze. Was that warning intended for him? Had that been Kevin Quirk? Or was someone *else* warning Kevin? Or warning a third person about Kevin?

Alan listened, wanting to hear the voice again. For a moment everything was hushed and insular, the special white quiet that exists only in snowstorms.

Alan took three more steps. The next sound he heard came from an area twenty feet or so in front of him, to his left. It was a dull thud.

"Get out of here! Shit!"

Again Alan stopped. Was that the same voice? He didn't think so. He crouched down close to the snowy ground. Who was warning whom?

In front of him, he could just discern the outline of the large boulders along the creek, but he didn't see any forms he could identify as people.

Alan kept close to the ground, scooting on his hands and feet in the snow. Suddenly, close by, though not right next to him, he heard the sounds of a scuffle.

"No! He has a gun!"

Alan stopped. That was the first voice again, the one that had warned about a trap. *Who has a gun?* He considered calling out to Kevin Quirk but realized he would immediately become a potential target for whoever had the gun.

After another dull thud, the muffled sounds of people fighting while wearing parkas and gloves abruptly stopped. With the suddenness of an apparition, someone came running from the direction of the noise. Whoever it was never saw Alan crouched close to the ground.

The impact sent the fleeing person flying and left Alan on his back, stunned. A handgun rested heavily against his leg. He pulled himself to sitting, tugged off a glove, and lifted the weapon.

Tentatively, he called out, "Quirk?"

From behind him, whomever he had inadvertently tackled jumped on his shoulders.

The gun went off.

The person who had grabbed him immediately let go.

Quirk, his voice so close to Alan that they could've reached out and touched, said, "Alan, damn you, run. Get out of here."

Alan turned to try to find the person who had tripped over him. He couldn't.

"*Kevin?*" he whispered.

"I said get out of here. Now."

Alan looked all around him, saw only white. Still clutching the handgun, he did what Quirk ordered.

He ran.

He expected to be stopped. He wasn't. He jumped into his car and started driving.

He felt like a complete coward.

NINE

When Sam Purdy and Lucy Tanner arrived at the Police Department on 33rd, Lucy parked the kid with the shitty Mazda on a bench in the lobby and told him not to move his ass. She stared him in the eyes until he flinched and said, "Yes, ma'am."

None of the personnel in the Police Department even said "good morning" to Sam or Lucy, not with the don't-mess-with-me looks on their faces.

They walked upstairs to the ballistics laboratory and entered without knocking.

Sam deposited the small evidence bags containing the cartridge casing and the slug on the laboratory bench of the department's fire-arms examiner, who was sitting on a high stool staring at the wall, wondering why the hell he had been called in the middle of the night to run tests on a handgun. He didn't see any reason that the tests couldn't have waited till morning.

Sam had known the criminalist for eight years but didn't know the man's full name. His name tag said G. Everett. Everyone in the department called him

Everett. Sam figured that the guy's kids called him Everett.

Lauren's Glock, already worked for prints, now tagged as ballistics evidence, sat on a plastic tray on the far corner of the worktable.

Sam lifted the tag on the gun and confirmed that it was the one Lauren had been carrying the night before. He pointed to his evidence bags and said, "Hey, Everett. My question is simple. Were this shell and this slug fired from that weapon? We'll wait for your answer."

Everett took a quick glance at Sam, another at Lucy, and decided to forgo whatever it was that he had been planning on doing during the next half hour.

"Have a seat, guys," he said. Neither detective took the suggestion. Sam was afraid he would fall asleep if he sat down.

Everett lifted the first envelope from the counter, opened it, peered inside, and then emptied the contents, a single brass cartridge casing, onto a clean sheet of lab paper.

"Have these been dusted?"

"No, sorry, Everett. I should have told you that. I'm tired."

Everett pulled on fresh latex gloves, carefully picked up the casing, and squinted at the head stamp. "It's the right caliber." Lifting a magnifying glass, he examined the specimen more closely. "And it's the same manufacturer as the rest of the load that I recovered from the magazine of the weapon." He gestured toward the Glock on the table.

With gloved fingers, Everett lifted the casing and

placed it on one side of his comparison microscope. He placed a control casing from a test firing he had done an hour earlier on the other side of the microscope. For almost ten minutes he peered through the lenses, adjusting dials, fiddling, and rotating his specimens.

"Tentatively?"

"Yeah," said Purdy, who was almost nodding off in the warm laboratory.

"It's a match. I'll get more specific when I haven't been up all night and I don't have you two breathing down my neck, but given the ejector and extractor markings, I'd say it's real likely these casings were both fired by the same weapon. You want me to get more technical about why?"

Sam shook his head. "God forbid. What about the slug?"

Everett changed his gloves and repeated the same procedure, this time placing a test bullet he'd fired earlier alongside the slightly misshapen bullet that came from the Mazda.

"Bullets are both copper-jacketed but the nose is deformed on yours. What did this impact?"

"Safety glass for sure, I don't know, maybe a little sheet metal."

"Did it pass through anything first?"

Sam shrugged his shoulders. The act felt like hard labor.

Everett was silent for at least five minutes as he finessed the controls of the microscope. Then he said, "Again, tentatively, another match. I have to confirm the measurements of the lands and grooves but there're good impressions to work with in the copper. I'll bet a Dr Pepper on a match. Both bullets from the same weapon."

Everett stole a glance away from his microscope and eyed the two detectives. Everett didn't know whether or not he was telling them what they wanted to hear. Scientifically, it didn't matter to him one way or another, but he liked his job best when performing his science made the detectives happy.

He asked, "Is this good news or bad?"

"For whom?"

Everett shrugged, he'd said enough. Sam Purdy, one of his favorite detectives on the force, was acting as though he were in serious need of a root canal.

"It's good news for you, Everett, because we're going to get out of your face. Thanks for your help."

Everett said, "Are you leaving these with me?"

Lucy said, "Absolutely."

"You have to sign for them. I need to get the casing dusted for prints."

Lucy scrawled her signature on the tracking forms.

The detectives walked out of the laboratory

Everett exhaled as though he'd been swimming underwater for five minutes.

Sam brought Lucy a cup of coffee. She was sitting with her feet up on his desk in his cubicle. He slouched back on a nearby chair.

"Now what?" she asked.

"We have to find Scott. Tell him he's made a little mistake."

Lucy said, "I'm glad this disaster is his, not mine. Imagine—falsely collaring a DA? Not on my tour, shit. This is going to smell for a long time."

"Scott's a good cop."

She raised a hand in self-defense. "No argument. I like Scott. I feel bad for him. Based on what you've told me so far, I would've brought her in, too. I just don't envy the shoes he's in."

"Lauren's not going to be vindictive."

"Woman has an acid stream in her blood sometimes, Sam. I've seen her on fire. You have, too."

Sam shook his head hard from side to side and rubbed his eyes. "Lauren's mellowed, Luce. She doesn't piss fire like she used to. She appreciates cops who do their jobs. Scott's been doing his job all night long. When she sees that, they'll kiss and make up. Listen, what do you say we arrange to get her released? I want to go home and get to bed. Let's find Scott."

Before Sam had a chance to pick up his phone, Scott found them. He was returning from the search of Lauren and Alan's house. He seemed jacked up about something.

He leaned over the divider between his cubicle and Sam's and said, "Searched her house, found *nada*. Nothing. Did get to watch Fuchs get chased around by a giant pink bunny rabbit on a John Deere, which was almost worth the price of admission. You know that annoying little doctor from the hospital? The one whose husband was diced at the Boulder Theater? She's a matinee all by herself. But we didn't find anything during the search.

"This shooting on the Mall, though, it's fishy. Han's alarm company receives a silent warning about an intruder a good twenty minutes before this Morgan guy says he fired at the burglar. I'm wondering if Morgan wasn't the burglar himself, staged the whole thing, and fired the gun to cover his entry. And we have a solid lead that Ethan Han has been dating Emma Spire. Too many coincidences for me, I think I'm going to—"

"Scott, sit."

"Like I said, I have some calls to make, Sam. I have to track down the chief trial deputy. And I want to find Han. I'm thinking maybe he changed the security code on his alarm to trap one of his employees. Maybe later."

"Scott, *sit*."

The tone of Sam's directive caused Scott to focus. He walked around the gray partition and took the chair next to Lucy. The three people filled the narrow confines of Sam's cubicle. Scott Malloy felt his tired muscles begin to ache.

"Hi Luce," he said in a belated greeting. "You've been shanghaied on this, too?"

"Yeah. Understand it's been a long night."

"That's the truth. What's up, Sam? I'm kind of busy." Just then, Scott Malloy recognized the expression on Sam Purdy's face. "Oh God, you're about to tell me something that's going to make me wish I was dead. Are my kids okay?"

Sam sighed. He felt awful about adding to the young cop's burdens. Scott Malloy already looked like compost.

"It wasn't Lauren who shot your John Doe last night, Scott."

"What?" Whatever color was left in Malloy's face drained away.

"Lucy and I found the slug that came from her gun. It was a block and a half away. It hit a car.

Given the trajectory, there's no way it went through the John Doe first. We have to cut Lauren free."

When Scott finally spoke again he had slumped way down on his chair. "Tell me, go ahead. Go slowly, my brain is mush," he said.

Sam related the events around the asshole kid and the bullet-pocked Mazda and the vandalism complaint and the subsequent discovery of the shell casing by Emma Spire's driveway.

"What about ballistics?"

"Everett's already tentatively confirmed that both the shell and the slug were from Lauren's weapon."

Scott puffed out his cheeks and exhaled loudly. "Does Pons know yet?"

"Nobody knows but us."

"I'm roadkill. The brass is going to fry me up and cover me with gravy. My first capital and this is what I do with it. I collar a deputy DA and then I'm forced to cut her loose twelve hours later."

Sam looked at his watch. "More like ten, but who's counting?"

Scott was reviewing the night, replaying his treatment of Lauren, looking for anything she could use against him. He was busily convincing himself that he had been reasonable, even accommodating to her. He remembered, though, not letting her see the doctor before he took her to the jail. And he remembered she was kidnapped from the ER when he left her unguarded. That wasn't good.

"I'm roadkill. I'm a dead skunk."

Lucy said, "Sam will talk to Lauren for you, Scott. She'll understand what you had to do."

Sam glared at Lucy for offering his help without

talking to him first. He knew she was right, though; he would talk to Lauren on Scott's behalf.

"Sam has a gut feeling about where we should look next."

Scott attempted to make an optimistic face. He opened his eyes as wide as he could, but he ended up looking like a drunk trying to appear sober.

Lucy continued, "Emma Spire."

Scott groaned.

Sam asked, "Anyone know where the hell she is?"

"Not me. Give me that phone, will you, Sam?" Scott Malloy punched in the number of the hospital and was connected to the nursing station closest to Lauren's room. He identified himself and asked for Casey Sparrow.

"She's asleep."

"Wake her."

"She's in the patient's room. I don't want to disturb my patient."

"Wake her."

Two minutes later, Casey Sparrow snapped, "This better be good."

"This is Detective Malloy. Please get yourself and your client presentable. We'll see you in ten minutes. There have been some developments."

"What developments? She's sleeping."

"Wake her. Ten minutes." He hung up and turned to Sam with a half-smile. "None of this has been on my terms all night. The damn woman's under *arrest* and still she's been running this like it's a film she's directing. If it kills me, at least I'm going to release her on my own terms."

"Which damn woman you talking about, Scott?"

✛

Cozier Maitlin was sitting at the kitchen counter trying to make sense of Alan's story about shooting Kevin Quirk.

Across the room, Alan dipped bread into batter for French toast. Butter was beginning to foam on the griddle.

"How many do you want, Cozy?"

"At least three pieces. No, make that four; I'm starving. That's how it ends? After the gun went off, you just left the park and got in your car and came back here?"

"Yes. That's how I *thought* it ended. I was waiting for Lauren to come home so she could give me some advice about what to do. I didn't know if I had broken any laws in the park. I mean, it wasn't my gun and I certainly didn't intend to fire it. I certainly didn't think anyone had been hurt. But instead of coming home, she called me from the police department. And now I find out it was Quirk that was shot."

"Do you piece it together any differently?"

Alan dropped a slice of saturated bread onto the griddle. "I'm wondering if the shot must have hit Kevin Quirk. After he yelled at me to run, he somehow managed to get to his car and drive to Emma's house. To warn her. To help her. To blackmail her. I don't know what he was planning. When Lauren saw him, she was scared, fired a warning shot. He collapsed in the street. When the cops found him bleeding to death, everyone figured she shot him."

"Who ran him over?"

"I don't know. Someone who followed him to Emma's house from the park?"

"Who was in the park with you besides Quirk? Who was he scuffling with?"

"Whoever it was who stole the disc. And—I'm guessing here—Ethan Han. I think Ethan was the one warning Kevin about the trap."

Steam rose as Alan slid the last piece of dripping bread onto the griddle.

"This will be enough to get Lauren released, right?"

Cozy sipped coffee. "Perhaps."

"Why only 'perhaps'?"

"Who's going to corroborate your version? I can imagine that when they hear you tell it, it will sound to the police like a valiant husband pleading, 'please, take me, not her.' "

"Kevin will corroborate it."

"If he lives. And if his involvement in this wasn't criminal in the first place. Otherwise, he'd incriminate himself. He doesn't sound like the type."

Alan sighed, checked to see if any of the French toast was ready to be flipped. He said, "Ethan Han, then."

"Maybe, if Han was actually there. And if he's willing to admit it to the police."

"Can't I prove I fired the gun? Isn't there some test or something they can do to show I fired a gun?"

"You said you showered when you got home?"

"Yes."

"Then it's too late to test for residue or trace metals. Sorry."

"You don't even think I can get myself arrested? Damn it. I think I'm the guy who shot Kevin Quirk."

"It's very possible no one will believe you. You've seen for yourself what this amount of snow does to evidence."

"Then the gun will have to convince them. They can match it, can't they?"

"If they had the bullet. But they don't. The round that hit Kevin Quirk went clean through him. If your version is correct, it's someplace in the park, or in the creek. Or in a squirrel. Needle in a haystack." Cozy eyed his breakfast with longing. He thought it was browning up nicely.

"You have another problem with the weapon that I don't think you've considered. You don't know who it belongs to. Someone finds out you have it, they might say that you stole it and used it to assault Quirk. Intentionally, not accidentally."

Alan hadn't considered that angle. "If I'm not careful, this situation could blow up in my face?"

"Yes, easily." Cozy reached across the counter, grabbed the coffee pot, and refilled his mug. He glanced at his watch. "Do you get the *Daily Camera*? I want to see if the press has picked up on any of this."

Alan told Cozy where to find the box for the local paper. He pulled on his coat and boots and headed outside to the lane.

As Cozy walked back in with the *Daily Camera* still wrapped, Alan slid the entire first batch of French toast onto a plate. Cozy drowned the bread in syrup and began eating.

"You're my lawyer, what do you recommend I do?"

"Open a restaurant. These are delicious."

The phone rang.

"Alan? This is Casey. Something's up. Malloy just called. He's coming down here, to the hospital. I think you and Cozy should be here, too."

Alan looked at his watch as though he needed a reminder of what time it was. "What does Scott want?"

Cozy stopped chewing and listened to Alan's half of the conversation.

"He wouldn't say. My fear is that it's not good. He just said he'd be here pronto."

Alan felt the burden of his secret, the knowledge about what had happened the night before in Eben Fine Park.

"How's Lauren?"

"Same, I think, still sleeping. I haven't woken her yet. Want to know what I need from you? I need Emma. Tell me you found her. I'd really like to have that card in my hand when Scott gets here."

"We found her once, Casey, but we lost her again."

"Well, I'd love a few minutes with her, if you guys can pull that off, it will greatly increase my leverage with the cops."

Cozy could barely contain the thrust of his adrenaline. He inhaled the remainder of his breakfast while Alan called Diane Estevez and asked her to cover his practice for the day. Diane, of course, had a million questions. Alan provided a capsule version of what

had happened overnight and said he'd fill her in on
the details later.

The big Toyota was in four-wheel drive all the way
downtown. Cozy whistled some old Springsteen as
he unwrapped the newspaper.

Alan glanced over, read the bold type, and felt great
relief that his wife's name wasn't in the headlines.

"Anything there?"

"There's a small piece about a shooting overnight
near Chautauqua. But mostly the front page is all
about the snowstorm."

"Is Lauren's name mentioned in the article on
the shooting?"

"Don't see it. No."

"So far, so good then," Alan said, as he pulled to
a stop on Fifteenth Street, at the east end of the Mall.

Cozy asked, "Why are we stopping here?"

"Casey is adamant about talking with Emma.
Ethan's place is on our way. I thought I'd see if
she's there."

"I'll wait here. I want to try to reach Casey again,
see if she's heard anything new."

✛

The combination of megadose steroids and sleeping medication left Lauren feeling like a drunk who
had sucked down a half-dozen lattes. She absorbed
the sounds of Casey trying to rouse her, the words
registering with the dull impact of a head hitting
a goosedown pillow.

"What . . . Casey . . . who's coming? . . . what do they want?"

"Try and wake up, babe. I don't know what's up. All Scott Malloy said was that they would be here to see us in a few minutes. They must've found something. Some evidence, a witness. I don't know."

Lauren tried to think it through. "What time is it? Is it morning?"

"Almost six."

"It can't be good news, then. Scott wouldn't hurry over for that. Not at this hour. I bet he died. Kevin Quirk. They're coming to tell me it's a homicide now."

Casey didn't want to get into a pessimism contest with her client at five-thirty in the morning. "You want to freshen up?"

Lauren moved her eyes and thought the pain had diminished overnight. She still couldn't see well, only dark and light, some vague shapes in her periphery. Another of the myriad side effects from the steroids had kicked in—her mouth tasted as though she had been sucking on pennies. "We need to tell Alan."

"I already did. He and Cozy are on their way."

"Thanks. I think I just want to wash my face and brush my teeth. I don't trust myself walking. Will you bring me some water and a basin? Am I decent?" She picked at the armhole of her backless gown.

"Barely. Let me go find you a robe."

✛

Alan yanked open the lobby door of the Citizens Bank Building at the same instant that a cop was descending the stairs from Ethan's laboratory to see what all the shouting was about down below. The officer had been wrapping up the details of the investigation into the middle-of-the-night make-my-day shooting.

Alan froze a step inside the main doors. At the rear of the lobby J. P. Morgan was holding a gun, gesturing wildly with it, using it more like a pointer than a weapon. His gaze was focused on Emma.

"Ethan has it, Emma!" he screamed. "He has the disc. I don't."

Five feet from Morgan, Ethan was breathing deeply through his mouth, slowly opening and closing his fists, staring coldly at J.P. His voice rigid with rage, Ethan said, "J.P. has the disc, Emma. He's been covering his tracks since he took it. Put that damn gun down, J.P. Jesus, somebody is going to get hurt."

Emma sat on the floor across the room, leaning against a wall. She looked at one of them, then the other, her face an emotionless mask. To Alan, she didn't seem to be connecting with either of them.

She raised her head at the sound of feet on the stairs. Her eyes widened as she recognized that the approaching stranger was a cop.

He was young and confident and Boulder-naive and didn't consider for a second that he was walking into a room full of people with guns. Although he could hear a man loudly asserting, "Bullshit! Bullshit! I don't have it, he does," the cop was halfway down the stairs before he could see the tall man at the rear of the lobby gesticulating with a revolver in his hand.

The cop tried to yell, "Police! Drop your weapon!" while he fumbled to draw his automatic from his holster. His panicked words caught in his throat and lacked authority.

J.P. was distracted by the commotion on the stairs and, as he turned to figure out what was going on, momentarily leveled his revolver at Ethan. J.P.'s aim quickly followed his gaze up the stairs toward the cop, who was just managing to free his weapon and release the safety.

Alan opened his mouth to scream a warning to the cop about J.P.'s gun when he saw that Emma, too, had a pistol in her hand. What the hell was she up to? *Would she use that thing?* On whom, herself?

No time to think, the memory of his cowardice in the park the night before fresh in his mind, Alan sprinted across the lobby toward Emma.

He thought of Lauren.

The cop fired his weapon first.

The shot winged J.P. and ricocheted off the stone, its crisp bark drowning out his scream of, "Drop it, damnit! Police!"

The officer hadn't yet seen Emma's weapon.

Alan was almost at her side when her gun went off. His hand was close enough to the barrel for the tissue on his palm to be seared by the gases and hot powder. His momentum carried him through Emma's raised arm and her weapon came loose, skittering across the hard floor toward the foot of the stairs.

J.P. squealed, "Oh God, I'm hit! I'm hit! Don't shoot me. Don't shoot me. Don't shoot, please, please, please." He dropped his gun.

The cop stood still on the stairs, breathing deeply,

his face mottled red and white like the flesh of a cut strawberry. "Get down! Get down! Hands on your heads. Everybody. Down, goddamn it! Now!"

Gun at arm's length, he scanned the room to check for danger, noted Ethan Han's moans and sickening gurgle, flicked on his microphone, told dispatch there had been a shooting and that he needed backup and at least a couple of ambulances.

⟵⊹⟶

Casey was brushing out Lauren's hair when a crisp knock echoed in her hospital room. Before Casey had a chance to say, "Come in," Scott Malloy pushed through the door and said, "Morning, Lauren, Ms. Sparrow. Sorry to have to wake you."

Casey dropped the hairbrush onto Lauren's bed and stood tall next to her client.

Sam Purdy followed Scott into the hospital room.

"Hi, Lauren, it's Sam," he said. "I'm here with Scott."

A tiny smile crept onto Lauren's face at the sound of the friendly greeting. She said, "Sam, hi. It's good to . . . hear your voice."

Lauren's heart was pounding in her chest. Something terrible was about to happen.

God, she had shot him. In her mind she saw the light, the hooded monster, felt the jolt, smelled the burnt powder. She had pulled the trigger out of fear, and she had shot Kevin Quirk. *And now he's dead.*

Lauren's nurse pushed into the room and broke

the tension. "Is one of you gentlemen Detective Malloy?"

Scott Malloy said, "Yes."

"I have a call for you from somebody who's not happy you're ignoring your pager. You want me to transfer it in here?" The nurse spoke in a bored voice. It was almost shift change and she didn't feel like running errands.

"No, I'll come out there." He turned to Casey and Lauren and said, "Don't go anywhere."

Sam Purdy walked to the side of Lauren's bed opposite Casey and said, "How are you, Lauren?"

Lauren shook her head, shrugged her shoulders, blinked away some tears. Finally, she said, "Being sick is bad enough, Sam. Being under arrest is worse. I've had better nights, believe me."

Purdy couldn't see the benefit of leaving Lauren in this painful limbo any longer. The suspense that Scott's retreat was causing wasn't helping anyone.

He said, "Listen. Scott should be the one to tell you this, not me. But the legal part of this nightmare will be over soon. We're here to cut you loose."

"*Really?*"

"Really. You just need to worry about your health. About getting better."

She started to cry.

Casey embraced her, wiped away the tears, and picked up the phone to call Alan and Cozy. There was no answer.

After picking up his phone call at the nurses station Malloy returned to Lauren's hospital room.

Casey thought he looked preoccupied and wrote it off to fatigue.

Scott eyed Lauren, then Sam. "You told her?"

Sam said, "Just that we were releasing her. Nothing else. That's yours."

The sharp cut of approaching sirens filled the room. Malloy gazed out the solitary window. He made a decision.

"Would you please help your client into the wheelchair, Ms. Sparrow? The phone call I just received? There's someone downstairs who I think would very much like to speak with her."

Lauren cried, "Oh, God. Alan? Is Alan all right?"

"Your husband is fine," Scott said. "I saw him, not too long ago, at your house."

Lauren covered her mouth with her hand. Silently, horrified, she said, *"Emma."* She wanted to ask, "Is Emma Spire hurt? Did Emma try to kill herself?" But she couldn't ask. She still didn't know what it was safe to reveal about Emma's involvement.

Casey guided Lauren's wheelchair out the door. The elevator ride seemed to last an hour. When they arrived on the first floor, the peal of the approaching sirens was piercing. As the group neared the main desk of the emergency department, the sirens faded off in reluctant *whoops*, one by one.

Lauren was grateful for the weight of Sam Purdy's hand on her shoulder.

Scott counted the arriving vehicles as the sirens died.

Three ambulances. One, two, three patrol cars.

*   *   *

The ER staff had been alerted to the incoming trauma and were huddled by the automatic doors.

Doctors and nurses surrounded the first gurney and rolled it into the nearest trauma room. An EMT called out the particulars. Muffled voices drifted back into the hall.

Casey Sparrow asked, "Who was that? Did anybody see who that was?"

Sam said, "No, I couldn't tell."

Lauren said, "God, this is so frustrating. I can't see anything. Would someone please tell me what's going on."

Scott Malloy said nothing.

The patient from the second ambulance walked into the emergency room surrounded by four uniformed Boulder cops, two in front, two in the rear.

Sam Purdy looked at Scott Malloy, saw the sanguine expression on his face, and said, "Oh God."

Casey Sparrow leaned close to Lauren's ear and said, "Emma Spire just walked into the emergency room. Her arm looks like it's been injured."

Lauren tilted her head every way she could, desperately trying to see something, anything. "Emma?" she called. Then to Casey, Lauren said, "But it's just her arm? The rest of her is . . . she's—"

"She's surrounded by cops, Lauren. But she's walking under her own power."

They're protecting her, thought Lauren. Thank God. Alan must have put her on a seventy-two-hour mental health hold-and-treat. Thank God she's okay.

Emma heard Lauren's call and spotted the threesome standing down the hall just beyond the nurses station. In front of them she saw Lauren sitting in the wheelchair.

Without providing any warning to the police who were guarding her, Emma abruptly changed direction and began to walk toward her friend. One of the officers thought she was trying to run away and grabbed her roughly by her injured arm.

Emma screamed from the pain and almost collapsed. She grimaced, trying to erase the anguish. In a clear voice, she said, "I want to see her first. Lauren Crowder, the woman in the wheelchair."

Scott Malloy called to the patrol officers. "I'm Detective Malloy. It's okay. Stay there. We'll come down to you."

Casey pushed the wheelchair forward until Lauren was two feet from Emma. A nurse appeared from behind Emma with a second wheelchair and guided her into it. Emma cradled her injured arm in her lap and stared at Lauren.

Emma said, "I'm sorry, I'm so sorry you were caught in this."

"Emma? Are you okay?"

Emma said, "Yes. It's over, I think. I didn't have to—"

Casey was studying the cops' faces and didn't like what she saw. She faced Scott Malloy. "Detective, is Ms. Spire a suspect in a crime?"

"Yes," Scott said, "she is. There's been another shooting. She was involved."

Casey left Lauren's side and lowered her face to within an inch of Emma's ear and said, in a kind, but authoritative voice, "I'm a lawyer. Listen to me. Don't say another word. Not another damn word."

Casey's tone reminded Emma of one of her mother's more mordant admonishments.

Lauren asked, "What are you holding her for, Scott?"

"Ask her. Go ahead, ask her about her boyfriend."

Lauren said, "Ethan?"

Scott said, "Why am I not surprised that you knew that?"

Lauren looked up in the direction of Scott's voice and appeared to be considering whether to reply to his question. Instead she turned back toward Emma and spoke clearly.

"Emma, are you looking at me?"

Emma stammered, "Yes."

"Do you trust me?"

"Yes."

"You're sure?"

"Yes."

"I'd like to introduce you to someone. This is Casey Sparrow. She's a good friend of mine. And she's going to be your attorney. Do everything she says. Everything. Okay?"

"Yes."

Casey turned to the uniformed officers. She didn't miss a beat. "Is my client in custody, gentlemen? Has she been Mirandized yet?"

Scott Malloy turned away, shook his head in amazement at what was developing, and despite his best intentions, smiled.

"Here we go again, Sam," he said.

Sam pointed outside the glass doors of the ER, where a microwave truck from one of the Denver TV stations was setting up for a remote broadcast.

"Ha," Sam said. "And they said there wasn't life after O.J."

+++

J. P. Morgan was on the next stretcher wheeled into the ER. He had a compression bandage on his left calf and he, too, was accompanied by cops. He had pulled himself to a sitting position and was trying to make sense of what he was seeing. Emma was in a wheelchair, surrounded by a half-squadron of police officers. Ethan was nowhere to be found.

With forced calm, Morgan called out to the closest nurse, asking where Ethan Han had been taken.

The nurse was flustered. "Are you family?"

"No. I'm his friend, his partner."

"I'm sorry then, but I can't divulge any medical information to you."

"That's fine, just tell me where he is."

She looked at the cops beside him and then down the hall at the police presence huddled around Emma. "I'm sorry," she said again, shaking her head.

Morgan called, "Emma?"

Over the shoulder of one of the officers, he said, "Emma, where's Ethan? Is he okay?"

Casey interrupted. "Don't answer him, Emma." She directed herself to the newcomer, "Who are you?"

"I'm Thomas Morgan. Who the hell are you? Where's Ethan, Emma?"

"Please speak to me. Don't address my client."

Morgan's voice took on an intense cadence. "Your client? What the hell is—?"

Lauren noted the change in tenor in Morgan's voice. The new sound pounded her consciousness like a bass drum. In her mind, Lauren heard a vivid replay of the voice of the man who had kidnapped her from the treatment room in the ER.

She said, "Oh, my God, J.P., it was you."

✥

Alan parked his car in a no-parking zone and ran into the emergency room to find Lauren. Cozy was steps behind him. The first thing Alan saw as he burst through the door was the bright yellow back of J. P. Morgan's parka. The next thing he saw was the look of alarm on his wife's face.

As Alan was trying to comprehend the events in front of him he heard his name called from behind. He turned. Standing in the airlock between the two sets of automatic doors was Raoul Estevez.

In one arm, like a football, Raoul held a vanilla-colored piece of electronic equipment about the size of a small VCR.

Raoul said, "Diane said you called, and that there had been a shooting. I thought—"

Alan's eyes locked on the optical drive in Raoul's arms and said, "Oh, no. Oh, shit. Oh, no." Quickly, he recovered. "Raoul, turn around and get out of here. Go home. I'll call you as soon as I can. Go."

✥

Lauren was riding the crest of a steroid buzz. She didn't want to sleep, she wanted to talk.

Alan wanted her to sleep so he could take the dog for a walk and try to figure out what to do.

He'd driven her home from the hospital and guided her in the door and down the stairs. He'd undressed her and drawn a warm bath and scented the water and he'd gently shampooed and conditioned her hair. He'd toweled her off and massaged her skin with her favorite lotion. He'd found her softest cotton top and eased it over her head before leading her to bed where he fluffed her pillows and covered her with a duvet.

"Do you want some music on?"

She turned to the sound of his voice. Their eyes failed to meet. She said, "No, I want to know what you saw in the ER. You're keeping something from me."

He tried to change the subject. "First, would you please tell me what you were doing at Emma's house?"

"I thought if I was there I could talk her out of volunteering to be raped by whoever had the disc. Or at least I could scare the guy away."

"That's why you had the gun?"

She averted her eyes. "I almost always have the gun with me, sweets. I should have told you about it a long time ago, but I didn't think you'd react well to me carrying a pistol."

"That doesn't show a whole lot of faith in me."

"No, I guess not. But I think that's a different conversation for us."

"Yes, it is."

"What did you see in the ER, Alan?"

"I want to tell you. But before I do, I need to know something. What comes first for you? Are you my wife or are you a prosecutor?"

"What do you mean? I'm both. Are you in some kind of trouble?"

"Maybe. Some things happened last night that you don't know about."

Her throat was dry. She told herself it was the Solu-Medrol. She knew it was only partly true. If she could see she would reach for the carafe of water by the bed. She couldn't see.

"What did you do?"

"Wife or prosecutor, Lauren?"

"Hon, that's a complicated question when I don't know the circumstances."

"I know it is. The answer's complicated, too, and I don't want to put you in an impossible place. You may have an ethical obligation to disclose what I know to your colleagues, or even the police. I don't think you will want to do that. You may end up being in a better position not knowing what happened."

"Is it about you?"

"Yes. And about a friend of ours, too."

"Who? Emma?"

"I really shouldn't say."

"Why?"

"What are your obligations to your office if I tell you?"

"I won't know that until you tell me."

"See," he said, "that's why it's complicated."

She considered the territory before she asked, "Are you protecting yourself, or are you protecting me?"

He paused, reflected, and said, "Both you, and me, I think."

Lauren digested his answer before she said, "But you're definitely not protecting *us*."

Raoul phoned two hours later. Lauren was finally resting. Alan answered.

Without preamble, Raoul said, "Two nights ago, I came by the lab to see Ethan. Generally, he prefers to meet with me in the evening, the lab is quiet, he is more open to conversation, is more . . . reflective, or perhaps, contemplative. I don't know. I have a key, but the laboratory was unlocked. When I walked in, I heard music, some Beethoven I think, but I couldn't find Ethan. I knocked at the door to his flat but no one answered. I walked around the laboratory looking for him and then in the front room I found them, Emma and Ethan. They were . . . involved, amorously, you know? I saw that he was wearing the collar."

"Yes?"

"It frightened me. I know what the device does. I feared what he would do with the data he was collecting. That he would be impetuous with it. She is so famous. I felt I needed to put the data out of his reach temporarily while I asked him to consider the ramifications of what he had recorded. I feared he would be impulsive with it, mention it to someone, or worse, share it. Word would get out. It would be bad for him, for the company. For her, too. You know, for Emma. It would be most tragic for her.

"Instead, it was me who was impulsive. I waited in the lab, hidden. After they finished, you know . . . they went to bed. I took the drive."

"Did you tell him you took it?"

"I planned to, of course. I was going to call him the next morning. But immediately when I got home, I regretted what I had done. I was—what?—humiliated. I am not a thief. And Ethan was very upset the next day. The investors called early and told him they had decided not to increase their positions in BiModal. He was facing another fight with Morgan about an IPO. It was not the correct time to tell him I had the drive. Instead, I erased the data and was planning on returning the drive when I had the chance. You know, surreptitiously. I never expected . . ."

"You couldn't have."

Raoul's voice became airy. "When Diane told me you had called, what had happened, with Lauren, with the shootings . . ."

"You may need a lawyer, Raoul."

"Yes, perhaps you are right. I'm so sorry, Alan. I have ruined so many lives. And Ethan's technology, it dies with him for now. It could have done so much good. So much."

Alan made a light dinner and decided to reveal to Lauren what he could. He felt a wall being built, brick by brick, between him and his wife. He won-

dered how they would scale it, what the consequences would be if they failed.

He said, "Neither Ethan nor J.P. really had the disc
or knew where it was. That I *know*. A lot of the rest
is conjecture. You want to hear my version?"

She said, "Yes."

"Ethan told J.P. what had happened—that the
Emma disc existed and that it had been stolen. J.P.
saw an opportunity. He decided to use the missing
disc to blackmail both of them—Ethan and Emma.
By then, the investors had already decided not to
increase their stakes in BiModal. J.P. was worried
that Ethan was again going to insist on taking the
company public. But J.P. had no trouble convincing
Ethan that they couldn't launch an IPO for BiModal
until the Emma disc was recovered. It could have
been used against Ethan and the company with devastating results. Then J.P. had to make sure that the
disc *wasn't* recovered. That meant getting Kevin
Quirk off the trail."

Lauren finished for him. "But J.P. had another
agenda, too. He wanted Emma. He left her a note,
pretending to have the disc, to blackmail her into
sleeping with him."

"Yes."

Lauren brought her warm hands to her cold cheeks
and held them against her skin. "There's more, isn't
there, babe? You know who really has the disc, don't
you? You know who stole it?"

He tried to conjure a way to respond. He wanted
her to know. He didn't want to tell her. "Like before,
some of what I'm about to tell you is conjecture.
Some of it I know for sure."

"And I'm supposed to guess which is which?"

"No. You're supposed to see the wisdom of leaving it the way it is."

"Tell me your way, then."

"You got my message that Emma was at my office yesterday?"

Lauren nodded.

"Okay. After she left, Quirk stopped by, looking for her. He was on his way to Eben Fine Park—you know, at the mouth of Boulder Canyon?—to meet someone who said they had the disc. I think it was J.P. he was meeting."

"You think?"

"I think."

"So J.P. shot Quirk? But when? I didn't hear another gunshot up by Emma's house."

He paused, permitting the silence to say things he could not. "I'd guess that the shooting took place at the park. Maybe there was a . . . a confrontation of some kind. And a shooting. That's where Kevin was wounded, but he had enough stamina to drive to Emma's house. He wanted to warn her, I guess. J.P. followed him there from the park. Saw Kevin had collapsed in the street. Ran him over, to finish him off, make sure he was dead."

"Who took the disc, Alan? Who really has it?"

"I don't think you want to know everything I know, Lauren. I can assure you the data is destroyed. And that it was never copied. Emma's privacy is safe."

Even though she couldn't see him she focused her eyes like lasers in the direction of his voice. "Emma's in jail for killing Ethan Han. Geraldo has a wing reserved at the Boulderado. Court TV has a satellite truck at the Justice Center. Emma's privacy is in flames. Who stole the disc?"

"Please believe me when I say I really shouldn't tell you. God, I wish I could."

"You don't trust me with this?"

"That's not fair, and that's not it, and I hope you know it. I love you."

"Was Ethan a good guy or a bad guy? Was he going to blackmail Emma with the disc? Was this whole thing about her father and abortion rights? At least tell me that."

"I don't know."

"Really?"

"Really."

"Damn it. It would be easier to swallow this tragedy if I knew Ethan was evil."

Later, after dinner, Alan drove Lauren back to Community Hospital for her second dose of Solu-Medrol. The tension between them was palpable. After Lauren was set up for her treatment, Alan used a pay phone in a hallway near the ER to return a call to Cozier Maitlin.

"How's Emma, Cozy?"

"Fragile, at best. She needs help, your kind of help. Casey's with her. She looks dull to me, no guilt, no remorse. I'm afraid of what's going to happen to her when she realizes what she's facing."

"I don't think she meant to shoot Ethan, Cozy. I think she was aiming at J.P. That's what I told the police it looked like to me."

"That's what she's telling us, too. She says she was

protecting the cop from Morgan. It turns out the bullet that killed Han entered from behind. It was a deflection or a ricochet. Unfortunately, being a bad shot isn't the choicest of defenses for Emma. We'll probably need a statement from you about your assessment to get a court order for psych treatment."

"No problem. Are you still my lawyer, Cozy?"

"Absolutely. With the size of the retainer you gave me, I'm yours for life. How's Lauren?"

"Okay. Her vision's still bad. But the pain in her eyes has stopped. That's a good sign. I'm calling from the hospital. We're back for her next dose of medicine."

"Say hello for me. What's up?"

"The ambush in the park? I think it was Ethan Han's partner who set it up."

"The man Lauren fingered in the ER?"

"Yes. I bet the gun I ended up with is his. If I turn it in, the police can check that; can't they?"

"They can. If it was his and if it was registered. But back to our earlier conversation. Why should they believe your story?"

"Why not? It's the truth."

Cozy scoffed. "Because you can't provide corroboration or evidence to support it. You want to risk it? For what? Morgan's already in custody. The police think they can tie his car to the tire marks on Kevin Quirk's clothing. And, anyway, Erin's been busy. I sent her to Eben Fine Park. She found a computer memory device, something called a Bernoulli drive, in a suitcase under a picnic table in the park. Her babysitter's a computer nerd. He checked the drive for her, said there's nothing on it. It's blank. I'll be giving it to the DA in the morning."

Alan was gaining more respect for J. P. Morgan's inventiveness. "The drive Erin found is a fake, Cozy. It was left there to trick Kevin Quirk into giving up the chase. The one you have isn't the one with the data on it."

"How do you know that?"

Alan sighed. "God, Cozy, it's going to take a while to explain all this. It's complicated."

Alan felt Sam Purdy's presence before he saw him. The sensation was of a change in atmospheric pressure, as though a cold front was approaching.

Alan said, "Cozy, I'll need to call you back. Sam Purdy is here."

"Don't let me interrupt you. I'm sure whatever you're talking about with your lawyer is much more important than anything I have to say."

Alan hung up, stared at Sam's face a moment and then embraced him. "Thanks, Sam. There's no repaying you for what you did last night."

Sam permitted the hug but didn't return it. "That's probably true; there isn't. Showing some occasional faith in me might be a good place to start, though."

Alan felt the rebuke physically. He took a few steps back and sat on a waiting room chair. Sam took the one beside it. He was still wearing his coat.

"I'm sorry, Sam. Last night felt like one long plane wreck. I didn't know what to do. I didn't want to put her at risk."

"Put her at risk? I'm your friend, I'm her friend. You've been treating me like I'm a damn leper. It hurts. I've never given you a reason not to trust me. Never."

Alan looked away. "You're right, you haven't. Quite the opposite. You've always been there. Always."

"So why didn't you ask me for help?"

Alan's hesitation wasn't lost on Sam. "I'm . . . I was afraid that your role would be confused. You know. Yes, you're her friend, but you're a cop, too."

"So this was for my benefit? You wanted to keep me from feeling uncomfortable." Sam's Iron Range lilt carried the sarcasm gently, as though floating it on a breeze.

"No, that's not it."

"You thought she was guilty?"

"I didn't know what happened, Sam. The situation with Emma was really fragile. Lauren told me she fired the gun. I feared the worst."

He said, "Ah," and seemed to Alan to be considering something. "So, did you get any sleep? I slept all day. Been up only since dinner."

"I was interviewed by your colleagues for a long time about the last shooting. But I got a nap in. Couple of hours."

"So maybe you were so tired you weren't thinking clearly?"

"Last night? Absolutely."

"No, I was thinking more like today."

"What do—? I'm not sure what you mean."

"You never called me. I figured we had things to discuss."

Alan was wondering if Sam was fishing for some repeated profession of gratitude.

"Miss Emma? Remember her? After Ethan Han was shot and before Casey Sparrow told her to shut the hell up, Miss Emma mumbled a few things in the ambulance on the way over here."

"Yes?"

"About you and Lauren."

Alan jerked his eyes toward Sam. "Curious now, aren't you?"

"What did she say, Sam?"

Purdy stood and walked two steps as though he were going to leave. He pivoted neatly on one foot, like an infantryman. "See, this is what I don't like. You ask questions and you expect answers. I ask questions and I get bullshit."

A woman ran past them toward the nurses station leading a small child who was drenched in red blood. The mother's voice was panicked and adenoidal and impossible to ignore. "It won't stop bleeding. It won't stop bleeding. It's her nose, it won't stop bleeding."

The nurse at the nearby ER triage desk took in the scene as though it were as banal as the arrival of the next customer at a convenience store.

Alan watched the drama before he turned back to his friend and said, "What do you want to know, Sam?"

"Just what happened last night. That's all."

"Are you going to sit down?"

"Are you going to make it worth my while? If we're going to continue this silly dance, I'd rather do that standing up."

"I'm not sure I can be the judge of how helpful I can be."

"Why don't we start with the guy with the electronics under his arm? Here, in the ER, this morning? The one who knew your name. Why don't we start there. I thought I recognized him."

Alan swallowed. "Okay."

Sam shrugged out of his coat, sat. "What was he carrying?"

"An optical drive, for a computer. I think it's called a Bernoulli."

"And he is . . . ?" Sam was snapping his fingers, pretending his memory needed jump-starting.

"Raoul Estevez. You met him once, a few years ago. His wife is my partner, Diane. She was beat up in her house, remember?"

"Yeah, I thought he looked familiar. He helped us find some missing keys, right? Nice guy. He's a computer wizard, isn't he?"

"A very talented man, yes."

"He knew Han?"

"Had just started working for him."

"Emma mentioned a missing disc. Could this Bernoulli have been it?"

"It's possible. I'm not sure what she told you."

Sam recognized the diversion. "She told us not to blame you or Lauren for anything she did. That was sweet of her, don't you think?"

Alan didn't know how to respond.

"Why did your friend have this optical drive?"

"Part of his job, I guess. He told me he was making sure some data was secure."

"Data?"

"Data."

"Data it is, then. So he carries it with him to the emergency room after Ethan Han is shot? That keeps it safe?"

Alan shrugged.

Sam sighed. "It looks like I'm going to have to talk with him. Your friend."

"Yes."

"Why do I have this funny feeling that he's co-cooned himself with a lawyer already?"

"Because it's probably true. You know how it goes."

"Upstairs," Sam pointed directly at the ceiling, "we have a comatose ex-Secret Service agent named Quirk. Used to guard Miss Spire for the government. Almost died in front of her house. Shot, then run over a couple times. Talk about your bad nights. You know him, right?"

"Emma had called him for protection. Emma was attacked, almost abducted, last week, in the parking garage on Spruce. She wanted some security help. Lauren and I met Quirk. He's sharp."

"In the city garage? And the local police, they couldn't be trusted with this matter? We know that for a fact, right?" Sam's sarcasm was no longer gentle.

"Emma's call, Sam. She's terrified of the media, not the cops. She was afraid of leaks."

"I see. So, Emma Spire almost got abducted—that's the word you used, right? 'Abducted'?—so she calls for a little backup. Shortly thereafter she gets a visit from Lauren who shoots a gun into the air in a blizzard for some reason nobody has a goddamn clue about—I'm right so far, aren't I?'' Alan shrugged his shoulders. "Then this bodyguard gets himself shot and run over by a car, and while we're not looking, Emma somehow manages to *accidentally* dust her boyfriend while she's trying to protect a cop in the lobby of Han's building on the Pearl Street Mall? End of story? Nah. There's more, see. First there's this disc, this data, that I don't know shit about.

"Second, we get us an anonymous tip that maybe Emma has a motive to kill Han. Do you know Han was a local organizer for Operation Rescue? Just learned that, myself. Given what happened with her father, I'm thinking that maybe the shooting was a biblical retribution type thing—you know, an eye for an eye. Neat twist, don't you think?"

Alan shook his head. "I don't know Emma that well, Sam, but I don't think that's her style. I think she was trying to protect the cop on the stairs."

"She tell you that?"

"That's the way it looked to me. I was there, remember?"

"Right. You seem to be just about everywhere." Sam examined his shoes as though they were actually interesting. "You know," he said, "this Morgan guy claims he didn't shoot Quirk. Says Quirk ambushed *him* in the park. Morgan claims that when he tried to run away, he got into a fight with somebody else, some mystery man. Morgan lost his gun. He won't answer questions about running Quirk over. But says he absolutely didn't shoot him.

"Let's say for a minute that I believe him. Still leaves holes in the story. We had way too many gunshots in Boulder last night but so far none of them have been reported in Quirk's vicinity. Has to be one more. So maybe that was it. The one in the park, with Morgan's missing gun."

"Thanks to you, at least we know Lauren didn't do it."

Sam was disappointed at Alan's response. He focused his gaze down the hall. "Yes, thanks to me, we know that."

"What about the other shooting. The make-my-day thing? In the middle of the night at Han's flat?"

"We think Han set somebody up. Figured an employee was stealing from him so he changed his alarm codes. Morgan was caught in the web. When Morgan realized what happened, he tried to cover himself by faking a break-in and firing Han's gun at an imaginary burglar. That's how we have it, so far. We'll get the rest."

"That's interesting."

"Interesting? What's interesting is that Morgan says he left an item in a suitcase in Eben Fine Park last night. Now we can't find it. Shoe prints in the snow heading right to where he says he left it, but no suitcase. Don't know what to make of it."

"Do you know what it was?"

"You may not believe this coincidence—but he says it was a Bernoulli drive. Something about a meeting with a blackmailer. A business thing. Says that there are billions—that's billions, with a *b*—of dollars at stake. I'm wondering if your friend Raoul maybe found his Bernoulli in the park."

"Don't think so, no."

"Morgan also said he saw a big utility vehicle, maybe a Suburban or a Land Cruiser or a Land

Rover, in the parking lot at Eben Fine. Wouldn't have been yours or your friend Raoul's, would it?"

Alan bowed his head. He scratched behind his ear. He knew the next words from his lips would be either a lie or a confession. He was tired. He knew that Cozy would tell him to keep his mouth shut. But he felt the corrosive drip of his actions over the last twenty-four hours as though acid were leaking into his heart. His continued silence threatened to poison his marriage and would certainly destroy this friendship.

He decided to come clean. He said, "How about this, Sam? Lauren will be getting treatment for another hour or so. There are some things I need to discuss with her, alone. When she's done, can you clear the way for Lauren and me to visit with Emma at the jail—tonight?"

"What's in it for me?"

"You agree to that, and I'll tell you what's happened the last few days. There are some topics I've promised other people I wouldn't talk about so I'm going to be vague about those. But I'll tell you the rest. Everything I can. Maybe when I'm done with my story you'll feel that you have to take some action. Maybe you won't."

Sam's lips thinned, disappearing under his mustache.

"It's a deal then, assuming Casey agrees to make her client available. What kind of action are we discussing that I'm going to be taking?"

Alan shrugged "Police action."

"Police action?"

"You know, like arresting me."

"Arresting you?" Sam weighed the density of the concession Alan was making. He said, "But you're willing to trust me with that decision?"

"I don't think there's anyone more deserving."

Sam waited impatiently while Alan visited Lauren. After Alan returned, he kept his half of the bargain. Sam didn't ask a single question during Alan's rendition of events.

"So, are you going to arrest me, Sam?"

Sam looked out the window. "What, for giving a false statement to a peace officer?"

"What I'm telling you is true, Sam."

"Yeah? Let's see. You're offering me a ghost story, a scuffle in the park, and the accidental discharge of a firearm to explain away a train wreck. And I'm supposed to jump at it like I'm grateful? And even if I do believe you, what do I charge you with? Being a moron?"

Sam looked disappointed, maybe even hurt. Alan wasn't sure which. "The truth is the truth," he said.

"Is it? The evidence doesn't support your version."

"I have the gun, Sam. The one that landed in my lap in the park."

"You have a gun. How the hell do I prove that it was the one that shot Quirk? We don't have the slug."

"I'm telling you I did it. That should be enough. Quirk will tell you the same thing, too."

"Quirk's story doesn't jibe with yours, buddy. Sorry. He says you never got out of the car."

"Quirk's awake?"

"Was, briefly. We got a statement before the docs helped him go back to sleep."

"What else does he say?"

"That's my business."

Alan shook his head slowly. "Cozy Maitlin warned me that you wouldn't believe me."

"Maitlin's a damn good lawyer. Maybe you should listen to him. I'm sure you're paying him enough."

Alan felt his heart grow still. Finally, he understood what was going on.

"You know what, Sam? You *do* believe me. You know damn well I'm telling the truth. If you thought I was lying to you, you would nail me to the wall."

Sam snorted. "I can't do anything about what you believe, Alan. You're a damn shrink. You read tea leaves. I prefer evidence."

Alan sat way back on his chair. He said, "Thanks, Sam. Once more, I'm glad I trusted you."

Sam stared hard into Alan's eyes. "I'm glad you trust me, too. Now, let's go find your wife and get over to the jail. I have my end of a bargain to keep."

✛

They met in the deserted courtroom at the jail.

Since the media were camped out in the jail parking lot, Alan and Lauren were chauffeured in a police department van that snuck inside through the same garage entrance through which Lauren had been delivered to the jail a day earlier. Emma's lawyers were already waiting in the courtroom. Casey was leaning against the bar, her red mane the brightest thing in the room. Cozy was on the judge's chair behind the bench, acting imperial.

Lauren said, "Oh good, I can see some red over there. Hi Casey, is that you?"

"Hello, Lauren. How you doing?"

"Better than my last visit here. Let's leave it at that. Are Cozy and Emma here, too?"

"I'm up on the bench, where I belong. We're waiting for Emma. What's this all about? How did you get Purdy to let you see her?"

Alan helped Lauren to a chair and said, "That was my doing, Cozy. Sam has a lot of what happened figured already, so I offered him a deal. If he lets Lauren and me see Emma, I would tell him what's been going on."

"Even . . . ?"

"Yes, even the shooting in the park."

Lauren said, "Alan told me all about it, Cozy. I agreed he had to tell Sam."

"Well, I think that may be ill advised at this time. As your attorney—"

"Too late, Cozy. It's done But, as a consolation, you'll be happy to know that you were right: Sam didn't believe me."

Cozy swallowed his next question as the door opened and a female deputy escorted Emma into the courtroom. Emma was wearing jail blues and canvas sneakers and her arm was in a sling. Her hair was stringy and her skin had such pallor that her eyes stood out like wounds on her face.

The deputy said, "I'll be right outside. You have

as much time as you need. I've been instructed to cut you all some slack."

The instant the deputy was out the door, Emma glanced up, recognized who her visitors were and squealed, "Lauren, oh God, it's so good to see you," and ran over and hugged her. "How are your eyes?"

"The pain is better, thanks, Emma."

"How did you talk them into letting you see me? I haven't even been arraigned yet."

Alan said, "It's a long story. Too long for now. We wanted to see you so we made some arrangements with the police. Are they treating you okay?"

"I'm in a holding cell, by myself. Casey said to be grateful, that I'm receiving special treatment. So I'm trying to be grateful. I'd rather be home."

Lauren said, "Emma, we're here tonight because of something that concerns Alan. Last night he was helping Kevin Quirk locate the missing disc, and there was a fight, and Alan ended up with a gun and a shot was fired accidentally. It looks like it may have been the shot that wounded Kevin. Alan just now told the police about it and we wanted to tell you in person. It implicates you and Kevin."

"Alan shot Kevin? But you were arrested for that, Lauren. Alan, did you let Lauren spend a whole night in jail while . . . ?"

Lauren defended her husband. "Alan didn't know Kevin had been injured. He didn't know anybody had been hit. He and I both thought I was the one who shot Kevin."

Emma said, "How does this implicate me? I wasn't even there."

"I had to tell the police about the missing disc,

Emma," Alan said. "There's no other way the story makes sense."

"Oh." She looked even paler than before.

Casey said, "Morgan probably already told them, anyway, Emma. It's okay. We'll deal with it."

"How?"

Alan explained, "My friend Raoul took the entire drive from Ethan's lab that night, right after . . . you know, the data was recorded. Raoul erased it himself. There are no copies. I told the police that the disc was a 'digital recording of a personal nature' or something like that. They don't need to know what was really on it; they just need to know that it was something that could have humiliated you. The press may pick up on it for a while, but they'll let it go eventually. You're just going to have to ride it out by reminding yourself that there's no data out there."

"There are no copies?"

"No. There are no copies."

"You're sure?"

"Absolutely."

"Then I don't care. I don't think it makes much difference to me now." She picked at her jail togs. "I'm not going to have to fend off the paparazzi for a while anyway. But I feel terrible that you're involved now, too, Alan. I'm so sorry."

Emma stood, the color back in her face. She took a hesitant step forward toward Alan, turned away, then back toward him again. "In the lobby, this morning, when you knocked the gun out of my hand, whom did you think I was going to shoot?"

Alan glanced at Casey, then back at Emma. "I already told the police I thought you were trying to protect the cop on the stairs."

"No, no. I appreciate that, but, right now, I don't want to know what you concluded I was doing. I want to know what you thought I was doing when you lunged for the gun."

"I wasn't sure, Emma. Things happened too fast. I saw the gun and I thought you might shoot yourself. I guess I even thought you might be distraught enough to kill Ethan."

With her good hand she pulled her hair away from her face. "You want to know what I was thinking? I was thinking about Nelson Newell, and his righteousness when he shot my father. How sure Newell was that he was justified. And right then, I think, maybe, I could have convinced myself I was justified in killing Ethan and Morgan for toying with my life. They were standing there knocking my well-being back and forth between them like it was a damn tennis ball. The gun gave me the power. I'll admit that." Emma's composure began to evaporate and tears formed in her eyes. Her voice shook. "But when J.P. raised his gun toward the cop, everything became different. And all I wanted to do was save him, the cop. That's all. In the end I just wanted to stop the killing."

Lauren said, "You did save him, hon. You did."

There is no jury box in the jail courtroom. Emma was directing her comments toward the bench, toward Cozy.

"No. You don't understand. I wanted to save my father." Her voice turned small. "Do you know that . . . I was too late to save my daddy? I tried to save him. I did. But I couldn't. Everybody thought I was so special that day, but I didn't do anything. Nothing. My daddy died. He died in my arms." She pressed her eyes shut to force some image to disappear. "Today, though, this morning, I saved someone. That's good. I'm so sorry Ethan had to die, but I don't really feel that I killed him. Maybe tomorrow I will. But I know what was in my heart when I squeezed the trigger. Isn't that what matters? What's in your heart?" Her words were jerky, buffeted by her tears. "What's in your heart? That's what matters. Right? Right?"

Lauren stood and found Emma by tracking her cries. She eased Emma's head to her shoulder and comforted her until the memories softened their grip.

The walls of the back of the courtroom are glass. Casey and Cozy were in position to see Sam Purdy and Scott Malloy enter the adjoining corridor. Cozy rapped the gavel to get everyone's attention. "Visitors," he said. For Lauren's benefit he added, "Sam Purdy and Scott Malloy are here."

Scott pushed the door open and proceded Sam into the room. "Sorry for the intrusion, everyone. We'll be brief."

Cozy said, "This can't wait?"

"No. It shouldn't wait."

Malloy approached Emma and pulled two photographs from a manila envelope. He held one in each hand. "You recognize either of these men?"

Emma took two steps away and whispered something to Casey, who replied, "It's fine, go ahead."

Emma nodded. "Yes. They're the two kids who

tried to kidnap me last week, in the parking garage at Eleventh and Spruce."

"Figured that. Punks. Thought you would like to know they're in custody. Pulled the same stunt in the garage on Walnut two days ago."

Breathless, Lauren asked, "Was anyone hurt?"

Purdy said, "No. No one was hurt. They let the woman go a few blocks from the garage. They wanted the car and the money."

Cozy stared at the two cops, who weren't making any effort to depart. He said, "What do you really want? That could've waited until morning. You two didn't get all dressed up for that little demonstration."

"You're right, Mr. Maitlin. We didn't." Scott Malloy stuffed his hands in his pockets and walked three steps toward the bench before he continued. "Ballistics evidence confirms Ms. Spire's version of events in the bank lobby this morning. It appears she wasn't aiming at Ethan Han. Her shot missed Morgan by no more than a couple of inches."

Casey said, "And?"

"And . . . the bullet the surgeons retrieved from Ethan Han's lung came from the police officer's weapon. Not from Ms. Spire's. To make a long story short, she's free to go."

"I didn't shoot him?"

"Apparently not, Ms. Spire."

"I can go home?"

Scott Malloy said, "You can all go home. As a matter of fact, I can't tell you how happy it would make me if you all just got the hell out of here."

ACKNOWLEDGMENTS

When I needed legal help, I had four talented volunteers. Paul McCormick, Peggy Jessel, Donald Wilson, and Harry MacLean generously offered their wisdom and their experience.

I received law enforcement instruction from professionals who work for a variety of jurisdictions, and I am especially grateful to Sergeant Tom Groff of the Boulder County Sheriff's Department, Detective Carey Weinheimer, Detective Melissa Hickman, and Virginia Lucy of the Boulder Police Department, and Detective Stephen Adams and John Graham of the Arvada Police Department.

Steven Miller, M.D., provided invaluable assistance in focusing my thinking regarding technology and entrepreneurship, and Terry Lapid, M.D., and Stan Galansky, M.D., were on call for all fictional medical emergencies.

Early readers of the manuscript hit the potholes that I didn't even know I'd created. I'm grateful to Lee Miller, Kay McCormick, Mark Graham, Vicki Emery, Elyse Morgan, Ann Nemeth, Greg Moody, and Ellen Greenhouse, all of whom volunteered for that hazardous duty. And my special thanks to Patricia and Jeffrey Limerick, and to Ann Crammond and the real Larry Arbuthnot for being good sports.

Having Al Silverman as an editor and a friend is a true honor. His skill is exceeded only by his graciousness and loyalty. The longer we work together, the wiser he seems. Elaine Koster, Michaela Hamilton, and Joe Pittman at Dutton/Signet provide me with a rare gift—they allow me plenty of rope, and trust that I'm going to fashion something with it that doesn't closely resemble a noose.

Lynn Nesbit, Eric Simonoff, and the professionals who work with them at Janklow & Nesbit Associates invigorate me. I'm terribly grateful.

My family's love is responsible for the creative air I breathe. To Rose and Alexander, to my mother, Sara White Kellas, and to all the Walshs and Whites from County Kerry to New England to the Left Coast, my loving thanks.

Don't miss Stephen White's
newest thriller

Critical Conditions

coming from Dutton
in March 1998

Adrenaline affects my friend Adrienne in the same paradoxical way that Ritalin affects hyperactive kids. It seems to calm her down.

On Saturday morning, as I was pushing my bicycle in the front door after doing ninety hard minutes on the hilly roads of eastern Boulder County, the phone rang. I was tempted to let the machine catch the call; I wanted to get out of my sweaty Lycra, I needed fluids, and I was desperate for a shower. But I answered anyway, hoping it might be Lauren with some news about her mother.

Adrienne said, "Hey, Alan, how you doing? It's me." The casualness of her greeting alerted me that something might be up; as often as not she didn't even bother to say hello when she phoned. "Hey, you doing anything? You busy right now? I have someone I think you should see."

I paused a second as I greeted my dog, Emily, who was pushing her flank against me forcefully, as though I were a sheep she was planning to herd to a different pasture. My pause was also intended to allow Adrienne an opportunity to explain what she wanted. When she didn't, I said, "I just got in from a ride. Where are you, at your house? What's up?"

Adrienne, a urologist, and her young son, Jonas, were our only nearby neighbors. They lived just up the hill from Lauren and me, in a renovated farm house set on a rise across the gravel and dirt lane.

"No, I'm at the hospital. Been playing Zorro with bladder cancer in the O.R. since seven. Just when I finished up the operation, Marty Klein found me and asked me to consult on an E.R. case, an adolescent female overdose. You know Marty, don't you?"

"Yeah, I know—"

"I'm still here doing the consult and I think you should see her, too—the kid."

"Isn't there a psychiatrist on call for that?" Although I did occasional psychological liaison work at the hospital, I didn't routinely consult in the hospital E.R., probably hadn't seen a case there in two years.

Impatience crept into Adrienne's voice. "I didn't say I think *somebody* should see her, Alan. I said I think *you* should see her. Can you hear the difference?" She paused. "Anyway, Levitt's on call."

Whenever Adrienne had an impulse to assail the mental health profession—not an infrequent urge on her part—Natt Levitt, M.D., was her incompetent-practice poster child. His name at the top of the E.R. on-call roster helped explain why I was being drafted to see the adolescent overdose.

I asked. "What's the kid's condition?"

"She's critical. Her vitals are . . . her vitals are shit. Consciousness is waxing and waning. Her kidney function is way whacked, and she has gross hematuria, which is why Marty wanted me on board. She's on her way to the ICU soon."

The severity of the girl's condition was unnerving.

Adolescent suicidal behavior is a crapshoot. Sometimes it's manipulative and benign; sometimes it's lethal as hell. Sometimes the kid screws up and actually kills herself when she doesn't really intend to.

I asked, "Why does she have blood in her urine? She take aspirin?"

"Don't know what she took. But ultrasound indicates a perinephric hematoma. We'll confirm with C.T."

"Which means what in English?"

"She has a mild renal contusion, a little rip in her kidney. So she's bleeding into her bladder."

"What can cause that?"

"Fifty different things. Little traumas. Falling out of bed, tripping over a cat. Punch in the gut."

"Any idea about the precipitant? What does the family have to say? Did she just break up with someone? Problem at school? What?"

"We don't know anything. Family isn't here. Police say a frantic kid—called herself a girlfriend—found the patient unresponsive, called 911. The friend left the front door of the house open for the ambulance, but she wasn't there when the paramedics arrived. The kid's parents are nowhere to be found. The police are trying to find everybody involved. But we're pretty much in the dark."

"Has she been oriented enough to say anything since she was brought in?"

"Not to me. Marty said she asked about her sister. Twice, I think he said. She said, 'Is she all right?' Something like that."

"And her sister's not around?"

"No, I haven't seen anybody with her, you know, visiting."

"Has anyone checked the house for the sister? This could have been some kind of suicide pact."

"I hadn't thought of that. The police went over to the house after the ambulance picked her up. I'll phone and make sure that they looked around real well."

"The kid hasn't spoken to you, Ren?"

"No, since I've been down here she's been in the ozone."

"Is she going to make it?"

"She's just a girl, Alan. She damn well better make it."

"What did she take?"

"Like I said, we don't know; it's polydrug, probably a cocktail. She responded to Narcan, so some narcotics for sure, and it looks like three, four, five other drugs, maybe more. There was a lot of stuff in the house. We'll be sorting out the toxicology for a while."

"Why—"

"Because I think you're the right one to see her. That's why."

"That's not what I was about to ask." It actually was, but I wasn't about to admit it. "What about the attending? You said it's Marty Klein? Is he okay with me seeing his patient? He's the one who'll have to absorb the flak when Natt Levitt finds out he wasn't called first."

"Done. Marty doesn't like Natt any more than I do. Does anybody like Natt? What keeps him around? I don't get it. Since when is having a medical license supposed to provide as much security as having tenure? But Natt's not your problem, he's mine. The order is written."

"Well—"

Adrienne laughed. "Most of the time I'm irresistible, aren't I?"

Adrienne was a true friend. And she asked few favors, professionally or otherwise. "Yes, Ren, you are." I glanced at my watch. "I have to shower first. I'll try and be there by eleven."

"I'm sure she'll be in the ICU by then. Look for us upstairs. And, Alan, one more thing."

"Yes."

"I don't think it's too likely you'll get reimbursed on this."

So what else is new? "No insurance?"

"Worse, I'm afraid. We're not totally sure of her identity, but if she's who we think she is, admission records for a previous E.R. visit for a finger laceration show that, back then at least, she was MedExcel. Are you a provider?"

"I was. MedExcel and I didn't see eye-to-eye."

"What do you mean?"

"Slight difference in philosophy. They wanted to run the treatment, and I sort of thought that was my role. I wanted to be paid, and they thought that was pushy of me. Little conflicts like that."

Her tone was mildly admonishing as she said, "You're just too sensitive for the current managed-care environment. There are worse companies than MedExcel, let me tell you."

"I don't want to know about them."

"But you'll see her anyway?"

"Sure, I'll send you the bill. Ren. You're rich."

She found my threat amusing. "Go right ahead. If you think insurance companies are hard to deal with, wait till you try to get a dime out of me."

I took a quick shower and thought about Lauren. She was, I guessed, sitting by her mother's bedside in a hospital in eastern Washington. Had she been home, I think she might have said something to caution me about what I was doing.

I ate a banana and some toast and peanut butter, and poured a cup of coffee for the road. Emily's dish had plenty of fresh water.

I have found every intensive-care unit I have ever visited to be an eerie place. Almost by definition, ICU's are hallowed temples of tragedy or triumph. The final results of the labors there are binary, either a zero or a one. The practitioners are either heroes or they are failures. The mood in the space, in the area that exists between the linoleum tiles and the ceiling tiles, is subdued, as though the players—the doctors, the nurses, the therapists—don't ever pause to acknowledge the immense stakes that are always on the table.

I greeted the ward clerk in the Community Hospital ICU, identified myself, and asked where I could find the new transfer from the E.R. Without looking up from a duty roster, he asked, "Which one?"

"Adolescent OD. Female. Don't have a name. I'm Dr. Gregory, for a psych consult."

He raised his head and gestured toward the far corner and said, "Ms. Doe. She's in bed four." As I walked past him, he said, "Good luck." In the vernacular, I assumed he meant that for her more than for me. A dividing curtain was partially pulled in front of the bed in the distance so from the nursing station I couldn't see much more than the foot rail.

I asked, "Is her chart here?"

"No, her nurse has it out there."

On the far side of the bed a stocky woman with red hair wearing a brilliant chartreuse top was adjusting the controls on an infusion pump. I wondered where Adrienne was.

I turned back to the ward clerk and asked, "Is Dr. Arvin here?"

"Is he the attending?"

"No. She's the urologist."

"The little one?"

"Yes."

"She's over there, I think, with the patient. Was a few minutes ago, at least. I haven't seen her come back out, but I was in the john for a minute."

A glass wall separated the nursing station from the eight ICU beds. The moment I was through the glass door into the unit I was confronted with the familiar but disconcerting smells and sounds of last-chance medicine. My breathing grew more shallow.

I found Adrienne behind the drawn curtain. She was sitting on the edge of a chair, her eyes fixed on the monitor above the bed. The indicator for number of respirations per minute read a sharp red 09.

Way too low.

She was holding her new patient's limp hand.

Adrienne didn't turn, but she knew I was there. She said, "I didn't tell you before on the phone but, downstairs? She was in cardiac three. When they brought in her, that's where they took her. And that's where I saw her. So this one's special to me. Okay?"

Adrienne had become a widow in cardiac three, the number three cardiac treatment room of the emergency room. Peter—her husband, my friend—had died in cardiac three after a brutal knife attack.

I said, "Okay," and touched Adrienne on the shoulder. With her free hand she felt for my fingers.

Staring at the bright red numbers on the monitor, I stated the obvious, and I gestured at the pale figure on the bed. "She'll be on a ventilator soon, won't she?"

Adrienne nodded gravely. "Her gag reflex is gone; she's stopped controlling her airway. They're setting up for the vent right now."

On masking tape at the end rail of the bed someone had written, "Doe, M." in bold capital letters.

M. Doe was a tall girl. In unconsciousness she seemed to stretch out over the length of the hospital bed. Monitor wires snaked from the upper end of her torso, which was immodestly covered by a pastel hospital gown that had seen about fifty too many washings before it had been pulled over her thin frame.

"Do you mind covering her up a little better please, Ren?" I asked.

The nurse turned and said, "I'll do it."

I thanked her and introduced myself. She smiled at me with a patronizing face that said, "We have a lot of work to do before you're going to do any good."

An automated blood-pressure cuff began to inflate

on the girl's upper arm, a drain gurgled, and the infusion pump measured another dose of fluid into her IV tubing. A nice little ICU symphony.

Adrienne said, "Don't you think she's lovely? I think she's really pretty."

My first thought was that, in these circumstances, no one was lovely. But I said, "Yes, she is," trying to imagine what M. Doe had looked like twenty-four hours earlier, and what events, what pain, had brought her here.

The child moaned and rolled her head to the side. She coughed once, a tiny cough, an infant's cough, before her eyes opened slowly and froze on me. Her eyes were puzzlingly clear, the same luminescent purple as my ex-wife's. And like Merideth's always had, this girl's eyes pierced me instantly in a way that compromised my balance.

"Hello," I said, moving forward half a step.

She blinked once before her eyes closed again.

Adrienne said, "She's done that a few times so far. Don't be fooled, it doesn't mean anything."

"Is she responsive to pain?"

"Was earlier, now only minimally to deep pressure. But I haven't played any Barry Manilow CD's yet. That might get a scream out of her."

I smiled.

Behind us we heard the squeak and drone of rubber wheels on linoleum. I turned and saw Marty Klein accompanied by a scrub-suited doc whom I didn't know. Behind them, a respiratory therapist was pushing a ventilator and a treatment cart our way. I said, "Hello, Marty."

He nodded. In other circumstances, I knew we

would end up talking about bicycles, my passion, and golf, his. Not this time. He said, "Hi, Alan, thanks for coming, sorry she's not too talkative. We're here to get her on the vent. Step out a minute, please. Okay?"

"Of course." I had no desire to watch what he was about to do. None.

Adrienne asked, "Marty, do you need me?"

"No, Adrienne. We're fine. I'll have somebody call you with the kidney functions as soon as they show any change."

"You have my home phone?"

"It's on the chart, right?"

"Yes. I want to talk with the parents, too. When you find them."

"I'll find you, don't worry. Get out of here. Go play catch with your son or something," he said as he pulled the curtain farther around the bed.

I began to follow Adrienne away from the bed when I remembered why I was there. "Just a sec," I said. I walked back and reached inside the curtain and grabbed the chart and flipped a few pages. Beside me, Adrienne had begun pacing. I think Marty's admonition about spending time with Jonas had some special meaning as this young girl hovered near death with her parents nowhere to be found.

"You have a pen?"

She gave me one. I used it to sign on to the case and then scribbled a brief progress note that reported an apparent overdose, an unconscious patient, absent family, and no progress. On the order sheet, I wrote, "When patient attains consciousness: Suicide precautions should be in place, including 1:1 staffing × 24 hrs." I also left instructions that I be called immediately when the parents were located or the patient became oriented.

Adrienne glanced at my notes. "You're ordering a full-time one-to-one? Nursing staff's gonna love that. And MedExcel? Yeah, they'll be thrilled. They're going to reimburse on this, mmm-hmmmm, sure. Probably cutting that check as we speak."

"She may not be done trying to kill herself, Ren."

"I know that. I'm just giving you a hard time. With Lauren out of town, somebody needs to, right? You heard from her?"

"Not this morning, no."

"You'll let me know?"

"Of course, thanks."

I turned back to the admissions data. The data field was mostly blank. But the first line read, "Doe, Merritt."

Out loud, I said, "Her name is Merritt."